THE WRITING IN THE WATER

OTHER TITLES BY JOHN AJVIDE LINDQVIST

Let the Right One In

Handling the Undead

Let the Old Dreams Die

Harbor

Little Star

Let the Old Dreamer Die

I Am Behind You. The First Place

I Always Find You. The Second Place

X. The Last Place. I Am the Tiger

Our Skin, Our Blood, Our Bones

Fail Again, Fail Better. Notes on Horror and Writing

Border

The Kindness

Alternative Facts and Birds—illustrated by Mia Ajvide

The Reality

THE WRITING IN THE WATER

A THRILLER

JOHN AJVIDE LINDQVIST

TRANSLATED BY MICHAEL MEIGS

Previously published as *Skriften i vattnet* by Ordfront publishers in Sweden in 2022. Translated from Swedish by Michael Meigs. First published in English by Amazon Crossing in 2025.

Published by Amazon Crossing, Seattle
www.apub.com

EU product safety contact:
Amazon Media EU S. à r.l.
38, avenue John F. Kennedy, L-1855 Luxembourg
amazonpublishing-gpsr@amazon.com

ISBN-13: 9781662525049 (paperback)
ISBN-13: 9781662525032 (digital)

Cover design by Jarrod Taylor
Cover image: © Mos-Photography / Getty

Printed in the United States of America

For Mia, my Mia
Always and forever

PROLOGUE

MIDSUMMER EVE 2019

The table on the dock is set for the feast. Everything required for a Swedish Midsummer Eve meal is here. Herring, boiled potatoes, and aquavit, as well as meatballs and ham in case the herring turns out to be too exotic for the guests from far away. Fine china is set out on the brilliant white tablecloth. A couple of miniature Swedish flags on tiny staffs stand at the ends of the table, fluttering slightly in the sea breeze. It's a perfect day.

Hosting the party are Olof Helander and his wife, Gabriella, owners of Knektholmen island, scarcely a kilometer from Tärnö in the Stockholm archipelago. Their "cabin" on the rise beyond the dock is an architectural marvel with a sixteen-hundred-square-foot open interior and panoramic windows overlooking the water. Olof's business arbitraging emissions rights and climate compensation payments financed *that* part of this opulent spread.

The four guests seat themselves with cries of delight. They include Chen Bao, who does business in climate-related affairs in China, his homeland, along with his wife, Chen Min. The party is rounded out with Cédric Montaigne, member of the European Union Parliament with responsibility for coordinating climate work between EU members. His wife is Suzanne.

The host taps his glass and welcomes them in English, adding a couple of phrases in Chinese and French. He lifts his little glass of aquavit and obliges them to learn to toast one another by saying *skål* in Swedish, an exercise that provokes laughter and an embarrassed titter from Chen Min. She hides her mouth behind her hand.

At one end of the table, hidden behind a pair of large sunglasses and looking away, is Astrid, the Helanders' fourteen-year-old daughter. She despises this artificial festivity, and only because Olof had threatened to change the Wi-Fi password had she been convinced to attend and "represent the family," as her father expressed it. She despises this forced joviality, she hates the guests' dutiful inquiries of her, and she was about to implode with disgust as tipsy grown-ups hopped around the homemade Midsummer pole learning the typically Swedish dance Little Froggies. Above all, she's nauseated by the fact that there's meat on the table.

Before the guests sat down to eat, Astrid took a snapshot of a slice of meat and posted it on her Instagram account with the title "Midsummer is Murder." She regularly posts images, brief videos, and texts about veganism and animal rights. She has nearly four thousand followers.

Astrid checks her mobile phone and sees it's 1:15 p.m. She'll give this "representing the family" business another fifteen minutes max, then Papa can say whatever he wants. She looks out over the water. Its surface glistens like a mirror. The only sailboats in sight have their sails furled and are using their motors instead.

"Helan går, sjung hoppfallerallan . . ."

Olof is on his feet. Astrid squeezes her eyes shut as if in pain. Her father undertakes the task of teaching his guests that "typical Swedish song." They imitate him in a cacophony of different accents, and Astrid tells herself, *Ten minutes; no, five. Only five minutes more, and I'm out of here.*

To get through those five minutes, Astrid taps the FaceTime icon and calls Algot, a kid in her class. She knows he's infatuated with her.

She could use some adulation on a day like this. As the signal goes through, Astrid stares out at the glittering water. Its golden glimmers are reflected in her sunglasses. She hears the faint sound of an approaching motorboat.

What the hell are they doing?

Astrid lowers the telephone and sees Algot grimacing and tilting his head, trying to make out what's happening on Astrid's end of the line. The grown-ups are still at it with their infantile and "groundbreaking" interpretation of "Helan Går." Astrid shakes her head and lifts the phone so Algot sees her. "You don't want to know."

"Okay. You post anything new?"

"Mm-hmm. Just did."

There's a clatter as Algot turns on his computer. His pimply face lights up. "Midsummer is Murder. Nice! Eighty likes already. And here's mine."

Algot is pleasant, smart, and encouraging, and Astrid really wishes she could return his affections, but she has much to deal with to maintain her own sanity. Anyway, she's begun to suspect she's asexual. She's never felt attracted to anyone, unless maybe that time when she was eight and had a crush on Edward from *Twilight*, mostly because all the other girls did.

She asks Algot what he's up to. He says "Nothing special" just as an open motorboat approaching the dock glides into Astrid's view. Are they expecting more idiots for this party? The motor shifts into reverse and then into neutral, and the boat stops fifteen feet away. Astrid looks up.

What the . . . ?

Two men are in the boat, both wearing black hoods. Now they lean over, and each lifts a . . .

"What the hell—*goddamn it!*" Astrid screams and throws herself under the table just as the men open fire with automatic weapons. She presses her face into the warm planking and hears glass and porcelain shattering above her and meaty impacts when rapidly fired bullets strike human bodies. Beyond the din of the chattering weapons, Algot is shouting, "What's happening? What's going on?"

The shadowed space beneath the table is ripped as bullets penetrate the tablecloth at the far end, releasing thin beams of sunlight that dapple Astrid's head. Her right hand is jolted, her phone shatters and disappears over the edge of the dock. A splinter slices Astrid's cheek. She hears the phone splash into the water.

I'm going to die, I'm going to die . . .

The stink of herring and aquavit fills Astrid's nostrils. Bodies slump or are flung from the chairs around her, but the firing doesn't stop. Blood splashes across the white tablecloth. Astrid realizes any random bullet will split her skull wide open. That's her last rational thought. She rolls off the dock's edge, following the phone, and falls toward the water.

She breaks the surface and sinks into the icy dark. Her wide-open eyes see algae and waving seaweed. Her mind goes blank. It's quiet down here, it's beautiful. She should stay. She hooks her right leg around two dock supports to keep from rising to the surface.

Silence and peace. Everything's okay here, just a little dark. Incredibly, she's still wearing sunglasses. Astrid shakes her head at her dumb luck. *They didn't break! Sweet . . .*

I

Julia and Kim

1

Julia Malmros first met Kim Ribbing while doing research for the Millennium novel she'd been invited to write. After David Lagercrantz declined to deliver yet another installment, the wildly profitable franchise was left hanging until the publisher could find an appropriate author to keep the adventures of Mikael Blomkvist and Lisbeth Salander going.

Julia was the first writer they turned to. Her four novels about Detective Superintendent Åsa Fors had been well received both in Sweden and abroad; they'd been published in almost forty countries. Her popularity was due to many factors, but particularly her ability to describe crimes in realistic detail. Julia had a twenty-year police career behind her, devoted initially to pursuing white-collar criminals. Later she worked in the violent crimes unit, before metaphorically putting down her police baton and picking up a pen.

Well, it hadn't been quite that simple. There had been a transition phase. Julia had remained with the police until after her second Åsa Fors book came out. That was her big breakthrough, and it had earned her so much that Julia felt secure handing in her resignation and dedicating herself entirely to writing.

And now they were offering her the Millennium series. She was flattered, though hesitant and a bit intimidated. She knew expectations were high all around the globe, and if she accepted, her life and finances would be altered. She'd read about Lagercrantz and the royalties that made him as wealthy as Scrooge McDuck.

But what use would Julia have for that kind of money? Her novels had already earned her enough to buy a corner apartment overlooking the Järntorget in Stockholm Old Town and a Toyota Prius she rarely used. She'd renovated her summer cabin on Tärnö and paid for a new dock there. What more could she need? Okay, she could hire some company to construct a swimming pool there, but was risking her reputation worth the opportunity to take an occasional morning dip?

It was vanity that eventually motivated her decision. She'd do it simply to show them she could; she'd rub their faces in it. Julia didn't know who "they" were, but "they" were certainly lurking out there somewhere. She was extremely well regarded both by readers and reviewers, but there had to be doubters. *Julia Malmros? The Millennium series? Ha!*

Only one thing intimidated her: Lisbeth Salander. Julia had read all the Millennium novels and knew that hacking and electronic espionage were often essential to the plot. She believed she could manage Lisbeth's character, but what about the programming and hacking? Julia had learned enough about computers to use them to detect tax fraud, but those skills were hardly relevant to the challenge and, besides, they were dated. She was going to need help.

Julia asked the publisher to come up with someone with the computer skills she lacked. Her novels were always meticulously researched, and it would be stupid to try to wing it with the eagerly awaited Millennium series. In the meantime, she sketched out a plot.

Her Åsa Fors books were anchored in everyday Swedish police procedure. Her concept for a new Millennium novel was to indulge in a wilder, more elaborate plot. International intrigue, maybe set in some of the places she'd visited on vacations abroad.

Mexico was the first location that came to mind. Drug cartels infiltrating politics and murdering inconvenient journalists; that was something for Micke Blomkvist. Stir in something about the border conflict with the United States. Salander could break into the cartel's network and sabotage their shipments. Chases and conflicts, motorcycles tearing through the jungle, a showdown aboard a smuggling vessel. Plenty to sink your teeth into.

Julia followed her usual practice of scribbling random plot ideas on sticky notes and posting them on her office wall. When she'd generated about fifty of them, she arranged them in clusters and possible sequences. The skeleton plot began to move and wave at her like a Día de los Muertos puppet. She nodded and smiled to herself. *Millennium, motherfucker!*

The publishing house responded a week later. It hadn't been easy to make contact with a competent hacker; they didn't exactly post their services in classified ads. Quite the opposite. Through a friend of a friend and so on, they'd managed to come up with a Kim Ribbing, a pro at testing firms' data security by hacking into their networks to demonstrate their weaknesses.

"Ribbing?" Julia said. "Like the aristocrats? Like Magdalena Ribbing?"

"No idea," was the answer from managing editor Louise Granhagen, who always sounded like she was struggling for breath.

"And—Kim?" Julia went on. "Is that a man or a woman? Guy or gal?"

"Haven't talked to the individual myself," Louise wheezed. "But the suggested rendezvous is the Espresso House on Västerlång Street. Tomorrow at noon. That okay?"

"Sure, that works. But how do I recognize him? Or her?"

"Work it out."

After they ended the call, Julia sat down at the computer to draw up a list of questions to take up with the "individual." She drew a blank; she didn't know where to begin. She decided simply to ask Kim Ribbing to give her the basics about hacking and hope to quiz them about any she didn't understand.

Julia was at the café ten minutes early the next day, armed with her notebook and a ballpoint pen. She ordered a cappuccino with an extra shot of espresso and took a table by the window. It was the end of January of 2019, and people outside were wading grimly through snow and slush. Practically all of them were wearing the snug down jackets that had become the daily uniform of the middle class.

Julia didn't see it happen, but when she turned away from the window, a person was sitting opposite her. A person who made her eyes widen in surprise. "Kim?" she asked and got a nod in reply.

Kim Ribbing's appearance was remarkable. He—since it was a him—had coal-black hair, carefully combed, that reached to his waist and framed a face as starkly white and fragile as porcelain. If you tapped it too hard, maybe it would shatter. His lips were thin, his nose was small and a bit crooked, but his eyes were the most striking thing about him. They were large and so light blue they were almost transparent. In contrast with his stark black hair, they seemed illuminated from within.

Julia's gaze moved from Kim's face to his torso. What she saw was even more contradictory.

Kim looked like a for-real hard rocker, or—why not?—a death metal fan, but instead of a leather jacket and Entombed T-shirt, he was wearing a thick old-fashioned overcoat with wide lapels and, under that, a black turtleneck sweater imprinted with an image of Skalman the turtle, from the Bamse children's cartoons.

That was so disconcerting that Julia couldn't help exclaiming, "Skalman?"

"Mm-hmm," Kim said. "My idol. Who's yours?"

Julia had no real idol, as far as she knew, but so as not to duck the question, she replied, "I don't know. Maybe . . . Malala?"

Kim nodded at her choice of the Nobel Peace Prize winner. "She's good. But not like Skalman."

Julia couldn't tell if Kim was just pulling her leg, testing her to see how willing she was to play along. He looked somewhere between twenty-five and thirty, as much as thirty years younger than she was, so maybe he possessed a different generation's sense of humor. Or maybe he was just bizarre.

Julia considered quizzing Kim about his relationship with Li'l Hop the Bamse bunny but decided to cut to the chase. "They tell me you're a . . . hacker?"

"Cracker, actually. But okay, 'hacker,' if you prefer that."

Julia opened her notebook. "What's the difference?"

"A hacker is someone extremely interested in computers and programming. A cracker is somebody who gets past a network's security systems. He can be a good guy or a bad guy . . ."

Kim lectured and Julia took notes. As she'd hoped, she came up with follow-up questions, prompting Kim to describe in detail what a Trojan horse was and how macrocode functioned. He was patient with her knowledge gaps, and Julia was enchanted by his graceful hand gestures as he explained things. He moved with the precisely calculated grace of a dancer.

An hour of this left Julia's head spinning with all the new terms and their interconnections. Even so, she thought she'd gathered enough to fake more knowledge than she really had. It was chiefly a matter of inserting the terminology early in the text and then luring the reader into accepting the rest. Julia put down her pen and rubbed her eyes.

"Why do you want this stuff?" Kim asked.

"The firm didn't tell you?"

"Nah. Just told me who you are. And that you needed help."

Julia looked around, then leaned forward and lowered her voice. "It's top secret, of course, but I'm going to write a new Millennium novel."

If Julia had hoped to impress Kim, she was disappointed. He didn't even lift one of his thin eyebrows, just said, "What's wrong with your own stuff?"

"Have you read them?"

"The first one. Didn't think much of it."

"The second one's better."

"Okay, if you say so."

Julia felt a bit offended, both by Kim's indifference to her big project and his opinion of her debut novel. Okay, she had to admit that one hadn't been so brilliant, but a person shouldn't *say* so. In a sour tone, she commented, "So, you're the guy who can tell me what's wrong with my novels."

Kim shrugged. "They're better than most."

"You said you thought it wasn't good."

"Most novels are trash."

Julia had led several hundred interrogations during her career with the police. Some people cracked like an egg after a little tap; others required tougher, lengthier treatment. And then there were those you never managed to break because they eluded you. Kim seemed to belong to the last group. Julia couldn't figure him out. He looked so fragile, yet there was something unapproachable about him that bewildered her.

"Thanks for the help, in any case," Julia said. "It was valuable. I might come up with some more questions later. Can I—"

Kim held up his phone, asked for her number, and rang it. She saved his number in her contacts as "Kim Cracker" before asking, "What do we owe? How should we—"

Kim made one of his elegant, sweeping hand gestures. "No need."

"But surely you want *something*?"

For some unknown reason Kim's face darkened. "I have everything already."

"Imagine that!"

They picked up their coats from the chairbacks and put them on. Kim's lapels were of black wool, evoking for Julia a photo of the painter Anders Zorn in something almost identical, taken perhaps a century earlier. There was also something ancient in Kim's icy-blue eyes, as if a much older being were sitting inside his head and peering out.

They stepped onto the slushy sidewalk. Kim took out a pack of Camel Blue cigarettes, opened it, and held it out. She'd been a heavy smoker for more than twenty years but had mostly stopped five years earlier. Maybe an infrequent ciggy in social occasions like book fairs, but otherwise nothing. Oh well, you could call this a social occasion. Julia worked out a cigarette. Kim lit it with a Zippo before taking one for himself. They smoked in silence for a while, then Kim asked, "You live nearby?"

Julia gestured toward Västerlång Street. "Yes. Toward Järntorget."

Kim nodded. With a tone as casual as a comment on the weather, he asked, "Want to have sex?"

Julia gasped in surprise while inhaling and went into a coughing fit. Trying to come up with a reply, she kept it going longer than she really needed. At last she said, "You know I'm a lot older than you, don't you?"

Kim's eyes widened. He looked genuinely puzzled. "So?"

"Well, just so you know."

"What do I need to know? That I won't . . . become a father?"

Julia cleared her throat again. "Maybe we don't need to decide right away. We can have a glass of wine or something . . . we'll see how it goes."

Kim's expression made it clear he found such socially acceptable behavior completely meaningless. Julia sucked in so much cigarette smoke that it overwhelmed her nicotine-deprived brain. She hadn't gone to bed with anyone in more than a year, when she'd gotten thoroughly drunk at the book fair, and the mere mention of sex made her belly quiver. She sneaked a look at Kim, who was studying the sign of a souvenir shop, apparently unconcerned. Moose wearing Viking helmets.

Julia kept herself fit by watching her diet and training at Itrim a couple of times a week. If her weight went over 130 pounds, she punished herself by reducing her intake to protein shakes until she was back down to 123, her optimal weight. She was entirely comfortable with her body and knew she looked very shapely, considering her age. "The attractive thriller writer," as her sex partner at the book fair had called her. "That lovely cop lady" was how her former husband, Jonny, used to tease her on those rare occasions he was in a joking mood.

Julia wasn't easily frightened. She could keep a stone face if some drunk hooligan came weaving up to her or remain icily indifferent to the worst threats. Even so, Kim gave her an uneasy feeling. Maybe it was less because he was so much younger than the fact it was *him*, a man who mystified her.

Still, it was tempting . . .

2

They finished their cigarettes and went down Västerlång Street without a word. Julia had never received such an unexpected proposition of sex, at least not in the middle of the day, and it left her speechless. But she felt they should chat a bit, otherwise this would feel too artificial, a transaction in utter silence. In a chirpy voice she asked him, "How did you get to be so good at computers?"

"Had a job. Till I figured it out."

"Huh! And then what?"

"I quit."

"And what job do you have now?"

"Nothing."

"But . . . how do you make ends meet?"

"Like I said before. I already have everything."

They got to Julia's apartment building. She tapped in the entry code and pushed the heavy door open. The marble of the staircase leading up to her floor had been worn by several hundred years of footsteps. Julia liked the building's distinctly historical feel and was more at home there than she'd been in the Bagarmossen apartment she'd shared with Jonny for twenty years.

Julia's apartment was a thousand-square-foot four-room place that had cost her the equivalent of just over a million dollars. The view toward Järntorget from the corner window of the living room probably accounted for much of that. Kim hung his overcoat on an elegant wrought-iron hook Julia had purchased in Italy. She was always careful to bring something for the apartment back from her travels, to incorporate her memories into her living space.

Julia glanced toward the half-open bedroom door where her bed was nicely made. Her abdomen contracted and sent a warm wave downward. She felt her throat tighten and realized she was nervous. *How banal!* Wouldn't be stupid to have a glass of wine. Kim made no comment about the apartment, which was tidy and stark, furnished with pieces from Länna and Mio and a few practical items from Svenskt Tenn. Only in Julia's office was a bit of chaos tolerated.

They went into the kitchen. Julia uncorked a bottle of Barolo. Kim plopped down at the little dining table by the window, picked up the binoculars from the sill, and raised them with an inquiring look.

"Ah, those are a bit naughty," Julia said, filling two large glasses. "Not sure that I want to ex—"

"Then don't."

Julia set the glasses on the table and seated herself opposite Kim. There was something disarming about his directness, so she decided to tell him anyway. She pointed at the Gyldene Freden restaurant, visible at one corner of the square.

"Right there is the Gyldene Freden. The Swedish Academy meets on Thursday evenings and afterward they go there. Sometimes they come out later, a little worse for drink. That's when I sit here and spy on them to see if . . . well, whether Horace Engdahl falls on his face in the street. Hasn't happened yet, though."

"I understand."

Julia took a big gulp of wine, trying to wash away her acute embarrassment. "Does that sound crazy?"

"Lonely, more likely."

Julia didn't have a large circle of acquaintances, just a few friends she met individually from time to time. It's true she was relatively alone, but that was her choice, wasn't it? But she understood how the notion of a woman sitting at her kitchen window to spy on tipsy academy members might be taken.

"How about you?" she asked. "Are you lonely?"

"Yes," Kim said, again just as direct. "I'm extremely lonely."

When he got to his feet, Julia made sure to take another big gulp of wine. Kim leaned over her, took her face in his hands, and kissed her. Something magic happened when his lips met hers. Though his had looked thin and tight, they seemed to dissolve, expand, and become soft and moist. She responded to his kiss and put her hand to his groin where something bulky began to harden.

"Okay," she whispered. "All right, then."

They went to the bedroom, Julia intent on holding on to the numbness created by the half glass of wine. When they reached the bed, Kim pulled up her blouse.

"Sorry," she said, "I need to do that . . ."

She felt awkward and wanted to get past the foreplay as quickly as possible, so she turned her back to undress. She heard rustling and zipping sounds behind her as Kim's clothes also fell to the floor. Julia covered her breasts with her arms, a childishly puritanical gesture, and turned around. What she saw then made her gasp.

She'd seen just about everything during her police career, but this was new. Kim's entire body was covered with a web of large and small scars, hundreds and hundreds of them. No surfaces had been spared except for his face, his penis, and his hands. A big scar was evident halfway up his neck, and maybe that's why he'd been wearing a turtleneck. His body looked as if someone had used it as a chopping block every day for several years.

"Good Lord!" Julia exclaimed, scarcely audible. "How . . . ?"

"Someone else started them," said Kim. "Later, I continued."

"Wh . . . *who?*"

"I prefer not to talk about it, if that's okay."

"Of course, I just . . ."

"I don't do it anymore, in case you're wondering. That was a long time ago."

Julia nodded. Kim stepped forward and took her into his arms. She placed her hands on his back and brushed her palms over his welted, striated skin. *How could he possibly have managed to cut himself so many times—on his back?* She felt his penis press warmly against her belly. She took it in her hand and sensed it was a big one, just as she'd suspected. Without releasing him, she moved backward to the bed, sprawled out there, and opened herself to him.

3

It wasn't the best sex Julia Malmros had ever had, but it was definitely one of the most interesting bouts. Although she and Kim were essentially strangers, he was quick to respond to her signals. They found a rhythm and played variations on it. The most intriguing part of it was the sensation of running her hands over his skin. He didn't feel human. The closest comparison she could imagine was a reptile, and strangely enough that excited her even more, even though she'd never imagined coupling with such a thing. No, it was the nonhuman aspect that excited her lust, the sense of making love with "the other." There was something . . . *transcendent* in the experience.

Another contradiction was the firmness of Kim's body. You might have expected his slight form to be weak, even anemic, but beneath Kim's scarred hide, his muscles moved like an ensemble of closely bound cables that stretched and contracted under Julia's inquisitive fingers.

When it was done, Kim pulled out of her without a word and went to the bathroom to wash himself. Julia lay there and wiped herself with a corner of the sheet. She'd already thought of changing the bed linens. The toilet flushed and barefoot steps sounded in the hall; she suddenly felt shy and crept under the duvet. Kim entered the room. She was fascinated again by his body, an unimaginable map of accumulated pain.

Julia bumped over to one side to give him room, but Kim started pulling on his clothes. When he'd finished, Julia spoke up. "Was that it?"

"What do you mean?"

"Just what I said. Was that all there was to it?"

"I don't understand. I asked if you wanted to have sex. You said 'maybe.' Then you wanted to. So we did."

Julia couldn't conceal the disappointment in her voice. "Okay, then."

Kim seemed about to leave, but he paused and sat on the edge of the bed. "So does this mean you want to have . . . a relationship?"

"I never said that, but a person usually doesn't go rushing off afterward. Are you always like this?"

"Haven't done this often. Can't claim to have a modus operandi."

Kim lowered his chin so that his long black hair fell forward and completely covered his face. For a moment it looked as if something from a horror film had invaded Julia's bedroom.

She refused to be frightened. Instead, she asked, "*Why* did you want to go to bed with me?"

"Just wanted to."

"Not because you *like* me or something like that?"

Kim shrugged. "I like you fine."

What had Kim said? That he was "extremely lonely." Not so surprising, since he seemed clueless when it came to social behavior. Or simply didn't bother. Whatever the reason, he was ill-prepared to establish or maintain human relationships.

"You can leave," Julia told him. She rolled over so her back was to him. He got up. He sat down again.

"Let's think about it," he said. "Let's suppose we lie here and have a little conversation postcoitus, which is what I think you mean. Then you'd ask me about things I have absolutely no desire to discuss. And we'd both be in a bad mood."

"Mood's not so good right now either," Julia muttered.

Kim sighed. "What do you want me to do?"

"You can at least give me a kiss on the cheek and say, 'See you later!'"

She heard a rustling as Kim got up and went around the bed. He squatted next to Julia and dutifully put his lips to her cheek. When she looked up, she saw his eyes filled with tears.

"What's wrong?" she asked.

"It's just . . . sometimes I wish . . . I wish I didn't exist. I'm so . . . awful. Broken. But that's just how I am."

Julia reached out to touch his face, but Kim recoiled and quickly wiped his eyes. He made as if to leave, but Julia stopped him. "One more thing. How old are you?"

"Twenty-eight. Why?"

"No reason. Just wanted to know."

"Okay. Good luck with the book."

"Thanks."

4

The splendidly impressive Roshult estate stretches out along Vätternstranden. Beyond the entry an extensive lawn runs down to the brightly glittering lake. It's a beautiful summer morning.

A boy appears between the columns holding up the so-called reception terrace. He's seven years old. His hair is blond and curly, his freckled face is delicate. A little cherub. Though the lad's eyes are so bright blue they rival the clear sky overhead, his little body seems weighted down as he walks with determined steps down to the lake.

The boy is wearing a fleecy moss-green bathrobe with deep pockets. As he approaches the lakefront, he begins collecting rocks and filling those pockets. When they're too full to accommodate any more stones, he steps into the lake.

He shivers when the cold water touches his skin, but he takes another step anyway. And then another. About fifteen feet from the shore, the skirts of his robe float upward, but the weight of the stones holds down the rest of it. The boy keeps walking. The water's up to his chin after another fifteen feet. He keeps going.

5

Julia lay on her side until she heard her front door open and then close. The bed smelled of sweat and body fluids. She got up, put on a morning robe, pulled off all the sheets and pillowcases, and stuffed them into the laundry hamper. Then she stood in front of the bathroom mirror and examined herself. This was how a woman who'd just had sex looked. Miserable.

The dimples on either side of her mouth had become wrinkles, and now she had pouches under her eyes. She'd always had a sharply defined jawline; it was still there but looser now. Someone might see her face as sweet, with those big brown eyes, the small pug nose, the mouth Jonny once called "French." She looked hard and sensual, both together, even though her features had become less defined with the passage of the years.

She prided herself on her hair. She released the clip that held it and let it cascade to cover most of her back. She'd turned forty before her first gray hair appeared. More had followed, and now, at fifty-eight, not a single strand was anything but ashen gray. She looked like the fairy-tale Princess Tuvstarr who'd left her dream castle to explore the world . . . and now was a pensioner.

But the prince never appeared.

Julia left the bedroom, went to the kitchen, sat at the table, and drank the rest of her wine. Then she took Kim's glass. He'd taken no more than a sip. Though it was only a little past two o'clock, clouds had gathered over Järntorget and in Julia's heart. She took a gulp of wine and realized she was feeling really low.

Had she been expecting something more? Well, not much more than an afternoon of caresses and conversation and eventually a slightly melancholy farewell. She hadn't intended to "become a thing" with a twenty-eight-year-old who'd freely admitted he was broken and idolized Skalman the turtle.

So why did this trouble her so?

There *was* something special with that Kim Ribbing, a kind of . . . candor. Most people were constantly focused on the impression they were making, on what they were going to say next. Kim was aware and attentive. That had been evident in his lovemaking, if not elsewhere. Julia had had a succession of sex partners in the years after her divorce from Jonny, and all too many of them were trying so hard to impress that they merely put her off. Kim wasn't like that. He was present. With the body of a reptilian gymnast.

It's useless to cry over spilled milk.

Julia's lips curled in a bitter grimace. It was astonishing how little comfort was to be found in so-called folk wisdom, and, besides, who the hell would stand there and wail because a little milk had been spilled. *A psychopath, that's who.*

Her mobile phone rang. When she saw it was Jonny, she thought about ignoring it, but she knew him: He'd call and call till she picked up out of sheer exasperation. So she took the call. "Hi, Jonny."

"Hey, sweetie, how are things?"

"Please. Don't call me 'sweetie.'"

"Sorry! Old friend, then."

True, all too true. Jonny and Julia had met during police training school, married when they were both twenty-four, and three years later Jonny had started calling her "sweetie." On the list of thousands of reasons for the divorce almost twenty years later, that "sweetie" was cause number one.

"Has something happened?" Julia asked.

"In fact, yes. Do you remember Edward Dahlberg?"

"Sure. What's up with him?"

That had been one of the last cases Julia worked before resigning five years before. A Swedish marine biologist employed in the Norwegian oil industry had left his home in Stavanger one day and was never heard from again. They'd collaborated with the Norwegian police and come up with nothing at all. The man had vanished from the earth without leaving a single trace.

"He's surfaced, so to speak," Jonny told her. "A trawler out on the Stavanger coast fished him up."

"They confirmed his identity?"

"Yep. Of course, there's not much left of him except bones, but the dental work was there and the DNA was available, so it's him, for sure."

"That's a hell of a thing." Julia had left police jargon in the past for the most part when she slammed the door of the Kungsholmen police station behind her, but it tended to come back when she talked with Jonny. "Got anything suggesting the cause of death?"

"Mm-hmm."

Julia sighed in annoyance. Jonny's job, like hers in the later years, was that of detective superintendent, and though he didn't know it, the others had nicknamed him "the Cat." Not because he was agile but because he tended to pussyfoot around controversial matters.

"Come on, Jonny," Julia said. "Spill it."

"We might say that certain circumstances indicate he didn't go into the water of his own free will."

"And those circumstances are?"

"Oh, for example, the skeleton's hands and feet were bound with plastic cable ties. Arms behind the back."

"Weights?"

"No indication of that. Presumably the poor devil was tied up, simply tossed into the sea, and left to his fate."

"Oh, my. That's hard."

"To say the least. Now for my mission. Now that we're certain it's a murder case we checked your notes. So, somebody might have been after him?"

"My report's in the system."

"Sure, but now I'm asking. So, about six years ago, was there anybody you can remember? Some suspect who stood out and you couldn't eliminate? You already know that I admire your fine instincts."

That last comment was untrue. The times they would discuss cases, Jonny groaned whenever Julia spoke about an intuition or a vague feeling something just wasn't right. Jonny wanted to have everything in black and white and preferred to catch a criminal red-handed. He preferred photographic evidence. Julia didn't bother to contradict him but instead let her thoughts fly out to Stavanger and the missing—now confirmed murdered—Edward Dahlberg.

She'd spoken with a host of people, both at the Statoil headquarters and out on the oil rigs where Edward had spent most of his time. No one had anything to say about the man other than that he was a conscientious and relatively stiff marine biologist, extremely devoted to his work and a skilled diver to boot. Nobody had heard he might have clashed with anyone or might be contemplating suicide.

"No, sorry," Julia said. "We followed up every lead and found nothing that I can think of. It was completely inexplicable. He just disappeared."

"Hmm. Okay, well, as you know, we have to open the investigation again, this time as a criminal case."

"Right. Good luck. Let me know if you come up with something."

"All depends. You know the drill."

"Yeah, but . . . good luck anyhow."

"How are things otherwise?"

Julia's stab at ending the conversation had failed, as usual. Jonny would ring up as soon as anything had the faintest connection with any of the cases she'd worked on. He seemed more interested in her these days than he'd been as her husband in the later years of the marriage.

Julia's interests for the moment were Millennium and Kim Ribbing. The first of those she wasn't allowed to discuss, and the second she wasn't willing to share, so she said, "Everything's just fine. Now I have a little something I must—"

"Would you like to get together sometime?"

"Jonny, no. I already told you . . ."

"You could change your mind."

"I haven't, Jonny. Goodbye."

Julia cut the connection. No dramatic event had brought their marriage to an end; it was a classic case of the persistent dripping of water on stone. It came down to the fact that Julia had found living with Jonny so horribly awful that she couldn't put up with it anymore.

6

Julia took a long shower and then vigorously rubbed her face and hair dry with a terry-cloth towel. She dressed in comfortable clothes and draped the towel around her shoulders so her wet hair wouldn't drip onto her sweater. Then she went to her office.

The apartment's smallest room measured about eight feet by twenty. She could see the interior patio through the office window and glimpse a patch of the now overcast sky. Julia had placed sticky notes on the unadorned walls, and floor-to-ceiling bookcases covered the rest. Five shelves were reserved for all the translations of her own novels; a writer deserves a bit of indulgence, after all.

Julia dropped into the ergonomic office chair at the enormous desk she'd bought when a shuttered factory's furnishings had gone on auction. It took up a quarter of the room. She liked having the vast surface so that she could surround herself with documents, books, desk ornaments, and pens. It gave her the feeling of being seated in an authentic writer's den.

She flitted from one sticky note to another, adjusting them to fit into the outline she'd begun to formulate, wrote out a nighttime conversation between Mikael and Lisbeth to evaluate the tenor of the dialogue, searched the internet for information on Mexican drug cartels, and pondered whether Lisbeth should discover a mass grave outside a ghost town. Julia shut down her laptop at half past seven and stretched.

There. Now she felt better. Every time she got involved in constructing a plot, the real world and its troubles faded, and with the magic of the alphabet she conjured forth something that hadn't existed before. On those infrequent occasions this went *really* well, she wouldn't even be conscious she was writing. She could remain in that state an hour or two before waking, thinking she'd written only a couple of pages and being astonished to see she'd produced ten. That hadn't happened today, but she'd gotten the outlines clearer in her mind and the story was much more vivid for her.

Dinner. She couldn't face preparing something, so she'd have to go to a restaurant, as she did two or three times a week. Fortunately, Stockholm Old Town offered plenty; that was one of the best aspects of living there. The hordes of summer tourists constituted one of the worst. The streets were far less populated in winter, but most restaurants were still open. Except for the ice cream shops, of course.

The melancholy and dissatisfaction left by Kim's visit stuck their claws into Julia as soon as she stepped outside her door. She was dismayed by the sterile sound of her heels clicking against the marble tiles. She saw herself as a lonely woman. After the divorce from Jonny, she'd imagined she'd be free to travel the world and let her long gray hair wave in the breezes of places she'd dreamed of visiting.

She'd really made an effort, wandering through Italy, Spain, Greece, and Latin America. She'd had a few short-lived romances, but she spent most of her time alone. And it was somehow simpler to be alone outside Sweden, sitting in some piazza with a bottle of white in an ice bucket and watching folks passing by.

Back home, on the same streets every day with slush underfoot, she felt more . . . isolated. Though Julia managed her days quite well, there was nevertheless a part of her that was discontented with her solitary existence. One good thing about the Millennium project was that it would probably put her into contact with the broader world again.

Julia was so engrossed in her thoughts of an alternative future that she almost stumbled over the figure sitting hunched in the elaborately arched entryway. A pair of brilliant blue eyes looked up at her.

"Kim? What are you doing here? How long have you been sitting here?"

"Couple of hours."

"Whatever for?"

"Damn it," said Kim, shaking his head so that his long black hair billowed around him. "Damn it to hell."

7

Kim and Julia spent almost all the next two days in bed together. Of course, they used the bathroom, drank water or wine, and ordered carryout from various restaurants, but their abode for most of the next two days was essentially the bed Julia would remake with clean sheets into which they cast themselves to get on with the business of soiling them again.

She couldn't understand that explosion of passion or why Kim attracted her so madly. Maybe it was the old notion that opposites attract. She and he couldn't possibly have been more different, and maybe Kim, too, was drawn by the attraction of "the other."

Julia was careful not to ask questions that might arouse those bad feelings. But even though they made love over and over throughout those two days, it wasn't exalted or affectionate at all. There was a freaky desperation in their grappling, as if they both were striving for something that couldn't be achieved through physical contact. Like trying to chop wood with a hammer, smashing wildly and getting nowhere.

They chatted about the outside world and trivial things. Their favorite places in Stockholm, how many street names they could recall, children's programs from the 1970s, and the comic films about the rural character Åsa Nisse. Astonishingly enough, Kim had seen all nineteen of them and could flawlessly recite each plot, though all were variations on the same themes.

Passing remarks and random details from Kim gave Julia a little material with which to construct a fragmentary picture of his background. Yes, he came from a very wealthy branch of the Ribbing clan. His parents had perished in a boat accident when Kim was fourteen, and the inheritance had provided him more than enough to live on for the rest of his life. In his youth he'd trained intensively as a gymnast, which explained the flexibility and assurance of his movements. He'd begun his training at the age of ten.

Julia told him about growing up in Alvik, where her father was a police officer and her mother was the secretary at the police station. Her papa was eighty years old, still alive, though bedridden at home, with caregiver visits four times a day. She'd been married for twenty years to Jonny Munther, whose last name sounded exactly like the Swedish word for "happy." She summed up their marriage in a few sentences and commented what a relief it had been to shed that "Julia Munther" name—"Jolly Julia" had made her sound like a perky giantess in one of those stupid 1930s comic films. She told him about the cabin on Tärnö in the Stockholm archipelago where she liked to spend her summers.

The real elephant in the room stood there watching as they rolled around. Each embrace and caress brought Julia in contact with Kim's alien skin, striated and knotted like that of a desiccated mummy. He didn't comment, and she didn't ask. When Julia cautiously mentioned his crooked nose, he said, "I took up boxing for a while." They didn't discuss it after that.

Julia set an alarm for the morning of the third day because she had an appointment with the publishers to let them know at last whether she was willing to wade into the Millennium morass. She got up and dressed carefully, making it a bit casual so as not to appear too eager, while Kim lay in bed and watched. They'd devoted two days to exploring every crook and hollow of each other's bodies, but strangely enough, Kim's pale blue gaze as Julia put on her bra made her feel oddly shy.

"How are you doing?" she asked as she buttoned up her white blouse. "Will you stay here, or . . . should I leave a key so you can lock the door?"

"No idea," Kim said. "All depends. Leave me a key."

One more thing they hadn't discussed: where this was going, if in fact it was going anywhere at all. It was hard to imagine a future for them, so it was better not to talk about that. Julia realized that by offering Kim a key to her place, she'd just taken the first step toward an implied ongoing relationship.

"Actually, where do you live?" Julia asked, not knowing whether that question would break the mood.

"Can't say I live anywhere, *actually*."

"But you must have some kind of roof over your head?"

"Hotels. I live in hotels. Different ones."

"Wow. Since when?"

"Since I . . ." Kim stopped and grimaced at what he'd been about to say and obviously reformulated his answer. "Since I was allowed to live on my own."

"That must cost a lot."

Kim shrugged. Julia didn't know the extent of his fortune, but from comments he'd made, it was clearly much greater than her own. And she had ten million kronor tucked away in various accounts.

Even though Kim had come as close to Julia as was humanly possible, there was something in his attitude as he lay in her bed that said a goodbye kiss wouldn't be appropriate, so she just gave a little wave and said, "See you sooner or later." Then she left the bedroom.

8

There was jubilation at the publishing company when Julia accepted, followed by champagne toasts. She told them of her plan to write it with a more international scope, focusing on drug cartels and muzzled journalists. That concept was accepted enthusiastically. With the help of a couple of flutes of champagne, Julia described the scene where Lisbeth Salander sneaks through the ghost town in the Mexican desert with the cartel thugs on her heels. Everyone was delighted and assured her this was the beginning of something fantastic.

Julia felt she was in a dreamworld when she came out into the street, where a mixture of rain and snow was falling. First the consuming passion of the days with Kim; now these agreeable songs of praise for her inventiveness as a writer. Three glasses of champagne on an empty stomach in the middle of the day made Julia Malmros a bundle of nerves sensitive to the touch of every snowflake landing on her fevered skin. She leaned against a wall and clung to a downspout, feeling about to float into the air.

Easy! Stay focused!

Julia looked down and breathed deep. She heard splashing sounds and looked up. A dowager with a little poodle on a leash was staring grimly at Julia with an expression that labeled Julia *a full-grown adult, drunk at this hour of the day!* No, that wasn't right; that was before. Now it was *Look at Julia Malmros, smashed already. This'll be something to tell my friends!* Julia tried to manage a reassuring smile, but the woman sniffed and tramped away.

Okay. The publishers were on board. So far, everything was fine. There was only one "but": Now Julia had to get herself together and *write* the damned book. Her recent days had passed in a haze of physical lust that had left no time for rational thought. It was time to collect herself and reconstruct her existence, return to her routines. Julia had no idea how Kim Ribbing would fit into that.

9

That's why Julia had mixed feelings when she entered her apartment and saw Kim's boots still sitting in the hallway. Part of her wanted to plunge again into the sticky bubbling of body fluids, the hot breathing and the surging orgasms; another part wanted to don her dry, warm writer's garb and become Ms. Practical at her big desk.

Julia took off her outer clothing and shoes before entering the bedroom. She found Kim lying on his stomach, his face turned away from her. He was wearing earbuds, and she heard faint music coming from them. Julia was intrigued. She sidled toward him. When she was a couple of feet away, she recognized the song. Her eyebrows went up when she heard the lyrics about two dark eyes and how love's flames lit to warm and light up the singer's life.

Yet another astonishing puzzle piece in the mystery that was Kim Ribbing. Julia reached out and touched his naked shoulder. Kim shrieked and pulled away, twisted around, and glared at her with eyes wide in shock as he yanked the buds from his ears.

"Sorry!" Julia said. "I—"

"Don't sneak up on me like that!" Kim cried in a broken voice.

"I didn't mean to."

Kim rubbed his palms hard against his eyes, as if he was trying to peel away something stuck to them. Julia held her arms out, appealing for forgiveness, not knowing what else to do. Trying to bring things back to normal, she asked, "You were listening to Sven-Ingvars?" She couldn't believe Kim was a fan of the 1960s pop band.

"Yeah," Kim said and put a leg over the edge of the bed. "So?"

"So nothing," said Julia. "Only it's not what I would have expected, that's all."

Kim grabbed up his clothes from where they'd lain strewn around the bedroom floor since Julia first pulled them off. He dressed and finished by pulling on the black turtleneck shirt where Skalman the turtle stood holding up his index finger as if cursing or admonishing someone. *No, Li'l Hop. Thunder honey will give you a stomachache!*

It seemed to Julia that Kim was acting like someone caught doing something illicit, someone intent on fleeing to avoid a difficult situation. She sat on the bed and folded her hands in her lap. "You can listen to whatever you want, of course," she said. "I'm sorry I frightened you."

"Okay," Kim said. "Right."

He looked around one last time to see if he'd forgotten something. His gaze fixed on the corner between the wardrobe and the outer wall, and he froze. Julia turned to look. All she could see was the rectangle of the wardrobe door decorated with a circle, the windowsill, and a flowerpot.

"What is it?" she asked.

Kim pointed at that corner and said, "The pattern!" He shivered, put his hands over his eyes, and strode out of the bedroom. He stopped in the doorway, then he seemed to struggle mightily before he was able to step back in, approach Julia, and plant an almost aggressive kiss on her cheek.

"So long," he said. "It was great."

Julia nodded and remained seated on the bed. She heard Kim pull on his overcoat out in the hall. The front door opened and shut. Silence descended. Julia looked at that corner. She saw nothing remarkable, only the obvious collection of objects. She ran a hand over the surface of the bed and found dried stains. She'd have to change the sheets again. She thought about the lyrics again, the two dark eyes.

Julia's eyes were quite dark. Had Kim been thinking of her as he lay there listening to Sven-Ingvars? Was that why he chose the song, or was it a mere coincidence? And which possibility did she *want* to be true?

10

"Kim? Kim? Do you hear me?"

Bertil Johansson, the estate gardener, kneels by the boy lying face down on the lakeshore. Bertil's work coveralls are soaking wet and stick to his body as he rubs the boy's cold, chubby cheeks. It was by pure chance that he'd caught sight of the child's curly blond hair moments before the boy disappeared beneath the surface of the lake.

Bertil had gotten up early to get to work on the difficult task of pruning the entire vineyard. He'd been standing with his clippers in hand, about to snip off a branch, when he looked up and glimpsed something he first took to be a diving seabird. It took him a couple of seconds to realize that the twist of yellow wasn't feathers; it was hair. He'd thrown down his clippers and rushed toward the lake.

It had taken him thirty seconds to get to the shore, another half minute to wade and swim out to where he'd seen the head go under. He dove. What he found made him choke so violently that a stream of bubbles rose from his mouth.

Kim Ribbing stood on the lake bottom with his eyes closed and arms out as if in prayer. His blond hair swirled around his head like the halo of a sea god. Bertil couldn't understand how a seven-year-old boy could have so much self-discipline in the art of drowning himself.

There was no time for speculation. Bertil swam to Kim, seized his body, and ascended. Kim's eyes and mouth remained closed when his head broke the surface. Bertil shook him and shouted: "Breathe, lad! Breathe!" A couple of seconds passed, then came an inhalation that sounded like a sigh as Kim's lungs expanded. Bertil pressed the boy to his chest and backstroked his way to the shore.

"Kim? Kim? Can you speak? Are you all right?"

The boy still hasn't opened his eyes. Bertil's greatest worry is how the boy's grandfather, Count Sigward Ribbing, will react. He's stern, and Bertil knows that the count is quick to exact corporal punishment if his grandson misbehaves during the summer weeks the boy always spends at Roshult. A suicide attempt will certainly be viewed as worthy of punishment. Bertil takes an anxious look up toward the manor house. Fortunately, it's just past seven; the count usually doesn't rise before eight.

Bertil looks down and sees the boy has opened his eyes. They reflect the morning sky's intense sheen. If you could look into the face of an angel, its eyes would be just like these, full of heaven's splendor.

"How are you?" Bertil asks. "Why . . ."

"Don't tell," the boy mumbles feebly. "Don't tell Grandfather."

11

Champagne was still bubbling in Julia's bloodstream, and it would be a couple of hours before she was capable of writing. Some of her writer friends told her that a glass or two of wine allowed their imagination to take flight, but most of them, like Julia, needed to be stone-cold sober to achieve the level of concentration required for composition.

One time she'd come home after a tipsy evening at the Angel Pub and had been struck by something rare enough to be called *inspiration.* She'd been stuck in the middle of her current Åsa Fors novel, but in a flash of clarity she saw exactly how to resolve the problem. Even though her mind was blurry, she sat down at the computer and wrote four pages. Of course, when she looked them over in the morning, they were garbage. She had to throw them away.

No writing for now. So, what to do? Julia got up from her bed, went into the living room, and clicked the Spotify icon on her phone, which had a Bluetooth connection to the room speakers. She tapped "The Dead of Night" and started the song. She slumped onto the sofa. The accelerating drone of the music filled the living room and was interrupted by howling guitars and a pulsing bass line that pounded Julia's chest. Depeche Mode songs were the auditory opposite of a cold shower; they surged and blew away the cobwebs with monotonous, hammering rhythms, singing about being horny boys with corny ploys.

Julia paused the music. No, this wouldn't work. The song's raw, ragged tone didn't fit her mood at all. She took a turn around the room, looked out at Järntorget, then went back to the sofa and tapped *Two dark eyes* into the search field.

The guitars that opened the song resembled Depeche Mode's riff about as much as a rabbit resembles a rabid wolf. It was the same when you compared David Gahan's voice to that of Sven-Erik Magnusson. Julia grimaced in disgust as Sven-Erik began singing in his smooth Värmland dialect.

She was sneering at those corny lyrics when she realized her cheeks were wet with tears. *Good God, this is ridiculous!* She couldn't stand this kind of music, and anyway, it wasn't even summer! Even so, she listened until the end, and her tears stopped. It ended, and she played it again. This time she found a playlist of Sven-Ingvars's greatest hits and listened to them all. When that ended, her continued weeping left her feeling completely drained.

As a teenager Julia had been a *syntare*, a fan of Swedish electro-pop. Hair slicked back to one side, pink fingerless gloves, leather jacket—the whole works. She called people who listened to Depeche Mode and Erasure thumb-sucker synth fans, because she went in for DAF and Nitzer Ebb. Over time the electro-pop industry lost its aggressive edge, and then nothing but that gentler, more melodious variant remained. All those thumb-sucker songs.

You must draw the line somewhere, but she'd thought it was miles away from Sven-Ingvars. But here she sat, her eyes swollen and bloodshot. Goddamned Kim Ribbing! Julia ended her music program with "A Question of Lust"—maybe by way of apology—but that, too, made her break down in tears.

Only about two hours had passed. Julia took a deep breath and pounded her thighs. *Okay, that's enough!* Here sat one of Sweden's most lauded thriller writers who'd just been offered an assignment bound to make her a multimillionaire and send her several times around the globe. *Sit here and sink into a pool of tears to the sounds of ridiculous pop music? No, sir! Time to go back to work.*

When she sat down at her desk again, that feeling in Julia's throat wasn't a lump. It was more as if she'd swallowed a wad of cloth, something stiff and uncomfortable stuck halfway down. But she faced up to the task. She opened her *Millennium_notes* document and started figuring out the twists and turns of Mikael Blomkvist and Lisbeth Salander's love story.

12

"So, then, you're in a raging bloodstorm?"

Irma Ryding took a drag on her thin cigarette, then flicked the ashes into the slush outside the Angel Pub. Irma, eighty-one years old, claimed she kept smoking mostly "to keep up appearances." Her lungs weren't really up to it any longer, but she considered that she had an image to maintain.

Irma had started writing detective novels in the 1960s, before Julia was born, but she had been overshadowed by Sjöwall and Walöö's Martin Beck series. Unconcerned, she'd continued to hammer out a novel every year. She'd created enough of a readership for herself to live off the proceeds. And she had a pension as well.

"Bloodstorm?" Julia echoed as she took an unaccustomed puff on the only cigarette she was allowing herself on an evening like this. She'd bought a pack at the newspaper kiosk. Camel Blue, the real thing.

"Not talking about love," Irma told her. "Sounds more like a fever or a raging storm in the blood. Hot and restless and absolutely wonderful."

Julia had spent an hour over a glass of wine describing the days she'd spent with Kim a week earlier. Irma had listened, grim and attentive as always, and then they'd gone out to treat themselves to a little nicotine before ordering another glass.

Bloodstorm, Julia thought. Seemed like an excellent description of her condition. Her body quivered with unending, intimate, ticklish stress, as if hordes of ants were crawling through the tunnels of her arteries. She wasn't entirely sure Kim was the one who'd conjured up that bloodstorm, but she thought so. She was aching for *something.*

"Why not just call him up?" Irma asked, squinting at Julia with eyes that once had been as bright blue as Kim's but were now clouded with age. She had short-clipped white hair; it was true that the cigarette fit her image. She looked . . . cool. Tough-assed, *une grand-mère fatale.* Julia hoped she herself would project the same image thirty years from now.

"No way," Julia said. "I can't . . . there's no future in it for us. I'd be pitiful, atrocious."

"Future?" Irma sniffed. "What happened with all that 'friends with benefits' stuff?"

"That's not me, not really. And you know what? Afterward, I spent half the afternoon listening to . . . get ready for it . . . Sven-Ingvars!"

"So?" Irma shrugged. "The only people who dislike pop music are those who've never been in love."

Irma loved making up drastic, snarky aphorisms, but Julia thought she was out on thin ice with this one. She was about to respond, but Irma held up a hand to stop her. "I'm not particularly fond of that sticky sweet stuff, but Sture liked it, and sometimes, when he grabbed me and we waltzed around the kitchen floor, suddenly all that nonsense about 'hand' and 'sand,' 'missing' and 'kissing' sounded real. Of course, they're clichés, but even so, they describe real emotion, lots of times better than that stuff folks call 'hiiiigh aaart'!"

Irma's husband Sture had died of cancer a decade before, only a week after their fiftieth anniversary. Julia's impression was that theirs had been a very happy marriage. The following year was the first that Irma didn't produce a novel. She and Julia met for the first time on a book fair panel. They'd been friends ever since.

If there was anything Irma despised more than people who sneered down from their high horses, it was what she called *hiiiigh aaart,* more commonly referred to as "the fine arts." When the Swedish Academy members were embroiled in their most heated discussions, Irma would telephone Julia almost daily for the latest dirt. Julia could tell her,

"All the beloved brothers of the academy are standing around with their trousers down. Now they're getting their little butts spanked and howling so loud that our late lamented Gustav III must be covering his ears down in his tomb."

Julia took a last drag and dropped her cigarette in the slush, where it went out with a hiss. "Right, sure. Say what you like, but I can't phone him, it would be . . . and, anyway . . ."

"Yes?" Irma made an irritated little *Spill it!* gesture.

"He's carrying so much pain," Julia said. "And I don't know if I can handle that."

"Huh," said Irma, dropping her cigarette. "Then you'll just have to ride out your bloodstorm, that's all. Shall we go inside and guzzle some more?"

13

Sigward Ribbing would never learn of his grandson's suicide attempt, but he sensed something was amiss. The boy lurked around the estate walls, hanging his head, and the count found that extremely annoying. Something had happened. It was probably mischief that the ill-raised little bastard was up to.

The count swooped down on the boy the afternoon of Midsummer Eve. The house was deserted except for the two of them when he strode into the library where Kim was curled up under a table, paging through a book of Gustave Doré's illustrations of the Bible. The count was a tall, well-preserved sixty-year-old who had no problem dragging the skinny boy from his hiding place. He slapped Kim a couple of times. "What have you been up to? What?"

"Nothing, Grandfather. Nothing!"

"I can see it on you. Very well, then, up on the horse until you—"

"No, Grandfather, no. Not the horsey! Please, Grandfather, not the horse!"

The grandfather's face, always stern, split into a delighted grin. The boy's fear and desperation was a balm to his soul. And soon he'd enjoy even better pleading! The count dragged and carried Kim into what had once been a ballroom but now was used to store furniture and other items no longer in use. As well as the horse.

Kim's terrified bleats rose even higher in volume when the count pulled away the sheet covering the medieval torture instrument they used in the old days to subjugate unruly serving girls and disobedient peasants. A wooden trestle was hewn so it had a sharp upper edge; a carved horsehead was set at one end.

The count unhooked a heavy black coat with wide fleece lapels from its place on the wall. The garment had belonged to his father, a grim man with a taste for punishing people. The count thought of the thing as the "tamer's coat." Its weight on his shoulders gave him a lovely sensation of authority and righteous judgment.

The count seized his grandson by the waist and lifted Kim chest high. Kim flailed at his grandfather's face, but his arms were too short to reach it. The count turned halfway around and set the boy on the sharp wooden edge. Kim's yelling changed from cries of fear to cries of pain as the keen edge pressed into his groin. Kim wiggled and turned, trying to get off, and the count roared, "Sit still! Otherwise, you'll get the cat too!"

The count had used the cat-o'-nine-tails on his grandson only once. It wasn't useful, because it left scars on the boy's back. He believed he had Kim's parents in an iron grip, but even they might have their limits. The horse was the better option.

Kim sat rigid, his face distorted in pain. He no longer wept, he merely sniveled and hiccupped. He gasped and panted, and his face was red.

"Aha," the count said. "How much shall we hang on you today? Eh?"

"Nothing, Grandfather," Kim moaned. "Nothing!"

"Oh, but we'll need a little bit of help along the way if we want this cock to crow."

The count rummaged in a wooden box holding weights attached to leather straps. He chose two five-pounders and hung them from Kim's ankles. Kim began shrieking, and the count nodded in satisfaction. Those yells seemed to send the count's soul soaring into the sky on invisible wings. He felt a dry lump of excitement in his throat. He gathered the tamer's coat even tighter around him and chuckled. "Gallop, boy. Giddyup!"

Kim was forced to ride the horse for twenty minutes, and by the end of them he was little more than a mass of quivering flesh. His curly hair hung straight, drenched as sweat gushed from all his pores. When the count unhooked the weights, the boy fell over, hit the ground, and lay there face down on the dusty parquet.

Kim's body felt split in two. The only thing holding him together was white-hot hatred that spit and popped like a welding torch. Someday its intense flame would turn outward. That day would come.

II

Tärnö

1

It was the morning of Midsummer Eve. Kim stared out the window of his junior suite at the Hotel Diplomat toward Nybro dock, where the Waxholm company ferries were tied up, bobbing gently in the glittering waves. Five months had passed since he left Julia Malmros with his "So long, it was great." He'd started to phone her several times, but each time he'd regretted the impulse and put the phone down. She had never called him.

Or maybe she had. A few days after Kim left her apartment, he'd purchased a flight to Cuba, where he spent two months off the grid in a tiny village. No internet, highly unreliable mobile phone coverage. She might have tried to contact him. Kim had been gathering his strength for a job he planned to carry out when he got back to Sweden. Now it was done.

Kim put his forehead to the warm windowpane. He was fatigued not only physically but also to the depths of his soul. He'd scarcely slept at all as he finished profiling an extensive ring of pedophiles on the dark net who shared pornography depicting the most extreme forms of child abuse.

Thor was the browser used to access the internet's dark side. It shuttled traffic across a host of servers, so tracing messages back to their origins required so much time and patience that the users had almost always signed off before Kim got to them.

He did have an advantage over the Swedish police unit that investigated child pornography. He could use unconventional—okay, illegal—means to break into suspected pornographers' computers and phones to lurk and wait for them to go online again.

One of Kim's tactics was to present himself in a chat forum as a twelve-year-old boy who could be enticed by a groomer. He was adept at keeping up the conversations so that in certain instances, with the help of a program he'd devised, he could search the internet's millions of networks to identify the individual from word patterns typically used by that particular groomer.

When he'd gotten a hit and finally identified the IP address from which the individual was conducting the conversation, he kept the talk hot and heavy while working his way through the chatter's firewall. Pretending to be a twelve-year-old and simultaneously using the skills of an expert cracker was exhausting.

When he had total access to the other computer, he searched for emails where the malefactor shared tips with others with the same interests. He installed Trojan horses there. These would infect the pedophile's future messages to acquaintances and provide Kim back doors to their devices.

When Kim began his project several years earlier, his main aim had been destruction. He succeeded in extracting source codes of several file-sharing programs that "child lovers" used to share images and videos. He planted worms that would shut down their computers forever as soon as they downloaded something. Or he deleted that network's entire contents.

That approach turned out to be completely futile. It took only a day or two before news of the attack was posted in some other forum. The phenomena of child abuse and exploitation were as resistant to attack as cockroaches were.

So, Kim decided on an approach like that used by the police, albeit with additional unconventional methods. He'd assembled a folder with nearly four thousand pages of texts and images, evidence that theoretically should suffice to charge and convict 340 Swedish citizens. He didn't know if the evidence he'd collected by these means would be enough, but this was a job he had to carry out.

His exhaustion wasn't due only to the searching, the cracking, and the challenge of inserting spy programs. It was also due to all the filth he'd been forced to view. The quantity of material kept on growing; at the same time, it got steadily more appalling. It had become the rule rather than the exception that even infants were subjected to gross abuse to be documented and shared with thousands of individuals. All this was deeply depressing.

Kim sat down to his keyboard, skimmed through the folder he'd titled *Pedophile Documentation*, and then sent it via encrypted link to the digital crimes unit within the Swedish police's national operations unit. Then he spent an hour deleting every trace of the documents from his own computer. Getting busted now for child pornography on his hard disk would be the height of irony.

Kim looked up and stared at himself in the mirror. He looked like hell. The three months he'd worked on the pedophile networks had aged him a couple of years. He had dark-purple bags under his eyes, and on his head four inches of blond roots were apparent. He needed rest.

Rest.

When was the last time he rested, really rested, in the past few years? Completely let go and just let life go by? The first memory that presented itself was the sight of his own hand lightly clasping Julia Malmros's shoulder as she slept, his knuckles faintly lit by moonlight flooding through her window. Yes. Embracing her, Kim had enjoyed as profound a peace as could be.

Kim pulled the keyboard to him again, tapped *Julia Malmros* into the Google search box and clicked News. Titles of recent articles filled the screen, and at first Kim thought Julia's Millennium book had been a big hit. Then he took a closer look.

Kim did something he hadn't done for months and months. He threw himself back in his chair and laughed out loud. After he'd overcome his amusement, he shook his head and wagged an admonishing finger at the screen. "Julia Malmros," he said aloud, "you're in big trouble now!"

He remembered the location of the summer cabin Julia had mentioned: Tärnö. Kim packed a bag, then left the hotel room and set out for the Vaxholm ferry dock.

2

No doubt about it: Julia Malmros was up to her neck in trouble. Several sorts of trouble. It had begun a few days earlier, when she had a meeting with the firm's editor about the draft for the Millennium project she'd sent in three weeks earlier. The writing had gone surprisingly quickly, and she knocked out almost four hundred pages in just over four months, no doubt because the fictional world and characters already existed. All she had to do was find things for them to do.

Granted, it hadn't been *quite* that simple. The sections about Lisbeth Salander's expert hacking had given her problems because her pride had kept her from contacting Kim Ribbing. She used what little knowledge she had and faked the rest with the help of Wikipedia. A different expert would have to go over the relevant sections before publication. She assumed that Kim was out of the question.

She was pleased with the result. *Sandstorm*—her title for the novel—was at least as carefully crafted a work as her Åsa Fors novels. A tightly woven international thriller about drugs, corruption, and freedom of the press. She'd further developed the characters created by Stieg Larsson and elaborated by Lagercrantz.

Julia had always thought that Jan Bublanski's Jewish background was underexploited, so she let him grow a proper beard and quote Martin Buber. She gave him the allure of an Old Testament prophet. Perhaps inspired by her affair with Kim, she hotted up the relationship between Salander and Blomkvist. She'd thought it unnecessarily chaste in earlier installments of the series.

She'd been bothered by Mikael Blomkvist's unconcerned attitude toward women. Often they practically forced him to have sex, much to his surprise. That's why Julia let him get #MeToo-ed, a turn that, surprisingly enough, the publishing staff applauded for setting the narrative in unquestionably modern times.

Julia was quite pleased with her product, all things considered. It had a freshness and energy the Millennium world needed. Knock on wood, but she was convinced that it would be a big hit. And bring in enough for her swimming pool at Tärnö. One of those infinity pools.

So it was with a happy heart and high hopes that she turned up at the publishing firm to meet her editor for the first time. Oh, well, not exactly *her* editor. For this high-profile project, Helena, her usual editor, had been replaced by another Helena they'd headhunted from a larger publishing house. A specialist in detective novels, the woman was behind the scenes of several huge successes in recent years.

Helena Bergman, for that was her full name, received Julia in her office and offered coffee. She was a short, nervous woman with restless hands and squinty eyes produced by years of scrutinizing manuscripts. The general manager of the publishing house had declared she stood head and shoulders above anyone else in the business; if anyone could guide the Millennium ship into port, she could. Julia wondered how much they'd had to splash out to entice her away from that major publisher.

They began by chatting in general about how the assignment had gone, what it was like to work with already existing characters, and what David Lagercrantz was up to these days. Julia had gotten impatient by the time they'd finished their coffee. She went straight to the essential question: What had Helena thought about *Sandstorm*?

Helena folded her hands in front of her on the desk. "We think it's a really fine novel. Superb, really, but . . . could it have a different plot?"

Julia was expecting Helena's last word to be "title" and responded "Certainly!" because she herself wasn't entirely pleased with the title. *But hold on—a different plot?* "What do you mean, exactly?"

"Just keeping everything the way it is, but with a different plot."

"But . . . the plot *is* the novel. How can I change the plot but still leave it the way it is?"

Julia felt a sudden chill in her gut. The general manager had made it clear that Helena Bergman had the final word as far as Millennium was concerned. She'd had a good relationship with Stieg Larsson's father and brother, and was therefore, as he'd emphasized, the utmost authority and final arbiter. But the woman was clearly out of her mind.

The editor gave Julia a quick smile. "There's so much in it that's fine. The characters, the energy, the dialogues. The #MeToo business with Blomkvist is brilliant. And more."

"What is there about it that's *not* good?"

Helena put the fingertips of both hands together. "Yes, well, the Mexico scenes. I don't think they seem so . . . relevant. And it seems to me there are more coincidences, random happenings, than strictly necessary. And the mass graves and tortured women—entirely too morbid for this series. And the descriptions of Salander and Blomkvist's life together are somewhat . . . inappropriate for children. *Quite* inappropriate, in fact."

Julia had difficulty responding to each of her objections, but everything really fell apart with her assertion that "Mexico doesn't seem relevant." Julia certainly could have toned down the novel to be less vivid and easier to digest, if that's what was desired. Chaste sex and friendly torture, no problem. But when the very foundation of the story was called into question, that was it. Julia's gut now felt as if she'd swallowed a huge chunk of ice. "When it comes down to it, you just want me to write a different novel?"

"I'm *not* saying that. But a novel with a different plot."

Julia put a hand to her brow and closed her eyes. This was going nowhere. Not only was her gut freezing, now the back of her head was pounding. She held back her outrage and had to control her voice when she opened her eyes. "Okay. So, I spend almost five months writing a new novel and send it to you, you read it and decide it's not *relevant.* Now what?"

Helena's mouth turned down when Julia stressed the word "relevant." "We should have been collaborating more closely. That's how I generally work."

The last thing Julia wanted was to write a novel with this individual constantly peering over her shoulder. She'd rather give up the whole shitty business. In as calm a voice as she could manage, she said, "But how about if we do this: You, working with some advertising agency, come up with a plot that fits your needs. Something relevant. Give me a five-to-ten-page synopsis, and I write the book. Using my narrative voice and my unique expressions."

Julia's suggestion was entirely sincere. It was the only possibility she saw of avoiding a total flop. Despite that, Helena Bergman squinted at her with a look that seemed disgusted. "We've really never done anything like that."

"Then I don't see how we can go any farther."

"No. Nor do I."

Julia wished she could come up with some snappy reply to save face, but all that occurred to her was that song about leaving the table and being out of the game.

3

The icy lump in her gut had turned to nausea by the time Julia reached the street. She'd written what she thought was probably her best novel, and it had been dismissed as irrelevant. And worst of all was that there was nothing she could do. She couldn't take her draft to another publisher, because the publisher directly behind her had the rights to the Millennium franchise.

Four months of work, straight into the trash. She'd gotten an advance, of course, but it was only about 5 percent of what she usually received for an Åsa Fors novel. She'd wasted her time, and she felt so frustrated she wanted to cry. Even more pathetic was that she hadn't come up with a better parting line than Klas Östergren's quote of Leonard Cohen when he resigned from the Swedish Academy.

She took out her phone and rang Irma Ryding, the only person she'd allowed to read the manuscript as it progressed, because Irma was the only person whose opinion Julia trusted. Irma thought *Sandstorm* was brilliant, though she shared Julia's misgivings concerning the title. They'd tried to come up with a better one but in vain.

Irma answered with her smoker's rasping voice on the third ring. "Julia. How did it go at the publisher?"

"That's why I'm calling. Can we meet?"

"Oh, my, as bad as that?"

"Worse."

"Ten minutes."

No need to specify the meeting place. During the day, it was always the Café Gråmunken. Not a fancy place, but Irma liked it because it wasn't "overlit and full of jabber," which was her chief complaint about most other cafés.

By the time Julia got there, Irma was already seated at the table they usually took if it was available, far back in the corner with the least light and hardly any jabber. Irma grabbed the tabletop and rose to give Julia a hug. Then she held her at arm's length. "You look miserable, my little dear. Were they mean to our Julia? Here!" She waved at their table. "Cappuccino with an extra shot of espresso and a Danish pastry, will that help?"

Julia couldn't hold it in any longer. She burst into tears, almost literally fell apart. Irma embraced her and patted her head. It was so unbelievably wonderful to be called "my little dear" and comforted. The icy lump in her gut melted and the nausea lessened. She'd have stabbed nails into her eyes before she let Helena Bergman see her like this. Once her sobs had subsided, Irma pointed to a chair. "Sit yourself down. Spill it."

Julia told the whole story, everything, from the beginning, eliciting tsk-tsks from Irma. By the time she finished, she'd ordered and drunk a second cappuccino.

Irma leaned back and told her, "You know, a few years ago they tried to sic that Helena woman on me. That was before the big publisher recruited her."

"How'd that go?"

"What do you think? It lasted a week. She wanted to stick her nose into *everything*. I know some people are pleased with her, since there are some authors who can't write a word unless somebody holds their hand, but that's not me. It's not you either. There's *no way* you can work with her."

"No, I see that. But what am I going to do?"

Irma leaned forward and held up her index finger as she so often did when she intended to emphasize a pronouncement. "Here's what you should do. You invent two new characters who are enough like Blomkvist and Salander to put into your novel, but not so similar they can accuse you of plagiarism. Then you write a bunch of new pages to define and introduce those characters, and you turn right around and go back to the publisher."

"Is that even possible?"

"Of course it is. You can keep the book the way it is and just rechristen them Lösböth Söhlönder and Möckö Blömkvöst!"

Julia laughed out loud and her spirits lifted. Maybe something like this could be the way out.

Irma went on. "And there's more you can do. You take your book to Bonnier, the biggest publisher, preferably with a different title. They put it out there and it's a huge success, and then Helena Bergman can sit there and stew. Snipsnapsnorum! Mind you, that's *not* a suggestion for the title."

Of course, it wouldn't be as simple as Irma was making it out to be. Julia would have to revise the text completely, though she'd be able to use large sections of the main plot. It was doable; it would go a lot faster than writing an entirely new novel.

"There is another possibility," Julia said. "Helena Bergman could be right. Maybe it's a crappy novel."

"No way, José! You can forget that. It's a hell of a thriller. Well written. The only thing I might agree with if pressed would be that stuff about all the coincidences. But, hey, look at Dostoevsky. When you read him, he makes Saint Petersburg sound like a little village. People run into one another all the time."

"Now, remember, I'm no Dostoevsky."

"No, but you're Julia Malmros, and that's anything but a disgrace."

Julia took Irma's hand from where it rested on the table, kissed her knuckles, and exclaimed, "Irma, what would I do without you?"

"You'd melt into a little puddle, that's what."

4

They separated, and Julia went home. She took her place at the desk and had a hard think. She reread the first chapter of her manuscript, in which a women's shelter improves the security of its digital systems to make sure outsiders can't break in to get the identities of protected women.

Nothing said Salander was the only one who could handle that. Naturally, her speech patterns and distinctive manner of dressing had to be changed, but otherwise this character could be anyone at all, say, someone like . . . Kim Ribbing? Julia snapped her fingers. Of course! She could change the genders so the computer wizard would be a young man and the journalist would be an older woman, like . . . herself?

Julia got dizzy when she thought of inserting someone like herself into her action-packed plot. It was anything but obvious. Changing the genders was a good idea anyway. She'd have to think more about it. Her telephone buzzed and she checked the screen. A reminder she'd agreed to appear on TV4 in an hour.

She'd completely forgotten she was supposed to go to the studio to tape an interview with Malou von Sivers of *Malou after Ten* to chat about the Åsa Fors TV series set to premiere in the fall. She wasn't in the least pleased at the prospect of the interview. Malou's usual approach was to ask leading questions meant to elicit exactly the answers she'd decided were needed. But the production company had said an appearance with Malou would be great publicity, and Julia had accepted. It was too late to back out now.

As she chose the clothes and shoes for the interview, she felt bitterness gnawing at her again. The momentary enthusiasm at the prospect of revising the story and using new characters was subsiding. No matter how she turned it, it was a story custom designed for Blomkvist and Salander. Reworking it would take enormous effort. *God damn Helena Bergman. I hope her hair catches fire!*

Julia donned a simple light-blue blouse, jeans, and black sneakers. She mended her makeup and called for a taxi. She'd just have to swallow her humiliation for the time being and concentrate on crotchety old Åsa Fors. What did she really have to say about the TV series? Nothing, it seemed to her. She hadn't seen much but thought those scenes were lousy. She wasn't about to tell Malou that. She'd have to improvise. She was usually pretty good at improvising.

5

It fell apart with the first question. Malou led by describing the upcoming series and said, "But before we talk about that—you seem to have been under the radar recently. What have you been up to?"

Julia responded without thinking. She heard herself saying, "I've written a new novel for the Millennium series."

Malou's expression was one of genuine astonishment. "Wow! Nobody's heard anything about that!"

"No. It's a secret."

"And you're letting it out now?"

"Yes. I certainly am."

"How come?"

The cat was out of the bag. Unable to hold herself back, Julia told Malou exactly what had happened. She mimicked that idiotic remark "It's a really fine novel, but could it have a different plot?" Malou shook her head in sympathy and let Julia continue. For once, she asked almost no questions. She knew she had a scoop; she let the victim chatter on, hanging herself.

Julia described how she'd gotten the assignment, how small the advance was, how the editor had first praised her and then cut her down. She gave a general description of the plot and wished good luck to whichever other author got the assignment.

When she'd finished, Malou sat gaping at her before pulling herself together. "That was quite a story you told us, Julia Malmros. Now, here's Bobo Ståhl to report on the new trend, mindlessness."

The next guest planted himself on the sofa, and a studio flunky gestured to show Julia where to go. She stepped off the low platform, telling herself, *That was stupid. Really stupid.*

The program was scheduled for broadcast the following day, but someone on the *After Ten* production team must have leaked it, for Julia got the first call from a reporter by seven o'clock that evening. "Is it true that . . ." et cetera, et cetera. Hadn't Julia signed a nondisclosure agreement? Yes, she had. What would happen now? She had no idea.

The real storm broke after the broadcast. Hordes of journalists tried to reach her, some of them even calling from abroad. The publishing company phoned and told her Stieg Larsson's heirs were threatening to sue them and they'd countersue Julia. Maybe the heirs would sue her as well. Everybody would be after her for damages. Irma called to tell Julia she was a fool but she didn't love her any less for that. "Tough it out, girl!"

At half past nine that evening, Julia turned off her phone and drank a whole bottle of wine while listening to Sven-Ingvars. She wished Kim were with her. He'd probably have been wholly indifferent to her actions; maybe he'd even have approved. She'd scarcely thought of him during the months of writing, but she realized now that she missed him.

She went to bed and sought Kim's scent in the sheets and on the pillowcase, but he'd long since been washed away. She patted the pillow where his hair had spread out so wonderfully and wept for a bit. Then she fell asleep.

When she turned on her phone the next morning, she found more than fifty missed calls. Around eleven o'clock, someone knocked on the door. When she checked the peephole and recognized a reporter from an evening paper, she didn't respond. She went to her kitchen window, picked up her binoculars, and focused them on the newsstand in the square. Sure enough, she saw her name in huge letters on a couple of news placards. She lowered her binoculars and saw a few people in the square pointing up toward her apartment.

Tough it out, Irma had said. Julia crouched in her apartment and toughed it out with her phone off, ignoring sporadic buzzes from the intercom. After two days of this toughing it out, she checked her calendar and saw it was the day before Midsummer. She packed a bag to leave everything behind and flee to Tärnö.

6

The ferry was packed. Lots of people were going out to the islands to celebrate Midsummer. When Julia made her way through the main cabin to get to the aft deck, several heads turned to watch her, and she heard whispers behind her back.

She'd refused to read anything about the controversy and didn't know how the story had developed. They'd probably interviewed someone at the publishing firm, who declared that Julia's remarks on *Malou after Ten* constituted an unprecedented breach of contract. But would ordinary readers care about that?

Julia's assumption was confirmed when she looked back into the cabin and a woman of about the same age caught her eye. The woman smiled and gave her a thumbs-up, then raised a clenched fist to signal *Fight on!* Julia returned the gesture, though with less determination, but lowered her arm immediately, afraid that everyone in there would mimic it, as if Julia were a partisan resistance fighter instead of a spited little author. After all, it came down to no more than that.

As they docked at Tärnö and she stood with a group waiting for the gangplank to be lowered, an elderly man turned to her. "Everybody's going to want to read that book of yours, my dear."

A murmur of agreement sounded around her. She said, "Maybe I can publish it as 'fan fiction.'"

"As what?"

"Oh, never mind. But thanks."

The gangplank descended, and Julia escaped the need to explain further. As she walked up toward her summer cabin, she began considering her little joke seriously. Wouldn't that be the ultimate *fuck-you*? Making the novel available for free on the internet! Then, when the publishers hired another writer and that drudge's Millennium installment came out, people would compare it with Julia's free version and find it inadequate . . .

Julia's fantasies lasted only until she got to her cabin, where the grass was overgrown and the terrace was full of branches fallen from the elm tree that looked trashier with every passing year. Julia hadn't been there since the previous summer. She devoted that afternoon to shopping, cleaning, airing the bed linens, and vacuuming spiderwebs out of the corners. The place was in acceptable shape by evening.

She finished up by hauling her five-horsepower outboard motor from the storage shed down the steep path to the shore. By the time she got to where her little fiberglass boat lay upside down on a couple of trestles, she had to stop to catch her breath. She'd rarely gone to the gym during the months of writing, and she was suffering now for that neglect. She was breathing hard and her arms ached. She leaned back against the hull feeling ancient.

"Useless old woman," she muttered. She set down the motor. Clenching her jaws at the effort, she righted her boat, lifted the outboard, and clamped it in place. This arduous procedure had once been Jonny's responsibility. Driven by a grim *I can do this!* Julia even managed to fetch the gas can and fill the tanks, push the boat out, and yank on the cord until the motor started with a ragged roar. She patted its plastic cowling. "Clever girl!"

She used the last of her strength to drag the boat up on shore. Now she had her own means of escape, independent of the ferry schedule and people's inquisitive looks. She returned to the cabin, poured herself a generous dose of Famous Grouse, and went out on the terrace. She settled with a deep sigh into a lounge chair.

The chair responded with a protesting creak as Julia leaned back and sipped her whisky. She looked over the harbor where sailboats were tied up in a triple row, waiting for the Midsummer celebrations. Even the people in the shops had sneaked looks at her. After a couple of shots of aquavit, they'd probably start dancing around her instead of around the Midsummer pole. *No, thank you.*

Julia felt herself horribly uninterested in everything, but most of all in her second career. She'd become leery of the word "joyful," but that was just what the work with *Sandstorm* had been, more so than with the Åsa Fors novels. She'd really enjoyed the company of Lisbeth and Micke, which made her disappointment that much keener.

Maybe with new characters? Julia shook her head and poured another whisky. She was indifferent to them as well. Her only craving at the moment was for a cigarette, but she hadn't bought any, and there were none in the cabin. *Damn, how depressing.* She couldn't even rustle up a little cigarette. Self-pity crept over her. It turned into bitterness during her third glass of whisky.

Those bastards. Those son-of-a-bitch bastards.

She wasn't going to write any more Åsa Fors novels. If she did, she wouldn't let the bastards at that shitty firm publish them, no, sir. Feeling momentarily exalted, she poured a fourth whisky.

Should she take decisive action right here and now? Create a website for fan fiction and just throw *Sandstorm* out on the net? *There you go, all you Swedes! A little Midsummer present from Julia Malmros. Enjoy yourselves!* She chuckled to herself and rubbed her hands together as she swished the whisky around in her mouth. They'd be hopping mad at the publishing firm, and maybe Helena Bergman's hair *would* catch fire.

Julia was on her way out of the lounge chair to wreak her vengeance, but she got dizzy and slumped back. Okay, she was a little tipsy. She shouldn't make decisions when she'd been drinking. Wait until the next day and see if she was still convinced.

The hell with it.

For a while everything had seemed to be going really well. Now she was back to zero. In fact, she'd lost some ground. Unless she was mistaken, fan fiction was technically illegal, but no one complained, provided it was small scale. *Sandstorm* was anything but. That required another decision. She wondered whether the firm really was planning to sue and how much a judgment might be. Millions and millions of kronor? Would she have to sell her summer cabin? Her apartment? *Damn Malou for letting me blather on and on!*

Music and sounds of carousing came up from the sailboats in the harbor. Coming to Tärnö had been a mistake. Her loneliness intensified when people were partying all around her. It would have been better to hole up in her apartment and let the shitstorm blow over. There was a splash in the distance as someone fell overboard, followed by gales of laughter.

Oh, hey, Leffe was so drunk for Midsummer! He tumbled into the sea with all his clothes on! Oh, how we laughed!

These people were idiots. Julia reached for the bottle to fill her glass but managed to stop herself. She knew how her emotions worked. If she drank any more, her bad mood would close over her like a wet blanket and probably stifle her for days as she kept drinking in the effort to resist it.

She needed to rise to the occasion. Get herself up, not just wallow here like a bitter old woman mulling over her disappointments. Julia screwed the cap back on the bottle and got to her feet by grabbing the chair's armrest. The chair moved and she almost fell but managed to regain her balance. She raised her glass toward the partying.

Skål. *Cheers to you, fools!*

She got into the cabin and dropped her clothes in a heap on the floor. She crept under clean sheets and the thin blanket. The room seemed to spin around her. She tried to think of Kim Ribbing and the days of bloodstorm in her apartment. It was no use. Then she visualized the sex scenes she'd written for Salander and Blomkvist. That brought a tingling to her crotch, but when she touched herself, nothing happened. She wasn't even allowed a tiny bit of pleasure. She curled up on her side like an innocent little girl. Quite a long time passed before sleep came to her.

7

The first thing Julia did upon waking was check her phone. Only ten missed calls, one of them from Louise Granhagen, the head of her publishing firm. Julia got up, gulped down a couple of big glasses of water, set up the coffee maker, then stood there, holding her phone.

Now what? She should stand up for herself and focus. Might as well face the music. She clicked the return call button and gazed out the window. It looked like they'd have fine weather for Midsummer. Not that it mattered to her, but it was good for others. At least it wasn't snowing.

Louise answered after the second ring and didn't bother with the niceties of greeting her. All she said was "So it's you, Julia."

"Happy Midsummer, Louise."

"Spare me. You know what a mess you've made?"

"More or less."

Julia went to the window to look out over the bay toward Knektholmen, where her childhood friend Olof Helander owned an architectural marvel he called his "cabin." On the phone she heard Louise snort in disgust. "They were on us like hawks here, I want you to know. And after you made yourself scarce, we're the ones who had to take it on the chin. Damn you, Julia."

"The heirs? Are they going to sue the firm?"

After a couple of moments of silence, Louise replied in a somewhat calmer tone. "I don't think so, they don't want to be seen as . . . but do you realize how much damage you've done? To the brand?"

"What brand?"

"Millennium, obviously! What do you think we're discussing here? Donald Duck?"

Julia didn't see why she should care about the Millennium franchise any more than about Donald Duck, but she was smart enough not to say so. Instead, she asked, "How about you at the firm? Are you planning to sue me?"

Louise sighed. "Until further notice the official version is that we will, but no, we're not. You may not believe it, but I actually care about you. You idiot."

Julia turned her face away from the phone so Louise wouldn't hear her sigh of relief. She had no idea how comprehensive and time-wasting a civil suit might be, and she didn't want to find out. All she told Louise was "That's good to hear."

Louise added, "Unless you cause us even more trouble."

"I was actually contemplating putting it up on the internet as fan fiction."

Louise blew up. "You do that, and I'll set so many lawyers on you that you won't be able to see your hand in front of your face!"

"I won't. But Louise, I was *really* disappointed!"

"I understand that, I do, Julia. I also think it's a fine novel, but we don't have the final say."

"It's Helena Bergman's?"

"That's what it came down to, yes." As Julia drew in breath for a withering comment about Helena's professional competence, Louise forestalled her with a question. "When will you have something new with Åsa Fors?"

"It'll probably take quite a while. You might say that this author's self-confidence has just gotten a great big punch in the mouth."

"Then you need to shape up. I hate to admit it, but you're the talk of the damn town now, and if you're smart, you'll take advantage of it."

"You know perfectly well, Louise, that I'm not so smart."

"No. That has been demonstrated as clearly as anyone could wish. Have a happy Midsummer, you crazy person."

"Happy—" But the line was already dead.

The coffee maker was sputtering, and the aroma of coffee filled the house. Julia's mood lightened a bit. Louise had been as horribly angry as she'd feared, but she wasn't going to lose her cabin or her apartment. Not much was left of her earlier vow not to write any more Åsa Fors novels for "those bastards at that shitty firm" to publish. Whether she'd be able to write them at all was another matter.

She poured herself coffee and drank it on the terrace, peering down toward the harbor where tipsy amateur sailors were busy on board, setting up tables for lunch. Was it already that late?

After finishing her coffee, Julia clapped her hands decisively. *Now* was the time for shaping herself up.

She took a long shower, then dressed in a white linen blouse and matching trousers. She dragged the table out onto the hill in front of the cabin and set it with her only tablecloth. She took from the fridge the provisions she'd bought the day before. Herring, potatoes, and eggs. She'd brought the aquavit with her from Stockholm.

She boiled the potatoes and eggs and even took the trouble to put the herring in wine sauce and the herring in mustard sauce into bowls instead of just plonking down the tins. She laid everything out on the table just as the one o'clock ferry entered the harbor. Then she fetched the bottle of aquavit from the freezer and looked around for a napkin. The only one she found was printed with a crayfish motif, a leftover from a party she'd held for publishing friends in happier days. She tucked the napkin under her chin and went back out to the table. Everything looked as it should; the charade was complete. She sat down.

Julia had served herself potatoes and started to shell an egg when she heard someone walking up the gravel path from the harbor. The steps came nearer. Julia lowered the egg and tilted her head.

A few seconds later a mostly black-haired head came into sight beyond the edge of the hill, followed shortly thereafter by the whole of Kim Ribbing. He carried a bag with a battered leather luggage tag.

Julia could only sit and stare. Kim stood across the table from her, looked down casually at the table arrangement, the egg in Julia's hand, and the crayfish napkin tucked over her blouse. "My, my," he said. "This has *got* to be the most pathetic thing I've ever seen."

8

Kim had fetched a chair and seated himself across from Julia. She pointed to his hair. "You're . . . *blond*!" That label was so incompatible with the Kim she'd known, she felt she had to say it out loud for it to be true.

"Mm-hmm." Kim chewed a potato. "You've put on a bit of weight."

It was true. Julia had put on seven or eight pounds since their encounter. She'd often thought that she really should get back to the gym or take up jogging, but while working intensively on the Millennium novel, she simply hadn't. At the sight of Kim's trim figure slumped across from her, she had to resist the impulse to go find her running gear and head out for a jog.

Instead she went inside the cabin, found another shot glass, and set it on the table. She pointed to the bottle of aquavit. "Want some?"

Kim shook his head. Dismayed, Julia saw herself as a pudgy old lady sitting alone and swilling down even more calories. Kim leaned over and unlatched his valise, then pulled out a bottle of light brown liquid with the label *Selección de Maestros*. He uncorked it and filled both shot glasses to the brim.

The rum was fantastic. It filled her mouth with the taste of the setting sun. She examined the bottle. "You were in Cuba?"

"In Cuba. Right."

"What were you doing there?"

"Everything I could."

"You speak Spanish?"

"I do now."

"And why are you here?"

"Thought you needed some company."

Kim tossed back his rum and poured another, after which he leaned back and contemplated Julia. "I assume your feelings are hurt, but they don't have to be. You just showed them you had cojones. That nobody was going to fuck you over. Cheers!"

Julia clinked her glass with his and drank. The setting sun set her insides afire.

9

Julia had poured a third glass of sundown and noticed Kim was no longer so short spoken. He told her that in Cuba he'd lived in a shack on the beach, studied Spanish, gone diving and spearfishing with two newfound friends named Fly and Fedo. Coming from Kim Ribbing, that was information overload.

"After that?" Julia asked.

"After what?"

"Those months in Cuba. Then what did you do?"

Kim had had a spring in his step when he came up the hill, but he'd been sinking down in his chair as if yielding to a heavy weight. With Julia's question, he sagged and rubbed his eyes. "A project. Really don't want to discuss it."

"Okay."

As Julia put her glass to her lips, she heard a noise from the direction of Knektholmen she couldn't identify at first. Was someone already setting off Midsummer fireworks? But it was a popping, no, a hammering too rhythmic to come from skyrockets or firecrackers. She looked at Kim, who'd turned his head to listen over his shoulder, concentrating on the sound. He raised an eyebrow. "Am I hearing . . . a machine gun?"

"Hell!" exclaimed Julia and slammed her glass onto the table. "It sounds like it's coming from down by Olof's!"

"Olof?"

She was already on her feet and moving. "I'll show you the way." She headed down the steep cliff path.

They shoved her boat off the shore. The gunfire had fallen silent long before. Julia took her place at the helm and unwound the starter cord while Kim took the middle seat. The motor started on her third try. *Way to go, old lady.* Julia backed away from the shore and veered around toward Knektholmen. Over the racket of the motor, she shouted, "Olof and I were in the same class, best friends for years. He used to visit here when he was little, and he loved the place. After he grew up, he got really rich and bought that entire island. I've gone a couple of times to visit."

Kim nodded and stared into the distance. Far away, in a passage between two islands, he saw a motorboat roaring at high speed toward the mainland, a craft far more powerful than Julia's boat, which had a top speed of only seven knots.

It took no more than five minutes to cross the bay, and when they rounded Knektholmen's eastern end, Julia immediately saw from a distance that what she'd feared had occurred. And more. The luncheon table set up on the dock looked as if . . . as if someone had destroyed it with machine-gun fire.

Bodies lay sprawled across the table and the dock; the tablecloth was in tatters and drenched in blood. As they got closer, Julia saw that not a single dish, bowl, or glass was intact. Everything was in shards and splinters, and the table leaned at a crazy angle because a leg had been shot away.

Julia choked and had to cover her mouth to keep from throwing up when she thought she recognized her childhood friend lying shot to pieces at the far end of the dock, his hair a caked mass of blood. *Olle. Little Olle!* Julia spread her fingers and took a couple of deep breaths. "Good God. Who does this kind of thing?"

Kim's gaze was fastened to the dock as well. "Somebody who wanted to make sure he finished the job."

Afraid of contaminating a crime scene, Julia and Kim pulled her boat ashore about thirty feet away. A couple of neighbors appeared, peering around the corner of the house as Julia snatched out her phone and called 112. She related what she was seeing in a relatively steady voice, then asked the operator to hold the line. She approached the elderly pair, who were staring at the dock and shaking their heads in disbelief.

"Did you see what happened?"

The man, whose white hair stood out around his head, pointed a trembling finger toward the dock. "There was a boat. A motorboat. Two men in it. They shot . . . fired and fired . . ."

"Did you see what kind of boat?"

"I think it was a . . . Buster. Aluminum. Is that right, Vera?"

Vera said nothing but stopped shaking her head. Julia relayed the man's information to the operator and warned that unless the men had ditched their weapons at sea, they were likely to be armed and dangerous. She was assured the police would start a search and told to stay where she was. Julia stuffed her phone in her pocket and reluctantly turned to look at the dock. What she saw there shocked her. "Kim! What are you doing?!"

10

Kim Ribbing had seen and been subjected to more than his share of horrors in his life, but this topped them all. Sprawled bodies lay shot to pieces, flung about as if someone had mercilessly pitched them there, not caring how they landed. It was so grotesque that there was an astonishing beauty to it, and that's why it was so horribly fascinating.

The last supper.

Strewn among shards of glass and porcelain were hunks of flesh Kim couldn't identify. Several of the bodies had been drilled apart, and a small woman was missing most of her head, the contents of which were smeared across the dock. One man had a couple of fingers shot away and must have held a hand up to shield himself from an automatic weapon. Kim realized that the pieces of meat weren't from the bodies but were ham chunks just as blasted apart as everything else around and under the table. Hundreds of shots must have been fired.

A glitter from the bottom by the dock caught his eye. Carefully avoiding the human remains that in some cases had been sprayed the full length of the dock, he made his way to the edge and looked over. A mobile phone lay below. It looked like it had been broken apart, probably by the impact of a bullet.

Kim heard a noise he couldn't identify. A ticking sound, like from an old-fashioned alarm clock but faster. It came from one side, beneath him. He rejected the thought of a time bomb—these people had been thorough, but not *that* thorough. He lay flat and leaned over the edge to look.

A girl no more than thirteen or fourteen years old was clinging to the underside of the dock. Sunglasses were pushed to the top of her head, and black kohl mascara had dissolved around eyes wide open and shining brilliant white in the dark beneath the dock. The girl's lips were quaking, and the noise was the chattering of her teeth. A smear of blood ran down her cheek.

"Hey!" Kim called. "Are you hurt?"

The girl just stared at him without saying or doing anything. Her teeth kept chattering. Kim weighed the pros and the cons, found no cons, and slid over the dock edge just as he heard Julia Malmros shout, "Kim! What are you doing?!"

The water temperature couldn't have been more than sixty degrees, so it was no surprise the girl was shivering. Kim gasped as his black jeans and even blacker T-shirt took on the same temperature as the water. He swam three strokes and got a hold on the dock pilings close to the girl, who still wasn't reacting. Kim assumed she was in shock, both physically and psychologically.

"What's your name?" When he got no answer, he said, "I'm Kim, and I want to help you out of here. Okay?"

No reaction, but she didn't resist as he worked her icy grip loose from the pilings. She was all goose bumps. He put one of her arms around his neck, held her waist, kicked away from the dock and stroked with his free arm. He quickly reached shallow water. He moved the girl, carrying her more than supporting her, and brought her onto the dock. Julia came running.

"My God!" she exclaimed and put her arm around the girl's shoulder, just making the child huddle closer against Kim. "Astrid! Are you all right? Are you hurt? Did they hit you?"

"Don't think so," Kim said. "Except for that scratch on her cheek. Get a blanket."

Astrid refused to let go of Kim, so he held her until Julia came rushing back from the house with a blanket. Then Kim had to work seriously to disengage Astrid's embrace. "You need to let go now so we can warm you up. I'm not going away. I'll stay right here if you want."

Gradually, gradually, Astrid's grip loosened, and he was able to wrap her in the blanket. Kim carefully lowered her so she was sitting on the warmth of a rocky outcrop; then he settled there and sat with his arms around her until the first police patrol boat arrived five minutes later.

11

The summer at Roshult when Kim was ten years old, he overheard a couple of conversations between his parents and grandfather that made him understand how things were. The grown-ups thought Kim was out swimming, but he'd sneaked around the house and hidden in the room by the veranda. The door stood open and he could hear every word they said.

His parents expressed certain misgivings about Kim's uncommunicative behavior and the unexplained scars across his chest and belly. Grandfather was in the habit of giving Kim a little "souvenir" with his penknife when he released Kim from punishment. That had provoked questions at the gym where Kim was allowed to train several times a week. When the parents raised the matter, Grandfather's voice took on a threatening tone.

Kim learned that Grandfather owned the family's four-room flat by Östermalm Square and the parents didn't have to pay rent. In addition, he provided them with a generous allowance. Kim had wondered where the money of his unemployed, quite idle parents was coming from. Now he knew.

Concluding the discussion, Grandfather took up the matter of an inheritance. He'd spoken to his attorney and ascertained that there were procedures that could be followed if one had relatives one decided should not inherit. Grandfather explained that he greatly enjoyed the summer holidays Kim spent at Roshult, but if they were of a mind to deny him that little pleasure, well, then . . .

His parents were quick to assure Grandfather that wasn't their intention in the least, they'd just been wondering. Kim concluded that his parents were fully aware of what was going on. He'd tried several times to tell them what Grandfather was doing to him, but they'd just waved away his reports as fantasies and forced him to return to Roshult the following year. Sitting hidden by the curtain, Kim clenched his jaws to keep from screaming. He crammed his knuckles against his temples. There was only one way to understand this: His parents had sold him. To a sadist.

It was after that summer that Kim began to interest himself in computers, exploring the internet with an explicit goal in mind.

12

The police were somewhat short staffed. Partly because of the holiday, partly because the extreme-right True Swedes party had decided to hold a demonstration on the day they considered a hallowed Swedish tradition. Dealing with the event had involved a lot of police resources. They wanted to make sure it wouldn't get out of hand.

All available police boats were out searching for an aluminum Buster Magnum, so Jonny Munther got to the crime scene aboard a Sea Rescue Society launch about two hours after the crime. He'd called Detective Inspector Carmen Sánchez away from her Midsummer celebration to accompany him. She'd already had a couple of shots of aquavit, so a patrol car fetched her and delivered her to Stavsudda, where Munther and the launch were waiting.

They'd been working partners for three years. They were compatible. Jonny was easygoing, thoughtful, and methodical, while Carmen, fifteen years younger, was creative and imaginative, quick to throw out theories for Jonny to ponder. A plus factor was that she had no trouble winning people's trust. She was always the lead when dealing with the foreign born. She herself was born in Sweden. Her parents were from Chile, and she grew up in Rinkeby, so she was comfortably multilingual and cross-culturally sensitive.

As the launch left the dock, Carmen went forward to where Jonny stood at the railing, staring into the distance. "Did I get this right?" she asked. "It was your *ex* who rang this in?"

"My former wife. Right."

"I thought she resigned."

"Pure chance. It happened on the next island over from where we had our summer cabin. Where Julia *has* her summer cabin."

Carmen squinted at Jonny and didn't see much other than his usual attitude of a dog who'd gotten fed up with chasing the ball and really wanted to curl up in his doggie bed. She'd long ago stopped teasing him about having a last name that was practically a pun on "happy."

"And how does *that* feel to you?"

His voice was neutral. "I don't allow personal feelings to interfere with my work."

"Uh-huh. 'Cause you don't have any, or what?"

"I have plenty of feelings, but unlike many others, I keep them to myself."

Carmen took that as a dig. She knew that Jonny thought she was unsuitably passionate and driven by emotions. Once he'd said, "Stop being so damn Latino!" She'd pointed out he'd just made a racist remark, so now he limited himself to comments like "Can we be a little less South American now, do you think?"

Carmen left him to contemplate the horizon and decided to enjoy the trip before the shit hit the fan. She'd never been out in the archipelago. She inhaled deeply, enjoying the sea air, and watched as tiny islands with cabins painted red and trimmed in white flashed by. The cabins seemed scattered about like toys.

The launch slowed to steer toward a nearby dock. Carmen Sánchez straightened up, took a deep breath, and chased away her tourist's attitude. They were approaching a crime scene. Her wandering attention sharpened, searching here and there for anything unusual, any discrepancy, while she as good as memorized everything she saw and made a mental map of the area. They landed and set out toward the Helander residence.

13

Buoys anchored around a diameter of a thousand feet of bay were linked by blue-and-white crime scene tape in case there was evidence to be found on the bottom. The divers were at work. They'd already found a huge quantity of shell casings and a badly damaged phone. But no weapons.

Jonny and Carmen went to the foot of the dock where the police had taped off the land side. Two bodies slumped over the table, another lay splayed across the planking, head hanging over the edge with dull eyes staring at the sky. The other three slumped or sprawled in their chairs. A small woman with Asian features had the back of her head entirely blown off; her brains were smeared across the dock and had run down the side. Two crime scene techs in overalls and hairnets padded around taking photos while others were involved installing a tent over the crime scene, a job that should have been finished much earlier.

They weren't alone. Out in the bay, reflections glinted sporadically off telescopic lenses. Three boats with reporters and photographers had turned up, and more were probably on the way.

"They were taken completely by surprise," Carmen said with a nod toward the table. "Several never got out of their chairs."

Jonny rubbed the perspiration from his neck. It was hot outside. "Has anyone found out who the guests were?"

"Yes. One of Olof Helander's work colleagues told us. We have a list."

"Good. Since I find it extremely unlikely that *all* of them were the murderer's targets."

"Assuming it wasn't wholesale retribution."

"Yeah. Assuming that."

They left the dock and walked up to the house, where the police constable who'd been the first to arrive was waiting. He looked so young that he could have been mistaken for a summer intern. He introduced himself as Bill Skugge, then took out his notepad. Many younger and some older cops had switched to digital notebooks, but Bill Skugge was obviously of the old school.

"Did I hear this right?" Jonny asked. "It was Julia Mun . . . Malmros who called it in?"

"Yes, sir," Bill Skugge replied and read from the first page. "Along with a . . . Kim Ribbing."

"*Ribbing*? What kind of guy is that?"

"No idea. Got the impression that they were . . . you know, together."

Carmen checked Jonny from the corner of her eye. His expression was ashen. Carmen had come to understand from occasional comments that Jonny wasn't the one who'd initiated the divorce, and he would gladly have seen it canceled. Maybe his reaction was related to that. Carmen turned to Bill. "Witnesses?"

Bill Skugge checked his notes. "Two neighbors. Anders and Vera Josefsson." He pointed eastward. "They live a hundred yards over there and saw the sequence of events. From their terrace."

"Good. We'll need to talk to them some more. Do we have any idea how long the sequence of events, as you say, lasted?"

"When you say 'sequence,' you mean . . ."

"The shooting," Carmen clarified. "How long did the shooting last?"

"The neighbors say it went on for almost a minute."

Jonny Munther woke from the reverie into which Kim Ribbing's name had plunged him. "Do we have an idea how many shots were fired?"

Bill Skugge made a sweeping gesture that included the crime techs working the scene and the area around the house as well as the dive boats anchored a few yards off the dock. "They can hardly have found all the bullets and casings, but they think more than two hundred."

Carmen made a quick calculation and whistled. "If there were two perps, that means . . . about six shots a second. We're talking about fancy gear."

"In cases like this, you can't rely on the witnesses' estimate of the time."

"No," said Carmen, "but it's more common in cases like this that their recalled experience seems *longer* than the actual elapsed time. Not the other way around."

Jonny shrugged, his gaze inexorably drawn back to the dock. Those poor devils down there never had a chance when a hail of bullets blasted them to pieces. *Two hundred shots.* The killers had made sure they wouldn't botch the job. And come to think of it, were there any magazines large enough for that much ammunition? That was a question for later.

"This girl," Jonny Munther said. "The daughter, what's her name . . . Astrid. How is she?"

"Evacuated by helicopter to St. Göran's Hospital." Bill Skugge added in a low voice, as if sharing a shameful secret, "The psych ward."

"Did anyone interview her?"

"She didn't respond at all. Ribbing sat holding her until the helicopter arrived."

"Are they available?" Carmen asked. "Malmros and Ribbing?"

Jonny grimaced. He didn't like hearing those names pronounced together like that, as if they were a single unit, a couple. Which they might be, but even so, that didn't have to be said *out loud.*

Bill Skugge pointed toward Tärnö. "Malmros said we could just go over there to her cabin if we had any questions. Her phone number is—"

"I have her number," Jonny interrupted. "Now, let's go chat with the neighbors."

14

There were curious bystanders and a couple of journalists standing beyond the marked periphery on the land side as well. Jonny and Carmen ducked under the tape, and Jonny waved them away, making it clear he had no intention of answering questions. Fortunately, the Swedish journalists were sufficiently respectful, and the two police officers could continue their way to the neighbors' property without a pack of hangers-on.

One of the Josefssons was a serious gardener. Maybe both. The extensive flower beds on their grounds were well tended, and the grass looked as if it'd been clipped with nail scissors. Jonny Munther couldn't recall ever seeing a lawn that was so even and yet so lush.

The owners weren't in as good a shape. They sat beside one another in a swaying hammock, holding hands, and looked straight ahead with frightened expressions as if ghosts were dancing along their tidily raked gravel pathways. Jonny had seen this before in the wake of violence. Witnesses could appear generally collected just after the event. Then a clearer understanding of what they'd seen hit them, and the world as they thought they knew it was blown apart. That's where the Josefssons were now.

"Excuse us for interrupting," Carmen said. "But we really need to talk with you a bit. Is that okay? My name is Carmen Sánchez, and this is my colleague Jonny Munther."

Jonny usually let Carmen take the reins in situations like this. She was better at coaxing frightened or frantic witnesses to relax and open up. Anders Josefsson nodded and waved to invite them to take seats in the terrace's garden chairs.

Jonny Munther looked out over the bay. The Josefssons had probably been sitting right here. They had a straight line of sight to Olof Helander's dock, so the investigation had at least two reliable witnesses, assuming their memories were clear and they could express themselves—capabilities that traumatic events could disrupt entirely.

Carmen Sánchez was another one from the old school. She took out her notepad, which wasn't the usual spiral-bound type but the booklet kind with a soft cover that kids in primary school use. She clicked her ballpoint pen. "I can see this is difficult for you. You've just had to witness a horrible thing. But you'll understand that's why your observations are very important." Anders Josefsson nodded wearily. "Did you see the boat arrive?"

Anders cleared his throat. When he answered, at first his voice was low and hoarse. "I noticed it when it rounded the western end but didn't pay attention until it . . . came in slowly. Toward the dock."

Carmen directed her pen toward the point of land a couple hundred yards from the dock. "Over there, then. And when you say 'rounded,' you mean . . . ?"

"That it came from the south," Jonny put in. "Presumably."

Carmen jotted a note. Vera Josefsson whispered, "Have you found them?"

"Not yet," Carmen replied. "But we're searching. Okay. The boat slowed, approached the dock, and then . . . ?"

"Then they stood up," Anders said. His wife started sniffling. He pressed her hand, then completed the thought. "And they started shooting."

"How many of them were there?"

"Two. I told that other officer."

"Just double-checking so we get it right."

"It was horrible." Anders rubbed his eyes with one hand as if trying to erase the vision from his mind. "They were . . . cold as ice. Just stood beside one another in the boat and fired and fired."

"Excuse me," Jonny Munther said. "You said 'cold as ice.' What exactly do you mean?"

"Well . . ." Anders looked into the sky as he searched for the words. "Completely . . . collected, that's it. As if this was something they'd done before. Yes, like they were pros, if that's the way to put it."

"Can you tell us anything about their appearance?" Carmen asked.

"Just that they had that kind of . . . mask over their faces, like . . ."

Vera Josefsson leaned against her husband and whispered something in his ear. He nodded. "Ah, yes, that's right. Vera says they were short. I might not say so, but they were definitely not tall."

"Like . . . young men?"

"Yes, perhaps. They were, how do you say, slim. Fine boned."

The Josefsson couple had nothing more to say about the perpetrators other than the men had put their weapons down in the boat before tearing off toward the north. Jonny and Carmen thanked them and returned along a gravel walk so carefully raked that every step felt like an intrusion.

"Okay, then," Jonny Munther sighed. "Looks like it's time to take the bull by the horns and interview my ex. There's the devil at work. Why did it have to be her?"

Carmen gave him a snarky smile. "Thought you didn't let your feelings interfere."

"That's not a feeling. It's a statement of fact."

15

Julia Malmros and Kim Ribbing had been on Knektholmen for only about an hour—first, because Kim wanted to care for Astrid, who insistently clung to him, and then to be interviewed by the police officer. After answering all the questions not once but twice, they got aboard Julia's boat and returned to her cabin. Neither spoke on the return trip. They stared without seeing, thoughts turned inward. In silence they pulled the boat out and in silence they took the path up the cliffside to the house.

Only after they'd returned to the table and Julia had poured two glasses of wine they chugged down in silence did she say, "Goddamn it."

"Yeah," Kim said. "God damn."

Kim hung up his wet clothes to dry and borrowed one of Jonny's old bathrobes, which was far too big for him. They settled at the table and sat there in continuing silence, staring toward Knektholmen. Presumably the banquet table and the blown-apart human beings were still spread out on the dock. The technical team had arrived not long before Julia and Kim left the scene of the crime and were probably hard at work.

They'd been back at the cabin for five minutes when they saw boats head out from the harbor in the direction of Knektholmen. Kim picked up his phone and did a quick search. "They're on it," he said. "'Massacre in the Archipelago.' Maps and everything." He nodded toward the boats. "Thrill seekers."

Julia never could understand people's attraction to scenes of blood and violence like wasps to honey. What did they get from it? A kick? A self-congratulatory feeling of *At least it wasn't me*? Though, granted, you might say she earned her living by feeding that attraction. She had a thought and turned to Kim. "Is there anything in there . . . about us? After all, there were people out there with telephoto lenses, and . . ."

"Yep," Kim said. "You're there. 'Well-known thriller writer' and so on."

"What did they say?"

"Does it matter?"

Julia blushed. For a while she'd avoided reading about herself after the catastrophe on Malou's program, but previously she'd been in the habit of googling once or twice a week in search of positive comments about herself and her novels. Most of the time she found them.

"Curious, that's all," she said. "Making conversation."

Kim's look made her cheeks redden even more. *The hell with him!* After everything that had happened, she had a right to wonder what the popular perception of her was without Kim looking at her as if she was an egomaniac. So why was she blushing? Because she *was* a complete egomaniac. *Anyway, the hell with him.*

16

By the time Jonny Munther and Carmen Sánchez got to Tärnö via the Sea Rescue launch half an hour later, the mood at the table was quite surly. Neither Julia nor Kim had drunk anything more. Julia, especially, had a notion that if she did, the bitterness would well up, and there was no telling what would be said.

Kim had sat for a long time scrolling on his phone, his hair hanging before his face like a black curtain.

"What are you doing?" Julia asked.

"Looking up your buddy Helander."

"Finding anything?"

"Maybe. He had . . ." Kim looked down toward the dock where the big launch had just stopped to let off two persons. When Julia groaned and slapped a hand to her forehead, he asked. "What's wrong?"

"My former husband, that's what."

Julia should have guessed. When the Stockholm police got tasked with an investigation out in the archipelago, it was often eager beaver Jonny Munther who was called in. But for heaven's sake! Was she ever going to get away from that guy?

After Jonny climbed the hill, he stood staring at Kim as if observing a supernatural phenomenon. Meanwhile, Carmen Sánchez came forward and introduced herself.

"I remember you," Julia said. "Think you came on board about the same time I left."

"Could be," Carmen said. "And I've heard a lot about you."

Julia glanced at Jonny, who stood stock still as if glued in place. "Nothing very positive, I assume."

"At the station, I mean. And yes, mostly positive."

"It's just that—"

"That bathrobe!" Jonny groaned. "Why did you give him *that* bathrobe?"

"He was soaking wet and chilled after he pulled Astrid Helander out of the water. That's all that was available." Julia turned to Carmen. "I don't know if we can be of any use. It was all over by the time we got there."

"You know it was my favorite one," Jonny said. "All those summers, every morning swim . . ."

"You can have it," Kim said. "But I'm not wearing anything underneath."

Carmen gave Jonny a look so sharp you could have heard a *zing*. He shook himself and stepped away from the slope.

"This girl you fished out, Astrid," Carmen said to Kim. "Did she say anything to you?"

Kim shook his head and continued tapping his screen. "I saw a phone in the water, next to the dock."

"Yeah, we found it," Jonny said with a carefully expressionless voice. He mused and then added, "There are limits even to the incompetence of the police."

"How's it going with the crime scene search?" Julia asked.

Jonny instinctively pressed his lips together. Carmen gave her the diplomatic response: "The number one priority, of course, is to find the murderers. Second is locating the boat and the weapons."

"What kind of boat?"

"A Buster Magnum. Aluminum."

A couple of seconds passed in silence. Kim spoke up. "I saw it." He held out his phone to show a photo of the model in question. "One of these?"

"Right," Jonny said, doing his best to show no enthusiasm. "Where did you see it?"

Kim waved one hand. "Between two islands. Over there."

"Hold on," Julia said and went into the cabin. She brought a nautical chart and spread it out on the table in front of Kim, who put aside his phone and studied it. "This is Tärnö," she said. "And Knektholmen is situated—"

"I see it," interrupted Kim. He pointed to two small islands with a channel between them. "Right there." He ran his finger toward the mainland. "They went through there. Fast."

Jonny Munther took his telephone. "We have people in the islands asking around to work out the course of their boat, but every narrowing of the search area is . . ." The word stuck in his throat but finally emerged: "Welcome."

While Jonny rang in the information, Carmen asked, "Anything else? Julia, you know the ropes and what's worth mentioning."

Julia thought for a moment. "Those sounded like incredibly rapid-firing weapons."

"Yes, we confirmed that. Modern weapons. Anything else?"

Kim turned off his phone and put it on the table, then stared straight ahead with eyes seeing something other than the bay, the cliffs, the elm, and the birch trees around the summerhouse. Jonny had stepped to one side, and the tone of his voice as he spoke into the phone suggested something positive had happened. At last, Kim spoke. "The right side of the table. Seen from the land side. It seemed like the killers . . . were concentrating on that side. Worse injuries on the corpses over there."

Kim got up and went toward the house. Carmen brought up the photo of the dock she'd taken and spread her fingers on the screen to enlarge it. Kim's comment seemed to be correct. That's where the Chinese woman with her blasted skull was sitting, and there lay the man who was staring at the sky, Olof Helander, his torso and belly torn apart. Bones and messy intestines were visible in the bloody remains of his shirt.

And then there was the Chinese man, the woman's husband, who sat closest to the water. He was the one whose fingers were shot away, maybe when he made a futile effort to protect his wife before the bullets hit her face and tore it into an unrecognizable mess. Since this man was Chinese, one could conclude that the only man on the opposite side of the table was a Westerner. The medical examiner would have to determine whether that supposition was accurate at the postmortem.

If you had to guess, Carmen Sánchez thought, *you'd think Olof Helander and Chen Bao were the primary targets.* She knew it was unprofessional to leap to conclusions, particularly at this stage, and even worse to act on them. *Keep all possibilities open.* Maybe this was a reprisal only against little Chen Min with the blown-open skull. Not likely, but possible.

Jonny Munther ended his call and came swiftly back across the cliffside with a bounce in his stride. "Got to go," he said. "They found the boat."

"Where?" Carmen asked.

Jonny glanced at Julia out of the corner of his eye but decided it didn't matter if she heard. "Vassrugge, by south Stavsnäs."

Julia's eyebrow rose. "Down by Sjösala?"

"Exactly. Maybe we're dealing with a couple of Evert Taube fans."

It was rare that Jonny tried to crack a joke; when he did, his humor was generally terrible. The beloved troubadour, the Swedish equivalent of Perry Como, was hardly someone to associate with a brutal massacre. An uncomfortable silence ensued. Jonny cleared his throat, waved toward the house, and asked Julia, "You and . . . that guy? Are you . . . ?"

"Is that relevant to the investigation?"

"No, I just—"

"Then I have nothing to say."

Jonny was about to ask again, but he was interrupted when Kim came out from the house. He'd pulled on his almost-dry clothes. He held the bathrobe out to Jonny. "Here. Sorry, didn't mean to upset you."

"You didn't. I just . . ." Jonny's explanation of that "just" was lost in a noisy clearing of his throat, after which he and Carmen excused themselves and went down to the launch. Halfway down the path, Carmen glanced at her partner and saw him holding the bathrobe to his chest. Tears were in his eyes.

"What was that you were saying," Carmen asked, "about feelings?"

"There are limits," Jonny replied in a choked voice. "There really are."

17

Toward the end of the afternoon, Julia Malmros rustled up a simple omelet and a salad. She and Kim took their meal on the terrace, but neither had much of an appetite. They paid more attention to the cold beer from Julia's fridge than to the food. It was just past six o'clock, but the sky was as brilliant as at noon.

Kim pushed his chair back. Julia was confused to see him poking around in the cuffs of his rolled-up jeans. When he sat back up, he was holding a metal pipe with a mouthpiece. He worked with the object, pressed a button, and a yellow light came on. Kim nodded. He sucked on the mouthpiece and exhaled a bluish cloud that smelled of eucalyptus.

"So," Julia said, "you're using e-cigarettes now?"

"Vaping. That's what folks call it."

"Why do you carry it . . . there?" She pointed to his ankle.

"Only place it doesn't chafe."

Kim's jeans were skin tight over his slim legs, and the pockets were little more than decorations. You probably couldn't push a coin into them.

"The water didn't damage it?"

"Evidently not."

"Do you have a regular cigarette for me?"

He dug in his bag and tossed an unopened pack of Camel Blues on the table. He held out the vape. "In case I get tired of this."

Julia tore open the pack. The cellophane crackled, the foil liner ripped and gave way. Those small sounds made her aware of how *quiet* it was. She lifted her gaze and looked out over the harbor.

The light was beginning to wane. Most Swedes were revving up for lively bacchanals with clinking glassware and music and song that over the course of the evening would give way to yelling and crashes of overturned bottles.

None of that was audible now. All they heard was a murmuring from huddled-together groups on the docks. It seemed that the proximity of Knektholmen was dampening the festivities. No one wanted to party close to a massacre site. Julia's current dismal view of humanity lightened a bit. She lit her cigarette, the first in a long time, took a long drag, and waited until the first hit of nicotine took effect. Then she said, "Okay. Tell me."

"Tell you what?"

"What you found out. About Olle."

Kim sucked on the vape pen and blew a couple of smoke rings. "I didn't apply any . . . unconventional methodologies, but . . ."

Julia assumed that he meant those kinds of digital searches conducted outside the law, a.k.a. *hacking*. Kim watched the smoke rings dissolve in the faint evening breeze before continuing. "What I found isn't particularly strange per se, other than it suggests there *are* some things to be found."

Julia knew better than to interrupt Kim when he forgot his customary taciturnity and started putting longer sentences together, even joining them into a coherent exposition. She simply nodded.

"He sells—or, rather, sold—climate compensation rights," Kim said. "You know, payments from an international fund designed to encourage firms to reduce toxic emissions."

"I see."

"He comes up as the owner of two different firms, both registered in tax havens. So it's not possible to examine their books by conventional means."

"Dirty money?"

"Not necessarily. The reason many in that branch of technical activity prefer the Cayman Islands or Cyprus . . . is that relevant?"

"Tell me what you want to. I'm listening."

"Then to hell with that. It gets a bit more interesting when you look at *Olle's* personal finances." Kim said the man's name in a mocking tone, which Julia found inappropriate under the circumstances, but she let it pass. Kim continued, "He declares his income from a Swedish holding company that in turn has revenue from the other two firms. Relatively low income for the boss of a business with twenty employees. But . . ."

Kim waved the vape to emphasize the next point, contemplated taking another puff, but then poked it down into his jeans cuff. "In addition, there's a business he owns in partnership with that Chen Bao guy, headquartered in Shanghai. And that's a ghost. There's no way to get *any* information about it, other than that it's registered. The firm is called something typically cryptic: International Credentials and Holdings, Inc. Its address is a post office box in Shanghai. No more information than that. The rest is on the dark side."

"And how's that related to *Olof's* personal finances?"

"He has a six-room flat on Strandvägen—fancy!—and drives a one-year-old Tesla. I assume that the real estate and villa we saw today didn't just drop down from heaven."

"I think he said it cost about eighteen million."

"Yeah. And that doesn't fit with his declared income. Not at all."

"So, you think . . ."

"That his real income comes from somewhere else, and it's not far-fetched to assume it's from the ghost business in Shanghai."

"The one on the dark side."

"On the dark side. It presumably dumps its ghost millions into an account so ethereal that not even an exorcist could locate it."

"Could you?"

"Maybe. But why bother? It's not my case."

"Because you're interested. Because you saw those six dead bodies on the dock and want to understand why it happened. Got anything else you need to do right now?"

"Hmm," Kim said and reached for the cigarette pack. "Hmm."

18

It was getting toward eight o'clock, and it had been a long Midsummer Eve for Detective Superintendent Jonny Munther. His absence from the festivities made no difference to him, since he'd stopped celebrating Midsummer after the divorce from Julia. He hadn't been a party animal even before that.

Half an hour after the massacre, the prosecutor in charge, Liselott Ahrnander, named him to head the investigation. Then she hurried off to her own celebration on some island outside Stockholm, promising to get back in contact that evening. She'd briefly checked in around six for an update and reproached Jonny for not yet having put an entire investigation team in place.

For the moment it was just him, Carmen Sánchez, and Christof Adler who were directing the uniforms out in the field—or rather, on the water. Jonny had been planning for some time to call Christof into an investigation to see if he was any good. The young man's gaze had a childlike attentiveness that suggested he might be useful. Jonny was an experienced professional but not particularly qualified when it came to childish curiosity and sensibility.

Liselott had emphasized this was a high-priority case, and the media would be all over *Detective Superintendent Munther* if he didn't assemble a competent investigating team before the press conference scheduled for the next morning. Or someone else might get the job.

Jonny decided that Carmen, with her social skills, should work at persuading colleagues eager to enjoy the holiday to join the investigation instead, so he would have enough quiet time to go over what they already knew and prepare himself for the media circus. Public speaking wasn't Jonny Munther's favorite thing.

The discovery of the boat had yielded little. They hadn't even been able to find any footprints on the dry ground beyond the reedy grass along the shore. The techs had wrapped the boat in plastic and shipped the whole thing to the National Forensic Center in Linköping. It had been reported stolen from the Stavsudda harbor about nine o'clock that morning, so there was no trail to follow up.

In a grove of fir trees a hundred yards from the shore, they saw a few broken branches and found faint tracks of two pairs of wheels, so the perpetrators had probably gotten away on motorcycles. They hadn't passed any traffic cameras along the way, which suggested they'd planned their route carefully.

The most impressive—perhaps disquieting—find had come at about five that afternoon.

Everything suggested that the perps had spent the night on the relatively uninhabited southern side of Tärnö. Drag marks on the shore exactly matched the width of the boat hull, so the theft of that craft had probably occurred the previous evening and was discovered the next day.

Add to that: The lowest drag marks in the sand had been washed away. A twelve-knot wind had blown from the north the previous evening but had slackened to four knots before midnight. Four knots wasn't enough to raise waves high enough to wash away the tracks, so they could conclude that the boat had been dragged up on shore sometime between six and midnight. The drag marks from when the boat had been wrestled back out to the water were intact.

The shore was six yards wide, and after that the forest took over. Twenty yards into the woods they'd found hollows in the dry fir needles that showed two persons had been there, along with two broader depressions at the bases of large fir trunks. After that, nil. And nada.

Summing it up, sometime between 6 p.m. and midnight, two individuals had parked and hidden their motorcycles at Stavsudda, where they stole a boat and took it and their weapons to the south side of Tärnö. They dragged the boat up on land, went into the forest, and then sat *stock still*, each leaning back against his respective fir tree for twelve to sixteen hours. Then they got up, pushed out the boat, and left to do their deed. The ammunition they used, with a soft covering around a hard core, was designed to cause maximum damage to human flesh. These were assassins who knew what they were doing and had the tools to achieve their goal.

The police had scurried back and forth among the islands talking to people and had a generally accurate idea of the boat's route. At the morning press conference, Jonny would call on the public in and around Stavsudda to phone in any information about things seen the previous evening and the afternoon of Midsummer Eve. He didn't expect to get much.

At least he had enough to toss out to the detail-hungry scribblers to make them think the police work was revving at high speed, which was also the case. But Jonny could already hear the inevitable question they'd shout after he gave them the hard facts: "Do you know what the killers' motive was?"

That was the next stage of the investigation. First, you gather your clues before they turn cold, and then you try to figure out for yourself *why* that evidence existed. Carmen had quite a few ideas, but none they could share with the press.

Jonny leaned back in his chair. He hadn't gotten home that day, so the bathrobe hung in his office. He was seriously embarrassed by his behavior on Tärnö and promised himself not to repeat it. *Kim Ribbing,* Jonny thought to himself and sneered. If Julia wanted to get together with some kind of hard rock musician young enough to be her son, that was her choice. Jonny would have to keep the grinding feeling in his gut to himself.

Jonny got up and peered down the hall to make sure no one was around. Then he went and picked up the bathrobe, pressed a sleeve to his face, and sniffed it. It smelled of summer, the sea, and the salt-drenched cliffs. He sighed.

19

"I never met anyone better than he was at folding paper airplanes," Julia Malmros said. She yawned. It was almost midnight, and she was showing the effects of her lack of sleep the previous night.

Kim drank from his Selección de Maestros. "Better than whom?" For such a slim person, he had an impressive tolerance for alcohol. A few shots of rum and four or five beers over the course of an evening had no visible effect, while Julia was starting to feel a little silly.

"Olle," she said. "He had a book with a hundred different patterns, and he knew maybe half of them by heart. Some of his work rivaled the finest origami." She looked up at the sky, which, despite everything, had darkened just a bit, allowing the brightest stars to appear. She blinked sleepily and remembered a time when she and Olle were ten years old. Olle had produced a veritable flotilla of airplanes of different sizes and shapes that they took to the Traneberg Bridge. They threw the paper planes over the railing one by one and watched them sail down to the water. She thought about describing that memory to Kim but couldn't quite bring herself to do it.

Kim flipped a hand toward her closed laptop. "Makes sense. His firm is also involved in developing drones to measure air pollution."

Julia nodded and stretched, hearing her joints pop. She stifled a yawn. "Think I'll turn in. Didn't sleep too well last night." Kim just nodded. Julia lingered in her chair. They were at a bit of a decision point, but Kim showed no sign he was aware of it. Julia carefully asked, "What will you do?"

"Been staying up all night recently. Haven't been able to sleep for a while."

"Because of that project of yours."

"Hmm."

Julia intertwined her fingers and pressed them to her belly. She noticed to her displeasure a little pudge that hadn't been there six months earlier. Though she was aware she wasn't particularly alluring, she tilted her head shyly. "Just to clarify . . . how are we supposed to relate when it comes to"—she felt a sharp prickle of embarrassment and ended awkwardly—"to you-know-what?"

Kim's gaze was so piercing that Julia suddenly felt naked. If she'd had a bedsheet within reach, she'd have held it up to hide her figure and her furiously blushing face.

"Sex and living together?" Kim asked.

"Mm-hmm. I'm not saying. . ." She searched for the words. "I mean, there's no need, you don't have to . . ."

And she was supposed to be a writer! Oh, yes, inventing hot sex scenes for Blomkvist and Salander was no problem, but when it came to asking a simple question, all she could manage was to stammer incoherently. Soon she'd be reduced to babbling.

Kim held up a hand to halt her effort to speak. "I'm afraid that for the time being I have no access to the sentimental aspect of life."

"You sound like a priest."

"Okay. Just not fucking interested. Better? Sorry if it sounds like a cliché, but it has nothing to do with you. Really. I like to look at you. But right now . . . it's just not possible. I'm not there. Disappointed?"

"Not at all. . . or not much, anyway. I just want to know where we stand, so things don't get ugly or uncomfortable."

"For the time being, we're standing in a desert."

"Is that also related to your . . . *project*?"

"That's a reasonable conclusion."

"Okay," Julia said. "Now I know." She got to her feet and realized she was a bit unsteady. Halfway to the house, she turned back. "Thanks for coming. It's good to have you here."

"Even though . . . ?"

"Yeah. And feel free to come sleep in the bed. Even though. Good night."

"Good night."

Kim opened his laptop. His fingers flickered across the keyboard. Julia held in her gut on the way to the house but immediately despised herself for it. She shrugged off her clothes and crept under the sheets, hearing the rattle of Kim's typing out on the terrace, accompanied by quiet music from the laptop speakers. Siw Malmkvist, the 1960s torch singer, unless she was mistaken.

Julia had to admit to herself that she'd put the question to Kim out of a sense of duty. Even though from time to time she'd nostalgically recalled what Irma called the "bloodstorm," her body and emotions weren't ready for that. The scene on Knektholmen she'd witnessed had settled across her like a mute burning lump in her belly, and it was almost a relief that Kim had turned her down.

Julia closed her eyes, and the image of Olof Helander's bloodied corpse floated up out of the darkness. Even though they'd drifted apart, there'd been a time when they were very close. A sort of awkward shyness had kept her from telling Kim, but Olof Helander had been the first boy to kiss her and the first to caress her budding young breasts. That was all; they'd been only thirteen, but the memory was still vivid.

It was hard to make a connection between the shy boy with the paper airplanes and the man who'd been shot to pieces on the dock. Hands that had once caressed Julia were now bloody stubs. She squeezed her eyes shut, trying to push away that image. If there was anything she could do for Olof now, she intended to do it.

She turned onto her back and listened to Kim's clattering and tried to imagine those swift fingers lightly touching her, but Olof Helander's shredded hands intervened. It looked like this, too, would be a long, sleepless night.

Anna-Lena Löfgren had taken over from Siw Malmkvist. A warm melancholy stole into Julia's heart when she heard the lyrics about a summer when love was found and a journey begun together.

Oh, yes, my unknown sweetheart. If only it were that simple.

20

During Kim Ribbing's time in Cuba and while he'd been intensively tracking down the pedophile ring, he hadn't been in contact with the group of happy warriors who called themselves the HackPack. When he opened the encrypted mail server, he found a message that the HackPack had changed its log-in page because the previous one had been "compromised." In other words, infiltrated by some official authority, probably the US National Security Agency.

Kim sighed and called up the updated web page. Some of HackPack's members were nerds who'd been in on it since the start, and the new access portal was a free version of the Pac-Man game. The challenge was to click on one of the hundreds of dots the little yellow man had for food. The right dot was determined by a logarithm accessible only to HackPack members. Anyone who clicked the wrong one was locked out.

After making sure it wasn't yet midnight, he used his cursor to insert the date into the logarithm and learned that the correct combination was eight down and three to the right. He double-clicked the corresponding dot, brought up the log-in page, and tapped in his username and password.

He sent a quick greeting in English from his alias, Skalman, to let everyone know he was back. Within minutes about ten members had responded that they'd thought Kim was dead or under lock and key. The first response was from Moebius, who'd invited Kim into HackPack because they had a history and had even met In Real Life. Moebius always replied almost instantaneously, no matter the time of day. Kim guessed that he never really slept but just dozed from time to time before his screen.

Kim asked what had been going on lately and heard about members who'd gone to ground or come back, a coordinated attack that had almost broken a Spanish bank laundering dirty money, and the exposure of a troll den in Moscow. HackPack was generally driven by moral outrage combined with an affinity for disruption.

The most interesting development was an exploit that had humbled the high and mighty. Someone calling himself Ces had hacked the Mossad's main computer. The Israeli foreign intelligence agency was reputed to have the best data protection in the world, and no one had ever managed to defeat it before.

HackPack's members were delighted, especially because Ces had a sense of humor: Mossad's spy central was hidden in the basement of an anonymous business in Tel Aviv, and Ces had taken command of a digital advertising display on its front so that for a couple of minutes it blinked *MOSSAD! HELL YEAH!* in Hebrew before it was detected and the power cut.

Kim did find that entertaining; did anyone know more about that Ces? No, not any more than they knew about *that Skalman,* someone wrote. Kim had always been careful not to give any details that could be clues to his identity. Just like practically all the other HackPack members.

Kim spent a while making ironic comments and finished by asking whether anyone wanted to accept the assignment of checking out a firm called International Credentials and Holdings, Inc. headquartered in Shanghai. A longtime member calling himself Legion asked what Skalman wanted to know. Kim wrote *Everything* and added he could pay three thousand dollars, in Bitcoin if desired. It was indeed desired. He said *So long!* and shut down his computer, cutting off party band Thorleifs halfway through its "Don't Cry No Tears."

As the nearly undetectable dusk yielded to dawn, Kim poured himself more rum. A few gulls flew overhead, then glided out over the bay with cries that echoed dismally above the silent waters. He let the first rays of the rising sun spice the golden liquid before he took a sip.

He thought about Julia Malmros and her somewhat rounder figure. The change didn't matter to him at all. A body is a body, and she was lying in bed inside the cabin. The mere thought of naked flesh brought up extremely disagreeable associations. Maybe he'd been turned off for good. He wondered how long Julia would accept that.

Kim rubbed his eyelids to push away the unwanted images of tortured children. He'd been abused in all kinds of ways during his youth, and maybe worst of all was the abuse from those who were supposed to heal him.

21

A week after his fifteenth birthday, Kim was admitted for treatment at the Vamlinge Electroconvulsive Treatment Clinic in Vallentuna, north of Stockholm, an institution the patients often referred to as the "Big Watt." He'd been severely depressed for several months, and the foster parents he'd been assigned after his own parents' tragic accident were alarmed to see him alternating between extremes of self-punishment and paralytic apathy.

Neither drugs nor therapy had had the least effect during the month he'd been at St. Göran's Hospital. Kim took every possible opportunity to harm himself. Eventually it appeared there was no alternative but to send him to Vamlinge for ECT—electroconvulsive therapy.

The clinic director, the one who planned Kim's course of therapy, was Dr. Martin Rudbeck, one of Sweden's leading authorities in the field. His reputation would be seriously tarnished seven years later when it turned out he'd subjected youngsters to experiments so unethical that he was charged and brought to trial.

In short, the physician had used youths as test subjects—guinea pigs—to see how much electric current a young brain could withstand and to determine aftereffects and collateral effects. Those trials were much less about treatment than about research.

During the trial the media compared him with German concentration camp experimenter Dr. Mengele. Martin Rudbeck came to be known as the "Shock Doctor." He was found guilty, though the decision wasn't unanimous. He was later freed on appeal. His reputation had, however, been considerably diminished, and even though the appeals court hadn't confirmed his sentence, he was barred from using electroconvulsive therapy. He returned to the neurology ward where his career had begun.

Kim was profoundly apathetic the first time he was wheeled into the electroshock room. He didn't care what was happening. He didn't move as they stuck the gag into his mouth and attached electrodes to his temples. The red flashes and the blinding darkness that filled his skull made him cramp violently on the stretcher. It was as if his head had split, allowing a gleam of light to filter in.

The next day's evaluation confirmed Kim was doing a little better. For example, he'd regained the ability to move his tongue and lips and could form words. It seemed that parts of his brain previously shut down had now been endowed with a dim glow that allowed Kim to examine their contents.

That was when he opened up. Kim sat in an armchair across from Martin Rudbeck for an hour and told him about the abuse and torture to which he'd been subjected during his youth, frantically scratching his scarred arms all the while. Then he went to the toilet and threw up.

What Kim couldn't know was that his descriptions of extreme trauma had aroused erotic excitement in Martin Rudbeck. He really had a tough nut to crack here! Before him sat a conscious being so damaged by life that the boy quite simply no longer wanted to live. The doctor figuratively rubbed his hands in glee when he considered what results could be produced by applying the mysteries of electricity.

Kim's next session was one that would be discussed in court, where Kim was later called to testify. The norm was that two "applications" were done per session. In Kim's case, there were five. On the last of them, the doctor wanted to turn up the voltage so high that his assistants refused to continue. If they hadn't, Kim would probably have been electrocuted to death.

When Kim regained consciousness after the last application, his body was merely a network of flaming nerves. His muscles seemed to be permanently knotted. His chest was so contracted that he could hardly breathe. His white hospital gown was sopping and stank of sweat.

When they released the straps and helped him into a sitting position with his legs off the stretcher, he collapsed onto the floor in a heap. As after all those times his grandfather had forced him to ride the horse, his body was cloven and split into pieces; and as before, the only thing that held him together was the hot flame of hatred, directed this time at Martin Rudbeck.

22

Kim's jaws clenched and his eyes narrowed when he thought of Martin Rudbeck. Kim believed the Shock Doctor had gotten off way too easy, and Kim had long ago set himself the goal of someday augmenting that judicial slap on the hand with a little session of private justice. That time would come . . .

Kim pushed Martin Rudbeck's face and blank expression away with an intense mental effort. There was something lingering from the day's events, something Kim had intended to examine more closely. He opened his laptop and googled *Astrid Helander*. Much to his surprise, a long list of hits popped up. Most were links to a YouTube channel titled "Murder Machine, Inc." The same title appeared on Instagram. Kim clicked one with the title "Pigs vs. Pigs."

Horrifying photos flashed on the screen: swine penned so close together that they bit one another and blood flowed. Astrid appeared and narrated in a voice trembling with suppressed rage. The video continued with a swine breeder explaining how much better animal conditions were in Sweden than in other countries. The image froze, a pair of horns appeared on the man's head, and the word *LIES* spread across the screen. Astrid appeared again, admonishing with her index finger and reciting the facts.

So this was the true character of the stunned girl Kim had pulled out of the water. Kim liked what he saw and was glad he'd been able to help that now-orphaned young woman. Rage was something Kim understood. He'd lived in its grip for his whole life.

He clicked a video titled "God's mercy?" and was shown how kosher slaughter was carried out. A steer hung suspended upside down, rolling its eyes, tongue out, bellowing as a circular saw approached its neck. Not even after the blade had slashed its jugular and blood had spurted did it stop writhing in its death throes. Astrid appeared. Tears ran down her cheeks as she screamed curses against animal torture in the name of religion. Kim had made his decision by the time he shut down the laptop. He was going to visit Astrid the next day and get to know her.

The sun was high above the horizon when Kim Ribbing downed his last swallow of rum. He went inside, undressed, slipped into the bed, and pulled the sheet over himself, then huddled close to Julia. She moaned in her sleep. A few seconds later her hand slowly neared him and lay motionless on his chest. Kim pressed it cautiously and held on as he sank into a deep sleep.

III

Astrid

1

The press conference was almost frightening. It had been relocated to the largest conference room at police headquarters, and when Jonny Munther stepped up to the podium, he found himself looking out over a packed room. There must have been eighty journalists. A living wall of photographers stood across the rear wall as well as a forest of tripods holding television cameras. Even Chinese TV had turned up. He had no idea how many other nations were represented.

Liselott Ahrnander had asked him to do his briefing in English, but Jonny had refused. His understanding of English was perfectly good, but he spoke it awkwardly, and he was smart enough to realize that within minutes he'd bungle some phrase and would promptly turn up as a "stupid Swedish cop" meme. It wouldn't be the first time.

The task of summarizing Jonny's briefing for the foreign journalists had been assigned to William King, a Swedish police officer raised in England who referred to himself as a "criminologist" and was a friend of the media, to say the least. Every time some cop made a mistake, King's rosy round face popped up. Sitting smugly on a television-studio sofa, he explained what *should* have been done. He was quite popular. His many male admirers referred to him as "the King." Jonny had his own private nickname for the man: Babyface Billy.

Jonny understood Liselott's logic even though he disliked it. Babyface spoke perfect English, everyone thought he was terrific on TV, and—here's where Jonny *really* took silent objection to her reasoning—Liselott explained that for the general public, King's appearance would give the impression they were giving the case the highest priority and had assigned their best officers.

"Best officers?" Jonny had snorted. "The guy probably can't tell a pistol from a revolver. He's nothing but empty talk."

"In fact, I think he can," Liselott said with a sour expression. "And it's important for us to make a good impression. We're being watched."

She'd said the same thing in all sorts of goddamned ways all morning. Jonny Munther suspected her main concern was for the eyes on *her*, eyes she'd like to see beaming benevolently and gradually ushering her to eventual appointment as Swedish attorney general. She wasn't incompetent, but she was undeniably ambitious.

Not all was lost. The previous evening Carmen Sánchez had managed to contact Ulrika Boberg, a forty-three-year-old specialist in financial crimes and one of the Swedish police's most competent analysts. She'd assisted Jonny a couple of times in homicide cases involving tax fraud.

Not only was Ulrika an expert in ferreting out shady financial dealings, she knew a lot about international trade, industrial espionage, and cybercrimes, all of them likely to pop up in the Knektholmen murder investigation. It looked increasingly likely that this was a professional hit commissioned by an unknown party. It probably involved big money instead of something as tawdry as jealous revenge.

Add to that the fact that Ulrika lived for her job. She had no family. And she did her duty without complaining. The only hitch was that she was a little . . . unusual. Probably obsessive-compulsive. Couldn't look at a stack of pages without having to set them straight. Oh well . . . you must put up with that kind of tic if you wanted her sterling results. Jonny Munther had Ulrika on his left and Carmen Sánchez to his right. Down the table William King sat running his mouth and enjoying his time in the limelight.

Jonny tapped the microphone. "Welcome. On the afternoon of Midsummer Eve shortly after six p.m., six persons were shot to death on Knektholmen, an island in Roslagen archipelago . . ."

Jonny summarized as much as he was authorized to share with the media. He asked the public to report anything they might have noticed about the getaway boat or the motorcycles. His tone was crisp and factual. It took him less than three minutes. Lots of hands shot up. He chose one at random.

"The family has a daughter," a haggard-looking reporter declared. "What happened to her?"

"No comment."

They hadn't revealed the names of the victims, though of course the media had found them right away. Withholding Astrid Helander's name wasn't merely an ethical requirement; it was a matter of her personal safety. It was hardly likely the killers were targeting her, but that possibility couldn't be ruled out. They'd definitely intended to mow down everyone sitting around the table.

A journalist in the front row waved frantically, so Jonny pointed at her. The woman's face was flushed with excitement. "Is it true the writer Julia Malmros was at the crime scene?"

"No comment."

She didn't give up. "It's obviously her in the photos. Was she called in as an expert? Or is she a *suspect*?"

"No . . ." Jonny sighed. "No, she's not a suspect. She happened to be in the vicinity, that's all, and she came to the scene. And with that, I'll turn it over"—Jonny swallowed hard and said the words he didn't want to pronounce—"to William King."

"Good morning, ladies and gentlemen!"

2

Julia woke at about ten o'clock, before the dazzling sunshine reached her face. She felt well rested. Kim lay at her side, his back turned to her. He was covered by the sheet. His long black hair with blond roots spread across the pillow. She studied the shape of his body beneath the thin sheet. Those splendid shoulders, the almost imperceptible hips, the compact but muscular thighs and calves.

She brushed his shoulder with her fingertips and felt a quiver deep in her abdomen, a feeling that made her blush. She thought she might be able to coax him back to life, but then remembered Olof Helander's dead body was probably lying spread out on some chilly examining table in a morgue.

Julia sighed and slipped out of bed without waking Kim. Perhaps he suffered from some sort of PTSD. She'd never seen anything as horrible as that bloody scene on the dock the previous day. Since resigning from the police, she hadn't had to confront a single example of violence or death. She'd written such scenes, of course, but only now did she realize how screamingly different those were from the real thing.

Commentators generally considered Julia a hard-nosed author, one given to close, detailed descriptions of horrible events. Oh, sure, she might get horribly upset when writing about such things, sweat would run down her back, but once she'd finished writing, it was done with. The scene on Knektholmen was entirely different. It wouldn't go away; it was fixed in her mind.

Julia set up the coffeepot and switched on her phone. Once again, a whole long list of missed calls, more than the screen could display. The country codes showed that many were from outside Sweden. She was really in vogue now. Once the coffee was ready, Julia took her cup out onto the terrace and started blocking callers. She got through twenty, gave up, and phoned Irma Ryding.

Irma immediately responded as usual. "Julia! How are you doing, my friend?"

"Not great. Sitting here and blocking numbers so my damn phone will work if someone like you happens to call."

"I *did* call. As soon as I heard what happened."

"Sorry. Hadn't worked my way that far down the list yet."

"No problem. So—how are you?"

Julia stared in the direction of Knektholmen. Yes, how was she doing, really? There was no easy answer to that. So many contradictory feelings filled her that she was . . . was . . . "Shut down," she said. "I feel completely out of it."

"Hardly surprising. When a person witnesses something like that . . . I understand you were there?"

"I was. I saw it. Everything. And I don't know if I . . . did I mention that Olof Helander was a childhood friend?"

"I seem to recall he was more than that." If there was one thing Irma was *not*, it was senile. She had an astonishing memory for names and faces. At the bar during the book fair she could identify practically every writer who walked by. "My sincere condolences," she said.

"Thanks, but it's not grief I'm feeling. Shock, maybe. I don't know. Maybe I'm feeling completely inept."

"Hmm. And who's that person you had with you?"

"Kim. He's here now."

"Bloodstorm?"

"Not much of that for the time being, I have to admit."

"It'll work out. Give it time."

One of the many things Julia valued about Irma was her ability to put things into perspective. Irma had lived a long time and gone through lots of ups and downs. One of her daughters, a teenager, had died in a car accident; Irma had survived a difficult bout with breast cancer; her beloved husband had died. Irma had gone deep but had always come up again. "It'll work out" was one of her most frequent refrains.

They chatted for a long time. Julia spoke about some of her childhood memories of Alvik. They talked about what had happened on Knektholmen. Kim came out on the terrace after a while, wearing the same jeans and T-shirt as the day before. He had a small backpack over one shoulder.

"Hold on a minute, Irma," Julia said into her phone. She turned to Kim. "Are you leaving?"

"Mm-hmm. Eleven o'clock boat."

"Okay," Julia said. She kept her voice steady. "Coming back?"

"Tonight."

"Great. Have a good time."

"You too."

When Julia picked up the phone again, Irma said, "Open up FaceTime. Let's get a look at your new boy toy."

Kim was already on his way down the hill, but even if he'd been standing at her side, Julia wouldn't have obeyed Irma. It bothered her to be with a young boyfriend who wasn't her boyfriend at all. Julia apologized and said Kim was already out of sight.

"Well, well," Irma said. "I must say that I've heard more passionate dialogue in a Samuel Beckett play."

"It's not exactly . . . simple."

"Do tell," Irma said. "You'll see. It'll work out."

3

Kim sat in the harbor next to a pile of baggage, waiting for the ferry. He looked around at the few people at the landing and then at the ice cream stand where some youngsters were hanging out, ice creams in hand, then he glanced at a boathouse. Kim went rigid. There it was again. *That pattern.*

The erect rectangle of a boathouse wall with the circular form of a life preserver hung at one extremity. A wooden fish crate nearby. The rhomboid shape of the shadow cast by a street sign. He rubbed his eyes. The pattern was still there when he opened them again.

Over the last six months he'd seen exactly that same pattern present itself more and more often. In wildly different circumstances. In trash barrels, in painted house walls, in shop displays, in sand dunes along the shore. Kim had a photographic memory, and he was certain he'd seen exactly the same configuration of shapes.

It wasn't some psychotic deciphering of signs the world was sending to him and him alone. But on the other hand, that insistently repeating pattern made him suspect the world might be a construction, a creation whose creator had a limited number of building blocks to work with.

God?

Kim opened his laptop and called up the copy of Thomas Aquinas's *Summa Theologica* he'd started reading in Cuba. Kim had long ago given up hope that the treatise would provide answers to his questions. Nor did it get him an inch closer to any kind of faith; in fact, the opposite was true. What made him pick up where he'd left off was partly a determination not to abandon the project half finished and partly a growing fascination for the paradoxical, even absurd, nature of the undertaking.

Thomas had tried to prove something impossible to prove, to name the unnamable, and to describe precisely something that couldn't be put into words. His all-encompassing First Mover, *primum movens*, the essence of which the human mind was by definition incapable of understanding, was so all-powerful that it might just as well be . . . nothing at all. Everything in his argument was locked up in patiently chiseled contradictions, but even so, that clever little monk kept chipping away at his text. Kim respected the sheer effort of the project.

He'd come away from his reading with one conviction: A bearded old patriarch or cosmic elf was a far better God than the scholarly priest's precise and almost mechanical version that by manifesting its fullness became empty. If Kim ever managed to find faith at all, it would be the belief that old Uncle Beardy was the one who counted, every time.

The ferry tooted as it approached the landing. Kim closed his laptop and put it into his backpack. He looked up at Julia Malmros's house before he boarded. He lifted a hand in greeting, and she did the same. Despite the current coolness in their relationship, there was something fine in the fact that there was someone who waved farewell when you left and waited for you to come back. A place to come back to. Kim had rarely had such a place.

4

After Julia rang off from her chat with Irma and the ferry with Kim aboard had vanished into the distance, she went into the house and did something she'd sworn to herself she'd never do: She tapped Kim's full name into the Google search box. His insistence on privacy made this snooping feel like cheating.

But things were different now. The bloodstorm had been a searing encounter between two strangers with no promises made—*wham, bam, thank you, ma'am.* This time Kim had left, planning to return. They'd have a meal together, talk to one another. Maybe they'd sound like characters in a Beckett play, but still . . .

Julia needed to know who and what this young man was, more than the few words and bits of information he'd dropped, so with *Kim Ribbing* in the search field, she hit Enter.

She knew a search for *Julia Malmros* would bring up half a million hits, many related to the upcoming episodes of the Åsa Fors series. *Kim Ribbing* yielded only about a dozen. A couple from his early teenage years reported prizes he'd won in various gymnastics competitions. The rest related to the trial six years earlier of someone the reporters called the Shock Doctor. Kim Ribbing was called as a witness. Reading through the articles, Julia learned that fifteen-year-old Kim had been admitted to the Vamlinge institution, where he'd been subjected to electroconvulsive treatments that a rational person would consider torture.

Julia shut down her computer and found herself staring again across the bay in the direction of Knektholmen. Maybe this explained Kim's intense attention to Astrid and why the traumatized Astrid had immediately clung to him. A commonality of terrible pain.

And what about Julia herself? What should she do with this new knowledge? She was at a loss. Maybe just keep in mind that her very first impression had been correct: There was a fragility in Kim, something that had to be handled with great caution. She didn't know if she was capable of that.

5

Stockholm was considerably warmer than Tärnö. The asphalt radiated heat through Kim's rubber-soled sneakers as he approached the entrance to St. Göran's psychiatric ward. He didn't know why he'd come; he'd simply responded to a feeling, a bond formed under the dock as he looked into the severely traumatized girl's eyes. It was reinforced when he'd watched her wave her fists protesting the scenes of the kosher slaughterhouse. Something linked them. He saw something of himself in Astrid Helander. That was a good thing.

Kim pulled open the door. The air-conditioned reception area chilled the perspiration on his skin. A gray-haired woman in a white dress and a bitter expression sat behind the counter. Kim shivered involuntarily. He really, *really* disliked places like this. Several years of his youth had been wasted in institutions like this one, especially the cursed one in Vamlinge run by Dr. Martin Rudbeck, the budding or probably already bloomed sadist who justified his experiments by claiming he "just wanted to understand."

Kim gathered his courage, reminded himself he was a responsible adult now, and went to the counter. "Hello, there. I'd like to visit Astrid Helander."

"Are you a relative?"

"No, but . . . can you check with Astrid to see if she'd like to see me? I'm Kim. Kim Ribbing."

"I'm not allowed to provide information about our patients unless you can prove you're a family member."

"But she *is* here?"

"I'm not allowed to provide . . ."

"Yeah, you said."

The woman's sour expression darkened a bit more.

"So, what should I do? If I want to visit her?"

"If that's the case, I suggest you contact her next of kin."

"I assume you can't tell me who that is?"

"I'm not allowed to provide information—"

"Thanks for nothing."

He walked away, leaving the woman to stew in her own juices. It occurred to him when he came out into the parking lot that Julia probably knew who Astrid's closest relative was; otherwise, he'd have to search out that information. Back to Tärnö then, mission not accomplished. He was fed up with taking buses and thought about taking his Mercedes out of the garage to travel to Stavsudda in his own vehicle.

Kim turned to look at the entrance to the psych ward, remembering all the times he'd been marched in and out of doors like those. If only he'd had a hand grenade. At least once.

6

"You've got to be kidding," Jonny Munther told Liselott Ahrnander as he closed the door to his little office behind him. "Please tell me you're joking."

"It's from upstairs," Liselott said. "If there's a joker in the pack, you'll have to go up there and find out."

"And by 'up there,' you mean Lelle."

"Not just him. Plenty more."

Lennart Browall had been appointed Stockholm's police chief less than six months earlier. Jonny had nothing in particular against the guy, but Browall had one obvious weakness: He was very assiduous about projecting a positive image of the corps. Maybe that was why he'd been selected. Since Rakhmat Akilov's murderous truck attack in central Stockholm, the public's perception of the police had gotten worse, what with gang shootings, scandals in the suburbs, and historic lows in clearing up criminal cases.

When there were eyes on you, you had to demonstrate your effectiveness and be able to present your actions to the media and public in a clear and convincing fashion. What could possibly be better, then, than to bring William King on board and let him take care of the investigating team's contact with the media?

Jonny Munther put both elbows on the desktop and rubbed his right earlobe between his thumb and index finger. "So, then," he said, "is that idiot going to lead the investigation?"

"Of course not," Liselott said. "He's there as an external consultant, but otherwise he'll have the same authority and responsibility as any other detective."

"And you're saying I have to *report* to him?"

"Don't make a big deal of it, Jonny. You leave him in his little corner and tell him what to say to the reporters. That's all. If it makes you feel better, you can think of him as a press agent."

"Thanks. That makes me feel so much better."

Liselott Ahrnander smoothed her skirt, gave Jonny Munther a short nod, and left. Jonny remained seated, head in hands and with an earlobe so thoroughly kneaded that it ached. One thing he knew perfectly well: He had no use at all for William King.

The guy's specialization was the easiest to sell to the media: profiling, making sweeping generalizations, especially about murderers' likely backgrounds and characters in relation to a specific criminal act. If he got it completely wrong, he could always claim that his declarations were based on "statistical likelihood." That gave him plenty of wiggle room.

No profiling was needed for the Knektholmen murders. There was no need to fixate on any particular trail; everything indicated that the massacre had been carried out by two full-blooded professionals whose backgrounds and characters were essentially irrelevant. Sure, if William King could come up with, for example, information about their nationalities based on their modus operandi, that might be useful, but Jonny Munther doubted he could. Jonny's task force now had its own clown.

"Everything for the media!" Jonny muttered just as he heard a knock on his door. Carmen Sánchez peeked in. She'd just returned from a tour along Åkersberga Street. Jonny motioned her to a chair. "Yeah?" he said irritably.

"You a bit upset?"

"Never mind. Let's hear it."

Carmen opened her kiddie notebook and scanned a couple of entries. "Motorcycles were seen by at least four persons in Åsättra,

Roslags-Kulla, and Vettershaga. I marked the probable route on the map in the conference room; you can take a look later. The most significant report for our case is that the last observation was at the Görla industrial zone outside Norrtälje."

"Oh, damn. We should have guessed."

"If we had, we could have blocked it off. We didn't. Not then."

Among the installations in Görla's industrial park was the Norrtälje flight school. The helicopter used for the spectacular 2009 raid on a bank in Östberga had been taken from there.

"So they got away?" Jonny Munther said.

"Yep. Certainly looks like it."

"How about the bikes? The weapons?"

"We've brought in the Norrtälje police to help search the area, but nothing's turned up."

Jonny rubbed his eyes and shook his head. "Stolen boat, automatic weapons, masks, motorcycles, helicopter. This is looking like the best-planned murder I've ever worked on."

"And the hardest to crack."

"Right. Maybe we can sic the King on the media to discuss their childhoods."

"What are you talking about?"

"Don't get me started!"

7

Carmen left the room. Jonny remained at his desk. He knew Görla well; he'd grown up in Ersta, just outside Norrtälje. His parents' greatest desire for him was that their oldest son take over the farm. They'd been terribly disappointed when he left for the police academy in Stockholm.

Jonny's plan had been to get assigned to Norrtälje after training and pursue his career there so he could check in on the farm from time to time. Then he met Julia. She'd refused to "move out into the sticks," so Jonny stayed in the capital. His folks had resented him and his decision for the rest of their lives.

A foul taste gradually filled Jonny's mouth, bitterness against Julia for manipulating him into becoming a reluctant city dweller and then tossing him onto the rubbish heap. He was tempted to sit there nursing his resentment, but he chose to get up instead and go to Ulrika Boberg's office.

He found Ulrika with her eyes intent on her computer screen. She held up one finger, holding him back, finished reading, carefully inscribed something on a sheet of paper, then turned to him.

"Come up with something?" Jonny asked.

He'd set Ulrika onto collecting details about the six murder victims, focusing for the moment on the three men, especially on their businesses. Ulrika carefully aligned the documents in the pile before her, placed her pen exactly parallel to the upper edges, and folded her hands together on the desktop.

"Full report or summary?"

"Let's take the summary for now."

Ulrika nodded and provided a concise summary of the same information Kim had downloaded the previous afternoon. Like Kim, Ulrika had focused on the obscure finances and activities of International Credentials and Holdings, Inc. in Shanghai.

"Can we access any information about this firm at all?" asked Jonny.

"That depends entirely on the willingness of the Chinese chamber of commerce," Ulrika said with a grimace. "Which is usually quite limited, especially if a request is related to things that offer a negative picture of China."

"You think they might?"

Ulrika gave him an indulgent smile. "This obviously isn't the sort of enterprise set up to sell bedsheets for children's cribs."

Jonny thought the simile was strange but understood what she was saying. "And that third man, then? Cédric something-or-other?"

"Montaigne. Not a difficult name to remember."

"Why's that?"

"Never mind."

Jonny didn't get it. He suspected she was making some intellectual or pop-culture reference. He couldn't do anything about popular culture, but he'd decided to start exploring the intellectual stuff after the divorce. He'd consulted a list on the internet and started reading classic literature for the first time in his life. The first title that attracted him was, naturally, *Crime and Punishment*. Since then he'd been working his way through Dostoevsky. Pretty good stuff, really.

Ulrika took another page of paper from her desk drawer and placed it on top of those already before her. She tapped the edges to set them exactly in alignment. "Montaigne is interesting also," she said. "European Parliament member with special responsibility for the trading of emission rights. He's part of a little group advocating sharp reductions of those permits."

"Are we talking about a lot of money?"

"Yes. Take Sweden, for example. Currently we've reduced emissions by about twelve million tons of carbon dioxide equivalent; we can sell those rights. In round terms, they're worth about a billion."

"But doesn't that money revert to the government?"

"Not all. Quite a lot is passed along to the firms that succeeded in reducing their emissions. Otherwise there'd be no incentive for them to do so."

"Hard to see how that could be connected with a massacre."

"You asked if there was a lot of money involved. There is."

"But how does that link the Cédric guy to the two others?"

"Unlike Olof Helander and Chen Bao, he appears not to be directly linked, at least not as far as business activities are concerned. On the other hand, he was insisting in the EU Parliament that heavily emitting industries should pay a certain percentage of their profits into a fund for measures to limit global warming."

"The sorts of things Olof Helander was working on. And marketing."

"Exactly."

Jonny Munther rubbed his chin and looked out Ulrika's office window. Gusts of wind were agitating an elm tree's dense crown. He shook his head. "Hard to see that as a motive. Somebody else will pick up the torch now that Cédric's gone."

"I repeat: You asked if there was a link. There is."

"Good job. Conference room in five."

"Five *minutes*?"

"Right. In five minutes."

Ulrika shook her head. "If you say so."

Jonny stared at the floor on his way to the room where the team was scheduled to meet to share findings and conclusions. The deeper they dug, the more complicated things were getting. As was so often the case.

He found it difficult to imagine a firm would commission the murder of six persons if it faced the risk of losing its emissions rights or was about to be forced to contribute to the fight against global warming. The key point for the moment seemed to be Helander and Chen Bao's partnership—what it involved and where the money came from. If there *was* any money.

Jonny was supposed to telephone the Chinese ambassador after the meeting, a conversation he was definitely not looking forward to. Swedish-Chinese relations were at a new low, and he could hardly expect enthusiastic cooperation. Oh well—after all, two Chinese nationals had been gunned down, and that might be worth something. If you wanted to put it that way.

Jonny opened the conference room door and stopped short. William King stood at the whiteboard with his hands behind his back, studying the map where Carmen had traced the motorcycles' route in erasable marker, leaving open the possibility of corrections. William turned around with a patronizing smile. "Aha, *Detective Superintendent* Munther," he said and tapped his index finger on a couple of places on the map. "Why didn't you set the route here? Or here?"

Jonny Munther tried to recall a quote from Dostoevsky that counseled meek acceptance in the face of evil.

None occurred to him.

8

Julia Malmros got back to the cabin around half past five after enduring stares while shopping for dinner and found Kim on the terrace with his laptop on his knees. He must have gotten back on the five o'clock ferry. Julia stopped halfway up the climb to her cabin to listen to the music streaming from his Bluetooth speakers.

Again, it was some ordinary song from the Swedish top forty, but Julia didn't recognize the singer. The guy sang with such exaggeratedly thick diction that he was hard to understand. "I" became "Ayeee," and "You" was "Yuhh." Julia hadn't ever heard the song, but it clearly was something about "Ayeee" and "Yuhh." She shook her shopping bags so the bottles clinked together, a way of advising him of her arrival. Kim looked back over his shoulder.

"What is that tune? Who's singing it?"

"Sten Nilsson."

"Sten . . . the Sten in Sten & Stanley?"

"Mm-hmm."

"And you . . . like that stuff?"

Kim shrugged. "It works."

"Uh . . . just how does it 'work'?"

Kim thought for a moment. "I can't handle hard stuff. When folks sing about how unlucky they are or when guitars, like, shriek, it makes me sad. That music gets inside me and depresses me."

"But there's a lot of romantic disappointment in Anna-Lena Löfgren's songs too."

"Yeah, but she gives it a kind of soft touch, if you know what I mean."

A rare, fleeting moment—Kim had opened up just a little and let Julia peek inside. She thought she understood. When Anna-Lena Löfgren lamented a love forever lost, she sang a sad story, not a tale of emotional devastation. A sweet little melody.

Julia caressed the back of his head. He allowed it, even leaned back a little into her touch. Julia glanced over his shoulder and saw he was reading a dense, complicated text in English.

"And what's this you're reading?"

Kim didn't look up. He scrolled down another page. "*Summa Theologica*."

"*Summa* . . . you're reading *theology*?"

"Uh-huh."

"Why?"

"Entertainment."

Julia had a vague notion of what *Summa Theologica* was. She'd had a philosophy class in high school and remembered that this text, basic to Christian thought, was wide-ranging and horribly obscure. Kim Ribbing had to be one of the few people in the world who'd call it "entertainment," especially while listening to Sten & Stanley.

Julia took her purchases inside and put them into the fridge. When she returned to the terrace, Kim looked up from his laptop. "Who is Astrid Helander's next of kin now that her parents are dead?"

Julia thought for a minute and recalled a slim young man in a motorcycle jacket smelling of motor oil. Olle's big brother, four years older, named . . . "Lars," Julia said. "Lars Helander. Olle's older brother. I don't think Gabriella had any siblings."

"You need to give him a ring," Kim said.

"And say what?"

Kim briefly described the encounter at St. Göran's and said he needed some sort of authorization or that Lars needed to take him in to visit Astrid. Julia searched her memory and seemed to recall Olle had said his big brother was a dentist and still lived on Kungsholmen. There should be no problem looking up his phone number.

"How come you're so interested in Astrid?" Julia asked although she already had a pretty clear notion.

Kim shrugged. "Personal reasons." He picked up his phone, tapped the screen, and almost immediately Julia's pocket buzzed. She took her phone out and saw she'd gotten a message. A phone number.

"That's his," Kim said.

"So . . . you already knew?"

"Not for sure. Call him now."

Julia went inside and sat in an armchair. Only after she'd pressed the blue digits of the phone number did she realize that this had to be a condolence call. Lars Helander answered on the third ring. "Hello, this is Julia Malmros. Maybe you remember me?"

"Oh, sure, of course I remember you. Hello, Julia." Lars sounded heavy and tired.

"First I wanted to say how sorry I am . . ."

They exchanged a few remarks about what a fine person Olle had been, what good friends he and Julia had been, and how unbelievable all this was. Then Julia explained her real mission. She learned that Astrid had been institutionalized and hadn't uttered a word since the attack. Sure, of course Lars could write and sign an authorization if that was what she wanted, but he should also let her know that . . .

After the call ended, Julia sat holding the phone in her lap and staring at a little reproduction of Picasso's *Guernica* hanging on the wall. Screaming men, screaming animals. Then she rose and almost sneaked out to the terrace.

Kim closed the laptop and looked up. "And?"

Julia held up the phone to show she'd just made the call. "Okay. He'll do what he can. It's just that Astrid's just been transferred. To Vallentuna." Julia had to clear her throat. "To Vamlinge."

Her covert Google search had given her the background, but Julia gasped at the dark, flaming hatred that instantly flared in Kim's eyes. He grabbed the chair arm, his knuckles whitened, his lips turned into a snarl, and he hissed out the declaration Julia had feared and expected. "We're damn well going to change that."

9

"Maybe that wasn't so clever," commented Carmen Sánchez. "What you did with the King."

It was 8 p.m. and Carmen Sánchez and Jonny Munther were the only members of the investigation team remaining in the office. Both were bushed after the long day, and it was habit more than duty that had kept them in the conference room where Jonny had given William King a dressing down so harsh it left the walls vibrating.

"I can't stand that pompous, ugly son of a bitch," Jonny said. "What's the use of turning up late with his advice when we've already got the facts?" Jonny made an unsuccessful effort to mimic William King's piping little voice: *"Why didn't you do it like this?"*

"Actually, he was right about that."

"No, he was not! The officer in charge made exactly the correct decision to prioritize the search for the boat. At the time we had no idea where the thing might end up. If we'd known that it was heading for Stavsnäs, sure, then the ugly shit's 'helpful advice' would have been accurate. He can gloat all he wants, the cocky bastard."

Carmen nodded, apparently accepting Jonny's declaration. "Okay, but I think there's something you don't understand."

"There's a *thousand* things I don't understand. Millions! Why are we alive? Is it nature or nurture that creates—"

"Just shut up," Carmen told him. After several years of close partnership, Carmen Sánchez was the only one in the corps who could say such a thing to Jonny Munther and get away with it. Jonny shut up and let Carmen continue. "William King's not on our team to be useful or even a media liaison. Think about it: Why is he here at all?"

"To get in the way."

"No. He's sitting here *instead* of sitting somewhere else, for example on some TV studio sofa. Trust me: If he hadn't been pleased to be let into the tent, he'd be out there right now as an expert commentator for TV4, telling people what fools we were for failing to put up roadblocks. And worse. This way, he can't do that."

"As for the roadblocks—" Jonny began but broke off when Carmen threw up her hands and glared at the ceiling as if seeking strength. Jonny dropped his objection and just muttered. "Yeah, yeah, I understand. But I don't like it!"

"Nor do you have to. But here's some well-meaning advice: Use gloves that are a little softer when you handle the 'ugly shit,' as you call him. Otherwise, he'll get his panties in a wad and go storming in righteous rage straight to the TV studio. And we'll never hear the end of it."

"That guy doesn't storm anywhere; he takes a taxi. Okay, yeah, I hear what you're saying. But once this is all done, I'll hire a hit man to take care of him."

"Fine. What did the Chinese say?"

"The usual. 'This is a sensitive, extremely complicated situation, but we will see what can be done.' Which in plain language means they're not planning to do squat. Or at least nothing they'll come tell us about."

"Did the CSI guys get anything from the boat?"

"They managed to lift half a boot print from one of the cushions. It could be evidence if we had the boot to compare it with, but it's no help for tracking them down."

"At least we know they weren't barefoot," Carmen said. "And the girl, Astrid, is still not saying anything?"

"Not a peep, either to us or to anyone in Vamlinge."

"Why was she sent there?"

"They're supposed to be experts in treating PTSD in youngsters. Anything from the medical examiner?"

Carmen peered at a page in her notebook. "No surprises. All victims died following injuries directly related to hematomas . . . blah, blah, you know how they write. They were shot down, plain and simple. And that Ribbing guy's comment was spot on. The right side of the table was much more shot up than the left one. Suzanne Montaigne, sitting closest to the shore on the left side, would have survived if she hadn't been unlucky. One of the three slugs that wounded her went right through the jugular."

They sat in silence for a while, pondering the vagaries of fate and how a quarter inch one way or the other can make the difference between life and death. Jonny liked the fact that Carmen had caught wind of his antipathy for Kim Ribbing and now regularly referred to him as "that Ribbing guy."

Carmen checked her phone. "Nope, definitely doesn't get any more fun than this." She rose and picked up her bag. "What's on for tomorrow?"

"Thought about putting you on the victims' social media accounts, if you have no objection. Christof took a quick look a few hours after the shooting to see if there was anything directly related to the Midsummer lunch. But a closer review, farther back, is needed."

"Doubt it'll turn up much."

"I know. But suppose there's something in there we miss and Babyface Billy gets hold of it. He'll be in the back of a taxi before I can count to ten."

Carmen gave him a dry laugh. "Good night, boss."

"Good night, Carmen. Say hi to Bruno."

Carmen's tall, broad-shouldered figure disappeared through the doorway, and Jonny sent a mental note of thanks to her sheepdog Bruno. Carmen was an outdoors fanatic and had applied to become a police dog handler. Bruno had turned out to be a keen, talented tracker, but he lacked discipline and quickly lost interest.

Carmen had been offered another dog, but she'd bonded with Bruno by then, so she adopted him and aimed her career in a different direction. She'd taught Bruno to sniff out exotic mushrooms. In the autumn Carmen might arrive with paper sacks full of mushrooms as gifts for others in the unit.

Jonny Munther got out of his chair and studied the map where the boat's escape route was marked. He followed the dotted line back to the little island of Knektholmen. Nothing about that insignificant yellow blob hinted at the previous day's horrors. "The Midsummer Massacre," as one alliteration-happy headline writer had called it.

Scenes from Knektholmen flashed through Jonny's mind, blocking others he'd heard described secondhand. Astrid Helander in shock, sitting up on the hill with that Ribbing guy's arm around her shoulders. Wide-eyed, her hands shaking. What was the girl thinking now? Or doing? Would she ever recover? Remember who she was? Regain her personality?

10

At 10:30 p.m. Astrid was sleeping in her narrow bed in room 304 at the Vamlinge Clinic in Vallentuna. The room was warm, though beyond the lowered shade the window was open the maximum four inches allowed by the security lock. Astrid had kicked off the sheet and lay curled up only in her nightgown.

She dreamed she was floating in a sea of warm blood. All sorts of panicked animals were swimming around her, bellowing, neighing, squealing, and shrieking in terror as something dragged them under, one after another. She reached out to grab a Labrador's wildly thrashing paws, but they slipped out of her hands, and the dog disappeared with a last pitiful whimper. The noise ceased. She was all alone in the dark-red sea, and the only thing to be heard was slow, labored breathing. Astrid's eyes flew open.

She wasn't alone. An elderly man sat on a chair six feet away from her bed. His thin gray hair was combed over a nearly bald cranium. He was studying Astrid in the faint illumination of the night-light. She felt naked in her thin nightgown; she fumbled for the sheet and pulled it over herself.

The man scooted his chair closer before he spoke in a squeaky little voice. "Hello, Astrid. My name's Martin, Martin Rudbeck. I'm here to help. First we'll see if we can help you regain your speech so you can tell me how you're feeling." He leaned forward and put an unbelievably chilly hand on her foot. She yanked it away. The man nodded. "I want to *understand*."

11

"Wake up, Julia! The place is crawling with reporters!"

A small strong hand shook Julia Malmros's leg. She sat up and groggily rubbed her eyes. Kim Ribbing sat bent over at the foot of the bed, lit by the glow through the window of a summer night. He was wearing his black jeans and a T-shirt with a picture of Sven-Ingvars. After their meal he'd been absorbed in work on his computer, and Julia had gotten hardly a word out of him other than good night when she turned in around eleven o'clock.

"Reporters?" Julia said, shocked wide awake. "What . . . how . . . ?"

"Hundreds of them! They want to read your Millennium novel!"

Julia sank back into bed with a moan. "Funny, Kim. Really cool. What time is it?"

"It's late. Gotta go. I'm taking the boat."

"My boat?"

"Right. Or are there others?"

Julia's head spun as she tried to imagine Kim Ribbing navigating her little fiberglass boat across the bay. "Have you ever steered an outboard motor?"

"No. But I watched you."

"You have to open the fuel valve first, and—"

"Like I said."

"Want me to steer?"

"No. You have a different assignment."

"Is that so?"

"Here." Kim placed a little USB flash drive next to Julia's pillow and patted her cheek before getting to his feet. Julia had the feeling she should be asking a ton of questions, but for the moment she couldn't come up with any. She did find one before Kim got all the way out of the room. "What'll you do when you get to the mainland?"

"Bought a motorcycle in town today. It's at the port."

His steps resounded on the floor on the way to the front door when Julia came up with the most important question. "Where are you going?" she called.

"Guess!" Kim Ribbing said, opening the door. "Check the flash drive." The door closed.

Julia lay on her back, staring out at the cobalt-blue sky and remembering Kim's reaction when she'd told him about Astrid. She had a pretty good idea where he was headed. Julia sighed and sat up. *The hell with you, Kim Ribbing.*

Barely awake, Julia put on a robe and stuffed the flash drive into a pocket. She was on her way to the kitchen to set up the coffee maker, but curiosity took the upper hand. She went to her desk, turned on her computer, and inserted the drive. The icon for a new folder titled *International Credentials and Holdings, Inc.* appeared. Forgetting about coffee, Julia sat down and opened it.

12

Even without help, Kim had no difficulty dragging the little fiberglass craft to the shore in the feeble rays of a dim moon. The summer night was at its darkest—in other words, hardly dark at all. The bay was calm and no boats were active. He pushed the boat into the water, managing to keep his feet mostly dry as he leaped into the bow and dropped his bag in the bottom.

He sat in the stern, opened the gas valve, pressed the rubber fuel pump button three times, and pulled out the choke as he'd seen Julia do. He yanked the starter cord, and the motor fired up immediately. Before setting his course for the mainland, he made a detour to the port to collect the coil of heavy rope he'd stowed there the previous day.

Vamlinge's security systems were surprisingly inadequate for a server containing so much sensitive information about the patients. Kim hadn't had any trouble getting into the hard disk set for an hourly automatic backup. He lurked on the disk and sneaked into the system under cover of a system update.

Kim saw Astrid was in room 304. He studied the Vamlinge floor plan. Her room was on the third floor, six windows in from the left. Astrid's file noted she was "catatonic," the same label they'd given Kim when he'd been completely abject, uninterested in communicating or even moving.

Finally, he'd checked on her attending physicians, Tomas Berndtson and Wilmer Syd. Neither name meant anything to him, but he'd been away from Vamlinge for quite a few years. Presumably they were later hires. The thought of younger physicians prompted another consideration.

He spent quite a while trying to get into the system at Stockholm University, which was much better protected than the hospital's computers, but he did succeed. He flicked through the lists of students formerly enrolled in the psychology department. His neck muscles constricted when he saw that Martin Rudbeck had been faculty adviser to both Tomas and Wilmer.

Kim didn't believe for a second that Martin Rudbeck had ever intended to give up his "important research" in trying to "understand." Nothing indicated the stinking bastard had anything to do with Astrid Helander, but it was bad enough that two of his students had their paws on her. Maybe they were still being supervised by the sadist and had adopted his methods.

Kim shut down the hacked servers after installing a couple of Trojan horses that would make it easier for him to get in later if necessary. Then he opened Astrid's Instagram account.

The most recent posting had been a photo of a platter of meatballs and a ham, probably the one Kim had seen shredded across the dock. The title was "Midsummer is Murder." Kim's lips twisted in a grim smile. The kid was a comic. Kim went back through earlier postings and found more still captures and a few videos, all with content like that on Astrid's YouTube channel. Animals subjected to the most disgusting suffering. How did she manage to get these images?

Kim studied the list of Astrid's followers. There weren't as many as on YouTube, but it still took Kim five minutes to scroll through the names and pictures of morose-looking young chicks with garish makeup before he located @gabriellahelander. He clicked on Astrid's mom.

The mother's last image was also from the Midsummer celebration, but it was quite different. Sitting at the end of the table, she'd taken a photo of all the other guests toasting her with little glasses of aquavit. The bay was in the background. Astrid sat with her huge sunglasses at the far end. She was looking down at her phone. She appeared to be conversing with someone.

Who are you talking to, Astrid?

An absurd thought presented itself to Kim: *It was all a hit job set up by Astrid, her revenge on carnivorous parents and their guests, and in this photo she's giving the killers their final instructions.* Hardly likely. Judging from her destroyed phone, she'd been in the line of fire too, so maybe it was some other radical vegan who was responsible.

Kim had closed the page, checked his mail, and saw Legion had completed his assignment. Kim reviewed the files before copying them to the flash drive, packed the things he needed, and awakened Julia Malmros. And now here he was.

The steady putter of the outboard motor made him yawn. The boat plowed forward through the calm bay, and the islands on either side seemed to float past in slow motion. A few houses still had the lights on; here and there, people were sitting outside under strings of colored lights. Several naked men rushed out of a sauna, snorting and yelling as they plunged into the water. A teenage girl sat on a dock holding a fishing rod. She waved at Kim as he passed. He waved back.

As he had so often, Kim felt estranged from the calm, well-lit normal lives most humans seemed to enjoy. He didn't resent that fact. He didn't particularly like being himself, but he didn't want to be anyone else either.

He reached Stavsnäs an hour later and pulled the boat up on the shore about a hundred yards from the steamer dock. His Honda motorcycle was chained to a tree by the parking lot. He opened the top case and took out his leather suit and his helmet. Once he was clad, he climbed into the saddle, turned the key in the ignition, and rolled off toward Vallentuna.

13

The folder Julia opened held hundreds of unsorted files. It took her an hour to move them into folders she labeled *Deposits*, *Payments*, and *Other*. Many years had passed since she'd had any use for her training in the financial crimes unit, but now it certainly came in handy.

There was no way of determining from the files what International Credentials and Holdings, Inc. (ICAH) actually *did*. The few times a completed job was noted on an invoice, it was labeled "consultant services," a phrase just as ambiguous as "assignment."

While writing her third Åsa Fors novel, Julia had read a book about the goings-on at the New Karolinska Hospital. Hardly a single person responsible for its construction had been able to complete their assignment without ordering "consultant services," usually undefined. The money had kept trickling away. Perhaps there was still a group of consultants huddled in some Kafkaesque corner of the building, doing whatever it was they did. Conferring. Conspiring. Consulting.

More than anything, ICAH seemed to be a clearinghouse for funds transferred between various accounts. Over time they amounted to huge sums; her back-of-the-envelope calculation was that more than thirty million kronor had changed hands in recent years. Payments were made to accounts in tax havens with bank secrecy laws, so Kim was right: You'd need an exorcist to get a look into them.

Julia had no such magical powers, so she turned her attention instead to funds transferred *into* the accounts. Those appeared to involve firms with names as meaningless as ICAH itself. If they weren't payments for consultant services, they were for activities cryptically referred to as, for example, "Assignment 22C-32." Julia spent an hour wading through the mess of letters and numbers. Then she got up and loaded the coffee maker.

Just think: Less than thirty years ago, crooks and bandits used cash for all their shady dealings. Bad guys rushed into a bank with guns blazing and made off with bags full of banknotes. All those masked meetings in parking garages where stuffed attaché cases were passed from hand to hand. Maybe that was still happening in Eastern Europe, but here in the West the disguises were entirely different.

No rush. There was no evidence that proved ICAH was involved in illegal activities other than probable tax evasion, but there was a lot that *suggested* it. All these faceless transactions and smoke screens. In contrast to this chase after phantoms, the revelations about the Karolinska project had been old-fashioned, straightforward hide-and-seek.

Julia gave herself a big mug of coffee. In honor of the lateness of the hour, she even poured a little milk into it. Then she went back to her computer and the examination of deadly dull documents. She'd rather have been obliged to read the *Summa Theologica*.

Just after three, the sun had started to peek out behind the islands beyond Knektholmen when Julia's eyes fastened on the name of a firm. OnyxC. Four months earlier the firm had paid ICAH a cool million for . . . *wait for it!* . . . consultant services.

OnyxC.

Julia heard a little *ding!* in the back of her mind, something to do with the disappearance of Edward Dahlberg, the marine biologist who'd turned up six months ago in a trawler net. It came up in connection with the leasing of oil rigs Edward was employed to certify. There'd been a shell company owned by a holding group that in turn was owned by . . . Julia snapped her fingers.

Frode Moe, Norway's famous industrialist.

The shell company Onyx sheltered subsidiaries of the same name plus letters from *A* to *G*. It had been only one of the many complicated components of the vast Futurig concern. Frode Moe was the principal stockholder. Nothing had been found that suggested Onyx's activities were illegal, so the info had been filed in the *Dead Ends* folder.

Oh, really?

Julia's initial excitement at her find gave way to doubt. What was she thinking? The fact that Frode Moe had paid a million to a business jointly owned by Olof Helander and Chen Bao was proof he'd hired a couple of killers to mow them down along with their families? Would that be good for business?

Julia shook her head. She wasn't being objective here. During the investigation she'd had her doubts about the man featured so often on covers of business magazines wearing his traditional Norwegian hand-knitted sweater to show he was a man of the people. Perhaps it was her personal dislike for such types, but Julia's instinct told her there was something fishy about him.

But mass murder? Pretty far-fetched, don't you think?

She drank the last of her coffee, rubbed her eyes, and turned off the computer. She sat for a few minutes enjoying the dawn light filtering through the window and caressing her face. This was no grand discovery she'd made, but at least it was something. The next step was probably to ferret out what it was that Chen Bao's aboveboard business had been about. Julia grinned, imagining a bloodhound with her own face frantically sniffing through the tangled undergrowth of meaningless digital leavings.

Hold on just a minute . . .

Amazingly enough, it was only now that Julia Malmros asked herself the obvious question: *What am I doing, really?* She'd ended her police career—and now she was sitting here imagining she was a private detective?

She was. No doubt about it.

She was extremely talented at examining evidence of financial crimes, but her knowledge was dated. On the other hand, she'd been given access to material the police couldn't get at with conventional methods. It came down to the fact that she was sitting here breaking the law.

She closed her eyes and remembered Olof's quivering lips those few times under the Traneberg Bridge, his careful caresses. His small face and delicate features. The same face, torn apart. Then Edward Dahlberg's face rose before her, even though Julia had seen it only in photographs. His generally acknowledged competence and friendliness, his devastated family.

Julia opened her eyes. Millennium was gone and Åsa Fors wasn't even a dim shadow. Several interrelated factors made Julia want to support the investigation to the best of her ability, but when all was said and done, it came down to the fact that she simply had nothing better to do.

14

Astrid Helander had had trouble getting to sleep after that creepy old guy left. He hadn't touched her except for his momentary grasp of her foot, but she felt as if he'd rubbed himself all over her with his peering and his weird voice. He was still *intruding* even after he'd left the room, and she didn't want to have him there.

She hadn't answered his questions or uttered a single sound. It wasn't that Astrid Helander was unable to speak; she'd simply lost all will to do so. To test it, she had whispered "Mama" quietly, broken into tears, and then said nothing more. There was no point.

She'd often been on edge—or even on a collision course—with her parents, especially Papa, and there'd been times she'd wished they could just vanish out of her life and give her the space to do her own thing. But vanishing wasn't the same as being murdered. Right?

Astrid drew her knees up to her chest and felt guilty for the times she'd said she wished they were dead. Because now they were. She'd gotten her wish. *Happy now?* No, there wasn't a speck of happiness anywhere in her body. She felt like no more than a black hole into which that creepy old man had cast a fistful of maggots.

"Martin" had explained that their relationship was going to be completely off the record. Her doctors had been his students. They'd requested his expertise to help deal with Astrid's particularly troubling condition of complete withdrawal. There were certain *methods* at which Martin was better than anyone else, and his pupils would approve the use of them the next morning. To show her he meant business, he'd taken a photo of her with his mobile as she lay in bed. That confirmed it: the old man was a pervert. And Astrid was in his hands. She balled up her fists, crammed one into her mouth, and bit her knuckles.

Why couldn't she just meet her usual shrink? Walter Berzelius, whom she'd been meeting twice a week at Psychiatric Services for Youth, was a man in his sixties mostly out of touch with Astrid's world, but at least he was an understanding adult she could talk to. Astrid could even go so far as to say that she liked the guy. He was a good listener. So why wasn't she allowed to see him?

Astrid bit the knuckles of her other hand. In contrast with many young people with similar problems, Astrid had never sought to harm herself. On the other hand, she was proud that her willpower was so strong she could hold her breath until she passed out. Walter hadn't been disturbed when she told him; he took it as just one more detail of her life. Her parents would have gone *bananas* if she'd told them.

But now they wouldn't go anywhere or know anything. Not ever again. Astrid had been informed that Lars Helander was her guardian now. Uncle Lasse was okay, but when he visited and asked if there was anything she needed and she silently gestured she needed to get out of this place, he just shook his head unhappily and said the doctors knew best.

It was past 3 a.m. The faint morning light made its way through the narrow opening at the bottom of the window. Astrid pressed her face into the pillow. Her whole existence had been torn to pieces. Would she ever be able to cobble it together into something resembling a life? As she lay writhing in the darkness of her tormented soul, she couldn't see how that could possibly happen.

A swishing sound came from outside the window. Then a rustling, followed by a cautious rap on the pane. Astrid sat up and looked around. Her first thought was that *Martin* had returned and climbed up the wall like the despicable spider he was. She rejected that thought and cautiously approached the window.

She immediately recognized the face pressed to the glass. That man with the brilliant blue eyes and black hair. He'd found her under the dock and sat with her. Kim.

"Recognize me?" Kim asked. Astrid nodded. "Wanna get out of here?" An emphatic nod. "Thought so. Here, take this and unscrew the lock."

A Phillips-head screwdriver and an Allen wrench were thrust through the opening. Astrid grabbed the tools and squatted to work on the lock. Kim was right: The sturdy hook was fastened to the window frame with a bolt that the wrench fit, and the metal plate was affixed to the sill with four screws the screwdriver matched exactly.

It took Astrid five minutes to get the plate and the hook loose so she could push the window all the way up. She found Kim hanging outside from a thick rope with his feet braced against the building front. Astrid leaned out and looked down. The rope dangled all the way to the ground, three floors below.

"Think you can manage to climb down?" asked Kim.

Astrid nodded. She was a star in her gymnastics class and could climb the gym rope all the way to the top.

"Great," Kim said and slithered downward. "I'll wait for you at the bottom."

Astrid turned to look into the room, checked what she was leaving behind, and found less than nothing. Holding the rope, she hoisted herself up into the window frame. She grabbed the rope tight, swung free, and wrapped her legs around it. Quickly descending, she made her way to the ground and to freedom.

15

That girl's got a great grip, Kim thought approvingly as he looked up and watched Astrid swing out in her nightgown, set her legs around the rope, and confidently lower herself a few inches at a time in short jolts. Kim had fastened the rope securely around a rooftop chimney after jimmying the lock on the fire escape.

He hadn't been sure the locking mechanism would be the same as the one he remembered from his own time there, so as a precaution he'd brought some backup items from Julia's toolshed, including a hacksaw. It clattered when he put down his backpack to peel off his leather motorcycle outfit. When Astrid reached the ground, he held the suit out to her. "Here. Put this on."

Astrid didn't ask why, she simply did as she'd been told. The leather that had fit him like a glove wrinkled and buckled a bit on Astrid's slimmer frame, but it would have to do. Kim wasn't planning to crash; the suit was more to ward off the wind at high speeds than to protect her from an accident.

"Lars, your uncle," Kim said. "You like him?" Astrid nodded. "You trust him?" She waggled a hand: *Kind of.* Kim took out his phone and brought up the number for Lars he'd found the day before. "I'm calling him, okay? Then we go there."

Astrid tapped her wrist to remind him it was very early in the morning.

"This is an emergency," Kim said. "If you stay here, you'll get shock treatment. *Electrical* shock treatment, and believe me, you don't want that. Got a better idea?"

Astrid remembered the dirty old man. She didn't want him to touch her. She wanted electroconvulsive treatment even less. She shook her head.

Kim tapped the number. Fortunately, Lars picked up on the fifth ring. His voice was phlegmy at first but then cleared up. Kim explained the situation: He'd just taken Astrid out of Vamlinge because the place was run by men sicker than the patients they were responsible for.

Lars asked how he knew. Kim said he'd been locked up in the place and had barely escaped alive. Hearing that, Astrid tilted her head and peered at Kim. Her uncle seemed to accept the explanation and said he'd do what he could to keep them from taking her back. Kim said he'd call again when they were getting close.

"But—you know where I live?" Lars asked. The bedsheets rustled in the background.

"I know." Kim rang off and signaled Astrid to follow him to the motorcycle leaning against the hospital wall. He picked up the helmet hanging from the handlebars and gave it to the girl.

Astrid's response was a gesture: *What about you?*

Kim, wearing black jeans and a thin black T-shirt with the image of what looked like some kind of pop band, just shrugged. "Plenty of worse ways to die."

They rolled slowly away from the environs of the hospital but then sped up as they merged onto the road to Stockholm. Out on the E4, Kim really revved it up. The Honda roared and leaped forward, pushing Astrid back. She wrapped her arms even more tightly around Kim's slim waist.

They sped along the practically empty autoroute at eighty miles an hour. Kim's long black hair whipped across the helmet visor so that Astrid had to squint against the intermittent stabs of light from the rising sun. The odors of gasoline and awakening vegetation swirled up beneath the faceplate.

For the first time since Midsummer Eve, she felt a touch of life. With it came the desire to say something. She put her helmeted head against the rider's back, knotted her fingers together at his waist, and whispered, "Kim."

16

When Kim reached his eighteenth birthday, a large group assembled at St. Göran's to decide whether he still required supervision by the authorities. He'd been released from Vamlinge the year before and had gradually recovered his essential psychological functions. He could be considered almost human once more. The verdict was that Kim should still be followed but no longer needed a guardian to manage the vast inheritance from his grandfather's estate.

They offered Kim help renting or buying a place to live, but he declined. The last thing he wanted was to stay in one place; he'd had enough of that in recent years. Despite a certain amount of instruction by the hospital staff, he didn't consider himself capable of managing a dwelling place.

So, for the following year Kim made the rounds of essentially all of Stockholm's hotels. He never stayed in any of them longer than two or three days. His only possessions were a backpack with his laptop, toiletries kit, and a few changes of clothes. It was during that year he began to idolize Skalman the turtle, who carries on his back everything he needs.

From those hotel rooms he surfed around various internet communities, where he asked progressively more sophisticated questions about breaking through digital firewalls. Some of the members were passionate about the subject and eager to share their knowledge. Kim gradually tested his own abilities.

He started with simple things. He hacked an obscure page selling S&M outfits and filled it with comfy country styles by Gudrun Sjödén. Then he got into the website of the Royal Swedish Academy of Sciences and replaced their boringly technical reports with info about UFOs. His triumph was when it took him less than three minutes to penetrate the Swedish Railways online booking site and change every departing train's destination to the sleepy little town of Säffle in Värmland province.

He took no real pleasure in these exploits; he carried them out simply to show himself he could. Dr. Martin Rudbeck in Vamlinge had burned away something vital within him. He was living, but he was no longer alive.

Sometimes he went to bars to numb himself with alcohol. He might go home with some random woman, and he was mildly surprised to find he was capable of having sex even though he felt almost nothing. When it was done, he went back to the hotel where he happened to be residing for the moment.

One late night Kim stood at Theodora's bar on Kungsholm Street in central Stockholm. He'd just tossed back his third whisky when a hand was laid on his shoulder and a menacing voice spoke. "Hey, girlie, you wanna come sit with us?"

Kim turned slowly. By then he'd let his hair grow long and dyed it black. His body looked slight and the place was poorly lit, so maybe this guy was making a mistake. Kim looked into the eyes of a man half a head taller and about forty pounds heavier. The guy had brown curly hair and looked stupid.

"No, thanks," said Kim. "But it was nice of you to ask."

A grin split the guy's face. He waved a finger at Kim. "You know this isn't a club for queers, right?"

"Thank you. I'm aware of that."

The guy jerked a thumb toward the door. "Yeah, I bet! So beat it. Now!"

"And why's that?"

"Because you're a queer. Anybody could see that. Even across the street."

Kim sighed and had turned back to the bar fully intending to order another whisky when he felt a harder grip on his shoulder. The guy spun him around. Curly Hair's eyes were squinted in anger. "You gotta look at me when I'm talking to you. Or maybe you want to come along and take it out to the street?"

"I can do that," Kim said, which made the guy start and gape before he again jerked his thumb toward the exit.

"Come on, then, you pansy!"

As Kim walked toward the door, from the corner of his eye he noticed another lout getting up from a table, almost certainly the one who together with Mr. Curly constituted the "us" mentioned with the invitation.

Kim and the guy stepped out into St. Erik Street. It was early May, a dark evening with a fresh spring chill. Kim put his hands into his jeans pockets, which brought a sneer to the guy's face. "Chickening out, faggot?"

"Not really," said Kim.

The guy hesitated but then aimed a punch at Kim's face. A quick sidestep was all Kim needed to avoid it. When the man tried an uppercut, Kim took a little backward hop, and the guy's fist swished by a foot away from his chin.

The guy was breathing hard. "You gonna fight or not?"

"What do you think I'm doing?" Kim said and held out his face. The guy put all his strength into a right cross that would have broken Kim's nose if it had landed. Ducking to the side, Kim pulled his right hand from his pocket. The guy's forward motion made Kim's blow to his solar plexus even more devastating.

Curly Hair doubled up with a heaving groan. Kim kneed him in the face. When the guy's head flew up, Kim grabbed his shirt collar to keep him from falling backward and planted a right cross on his chin that bloodied two of Kim's knuckles. He let go and the guy fell into the street.

Kim was no stranger to brawling. In the various institutions where he'd been kept, it wasn't unusual for resentments to flare and turn into physical violence in the dayroom. Most of the time an orderly quickly broke it up. This was the first time Kim had tried out his abilities in the outside world.

He caught sight of the guy's buddy hurtling toward him from behind and sidestepped. This time Kim didn't bother with sparring. He pounded the buddy's soft parts while dancing around him. Maybe he got a bit reckless, since the second guy landed a hard right to Kim's chin that filled his mouth with blood.

That's when he first seriously began to think this was fun.

And so it began.

17

Kim parked the Honda outside Lars Helander's house at No. 8 Svarvar Street at half past four. Astrid climbed down from the passenger seat, took off the helmet, and handed it to him. In a voice raspy from disuse, she asked, "Why?"

"Why what?"

Astrid cleared her throat. "Why did you come get me?"

"Like I said. They locked me up there too."

"For electric shocks?"

"Mm-hmm."

"But . . . why?"

"Everything they could imagine."

Kim started to telephone Astrid's uncle, but she put a hand on his arm. "There was this guy there," she said. "Really disgusting old guy. When I was sleeping."

Kim's face darkened. "Let me guess—named Martin?"

"Yes. How did you know?"

"Martin Rudbeck. We know each other from long ago."

Astrid stepped back. "You're friends?"

Kim smiled bitterly. "Try the opposite. If I get time, I'll give you the miserable details. Anything else?"

There was a lot more, especially the fact that Astrid didn't want to lose this Kim who'd wrangled his way down from heaven when she needed it most and then escaped with her through the predawn light.

But she shook her head, so Kim phoned Uncle Lars to say they'd arrived and could he bring down a blanket or something?

"The suit," Kim said. "I need it." As Astrid reluctantly pulled off the leather that had so pleased her, he added, "One thing. About Midsummer Eve. Before . . . before it happened. You were talking on your phone with someone. Who was it?"

"How did you know—" Kim waved away the question. "Algot. Algot Mörner. He's in my class."

"Boyfriend?"

"*He'd* like that, but . . . no."

Kim nodded, took the outfit, and started pulling it on. "Where does he live?"

"24 Linné Street. It's—"

"I'll figure it out. Got a phone?"

"No. It was . . ."

"Sorry. That was stupid of me." He handed Astrid his phone. "You know his number?"

"Yes."

"Okay. Text and tell him to go out to the street in ten minutes. Give him some detail that only you would know."

Astrid thought for a moment, then composed the message, her fingers a tapping blur against the screen, then she returned his phone. The door opened. Lars Helander came out to the street with a blanket folded over one arm. Kim pulled up his suit's zipper and started the Honda.

"Do I get to see you again?" Astrid asked.

"I'll drop in." He rolled slowly off down the street as Lars put the blanket around Astrid. Kim stopped a couple dozen yards away. He looked back. "Hey. You."

"Huh?" Astrid pulled the blanket close around her.

"I like your videos."

18

Algot Mörner had three principal interests in life: computer games, masturbating, and Astrid Helander. Numbers two and three were usually associated with one another. He had never so much as touched her in real life, but in his fantasies their athletic couplings were extensive and inevitably naked.

He'd tried to call her countless times after Midsummer Eve. His dozens of texts were never answered. He understood from what he read in the papers that Astrid had survived, but beyond that, nothing.

Algot was awakened by a ping on his phone signaling an incoming message from some unknown number. He rubbed the sleep out of his eyes and read it. Come out to the street in ten minutes. Mumford rolls snot balls.

Algot grinned. The text must be from Astrid. Their physics teacher had a weird resemblance to the singer in Mumford & Sons. One time Algot and Astrid had discussed their suspicion that the teacher was always picking his nose and rolling snot between his fingers during class. Finally they'd checked his desk and found a myriad of nasty little dry balls squashed against the underside, so, yes, Mumford really did roll snot balls.

Algot was so eager to meet Astrid out on the street that for a moment he thought the leather-clad motorcyclist with long black hair *was* Astrid, magically transformed and come to fetch him. But of course it wasn't. The guy looked more like something out of a manga comic, kind of like *Ghost in the Shell.* Though come to think of it, so did Astrid sometimes. Hmm.

"Algot?" the guy said, making Algot's heart skip a beat or two. "Algot Mörner?"

"Uh . . . yeah?" said Algot, warily approaching.

"Astrid sent me. You were talking to her, right? On Midsummer Eve."

"Yeah. Right. How is she?"

"She's fine."

"Is she hurt?"

"No. Did you see or hear anything during the shooting?"

"I heard, like, when it started, but after that my screen went black."

The motorcyclist thought for a moment, then asked, "Can you tell me anything about how Astrid . . . how she seemed just before it happened?"

"Are you from the police?"

"I'm really not."

"So who *are* you?"

"A friend."

The guy didn't look like someone who'd have any friends. Algot hesitated, rubbed his neck, and shifted from one foot to the other. He couldn't understand how Astrid could have sent this weirdo, but the stuff about Mumford was proof enough the text was from her.

"What is it?" the guy asked. "You're thinking of something."

"Fact is . . ." Algot said, feeling his cheeks getting warm. "I, like, I . . . I *have* it."

"Have what?"

"The conversation. On video. I recorded it."

The guy's eyebrows rose. He leaned closer to Algot and examined him in a fashion that made Algot take a sudden interest in his own shoes. "You *recorded* it? Why?"

"So I . . . I dunno . . . just good to have."

Algot wasn't about to explain how a recorded FaceTime conversation with Astrid would be "good to have" or that because of all this business he hadn't used it in any unseemly way, because it ended so horribly.

"Let's have a look," the guy said in a tone that brooked no contradiction. He held out his hand. Algot was too intimidated to do anything but take out his phone, find the video in question, and give it to the guy. The cyclist studied the screen intently for a couple of seconds and then said, "I'm copying this on my phone."

Algot heard the swoosh of an outgoing message and asked, "I mean . . . is that permitted?"

The guy handed the phone back. "Does Astrid know you record your FaceTime conversations?"

"It's cool. Don't tell."

The guy started his motorcycle. "Recording them's not so cool. We'll see."

19

Even though it was only a few minutes after five, the heat in Stockholm was gradually rising as the sun climbed in the sky. Kim rolled slowly along Humlegården, parked the Honda in a motorcycle slot, and grabbed his backpack. He walked across the street and settled in the shade of what was probably an ash, his back against the trunk.

He took out his laptop, transferred the video from the phone, and examined it in full-screen view. Then he dug his vape pen out of his cuff and sucked on it as he watched the video again from the beginning. After watching a couple of minutes, he started to think maybe it was "cool." It was obvious Astrid Helander was teasing poor Algot. She pouted and just "happened" to turn her phone so that it was aimed down her cleavage and her breasts were visible.

"So then, what are you up to?" Astrid asked in a voice that suggested she wasn't particularly interested in knowing.

"Nothing special," Algot said, inhaling and about to continue, but just then Astrid looked up in surprise. Then she screamed, "What the hell—*goddamn it!*" and chaos broke loose. A dry rattling sound was heard in the distance as the image went dark and sounds of breaking glass and porcelain were heard.

"What's happening? What's going on?" Algot shouted. The rattling sound of gunfire and the smashing continued. Astrid's panicked breath was audible. A sudden flare of light, then a smashing sound, followed by blackness and silence.

Kim exhaled a cloud of smoke and moved the indicator to the point where the phone disappeared into blackness. He replayed the sequence at half speed. The rattling became perceptible as an uneven double rhythm, the automatic weapons' syncopated *ta-ta, ta-ta, ta-ta.* The sounds of smashing glass and porcelain became long drawn-out treble tones, and Astrid's breathing was a dark droning. Kim brought the screen close to his face.

He made out the contours of Astrid's face in profile under the table. After a couple of seconds the profile became more visible and better lit, presumably because the tablecloth was being shredded. The girl's face was twisted in a grimace of pure terror. Then—darkness.

Kim moved the indicator to a few seconds earlier in the sequence. The video began just as Astrid looked up. Her "What the hell!" was reproduced in such a deep bass that it sounded as if the host of the event could have been saying it. Kim noticed a movement at the upper edge of the image. He brought the screen close and squinted, holding a lungful of vape smoke.

There.

Astrid's huge sunglasses mirrored the waterfront. And a boat in which two men were standing. Kim bit his lower lip. There they were. The murderers. Kim loaded the video into the program Final Cut, zoomed in on that portion of Astrid's sunglasses, and spent a couple of minutes refining and cleaning the fragment that at normal speed would have played for less than a second. He put away his vape pen and viewed it at ultraslow speed.

The hugely enlarged images were blurred. There was no way of saying anything about the killers' identities, since each gunman wore a mask and hood. Nor could Kim identify the guns other than to guess they were identical models of automatic weapons. What most caught his attention was how erect and still the two shooters stood in roughly identical stances.

He didn't know what this was worth, but he'd done what he could. He saved the original video and the short sequence to his phone and was about to send it to Julia Malmros to relay to the police. Then he thought better of it; he called up the original video and cut everything except the youngsters' last remarks. No desk jockey at police headquarters was going to sit and drool over Astrid's fourteen-year-old breasts.

He sent a short text to Julia with the edited video. Then he sat under the tree for about half an hour. He closed his eyes and let his thoughts wander. They dwelled mostly on Astrid Helander. Sure, in addition to her righteous vegan rage, the girl was cute and a little clingy, but Kim couldn't deny he'd felt a bond with her. Like him, she'd encountered Martin Rudbeck's obsession with *understanding*, even if he hadn't managed to fry her brain.

It's coming, Martin. You'll get yours.

Kim's head lolled to one side. He slept for five minutes. He awoke feeling refreshed. He climbed aboard his bike and drove to the nearest Phone House, where he made certain arrangements before remounting and turning the front wheel toward Stavsudda.

IV

Tärnö 2

1

Julia Malmros was awakened by the *ding!* of an incoming text. She fumbled for her phone and saw it was almost six. *You can catch up on your sleep when you're dead.* She squinted at the screen and saw Kim had sent something. A text with a video attachment. Forward to rockin' Jonny. Julia sat up, put the pillow behind her, and watched the clip.

Goddamn Kim Ribbing.

Where did he get hold of this? Julia had guessed Kim was going to Vamlinge to liberate Astrid, so presumably this was from her phone. But psych patients weren't allowed to have phones, were they? Besides, Julia reminded herself, Astrid's phone was in pieces now in the hands of the police.

Whatever. Julia was no judge of what the blurry video might mean for the investigation, but it must be worth *something* to have some of the events captured as moving images. She did as Kim had instructed, forwarding it to Jonny after deleting Kim's text and writing her own: Sending as thanks for participating in ongoing developments. Julia.

She wasn't trying to take credit for Kim's find. By using her as an intermediary, Kim had made it clear he didn't want to be dragged into the police investigation. Julia had only just enough time to set up the coffee maker for the second time when her pocket buzzed. Since she'd blocked all unknown incoming numbers, she could use her phone again. This one was from a number in her contact list. Jonny Munther.

"Good morning, Detective Superintendent," Julia answered.

"*How?*" was all Jonny said.

"How *what*?"

"Julia, get it together. How did you get that video? And if you say a confidential source, I'll send the Coast Guard to burn your house down."

"That's probably not in their job description."

"Seriously, Julia, how?"

"Is that important?"

The silence on the other end lasted a couple of seconds. Then Jonny said, "Does this happen to be related in some way to the fact that Astrid Helander broke out of Vamlinge last night?"

"I know nothing about that."

"Is that Ribbling guy mixed up in it?"

"Like I said. But the video will probably be useful, won't it? What do your guys think?"

"Around here nobody's thinking. Except I knew, *I knew* this would turn into a huge mess as soon as I heard you were the one who called in the shooting."

"A mess? What kind of mess?" Julia asked innocently, but Jonny had already hung up with a groan. Julia whistled the Sjösala waltz as she turned on the coffee maker.

2

Jonny flipped a hand to signal Christof Adler to turn the lights in the conference room back on. The young man got up and did as he'd been told. Even though Christof hadn't come up with any brilliant suggestions, his mere obedience and willingness to help encouraged Jonny a bit. The entire investigating team around the table had just watched the phone video of the shooting. A frozen image of the two men in the boat remained on the big screen.

Jonny cleared his throat. "It looks like the best we can hope from this is an indication of what type of weapons these are. I sent the video to an expert in the national operations unit, and we hope to get a reply soon. As for—"

"Excuse me?" William King was holding up his hand.

"Uh-huh?"

"That video, where's it from?"

"We received it from Julia Malmros."

William King laughed out loud. "What? Did you call your *ex-wife* in on this case?"

Jonny squirmed. "I didn't call her in on anything. But she's the one who sent it. As for—"

"And the editing?" This time William King interrupted without holding up his hand. "The slow-motion edit? She did that too?"

Jonny quietly started counting to ten as he looked to Carmen Sánchez for help. She shook her head almost imperceptibly and mouthed, *Julia?* Jonny made a similarly restrained shrug and directed himself to King.

"I think we can concentrate on the content of the video for the time being instead of its . . . origins, unless there's *someone else* who objects?"

Before the situation got even uglier, there was a rap on the door. Jakob Lans from the national operations unit looked in. Lans was a self-proclaimed gun nut who subscribed to all the available publications about weapons, and there were plenty of those. He was a hunter, a member of a shooting club, and a collector with a vast array of weapons both modern and antique. "Is this a bad time?"

"Terrific that you're here," Jonny Munther said. "Come in. Find anything?"

"Not much of a challenge," Jakob Lans said. He walked to the screen and pointed to one of the weapons. "This here, my friends, is one of the world's most common automatic weapons." He looked around the circle of cops and made them wait for it for a couple of seconds. "To be specific, the Red Army's new standard weapon, the QBZ-95. Great firepower and, as you guessed, a rate of six shots per second. A really fine gun."

"The army?" said Christof, wide-eyed. "Could it possibly be the Red Army that—"

"No way!" Jakob Lans said, throwing up his hands. "As I said, there are *plenty* of these weapons out there, and a few have gotten away from the army. I have seen offers in . . . hmm . . . certain websites . . . showing they're available for purchase."

Carmen Sánchez tossed it out there. "But it *might* be the Red Army?"

"That can't be excluded. Nope."

Jonny slapped a hand to his forehead and thought, *Oh, fuck.* If the situation had been *complicated*, as the Chinese ambassador put it, this new information wasn't doing anything to unravel it. Besides, what did he know? The embassy might be *involved.* The thought flashed through his mind that he'd blamed his former wife for the mess that now was really getting worse.

Ulrika Boberg turned her laptop to show them a full-screen image of the QBZ-95. An intimidating and somewhat handsome weapon. "You can buy one of these on the internet?"

Jakob Lans's expression showed he'd like to begin his reply by saying *Oh, my dear . . .* but he held that back. "If somebody knows where to look, he can buy himself a battle tank on the internet. And one thing more . . ."

He cleared his throat long and loudly as if preparing to deliver a long lecture, but it turned out he was simply teasing them again. Once he was certain he had the group's undivided attention, he pointed to the screen. "Of course, I listened with earphones so that I—that's right, I wanted to double-check the soundtrack of the firing to be a hundred percent sure which weapon was involved."

Jakob Lans was never less humorous than when he grinned self-mockingly at his own nerdiness and ability to identify a weapon from its firing pattern. He moved the video cursor back to the previous second and turned the screen volume up to max.

They sat transfixed by the sight of the boat gliding slowly into the picture. Astrid Helander's "What the hell—*goddamn it!*" thundered through the room before the weapons began spewing deadly slugs with such explosive power that the conference room's glass wall vibrated visibly and people out in the central workspace turned to look.

Jakob Lans hit the pause button. "Did everyone hear it?"

"Yeah," said Carmen Sánchez. "Just after Astrid's exclamation but before the shooting started. Someone was saying something."

"Yep," said Jakob Lans. "Listen again."

Now that they all knew what to listen for, they heard it. One of the men said something to the other the moment before they started shooting.

"What's he saying?" William King wondered. "I mean, that *is* a man, isn't it?"

"No idea," said Jakob Lans. "What do you think?"

"Boat?" Christof suggested. "Late?"

"No, there's a kind of *s* in the middle," said Carmen Sánchez. "Lazy?"

"Strange thing to say," remarked Ulrika Boberg, "before you start shooting people. *Lazy*?"

Jonny Munther sighed. "Thinking about what we now know, or think we know, maybe we can come to a consensus that . . . it sounds like Chinese?"

"Yep," Jakob Lans said.

Five minutes later Geoffrey Chang from the vice squad arrived. He was an expert on image analysis and pattern recognition, and most of his work was in tracking down prostitution rings. In this case, however, it was his Chinese Swedish background that was required. He had a Chinese dad and a Swedish mom, had spent his first ten years of life in Chengdu, and spoke both languages fluently, as well as English.

Geoffrey was set before the computer with a pair of noise-reducing headphones. The group sat breathless around him as he viewed the video several times. Finally he took off the headphones, nodded, and said, "No doubt about it. It's Chinese."

This time Jonny Munther couldn't keep from saying it out loud. "Oh, fuck!"

"What's he saying?" Carmen Sánchez wanted to know.

"Yeah, he's saying *Låh tse*." With a sly smile Geoffrey explained, "That means something like awesome or brilliant, or maybe blinding."

Carmen tapped her own chest. "*Låh tse*!" Her guess had been phonetically the closest.

"Hmm," Geoffrey Chang responded. "But what might be more interesting in this connection is that it's a dialect expression used only in and around Shanghai."

3

Astrid Helander jumped in alarm when the doorbell rang just past ten. In a moment of childish panic she thought about hiding under the bed but restrained herself and pulled the blanket up to her chin as she heard her uncle's steps go down the hall. Lars Helander had canceled appointments at his dentistry practice in case his niece should need something.

The front door opened. Astrid heard her uncle talking with someone. She knew that *they* were bound to come looking for her, and naturally the first place they'd look would be her guardian's house. Her uncle had promised not to let them take her, especially after she described what had happened during the night.

Martin Rudbeck.

The man had sat on the edge of Astrid's bed and regarded her as she imagined a butcher would look at an animal destined for the chop. Evaluating her, wondering how much could be gotten from her. When all was said and done, to him she was just another chunk of meat. She imagined that butcher stabbing her uncle with his psychological knife and twisting it. But the front door shut, and immediately afterward there was a careful knock on her bedroom door.

"Astrid?" It was her uncle's voice. "Are you awake?"

"Yes."

Uncle Lars opened the door, came to her bed, and held out a little cardboard box. "This came for you. Delivered."

"What is it?"

"No idea," her uncle said and examined the box. "But it's from . . . what does it say here . . . Phone House."

"Okay," said Astrid and accepted the package. "Thanks."

Astrid waited until her uncle had left and shut the door behind him before opening the package. Inside was the latest model iPhone. No note or name of the sender. Astrid's own phone was in blasted pieces in the police evidence room, so she was grateful to receive this inexplicable present.

After finishing the basic setup, she looked through the phone and found no unexpected content, but before she downloaded her account from the cloud, an impulse prompted her to check the contact list. It wasn't totally virgin. There was a single contact registered, a phone number that went to a Sven-Erik Magnusson. That name somehow seemed familiar. She went out to the kitchen where her uncle sat reading the paper and asked him. "Sven-Erik Magnusson. Who's he?"

Uncle Lars took off his reading glasses and scratched his head a couple of seconds before answering. "Ah, yes . . . I think he's a singer with Sven-Ingvars, isn't he?"

"Sven-Ingvars?"

"The pop band. I think they're the ones who did that . . ." He cleared his throat and tried to imitate it: "*I want to be yours, Margareta . . .*" but stopped and shook his head. "No, I'm wrong, that was someone else . . ."

"Okay," Astrid said. "Thanks."

She remembered the shirt Kim was wearing when he got her out of Vamlinge, with the picture of old guys in crazy clothes making silly poses. That must be the connection, but there was only one way of making certain. Astrid phoned Sven-Erik Magnusson.

As Astrid expected, it was Kim who answered on the second ring. A droning sound was audible in the background. Astrid thanked him for the telephone, then asked. "Where are you?"

"In a boat. You?"

"In bed."

"Really? Great. But now you know how to reach me."

"Why'd you call yourself Sven-Erik Magnusson?"

"Private joke. Not so keen to put my own name out there." The engine sounds on the other end changed. They started stuttering and then stopped. "If there was anything else . . ." Kim sounded a bit stressed.

"Just wanted to thank you. For everything."

"Entirely my pleasure. Looks like I have something to take care of now."

"Maybe I'll call again."

"Do that. Bye."

He rang off before she could say anything. She sat for a while, running her thumb across the phone screen. Maybe she was a little infatuated.

4

It was just past eleven when Julia Malmros saw a boat rowed with strong, regular strokes toward her place on the shore. She went back to the article on Chinese solar cells she wanted to finish. Then she looked up again. The very incongruence of it had kept her from recognizing Kim Ribbing. She hadn't imagined him being able to sit and steer an outboard motor; even less could she have imagined him *rowing*. But there he came. Rowing.

Julia strolled down the hill, grinning and timing herself to arrive just as the boat reached the shore. Kim turned around and gave her a grim glance, sweat running down his face.

"Out of gas?" Julia suggested.

"You should have a reserve tank," Kim said. He wiped his brow on his shirtsleeve before climbing out.

"I do," Julia said and pointed to the seat in the bow, which had a hinged hatch. "In there."

"You might have said."

"When should I have thought of it? And maybe you could have asked."

Kim muttered something under his breath. They worked together stowing the oars and pulling the boat ashore then walked up the cliff path.

"Everything worked out?" Julia asked.

"Great." His tone was heavily ironic.

"Sent your video to Jonny. He got really excited. Wanted to give you some kind of commendation."

"You're joking. I hope."

"Of course. I didn't mention your name."

"Good."

Kim sank into one of the chairs on the terrace, breathing hard and hanging his head. It was unusual to see him so—what was the word?—"affected." He took almost everything with a strictly stoic attitude.

"Didn't know you could row."

"I can't. Found that out."

"Listen, I did some searching about Chen Bao and found out some things."

Kim held up a hand without looking up. "Not now. Can't handle it. Tell me later. Not now." He again wiped his brow and lumbered into the house. A few moments later Julia heard sudden creaking and the squeal of protesting bedsprings when he literally *crashed* into bed.

5

Julia remained where she was and twiddled her thumbs. Kim had every right to be tired, of course, but she'd been looking forward to reporting what she'd found. Nothing spectacular, but she was starting to see a certain pattern of guilt by association.

Most of the public information about Chen Bao's firm Klintec was in Chinese, but with a little puzzling through the firm's English website and various articles, Julia had constructed a relatively coherent outline of the business. Call it a skeleton.

In brief, Klintec traded in emission rights originating in China that were bought up by middlemen who sold them onward, for example to Swedish firms and government authorities. Greenbase, Olof Helander's firm, was one of Klintec's principal customers. Nothing wrong with any of that.

China's system for emissions rights differed from the European approach in that factories were rewarded when they emitted lower quantities of carbon dioxide equivalents than expected from their manufacturing targets. Thus, rewards were for efficiency rather than for positive effects on the climate. A factory could churn out as many greenhouse gases as it wished if it did so while achieving a maximum level of productivity. In other words, the Chinese government paid no attention to measures beneficial to the environment.

On the other hand, the Chinese were certainly no enemies of large-scale investments in green energy. And that was where Klintec came in.

For example, say Klintec invested several million in the construction of a park of solar panels, funds that might come from, say, a European airline wishing to brand itself as climate friendly, featuring happy little green men in its ads.

The problem was what's called "additionality," whether the project never would have materialized if those millions hadn't been on offer. That was hard to prove, and the gray zones were vast. China could claim that the authorities *really* weren't intending to build and erect air turbines on wind farms even if those long-term plans existed; they merely waited for a handsome contribution funded by "flight-shamed" Europeans responding to Greta Thunberg's pro-climate campaign. Thank you, oh thank you, *now* there'll be wind power here!

Odd, but not so surprising. On the other hand, China and several other countries also received climate compensation payments for *not* doing certain things. One of Klintec's greatest sources of emissions rights was the Chinese petroleum industry. Most of China's oil was found in the depths of the South China Sea, and PetroChina had recently commissioned the construction of Bluewhale, the world's largest oil rig. Meanwhile, PetroChina had canceled contracts for a couple of other rigs (which they really might not have intended to build) in exchange for several hundred million in climate compensation payments. As a gesture of thanks, they'd even spent a tenth of that amount to knock together a few thousand solar panels.

That's where Julia thought things began to get intriguing. Greenbase channeled money via Klintec to the Chinese government as compensation for *not* extracting oil. Futurig, Frode Moe's concern, thrived by extracting oil, principally in Norwegian waters with oil rigs constructed in—wait for it!—China.

That's what Julia saw as guilt by association. She didn't have a clear idea of the relationships, but there had to be a link somewhere. Too many interlocking puzzle pieces, even though she still couldn't see the big picture. But it certainly wouldn't show frolicking little green men.

Julia picked up her phone from the table and sat for a while contemplating the name "Jonny Munther." How strange that had once been her last name. She'd shared almost half her life with the man behind that name. It seemed inconceivable. She phoned and Jonny answered almost immediately.

"Damn it, Julia! Used to be you ignored my calls, now you're ringing me up every fifteen minutes when I've got so much to—"

"Was the video useful?"

"How did you get it? Tell me. Now."

"Can't comment about an ongoing investigation."

There was a terrible silence on the other end of the line. Julia had given the standard police response to the media and curious snoops when there were things better kept confidential. Jonny answered gently, as if speaking to a child. "Julia, you know you're not with the police anymore, don't you?"

"Right, thanks."

"Is that crystal clear? You're acting suspiciously like someone conducting a *personal* investigation."

"I am indeed. And I've got more."

"I'm hanging up now."

"You'll want to know this."

Another silence. Julia could really see Jonny sitting, rolling his eyes, and pulling at his earlobe the way he always did when he was upset. He finally answered. "Spill it, then."

"Not on the phone."

Jonny Munther's frustrated sigh rattled his phone. "Is it something really juicy?"

"Really do think so."

"When can you be in Stockholm?"

"The ferry leaves at noon, so in about two hours. But I want something in return."

"Can't comment about an ongoing investigation."

"Jonny . . ."

"On the phone."

They set a time and place and ended the call. Julia leaned back in her chair, looked toward Knektholmen, and nodded. "Private investigator." The term had always had negative connotations when she was with the police. Tinfoil hats, conspiracy theories, rights activists, and *private investigators*. Now she kind of liked the ring of it.

6

Too many monkeys.

Jonny Munther had seen it coming; he'd just *known* it. Get his ex-wife involved in his assignment to run a proper police investigation, and the whole thing turns into a whodunit. Jonny put down his phone and gave his earlobe a last pinch as he reminded himself that it wasn't really Julia's fault that everything was such a mess.

Jonny had had to go on his hands and knees to the Chinese ambassador with the request to set up collaboration with the Chinese police in Shanghai. Asked why, he'd been obliged to say that the technical aspects of the investigation were such that he wasn't allowed to explain. Oh, really; could he at least say whether some Chinese citizen was suspected of a crime? He couldn't answer that either, for the same reasons, but a collegial relationship with the police in Shanghai was really needed.

Perhaps the detective superintendent at least might explain to what extent the investigation would cast an unfavorable light on the Chinese government and cause lasting offense to the Chinese people? *Yes,* Jonny Munther had wanted to answer, *we're aiming to offend the entire Red Army,* but what he said was that at the present time he couldn't exclude the possibility. The conversation had ended with mutual wishes of continuing good health. Beyond that, nothing at all. Nada.

With the help of information from the video, they'd been able to consider the partial boot print found in the boat in a new light. Jonny had grabbed his head and rubbed his temples hard when the techs confirmed that yes, the print was made by a type of boot used by the Red Army twenty years earlier.

China, China, China.

The only small comfort was that at least it was an older model of boot, suggesting two *former* Chinese military types, soldiers who'd left the army for more lucrative employment. That would hardly be enough to satisfy the Chinese ambassador.

Jonny Munther glanced at his watch: 1:30 p.m. At three o'clock William King was to meet the press, and Jonny needed to brief him about what he could and could not say.

Too many monkeys jumping on the bed.

Jonny found William King at his computer in the conference room. William hadn't yet been assigned an office, because Jonny didn't want to view him as permanently installed.

"Got a minute?" asked Jonny and took a chair.

"Always, Detective Superintendent," William King replied with that tone of voice. Jonny couldn't decide whether it was submissive or sarcastic.

"The talk with the press," Jonny said. "You can give them what we know about the actual event and even the helicopter."

"The boat on Tärnö overnight? That they holed up there and waited? That's a nice image."

Nice image. Jonny grimaced, but even so, he said, "Yeah. Can't see what that might prejudice, all that kind of stuff is okay, but not a word—and I mean *not a single word*—about Shanghai or China or the Chinese."

"Okay if I mention *rice*?" Jonny's sour glare made William King hold up his hands and say, "Okay, not in the mood for jokes, apparently."

"You understand me exactly. The situation with China is as good as closed. I don't want to have it nailed shut as well."

William King nodded. "The helicopter. The individual who saw it take off in Norrtälje knew something about helicopters and identified the model, et cetera. Shouldn't we show a photo of that model and ask the public to report any observations? Where it seemed to be headed? We have the international media here, and they *might* have flown out of Sweden."

What most irritated Jonny about that suggestion was that in the general uproar he hadn't come up with it himself. No doubt William King was spinning opportunities for himself to star in media drama, sitting there and holding a photo, offering photographers something like that picture from the Palme murder investigation when Stockholm police chief Hans Holmér dangled a couple of Magnum revolvers from his index fingers. *A nice image.* It was a damn good idea, all the same.

"Sure," said Jonny. "Do that."

7

Kim Ribbing was totally disoriented when he awoke about 3:30 that afternoon. For a long, heart-stopping moment he had no idea where he was. He stared at the light-blue rectangle of the window, caught sight of a round knot in the pine planking, and thought for a second he was trapped in the pattern. Then the ceiling, walls, and bed shifted into a familiar configuration and single words: *Julia. Summerhouse. Tärnö.*

He couldn't remember undressing, but he must have, since he was in his underwear. He located his jeans and T-shirt on the floor by the bed, still damp from his sweaty rowing. He sniffed them and made a face.

Astrid. Vamlinge.

Okay, then. Now things were becoming clear. Kim got out of bed, looked through the kitchen window, and saw no sign of Julia on the terrace. Found a note on the desk. *Going to the city. Back this evening. J.*

Kim tilted his head. There was something intimate about that simple *J*, more so than if Julia had written *Kisses* or *Hugs* the way people do. Maybe because it suggested there was only one J in his life. Had she appropriated that letter of his alphabet? He kind of liked that notion.

Kim found a beach towel, tossed it over his shoulder, and took the cliff path to the shore. Though it was almost eighty degrees out, the water felt chilly when he stepped in. He waded until it was waist deep, let himself fall forward, submerged, and swam a few strokes underwater.

He burst through the surface suddenly and blasted water in all directions, an eruption of flying drops glittering like cold gems in the pouring sunshine. The fog in his brain was gone, and he was at home in his body again. He pulled off his underwear and rinsed it underwater before putting it back on. He had a couple of dry ones in his pack, but why waste them?

He went back on shore, ignored the beach towel, and stretched out on a warm rock to dry himself in the sun. His joints cracked; he relaxed. *That does it. Now it's okay.* He rested for a few minutes, and then it came to him: *Martin. Rudbeck.* The comfortable, almost liquid feeling of his body vanished as his muscles tensed in small knots of anger. He sat up again.

He had an idea. He spent a while trying to decide whether it was practical. It should be, with the help of a little bug Moebius had created and boasted about to HackPack.

Kim's skin was already dry as he climbed back up to the cabin, allowing himself the pleasure of wrapping the beach towel around his hips, since the air was warm and still.

After creating his bug, Moebius had spent about a month working his way into all the Swedish broadband operators and setting loose tiny little Trojan horses that galloped about and could provide backdoor access to the systems. With codes Moebius helpfully kept on hand, anyone could gain administrative access without being detected.

Kim logged into Moebius's digital treasure chest and got a hit with his first code. Telia. Martin Rudbeck procured his probably disgusting downloads from them. That was a bit of a challenge, since Telia was one of the largest internet service providers, if not *the* biggest ISP, so it generated millions of IP addresses every day. The search criteria had to be narrowed.

The first and most decisive reduction was no problem, thanks to Moebius's little horsies. Kim knew the Shock Doctor's address, so he could see which base stations in the immediate vicinity were pumping their traffic into his and others' logged-in devices. It got trickier after that. Thousands of IP addresses scrolled down Kim's screen, and it was impossible to determine which one or ones Rudbeck was using.

He took a quick look, reentered Telia as an administrator, and found that as he'd suspected, the doc's phone subscription was with the same provider. The number was unlisted, but with administrator access Kim saw it. Rudbeck used an ordinary Galaxy S8, so in Kim's guise as a fully cleared Telia administrator, it took him only about fifteen minutes to get into the phone. It was probably full of goodies, but Kim had a different mission.

He licked his lips. The good doctor really needed to get a hint that someone was sneaking around in his phone. Kim crossed his fingers and tried to adjust the connection setting. Bingo! If Rudbeck tried to use his phone on the mobile net, nothing would happen, but since the phone was now on a Wi-Fi connection, Kim could view the router's IP address. That router was directing traffic to all Rudbeck's connected devices.

Kim entered the IP number and found three devices connected to the router. He pulled up the one with the most usage, which should be the man's computer, even though for the moment that wasn't Kim's principal objective. The start screen was displayed; strangely enough, it was completely blank. He couldn't go any farther.

Kim tested a few standard approaches for getting over or under the firewalls. Nothing. More sophisticated methods. Nothing. Martin Rudbeck's computer might as well have been inside a Faraday cage and therefore, by definition, digitally inaccessible. There'd probably been updates in security systems during the time Kim had been off the grid . . . raising the question of just what the Shock Doctor was hiding inside his digital strongbox.

That problem would have to wait. Kim had been looking for something else. He crossed his fingers again and checked the third connected device. Bingo! As he'd hoped, Rudbeck was so up to date that he had a smart TV. The computer's security had provided the doc the equivalent of a Swiss bank vault, but protection for his TV was more like a plastic bag from Cuba. Poke it a bit, and it pops. Kim was inside in a couple of minutes.

Martin's model used a remote and had a camera. Kim got in and opened the camera feed in a separate window on his screen. When Martin Rudbeck's living room appeared, he threw out his arms and took a bow to an imaginary crowd.

Well, well. So this was the home of someone who enjoyed torturing children for the sake of science. "Tasteful," many folks might have said. "Vile" was Kim's verdict, since all he saw were objects or pieces of furniture used by Martin Rudbeck and therefore disgusting.

A big sofa with fluffy cushions next to an armchair draped with what seemed to be a Mexican blanket. An oval coffee table in blond wood in front of the sofa. A bookshelf crowded with leather-bound volumes. A blue patchwork rug on the floor. Viler than vile. Beyond the sofa a window looked out onto a glassed-in porch. Bright-green potted plants stood in a row on the windowsill. Foul.

No movement. Kim might as well have been looking at a photograph. The sight made his skin crawl, but Kim knew that was mere association. There was nothing in the picture to prove this was Martin Rudbeck's living room he beheld.

He'd just finished making a few modifications to the settings on the router and the television to give him personal back doors to the systems when a shadow fell across the living room floor. A couple of seconds later, behind the sofa and before the window there appeared a figure Kim knew all too well. Martin Rudbeck's graying comb-over fell across his forehead when he leaned over to water a flower. Kim pointed an index finger at the man's head. With his thumb he pretended to cock a pistol. He let the imaginary hammer fall.

Gotcha!

8

Jonny had proposed they meet at the McDonald's on St. Erik Street. Just a stone's throw from police headquarters but completely anonymous. Julia assumed that was because not for his life would he want others on his team to know he was consulting her.

Julia bought a coffee and found a table as far in the back as possible. Some of the many faces turned to watch her walk by; several of those persons leaned forward to say a word to someone at the table with them. People had sometimes recognized her in the street even before the program with Malou, but after it her impact as a celebrity had increased tenfold. Maybe Louise was right; maybe she should take advantage of it. Julia sat down, sipped her coffee. To keep herself amused, she tried to imagine the opening scenes of an Åsa Fors thriller.

Maybe something with gang wars and shootings; that would appeal to contemporary sensibilities. Perhaps . . . Julia twisted a lock of hair between her fingers and called up an image. A market square. Some man of foreign ancestry comes along carrying a couple of grocery bags. Suddenly he falls to the ground, losing the bags. Three oranges go rolling across the pavement. The man is dead.

Right. And why is he dead?

Her opening scene was really that of the three brilliantly colored oranges rolling across the pavement grate of a shabby plaza. Then came the grocery bags, then the man. But why did he fall to the ground, undeniably dead?

Because a sniper shot him.

Okay. Up on a roof or at an apartment window, there's someone sitting with a rifle equipped with a silencer and a telescopic sight. Someone like the gamer characters Mangs or Laserman but smarter and with better equipment. More shots follow. Maybe she would tie the deed to the True Swedes. Julia had long intended to include the growing extreme-right party in a novel, but she hadn't come up with a plot where they'd fit. Maybe this one would do it.

She drummed her fingers on the table. She'd done a decent amount of research to be able to write the sections about Lisbeth Salander and the women's shelter. Maybe that could be recycled. Put in a plotline about honor-based violence and women who were forced into hiding. Sensitive subject, but it might work.

Okay. Say that the fusillade blasts through a housing area . . .

Jonny came into the place and looked around. Julia lifted a hand and stopped musing, which destroyed the story. Whenever she called up an image and started asking herself questions about it, before long she had the beginning of a story. "Destroyed" certainly wasn't the right word, though; after all, conjuring up a tale was her talent and her profession. Without that ability, she'd never have been able to write.

Jonny bought a coffee and came to her table after looking around, probably to make sure he didn't have the security services tailing him. When he took a seat across from her, it occurred to Julia that every meeting they'd had since the divorce had concerned an investigation.

"So, then?" said Jonny. "What have you got?"

"Shouldn't we chat a little first? After all, you've been wanting to do that for a long time."

"Got no time, but okay. How's the boat?"

"The boat's just fine."

"Wonderful, wonderful. And how's it going with Mr. Ribbling?"

Julia knew Jonny was doing it on purpose but corrected him anyway. "His name is Ribbing, and it's going . . . so-so."

"Can't imagine what you see in a guy like that."

"What do you mean, 'like that'?"

"I mean what I say." Jonny swept his hand across the tabletop as if clearing off crumbs. "So. Enough chat for you?"

"Seems so."

"Great." Jonny took a gulp of coffee. "Oh, shit. Nothing wrong with the coffee at the station, but *this stuff* is what I call cop coffee. So, tell me."

"International Credentials and Holdings."

"Not news. We've got folks on it."

"Okay. And you're aware of the connection with Frode Moe?"

Jonny took a slug of the coffee he'd called disgusting. "Suppose for the sake of argument we say we aren't, due to certain . . . confidentiality problems."

Julia outlined the transfers to and from ICAH's account, the sums involved, and the fact that OnyxC, previously owned by Moe, was one of its clients.

"And all that—how'd you get hold of it?" asked Jonny Munther.

"Unconventional methods."

"Ribbling, then. You know this is nothing we can use, and as far as I'm concerned, it's not proof of anything illegal."

"I'm not saying it is. I just want to point out there's a connection leading in a certain direction. And Frode Moe also came up in the investigation into that marine biologist who turned up in a trawler net, according to you. It seems a bit . . . I'm assuming that you're informed about Klintec and Greenbase . . ."

"We are," Jonny said and gave the coffee one last chance. He shook his head and put it down on an adjacent table.

"Then you also know," said Julia, "that with this climate compensation payment for oil drilling and the construction of oil rigs there, and . . ."

"Yeah, we know. And that means?"

"I actually don't know what it means," Julia said. "But there's a bit too much that seems to be connected."

"That's not enough to arrest Norway's most celebrated businessman. Not by a long, long shot. But this is a hell of a thing you've got yourself into here. Is this your new career? Private investigator?"

When the term came out of Jonny's mouth, it had none of the positive vibe Julia had imagined. She shrugged. "You can't deny I was a good investigator. Why shouldn't I keep using those skills? Got anything that can help me with the job?"

Jonny Munther stared at the tabletop. As he pondered, his lips twisted and tightened as if he'd bitten into a lemon. He looked around and saw several people gazing in the direction of their table. Finally, he leaned forward and muttered, "You didn't get this from me. Or from anyone in the police. I hope you understand that."

Julia nodded, and Jonny leaned so far across the table that they were nose to nose. What kind of information could be so unbelievably sensitive? To keep from missing anything, she turned her head to one side so her ear was close to Jonny's mouth. He whispered, "*Shanghai.* It's practically certain they came from Shanghai. Could be they're former military."

Jonny Munther straightened up and spoke in a more normal conversational voice. "And so maybe you understand why this is sensitive?"

"Yes. Diplomatic sensibilities."

"You might put it that way."

"So how come you're telling me?"

Jonny gave Julia a side glance and said reluctantly, "Because I don't deny you were good as an investigator. But as a wife . . ."

"Maybe we shouldn't go there, Jonny."

"No. We probably shouldn't."

When Jonny Munther left for the station, Julia remained at her table and finished the coffee that she personally didn't think was so bad. *Shanghai.* Like oil, the city's name kept coming up here and there when you turned over the stones in this affair.

Fortunately, Julia had an excellent connection when it came to things concerning China. She flicked through her contact list and called up the number for Bruce Li.

9

Julia had needed to do a good deal of research for her third Åsa Fors thriller, *The Key to Paradise*. A Chinese businessman was found murdered at Stockholm's Grand Hotel. Clenched in his fist was a key, the sort used to wind up a music box. It was her only novel featuring international intrigue, and Julia had to learn about Chinese politics and business practices.

The publisher had gotten hold of Bruce Li at the Swedish Foreign Ministry, employed for his knowledge and his thoughts about China's future. He had foreseen clashes between China and the United States over trade and predicted Swedish-Chinese relations would worsen if Sweden awarded a Nobel prize to any unacceptable writer or opposition figure. He'd gotten both predictions right.

Winnie the Pooh was persona non grata in China because of his resemblance to President Xi Jinping. If Bruce Li had been the Chinese president, the comparison would have been with Eeyore the donkey. The man had the most woeful face Julia had ever seen, and his pessimism about almost everything was deep and lasting.

During the conversation they'd chatted a little about personal matters. Bruce Li had told her his greatest misfortune as a child had been his name. Champion fighter Bruce Lee had been at the height of his stardom in the early 1970s when this almost identically named boy had been only ten years old. All the boys in school bullied him and wanted to combat the swarthy little kid so they could claim afterward that by gosh, they'd given Bruce Li a whipping. That was probably the origin of his dismal view of life.

The Foreign Ministry employed him as a resident China expert, but it came out during their conversation that his principal talent was describing worst-case scenarios, an assignment for which he was eminently suited. All he had to do was tell his colleagues what he really expected would happen.

Bruce Li had grown up in Hong Kong and studied economics. He rose quickly through the ranks and was one of the architects of the market-economy reforms. Then the Tiananmen Square demonstrations occurred and prompted an ideological clampdown. Regarded as all too liberal, Bruce Li was suspect and lost his position. He soon realized he had reason to fear for his life, so he fled to Sweden in 1995.

He was intelligent and quickly learned Swedish. A few years later the ministry employed him as an occasional consultant. He was hired on a permanent basis not long after the turn of the century and became one of the most highly regarded China experts. People always heeded what he had to say, although they often took his pronouncements with a grain of salt. For example, China had *not* caused a massive bloodbath by invading Taiwan. "Wait and see," was Bruce Li's comment. "Just wait and see."

Julia had thanked Bruce for all the valuable information, and he'd surprised her by asking if he might invite her to dine with him sometime. He'd mentioned in passing that he wasn't married, but Julia wasn't receptive to romantic intentions. She'd declined in a friendly fashion. He'd phoned a couple of times later, but she hadn't picked up. So it wasn't entirely guileless of her to call him up all these years later to renew the contact, but she couldn't come up with a better alternative.

While the call was ringing, another idea for Åsa Fors popped up in Julia's mind. That wasn't unusual. She would imagine a shadowy basis for a story, and later—to paraphrase Stephen King's comment to an interviewer—the "girls in the basement" would get to work. Her unconscious mind solved problems for her on a freelance basis.

The sniper goes to showings of several apartments and manages to make copies of the door keys. That gives him access to several empty flats from which to carry out his deadly work. Julia gave herself a thumbs-up just as a voice with a dismal tone answered, "Hello, this is Bruce Li."

"Hi! Julia Malmros here. Maybe you don't remember me . . ."

10

Jonny Munther got to his apartment just after eight. He took the bathrobe from the plastic shopping bag on his arm as soon as he entered. He held it before him with both hands. The scents of sea and salt brought a little lump to his throat.

This wouldn't do. Was he going to pad around the apartment like a melancholy hound, always coming back to sniff his olfactory memories? It was pathetic, but what could he do? Burn the damn thing? That sounded a bit too drastic; and it *was* a good-looking bathrobe. Jonny put an end to the matter by angrily stuffing the garment into the washing machine and setting the temperature to maximum. That should be enough to sluice away the traces of the old days. As well as those of that Ribbing guy, of course.

He had a two-room apartment near Odenplan, an easy walk from police headquarters. Jonny had taken it five years earlier as a sublet from a colleague working in Spain. Said colleague had no intention of returning anytime in the foreseeable future.

Jonny had done almost nothing to make the place his own. He'd put his things into storage after the divorce. Since his colleague had left the place fully furnished, Jonny saw no reason to express his own personality—to the extent he had one—in the space. Everything was already there. The only major modification he made was to purchase a comfortable armchair for reading, where he could sit as he improved his education.

Jonny opened the freezer. From among the packages of prepared meals he selected meatballs with mashed potatoes and put it into the microwave. Jonny was perfectly capable of cooking for himself. His specialty was a slow-braised lamb stew he and Julia had usually offered when they had guests. But who bothers with all that when cooking for one?

Julia, Julia, Julia.

Why, really, had he shared the information about Shanghai? Her contribution hadn't been much, and Jonny found that stuff about Frode Moe hard to believe. She was grasping at straws. So, why? Jonny thought he knew. He glared grimly at the microwave timer as it counted down.

In all the years they'd both worked as police officers, not once had they taken part in the same investigation. It wasn't done, because *it might affect a person's judgment*, et cetera, blah, blah, blah. Was it such a terrible thing to do something together with Julia now that he had the chance?

He could always offer the same excuse he used for himself: Julia was—had been—a competent police officer, and it would be good to have someone capable of thinking outside the box working with the Kungsholmen police headquarters. But still, it couldn't be denied that he'd shared a significant detail of an ongoing investigation with a private individual. Didn't look good at all.

The microwave went *ding!* Jonny took out the plastic tray, pulled off the film, and put it on the table. He got his utensils, took a light beer from the fridge, and didn't bother with either a glass or a plate. He ate a couple of forkfuls and then picked up his paperback copy of Dostoevsky's *The Idiot.*

Jonny opened it at the dog-eared page and held it before him in his right hand as he shoveled his food in with his left almost without noticing. He shook his head. If there was an idiot anywhere around, it was him.

11

The last boat from Stavsudda docked at Tärnö at half past eight. Julia Malmros went ashore, her bag hanging from her shoulder and a plastic shopping bag in either hand. One held purchases from the Swedish government's liquor monopoly, and the other contained a selection of antipasti from an Italian delicatessen stall in the Östermalm Food Hall. A person has a right to luxury from time to time.

This was her favorite time of day, at least on Tärnö at this time of year. The long light of the summer sun made dwellings painted in traditional Falu red glow softly. Their windows reflected the choppy, glittering surface of the sea and sent flashes of light dancing along the steep hillsides. The salt tang of the cool evening breeze swept in from the Baltic and brought with it the murmur of voices from nearby islands. It was the time of day when the world seemed like a magical puzzle just about to reveal its solution. It never did, but the wonder of it remained.

Kim was sitting on the terrace with his laptop on his knees, wrapped in Julia's own bathrobe. From the speakers wafted the voice of Lasse Lönndahl, the Frank Sinatra of Sweden, singing "A Thousand and One Nights." Julia's shopping bags emitted a glassy clink as she sat them down. "You went swimming?"

"Yeah."

"Was it cold?"

"Uh-huh."

"Want a glass of wine?"

"Sure."

What was it Irma had said? She'd heard more passionate dialogue in a Beckett play. But even though Didi and Gogo often traded absurdities, at least they *conversed* with one another. She sighed, and Kim seemed to become aware of his own behavior. He looked up. "Sorry, I have a little . . . I'm looking for a place to live."

"Oh, really," Julia said, relieved. "Finding anything?"

"Uh-uh. I have certain requirements."

"What kind?"

"Pretty specific ones."

And Julia had to be satisfied with that. She carried the food inside and stowed it in the fridge. She filled a board with a generous selection of antipasti. A couple of oysters, two sorts of prosciutto, a few sliced sausages, a bowl of pickled olives. She opened a bottle of Italian white and took it all out to the terrace and set it out on the table. "Ta-da!"

Kim shut down the laptop and looked almost horrified at the abundance before him. "You didn't need to do that."

"Why not? I wanted to. Dig in."

Julia pulled off a strip of prosciutto, held it high, opened her mouth, dropped it in, and chewed. She poured a glass of wine and handed it to Kim. He took it, thanked her, and reached toward the board with the caution of a man about to pet an unknown dog. He chose an olive and chewed thoughtfully.

"What is it?" Julia asked. "Is there a problem?"

"Nope," Kim said. "I'm just so completely . . . not used to having people do things for me."

"You need to get used to it." Julia nodded to Kim's closed laptop. "Stockholm?"

"Preferably."

"See anything?"

"Not nearby."

"Not near Stockholm?"

"Not near what I need. What did you do?"

Julia didn't understand what could be so secret and mysterious about Kim's search for a place to live. She was put off by his reticence, so she limited herself to saying, "Met Jonny."

"Oh, yeah?"

"Uh-huh, and he had a thing or two to tell me."

Julia inspected the platter and chose a slice of dry salami, popped it in her mouth, and chewed with great concentration. Kim just looked at her. *Take that,* Julia thought. *Two can play that game.* She drank some wine, folded her hands in her lap, and looked out over the bay where pink-tinted clouds were reflected in the watery surface. Time passed. At last Kim said, "Julia. You're being childish."

"Oh, really? Just like you, then."

"No. You ask, I don't want to answer. That's what grown-ups do. But to start saying something and then stop just to be defiant—that's childish."

"You can be pretty childish too."

"Which is also a childish thing to say."

Julia stuffed another bit of sausage in her mouth and ground it between her molars. She tried to decide whether she should be offended. She came home with good things to eat and supplies from the liquor store, a super adult thing to do, and then she got called . . . But would she have preferred for him to say *Now you're sounding like an old woman*? No, she wouldn't have liked that. She let it go. "Okay, then. Jonny said it's almost certain the killers came from Shanghai, and they're probably soldiers or ex-military. I don't know how they concluded that, but that's what he said."

"The weapons," Kim said. "They're the Red Army's standard guns."

"How . . . how do you know?"

Kim gestured toward his laptop. "Those are easy to buy, so they must be basing their assumption on something more."

"Okay," Julia said. "In any case, I phoned Bruce Li at the Foreign Ministry, and—"

"*Who* did you call at the ministry?"

"Bruce Li."

"Aha, so *that's* where he disappeared to. Lots of folks wondered."

Julia giggled. There were plenty of conspiracy theories about Bruce Lee's early death, and some claimed that he was still alive, maybe hanging out in a UFO somewhere. The Swedish Foreign Ministry had never been mentioned in the speculations.

"Yes, his name has given him lots of grief," Julia said. "Anyhow, he's a China expert, and I have a meeting with him tomorrow. Want to come?"

"How could I *not* want to meet Bruce Lee? Maybe Elvis will be with him."

"You shouldn't make that kind of joke."

They sat there a couple of hours until they'd finished the antipasti, washing it down with another bottle of wine. They didn't talk much, just watched the twilight's desultory modulation of the skies. It didn't get dark, but clouds shifted through various subtle shades of pink and red as they lazily floated by, mirroring themselves as vainglorious images on the surface of the sea.

Just before eleven Kim stretched and yawned. "That's it . . . tomorrow's another day."

"Are you being ironic?"

"That's a simple fact. Good night."

Kim started to get up but sank back in his seat and gave Julia a penetrating look, as if she were a puzzle he needed to solve. Julia felt extremely enigmatic as she sat there in a slight haze, chewing the last olive. "What is it?"

"That project," Kim said. "That I worked on. It forced me to look at . . . things. Things that have made the sight of naked flesh, the feel of skin . . ." Kim shuddered as if he'd just received an electric shock. "Anyway. What I wanted to say is that it's fading."

"Fading?"

"Yeah. The images. They're just as vivid, but without the same . . . effect. Not anymore. They're still there but they're . . . fading."

Julia had an idea what Kim might be suggesting. She replied earnestly. "Meaning that . . . ?" She couldn't bring herself to say it.

"Don't think so," said Kim. "But maybe . . . eventually. Little by little."

"Little by little?"

"Yeah. Good night."

"'Night."

Jonny wasn't the only one as reluctant to commit as a cat prowling around a bowl of hot porridge. Julia remained in her seat and watched Kim's slim figure vanish into the house, heard the swish as he shed his clothes, and the creak of springs as he got into bed. She felt a little disappointed. Their bloodstorm had dwindled to a barely perceptible evening breeze that was hardly enough to rustle the leaves.

Or maybe . . . well, the images had faded for Julia as well. Olof Helander's massacred body no longer haunted her. When he did emerge from the shadows of her mind, the vision was mixed with that of the boy who made paper airplanes. She could handle that.

Julia took a gulp of wine and followed a thought, visualizing Kim lying in bed a few yards away. His scarred body, his soft hands. That familiar hot tingling sensation ran up her crotch and rose to fill her midriff with warmth. *Little by little.* Julia's throat dried up, and she found it hard to swallow. A new image filled her mind. Maybe it would be testing the limits, but as desire filled her, she succeeded in convincing herself it was possible. She rose and went to the toolshed to find a roll of duct tape.

12

It was far too warm in the bedroom for a blanket. Kim pulled the sheet up to his chin. He thought about houses as sleep slowly spread its mantle over him. He'd looked at hundreds of them that afternoon without finding any that was appropriate for his plans. Now he was engaged in drowsily creating one in his mind, a residence appropriate for a very special plan he had.

The walls floated, changed places; the roof rose and sank. The attic space and basement storage area appeared and disappeared. Maybe the best approach was to buy a piece of ground and have his imagined house constructed there? No. He had the resources but didn't have the patience for that.

Kim had almost drifted off when he heard barefoot steps coming into the bedroom. He'd thought Julia would sit up drinking wine for a while yet. Maybe this constant drinking was a bit too much, though he knew his own limits and never drank so much he lost control of his thoughts and actions.

In shadows lit only by gaps along the edges of the blackout curtains, Kim saw Julia was naked and was carrying a roll of some sort of fabric. She fastened her eyes on him. The whites gleamed in the dark when she opened them wide. He felt a stir of apprehension at the sight of this female night demon coming for him, this succubus. "What are you doing?" he muttered.

"Taking you at your word," Julia said and went to the window. "Let me know if it doesn't work for you."

There was a ripping sound. Kim saw Julia pull a length of duct tape from the roll she held. He saw her hands trembling a little as she taped over the gaps with jerky little motions. The room became totally dark. There was a thump when Julia dropped the roll of tape onto the floor.

"So," she said. "No skin to see, and . . ." The bed creaked and rustled. Julia stretched out over Kim. Only the sheet separated them. With a hot, breathy voice, she said, "No touching."

He couldn't see even the whites of her eyes in the total darkness. Kim felt her weight and warmth, heard her hot and heavy breathing as she rubbed against him. He didn't know if he wanted this or even if he thought it was acceptable. Even so, he felt an erection rising.

Julia felt it too. She whimpered, rubbed harder. There was a faint scratchy sound as her pubic hair rubbed against the sheet. Her warm breath across Kim's face had a malty smell.

"Julia . . ."

"Shh. No talking."

Through the thin fabric Kim felt the contours of her labia enclosing and grasping the tip of his penis, massaging the length of it, as she humped with increasing intensity. He threw out his arms and let her go at it. Julia's hair flicked across his face. An invisible glowing orb rose in his groin and burned away any thought of right and wrong.

Julia pressed her knuckles into his chest as her body thrust back in an arc. She released something between a growl and a whimper and thrust her pelvis violently against him. The orb burst, and a sticky warmth spurted across Kim's belly. He exhaled a long, hot breath as Julia rolled off him.

They lay a while in the blackness without saying anything or touching one another. Kim pressed his fingers to his forehead. "Julia, I don't know if . . ."

"I don't know either. But now it's happened. Okay?"

"Maybe. Probably not."

"That'll have to do."

They heard a quiet popping sound from Julia's shoulder joint when she reached out and brushed fingertips soft as feathers across Kim's face. "May I ask something?"

"Maybe."

"Why's your nose crooked?"

Kim sighed. "Little by little. Little by little."

13

Something had happened within Kim that night on St. Erik Street outside Theodora's. It wasn't that he enjoyed hitting other people; it was the combat, *the concentration. "Enjoyed" wasn't the word. He valued the fact that there was no room in his mind for anything other than what was happening in real time. Many years later he would have a similar experience with Julia Malmros. Similar but different. Or maybe essentially the same.*

His swollen cheek didn't bother him much. It was the whack that actually landed that had brought him instantly into the moment and made him feel alive. He felt like a phantom most of the time. But blood and physical pain aren't part of the spirit world. He'd been fully present.

Several days passed before Kim started to feel deprived. He wanted to experience it again; he hungered for it. He couldn't simply go around and provoke strangers into fights, but he assumed there must be others who felt the way he did. He opened his laptop.

Public internet pages mused on whether a real Fight Club *existed in Sweden. But on the dark web you could find times, places, and dates. Unlike the movie, people met in different secluded places each time to stay out of sight of the authorities.*

The first time Kim went to one, the meeting was set for a culvert under the St. Erik bridge, not too far from the place where he'd had his epiphany. He arrived just after eleven that Monday evening and thought either he'd got the venue wrong or the whole thing was a bluff. The site was under construction, littered with debris. Signs warned "NO ACCESS." A gaping hole in the fence showed only darkness beyond.

Kim stood and listened. Despite the noise of traffic crossing the bridge above, he heard faint groans and thuds coming from somewhere back in that darkness. He used his lighter for illumination, stepped over rusty iron scaffolding and construction trash, and advanced until he reached a metal door where another warning sign was posted. He opened the door.

It was impossible to see how big the room was, but judging from the echo of bone meeting flesh, it was probably a concrete hangar. Two floodlights set on tripods created a circle of light where two fighters with bare torsos circled one another. He saw many men in the shadows just outside the lighted ring.

Kim stood in the darkness until one of the men fell, sending up a cloud of dust to dance in the spotlight beams. The winner held up his arms in triumph, then asked the other guy if he was okay. He got a groaning yes and helped the loser get up. Kim stepped into the light. The floodlights dazzled him, so he couldn't see anything but a wall of black. "Can a guy join you?"

It got real quiet for a couple of seconds. A voice from the darkness replied, "And who are you?"

"My name's—"

"Uh-uh!" the guy stopped him. "We don't use our names. I'm asking again: Who are you?"

Kim thought for a moment, then replied. "Skalman."

His turtle answer provoked a certain amount of mirth in what Kim's adjusting eyes now perceived as dim shadows. Figures sniggered or chuckled as they shifted in the dark. There was a certain amount of amusement in his challenger's voice when the man replied. "You don't look like a cop, and that name proves it beyond a doubt."

Murmurs of agreement made Kim ask, "How's that?"

"The name's crazy. If you wanted to come here and, like, infiltrate, *you'd damn well have called yourself Mister Destruction or some shit like that." The guy stepped into the light as he finished speaking. Other than a swollen lip, a scar over one eyebrow, and the beginnings of a cauliflower nose, he could have been any man in the street. Jeans and blue polo shirt,*

a bit shorter than Kim, a perfectly ordinary-looking guy. Say, a cashier in a sports shop you'd forget as soon as you left. "You ever done this before?"

"Never."

He nodded and made a circling gesture toward the darkness. A different man came out of the dark with a couple of strips of cloth, nodded in greeting, and offered them to Kim. Kim nodded back. The man retreated into the shadows.

"Okay," Kim's interlocutor said while wrapping cloth around his knuckles. "Rules are simple. No hitting below the belt, no kicks. No hitting anyone who's down or kneeling. That's it."

Kim nodded and wrapped his own hands. The man waiting with his hands already bound peered at Kim. "You interested in knowing how a man signals he's had enough?"

"That's not going to happen."

The man chuckled, looked out into the dark, and pointed at Kim as if to say How about this guy! *Then he turned back to Kim and said, "You're a cocky devil. I like that. But, anyway, if it happens to . . .* happen *. . ." He emphasized that last word. "This is what you do." He raised a fist and tapped his own shoulder.*

"Hasta la victoria siempre," *Kim said.*

"Excuse me?"

"Nothing. Ready to go?"

"Off with the shirts first." He pulled his polo shirt over his head and tossed it out of the circle of light. He had a more compact, better-trained body than his ordinary appearance would suggest. Kim hesitated. He was wearing his usual long-armed knit shirt to hide his scars, and . . . shit on all that. *If he was going to do this thing, he might as well go all in. He pulled off his shirt and threw it behind him. A low murmur came from the bystanders, but that was all.*

"What—" Kim started to say, and a fist came hurtling toward his face. He managed to pull his head back just enough so that the man's knuckles barely brushed the tip of his nose, doing no damage.

They battled. This was something different from the melee on St. Erik Street. His opponent, who would later introduce himself as Styx, had both speed and technique. Kim took a blow to one ear that made his head ring and a cross that split his lip. He landed a lucky hit to one of the man's kidneys that made the guy groan, as well as an uppercut to the chin so the guy had to put his hands to the ground to keep from falling over.

They circled and sparred hard for another couple of minutes, until the man lowered his hands and said, "Okay. That's it."

"Had enough?"

The man grinned. "Not at all. Don't worry, we'll go at it again sometime. Others are waiting for their turns. This was just to see if you're any good."

"And?"

"You fight like a goddamn ballet dancer, but a damn tough one. You're in, Skalman."

Over the following months, Kim joined the group a couple of times a week. They liked to call themselves SFF, Stockholm Street Fighting. He fought in empty swimming pools, empty courts behind schools, under other bridges, and in storefronts slated for destruction. He handed more of it out than he received, but he got his share of black eyes, sore chins, and split eyebrows. It worked for him. In the white glare of the floodlights, he was as present in the moment as an actor onstage. As soon as it was over, he started longing for the next time.

He taught himself the noble art of not hesitating. Even before the adrenaline rush started, he entered the match as if it were already won, and once the rush took hold, he kept a cool head to seize the advantage when an opponent dropped his guard.

Members came and went. Some dropped out, others joined. Styx was the only constant; he transported the two floodlights to fight sites in his shabby van. Once he let it slip that during the day he really did work in a sports shop.

Everyone knew that when Kim's match with Styx finally took place, it would be a boss fight. They fought on the platform of the never-completed

Kymlinge underground train station in Järvafältet. Styx was the toughest opponent Kim had ever come up against, and it ended in a tie when neither of them could do more than stand sagging into one another as their blood and sweat mingled. Styx came away with a broken rib—not too bad for a ballet dancer—and Kim's nose was busted.

As Kim stood on the platform where trains never appeared, his hands on Styx's shoulders and their foreheads pressed together under a brilliant full moon as blood poured from his scalp, he thought, This is the peak. It doesn't get any better than this.

Then and there he knew it was the last time.

V

Stockholm

1

Astrid Helander sat before the mirror, teasing her hair. She hadn't paid the least attention to her appearance since her parents' murder. She dabbed black around her eyes. She had to go to Psychiatric Services for Youth in a couple of hours to meet Walter, and he would drive her to the police station. The police had offered to talk to her at psych services, but Astrid refused. The room where she and Walter sat and talked was her refuge.

More kohl. Astrid had been hallucinating that she had no face at all, so she painted one on. Her makeup and clothing had sometimes made people dismiss her as emo, but those were mostly women a bit older than she was. The younger ones preferred e-girl, which Astrid found easier to bear. E-girl wasn't as limiting and could include the whole spectrum from punk to skate and even all the way to grunge. The only common denominator was clothing style. Garments were always loose fitting.

She was no e-girl now. She was a mask painted on a vacuum. She remembered how Kim's hair had flicked across her face as they plunged through the early morning like something out of an Amy Winehouse video. A slight smile flickered across Astrid Helander's lips as she applied the kohl stick to the corner of her eye and farther out.

She'd googled Kim and read about his successes in gymnastics and his appearance at Martin Rudbeck's trial. His shirtsleeve had glided up, revealing his scars as he clung to the rope outside her window in Vamlinge. Kim had probably gone through a hell even worse than her own; even so, he'd come out the other side as a functioning human being.

Kim, thought Astrid as she painted her lips pink. *Remember Kim. He got through. You'll get through too.*

2

Julia and Kim sat in silence on the ferry's upper deck. They'd neglected to set an alarm and had awoken fifteen minutes before the scheduled departure. They'd barely had time to gulp down their cups of instant coffee before dashing out of the house. Not a word had yet been exchanged.

Kim worked his vaping pen out of his jeans cuff, took a drag, and exhaled a thick cloud of vapor that swept around the passengers in the stern before dissipating. An elderly lady got up, went up to Kim, and pointed sternly at the sign showing a cigarette crossed out in red.

"It's just steam," Kim said. "Not smoke."

"Nevertheless, it's prohibited," the lady said.

"But why . . ." Kim started to protest, but then shrugged and put away the vape pen. The dame left, muttering something about "hooligans."

"You have to choose your battles," Julia said.

"Right," said Kim. "Speaking of that. About last night."

"Wouldn't exactly call it a *battle*."

"Felt a bit like one."

Kim tried to catch her eye, but Julia looked away and noticed a Jet Ski zooming back and forth across the ferry's wake. She pointed. "Look at that jerk. I think they should declare open season on assholes like him."

"You don't want to discuss it?"

"Rather not."

Kim accepted that, and they remained in silence for the rest of the passage. Julia was ashamed of her behavior the previous night. It was very unlike her to . . . *grab* like that.

Kim leaned toward her as they approached Stavsudda. In a low voice he said, "I don't know how you feel about it, but I'd really prefer to be something more meaningful than a dildo."

Julia wanted to tell Kim that being close to him was what was keeping her away from the edge, preventing her from collapsing, but instead she replied, "Isn't as if I raped you, exactly."

Kim wrinkled his nose. "It was about as close as you can get when it's the woman doing it to the man. It was assault, no matter what you say."

"You could have said no."

Kim stared at her. For a long time. Julia refused to look back, because now she was really feeling ashamed.

Julia toyed with her long hair gathered in its sloppy braid. Nothing more was said.

3

The tip had come in that morning. Somebody in Karlstad had seen the helicopter land for refueling, then take off and head westward, presumably toward Norway. They'd gotten no tips from the neighboring country, however, but the attack probably hadn't been as much of a scandal there, even though it was one of the lead news stories. Jonny Munther had given Carmen Sánchez the job of contacting the Norwegian police for help going through airline passenger lists to identify Chinese nationals who'd recently left the country.

Norway, Jonny said to himself, tapping a pen on the map of Scandinavia tacked to the wall. *Norway. China. Oil. Moe.*

"What's on your mind?" asked William King.

"Nothing," said Jonny. He had no intention of sharing his former wife's crazy theories with the group. He'd discreetly asked Ulrika Boberg to keep an eye out to see if Frode Moe's name came up anywhere in the digital records. That was as far as he intended to go.

Ulrika hadn't found much except the fact that the drone activities of Olof Helander's Greenbase firm were more lucrative than they'd first appeared. The man had patented the monitoring equipment for drones that measured emissions and pollution. The money for licensing agreements was washed through various companies in tax avoidance schemes so sophisticated that they bordered on tax evasion. That had little bearing on their investigation, however, and Ulrika had passed it along to her colleagues at the Tax Fraud Unit.

The team had confiscated all the deceased individuals' computers and phones. Nothing was found there either, unless you counted Cédric Montaigne's extensive but off-putting interest in gaunt women in bondage and Chen Min's almost manic acquisition of porcelain cats. Astrid Helander's phone had been so badly smashed that the techs had extracted only her contact list.

There was a glimmer of hope. The Chinese had softened their position. The case was news even in China, and interest in the articles had taken off when it turned out that the Chen couple's son had vanished. Thirty-year-old Danny Chen resided in Shanghai (no surprise) and hadn't been seen since the news that his mother and father had been murdered. Now the newspapers knew about it. Had he been eliminated, or had he decided to go underground because he knew something significant?

The Chinese ambassador had personally phoned Jonny that morning. After inquiring about his health, His Excellency had said he'd been in contact with the police in Shanghai and that a collaborative undertaking with the Swedish police wasn't at all inconceivable. It was simply a matter of coming to an agreement on the modalities. If all went well, a couple of Swedish officers, men or women, could be admitted to Shanghai the very next day.

"Who or which?" Carmen Sánchez asked.

"I thought immediately of you," said Jonny. "You have a way with people, and as far as I know, you haven't been abroad for a while. And you can take that guy Geoffrey Chang who helped us with the video. He seemed pretty smart. If vice will loan him to us. What do you say?"

"I say yes, and I say thanks. And I agree. He did seem sharp."

William King put his hands together to form a heart—"Ting, tong, Chinaman!"—and thereby forfeited any shred of goodwill Jonny Munther might have had for him.

4

Bruce Li had explained it was necessary their meeting be completely off the record, and for that reason he'd insisted on meeting Julia at the teahouse in Kungsträdgården. She and Kim had arrived fifteen minutes before the stipulated time and both had finished a triple espresso, which lightened the mood between them a little. Julia put down her empty cup. "Sorry if I was a little hard with you."

"You mean last night? I have an impressive bruise on my hip."

"Me too. But on the boat, I mean."

"Yes?"

Julia had really intended to offer an apology for her wanton behavior, not to explain it. With her index finger she twirled her cup around and around on the saucer before admitting, "I don't know what I should say. It's some kind of . . . desperation. A shriek. Inside me."

"So you did your shrieking on me."

"Yes. That's exactly it. Since you were available."

"Not so sure I want to be just 'available.'"

"I understand that."

It seemed almost inconceivable that Julia's profession involved expressing herself and she was extremely skilled at it. When called upon to explain her own emotions, she found that her speaking ability regressed to that of a five-year-old. Julia leaned over, put her face into her hands, and murmured, "'I'm leaving the table. I'm out of the game.'"

"What are you saying?"

Julia looked up. "Sometimes . . . it's a feeling I just want to . . . like Klas Östergren did when he resigned . . . but with *everything*, you understand?" She balled up her fists and tried to come up with a better explanation.

Kim looked out over the water and said, "Oh, my goodness."

Julia turned and saw Bruce Li sluggishly making his way between the tables. His expression was woeful enough to make you think he'd just learned that his whole family had been liquidated. His suit, much too heavy for the summer warmth, hung like a sack on his frail, sloping shoulders. He seemed lost in thought and shook his head from time to time as if recalling some especially lamentable fact.

When he reached their table, Julia stuck out her hand. "Hello, Bruce!"

"Yes, yes," said Bruce Li and shook her hand without the least enthusiasm.

Julia gestured toward Kim. "And this is Kim Ribbing. Hope that's okay with you."

Bruce Li shrugged in a way that showed it wasn't okay in the least, but he'd have to put up with it. Julia assumed he'd been looking forward to an intimate tête-à-tête. Insofar as Bruce Li ever looked forward to anything.

"Have a seat," Julia said. "Would you like something? Coffee?"

"No, no," said Bruce Li. "Bellyache." He dropped onto a rickety garden chair with a groan as if sinking into an armchair. He took a handkerchief from an inner pocket and wiped his sweaty face. Julia pushed her untouched water glass toward him. "Maybe a little water?"

"Did anyone drink from it?"

"No."

Bruce Li took the glass and examined it carefully to ascertain that Julia wasn't deceiving him. He took a couple of deep gulps. That seemed to perk him up a little.

"So, then," he said. "How much do you know about the story?"

"I know they came from Shanghai," said Julia. "This is highly confidential. The police are extremely strict in seeing that—"

"We know that already," Bruce Li said.

"We? Who's 'we'?"

"Me. My contacts at the embassy. A few others."

"Why was I made to think it was a big secret?"

Bruce Li sighed and replied as if it was his onerous duty to instruct a child. "Knowledge is one thing. *Public* knowledge is something else."

"They don't want it to come out in the media and harm relations with China?" said Kim.

Bruce Li pointed at him as if to say *Hear! Hear!* Julia nodded. Most secrets were like smoke, anyway. They tended to slip out. The smell of them could be detected, if nothing else.

"You know about Danny?" asked Bruce Li.

"The son?" said Julia, who'd kept current with her phone. "Who's dead or vanished?"

Bruce Li shook his head. "Not dead. Not according to my China contacts. Disappeared, yes. But not dead." He looked over Strömkajen where the Vaxholm ferries were lined up. "I met Olof Helander a few years ago. He wanted advice about doing business in China." Bruce Li's expression lightened so that he looked merely dismayed instead of deeply grieved. "He invited me to his Midsummer Eve party that year."

"Aha," said Julia. "Was it a good time?"

Bruce Li shook his head, and gloom settled over him again. "Didn't go. The sea." He made a waving motion to indicate how the choppy sea disagreed with him.

"Those business affairs," Julia said. "What kind were they?"

"Unless I don't remember correctly, he was going to manufacture drones, and he was thinking about doing it in China. I don't know how it turned out."

Bruce Li grimaced as if his lack of knowledge bothered him, and his face wrinkled in a sad expression Eeyore would never be able to achieve even in his darkest days.

"The son," Kim said. "Danny. Would it be possible to contact him?"

Bruce Li regarded him and raised his thinning eyebrows. He shook his head and seemed about to make a pronouncement about impossibilities, but he paused and furrowed his brow. "Hard," he said. "Maybe not impossible. I know someone who *might* know someone, and . . . Yes. In that case. But I suspect it must happen in some designated place. He is obviously not eager to show himself in public. Anyone could understand that."

Julia spoke. "So, if someone from the police in Shanghai . . ."

She was stopped by the sight of Bruce Li's eyebrows shooting up to the maximum. He waved away the suggestion. "Not the *police*," he hissed. He looked around as if Julia had just said something extremely dangerous. "No one relies on . . ." He changed the subject. "I think, anyway, that he would find it easier to trust a Westerner, the way things are now."

"Okay," said Kim.

"Okay, *what*?" asked Julia.

"Okay, I'll go."

"*You*? Why should you—"

"Got nothing special to do, and anyhow," Kim said with a shrug, "I guess it fits in with the little pause we're in right now."

Bruce Li looked back and forth between Kim and Julia before clearing his throat and saying in a low voice, "You will excuse my intrusiveness, but does there happen to be a romantic relationship in evidence here?"

"You might put it that way," said Julia, not knowing if that was still the case.

"I understand," said Bruce Li and looked a tiny bit more disappointed, if that was even possible. "I wish both of you long life and good health. Let's concentrate on business."

5

Astrid Helander was already seated there with her psychologist Walter something-or-other when Jonny Munther and Carmen Sánchez entered the conference room. Astrid's eyes were so ringed with black makeup that she looked like a panda cub. Her lips were bright pink. Jonny assumed it was a sort of protective coloration. He placed a thin sheaf of pages on the table and seated himself beside Carmen. She took out her notebook.

"Thank you for taking the time to speak to us," Jonny said. "And I'm sorry for your loss."

Astrid nodded without taking her eyes off the cloth draped over the team's whiteboard. She pointed at it. "You have pictures behind that?"

"Yes. We do have photos," Carmen Sánchez said. "But I don't think it's a good idea for you to see them."

"I most certainly agree," said Walter.

"Don't want to either," said Astrid. "Just wondered."

Jonny Munther looked through his notes summarizing the details of the investigation but put them down. "Just wondering. Was it Kim Ribbling who got you out of the clinic?"

"Ribb . . ." Astrid started to reply but stopped and turned to Walter. "Do I have to answer that?"

Walter smiled. "I'm a psychologist, not an attorney."

"This isn't an interrogation," Carmen Sánchez said. "You're not obliged to answer *anything* you don't want to."

"So, I won't."

Jonny seemed to want to insist, but Carmen gave him one of her looks. Jonny nodded, let his shoulders slump, glanced at his summaries, and said, "First of all, this video . . . I mean, we got a video made with your phone, and on the—"

"What?" exclaimed Astrid. "What are you talking about?"

"Someone sent it in, and it mostly shows you when you—"

"But I didn't video anything, and even if I had . . . I want to see this video!"

Carmen Sánchez looked at Jonny. He shrugged. Walter asked whether the material showed anything of what had happened to Astrid's parents. When Carmen assured him it did not, he said it was up to Astrid. She wanted to see it, so Carmen opened her laptop, called up the video, turned the screen toward Astrid, and tapped the space bar.

"What the hell—*goddamn it!*" Astrid's voice screamed through the speakers. The Astrid in the room with them flinched at the sudden burst of automatic weapon fire. Since the seven seconds of video didn't show anyone dying, Carmen let it run to the end.

"I don't understand," said Astrid. "I don't . . ." Her expression changed as the light dawned. "Algot," she said and nodded. "Algot, that little perv."

"You'll need to explain that a bit," Jonny Munther said. "Who is Algot?"

"Kid in my class. Long story. Completely irrelevant."

"It's better if you let us decide what's relevant," Jonny Munther said.

"Take my word for it," said Astrid. "Teen hormones. Nothing there for you."

"But can't you just—" Jonny persisted.

Carmen interrupted. "Okay, so let's continue. I understand this is difficult for you, but did you *see* the gunmen?" Astrid nodded. "Can you describe them at all?"

"It's just that I saw them only a second before I . . . before I hid under the table." Astrid's expression suggested she was embarrassed to confess that.

"It was good that you did," Carmen said. "Unbelievably resourceful, really."

"Resourceful? What does that mean?" Astrid asked.

"That you managed to keep a cool head in a difficult situation," Walter suggested.

"The murderers?" Jonny Munther reminded her.

"I don't know what to say. They were small men. You know, like, yeah, lots of kids my age." Astrid made a face that showed her opinion of kids her age.

"If you had to guess their nationality, what would you say?" asked Carmen Sánchez.

Astrid squinted at the ceiling for a moment, then said, "I dunno. Maybe from Vietnam or Thailand. But I couldn't tell."

Carmen sneaked a glance at Jonny Munther and saw him purse his lips. Each successive clue pointing eastward tended to dismay him more. He pulled himself together and said, "Of course this is hard for you, but I must ask. Can *you* think of anything about your papa's professional life that might lead to . . . well, yes, to his murder?"

Walter gave Jonny a disapproving look. "That was a completely unfeeling way of asking your question."

"I beg your pardon," Jonny said. "I don't know how else to—"

"It's okay," Astrid said, again looking up at the ceiling. She frowned and turned to Carmen Sánchez. "Do you have his iPad?"

Carmen leafed through the inventory of confiscated items and found that the police were holding two computers and two phones. "No," she said. "No iPad listed."

"Uh-huh," Astrid said. "Thought so. I saw it only twice. First time I said something like, *Hey, you have an iPad, I didn't know that,* and he told me he'd borrowed it, that was all, but I could tell he was lying. And besides, I saw it again a few months later when he forgot and left it out on his desk."

Carmen asked, "Do you have any idea of what he might have had on it?"

"Nah, but probably something he was worried about. It was locked with a password *and* fingerprint recognition."

"You tried to open it?"

"Mmm. . . a person gets curious. When something's so awfully secret. But no luck."

"Do you know if he had it with him on Knektholmen?"

"No idea. Didn't see it, so it could be anywhere at all. Sorry."

"Really no reason at all to be sorry," Jonny Munther said. "That was useful information, and we will—"

William King threw open the conference room door without bothering to knock. "Now all hell has broken loose!" He was holding an open laptop.

"Excuse us," Jonny said. "We're in the middle of—"

"You'll want to see this," said William King, giving Astrid and Walter a side glance. He positioned the laptop on the table so that only Jonny Munther and Carmen Sánchez could see the screen. Jonny caught just a few words of the headline on the daily *Aftonbladet*'s website, but that was enough to confirm that hell indeed was loose: Chinese, Soldiers, and Knektholmen.

"Oh, my," Carmen Sánchez sighed. "Well, that's smoked it."

6

Kim sat in the Rival Hotel lobby at Mariatorget with his laptop and a small glass of Punk IPA. Julia Malmros had gone to visit her father, and Kim had booked himself a single at the Rival. Their previous congeniality on the island had mostly disappeared, and Kim had early morning plans anyway. He'd already bought his ticket.

Kim was extremely sensitive about any intrusion into his privacy, and what Julia had done the previous night was certainly an intrusion; she'd used him as if he were a machine. That had put Kim off, and the situation deteriorated further when Julia treated it as unimportant. As if women were somehow incapable of abusing men.

Kim shook his head at that attitude. You might as well call it female chauvinism. It was time to take a break from Julia Malmros, distance himself, stand clear, and examine that relationship to decide what it was worth.

Kim's screen displayed the *Aftonbladet* article. The report that Chinese soldiers had carried out the assault had come from a "reliable source" in the government, so Bruce Li had probably been right: Lots of people knew. Kim assumed this was complicating things for the police, and he wasn't likely to run across DS Munther in Shanghai.

As so often before in his life, he didn't really know why he'd volunteered to take the trip. Perhaps he just needed an excuse to escape from Julia for a while. Or it could be that he was a thrill seeker. Maybe he simply had nothing better to do. Taking a trip to the other side of the world meant not having to deal with a pile of practical problems.

Kim took his phone and pulled up the Hemnet real estate site, where he limited his search to villas in central Stockholm or the vicinity. Not many were available. A couple of new listings had appeared. Kim noticed a residence encircled by a tall iron fence. He read the description and viewed several photos. He phoned Jenny Martling.

Jenny had handled his financial affairs since he reached his majority. She managed his fortune, filed his taxes, and generally assisted him. Under her competent administration, Kim's wealth had almost doubled over the last ten years. He trusted her completely.

Jenny picked up almost immediately, as usual. "Hi, Kim. Everything going well, I hope?"

Kim wasn't good at small talk and Jenny knew it, so he went straight to his request. "I need help with a thing."

"That's what I'm here for."

"Good. I want you to buy Haiti's embassy for me."

She was silent for a couple of seconds. "Let's try that one more time."

"Haiti's previous embassy in Stockholm. It's for sale. I want to buy it."

"What are they asking?"

"Does it matter?"

"No, as long as it doesn't involve . . . actually, no, it doesn't matter."

"Okay, good. Can you arrange it ASAP?"

He heard the rustle of a pen on a pad as Jenny inquired, "Are you intending to . . . reside there?"

"Yes. So, it'd be great if you could take care of getting it furnished too."

"Furnished?"

"Yeah, with furniture, you know. Chairs, a table, a bed, stuff like that. You can invoice double your usual fee."

"Really no need for that, but what *kind* of furniture, what style . . .?"

Kim sighed. "Find pictures in some design magazine and tell somebody to use those. *Furniture.* Or use your own judgment, something you like."

"Aha, I see," said Jenny unhappily. "Yes, uh-huh, I'll take care of it."

They ended the call, and Kim took a sip of beer. He wanted to vape a bit but assumed that it was prohibited. He scrolled through the photos of the former embassy and closely studied the descriptions. The place looked perfect for his needs.

Furniture.

Kim had left his bag on Tärnö, so he planned to buy the things he needed at Schiphol Airport's duty-free shops in Amsterdam when he changed planes. He needed to buy clothing. It didn't matter what kind, provided it fit. He would have something to eat. What kind of food wasn't important except that he needed to be nourished. And when he came home, he'd have furniture. It didn't matter what kind, provided he could use it to sit on, lie in, or stow stuff. People put entirely too much energy into the wrong things.

There was one aspect of the Shanghai trip that Kim hadn't adequately considered: the fact that it could be dangerous. If he was going to meet a person in hiding with significant information about a massacre, it seemed possible others would be looking for that same person.

Kim pondered that for a while, then sent a message to Moebius, who'd invited Kim into HackPack because they had a history and had even met In Real Life. Moebius messaged him back in just a couple of minutes to confirm that he could take care of what Kim had requested within an hour or two.

Kim left the hotel and went to look for a hair salon where he could have his ends trimmed and his long blond roots dyed. He'd idled around enough now. It was time to get back to being who he wanted to be, at least on his exterior. His inside was a lost cause.

7

"And it wasn't you?" Jonny Munther stared straight into William King's eyes.

The man held up both hands as if a gunman were threatening him. "I swear on my mother's grave."

"Is your mother dead?"

"You can verify with the civil registry if you doubt me."

Jonny grasped the sides of his desk and rocked back and forth. As he'd feared, the *Aftonbladet* report had made the Chinese slam the door they'd opened just a crack. No hope now they'd cooperate with the Swedish police.

"If you think it was me," William King said, "did you wonder even for a second *why* I would do such a thing?"

"Let's be frank," Jonny Munther said. "I don't trust you any farther than I can throw you."

"Okay, that I maybe can understand. But, well, damn it, why? What have I done to deserve it? 'Follow the money,' as they say in English. Okay, it's not a question of money, but when all is said and done, it's still a matter of who stands to gain."

Jonny Munther fixed his gaze on a Marc Chagall print hanging on the wall. A couple in a loving embrace hovered contentedly above a roof. Their situation was just about as remote from his as could be imagined, considering he was standing on dry land and arguing with a person he disliked.

"The killers, obviously," said Jonny Munther. "Since this hinders the investigation, to say the least. But I doubt they tipped off the *Aftonbladet*."

"Okay," William King said. "And what's our side going to do now?"

"Turn over that part of the investigation to the Chinese police."

"Exactly. Could that have been the reason?"

Jonny stopped rocking. No matter how much he distrusted William King, he had to admit the guy wasn't stupid. He had a point. The *Aftonbladet* had said the report came from "within the government," a comment so ambiguous it could mean just about anything.

"You mean the Chinese want to take over an investigation that's troublesome for them so they can bury it?"

"Something like that, yes."

"Hmm," said Jonny Munther. "As long as it wasn't you."

"I swear by all that I hold holy."

Jonny doubted that William King held anything holy, but Jonny believed him anyway.

8

"Cool, huh?"

The object dangling from Moebius's fat index finger looked like a minuscule ruby set in a metal frame. It dangled from a thin silver chain. Kim Ribbing wound the chain around his own index finger and inspected the pendant. The ruby was no larger than the nail of his little toe, but hidden behind it was a digital tracker that, considering its size, was extremely powerful.

"Got it delivered ten minutes ago," Moebius said. "Not cheap, this thing."

"Software?"

"Sure. Man, I feel like Q. That make you James Bond?"

Moebius took back the necklace. The pendant looked tiny in his big mitt. On his computer, a hulking machine that could have steered a space station, he opened a program called Tracksuit. An empty white field appeared against a blue background. He held up the ruby. "Couldn't be simpler. Emergency situation? You press right here." Moebius's clumsy fingers eventually managed to press the ruby into its setting. A shrill alarm signal erupted from his computer, and the white field was instantly populated with numbers that Kim assumed were coordinates.

"Okay," said Kim. "So, why—"

Moebius held up an index finger to stop him. "Wait for it."

Kim waited. Three seconds later, Moebius's phone buzzed angrily, just as the computer had done. He held it out, and Kim saw the same coordinates. Moebius moved the computer cursor to a red dot labeled Received. He clicked it, and the alarms on both devices stopped. Moebius held out his hands like a circus ringmaster who'd just shown off his leading attraction.

"Why isn't there a map?" Kim asked.

Moebius's smile turned upside down. "What do you need a map for?" he grumped. He copied the coordinates, pasted them into Google Maps and pressed return. A map of Sundbyberg appeared on the screen with a red marker hovering over the building containing Moebius's tiny efficiency apartment. "Takes five seconds, max. How lazy can a guy be?"

Kim looked around the flat. A layer of dust covered every surface. Dust bunnies the size of fists lurked in the corner and along the baseboards. Piles of pizza cartons lay on the floor; Kim knew Moebius had them delivered because he found it difficult to go out in public. He'd gained weight since Kim last saw him. Even though Kim knew the squalor was directly related to Moebius's mental health conditions, he found it a little funny to be called "lazy" by the man.

"How do I reboot it?"

Moebius pointed to a tiny hole on the back of the pendant. "Stick a tack or something in there."

Kim found a paper clip among the piles of stuff on Moebius's desk, straightened it, inserted it in the hole, and pressed. The ruby glided back into its original position. He opened the lock on the silver chain and put it around his neck. After a little fumbling, he managed to fasten it.

"Nice," said Moebius. "Sexy lady!"

"Thanks. Just one more thing. Could you fix it so a Jonny Munther of the Stockholm police can have that Tracksuit software too, and you can explain to him—"

Moebius's index finger was up again, this time waving back and forth. "No way, José. Never gonna talk to the *police*. Uh-uh."

"Okay. Then contact Julia Malmros and get the program to her, so *she* can contact the police if something happens."

Moebius looked horrified. "I have to?" For Moebius, any new human interaction was intimidating.

"Yeah," said Kim. "I'll send you her number. She needs it for both the computer and the phone, like you."

"It installs on the computer, then the computer forwards any alarms to the phone."

"Okay, sure. And it's not going to track me if I don't *want* to be tracked? If I don't press the button?"

"Nope."

Kim went to the kitchen for a glass of water but stopped in the doorway. The oven there, the drawer over there, a rhomboid-shaped trivet, a pile of unwashed plates, a circular tray. *The pattern.* He stood staring for a while, then turned. "Moebius. What if everything's just a simulation?"

"What do you mean?"

"Textures that keep repeating. Like everything is artificial and existence is a kind of test drive."

"And we're supposed to exist in somebody's computer program? That's just *The Matrix.*"

"No. Not a program. A simulation."

"Sorry, you lost me there."

Kim eventually found an almost clean glass in the cupboard. He filled it and gulped the water down. A worried Moebius peered at him from the gigantic desk chair that looked like a relic from the bridge of the *Enterprise.*

Kim put the glass down among the other dirty dishes. "You hear anything more about that guy Ces?"

Moebius grinned a little. "*Mossad! Hell yeah!* The HackPack guys can't get enough of it. Don't know why, but lots of them think Ces is a woman. They can't wait to see what she'll come up with next. Hope it'll be something with NASA."

"Why NASA, specifically?"

"No reason. NASA's cool, that's all."

Before leaving, Kim asked, "Bitcoin, as usual?"

"Naw," Moebius said, rubbing his hands together. "Gold. I want gold."

"You mean . . . *gold* gold? The yellow metal?"

"For sure. Starting a collection. Gonna sit here in my hidey-hole like Smaug."

"Fits you perfectly. Take care of yourself."

"You too, Skalman, you too. Say hi to Granny."

9

Julia couldn't believe it; the odor in the stairwell of the building on Margretelund Street in Traneberg was the same as she remembered from childhood. It was probably the musty smell from Papa's apartment. The home services visitors never had the time to do the full cleaning job that was needed, and Julia, to her shame, had never done it herself. She came up with various excuses, but the real reason was that she found it disgusting.

She rang the bell a couple of times before opening with her own key. Papa could still get out of bed to go to the toilet without assistance, but he had to use a walker, and that took a long time. He spent most of his day sitting up in bed watching nature documentaries and snooker.

"Hello!" called Julia from the hall. "It's me!"

Each time she entered her father's place, Julia felt that moment of uncertainty, wondering whether he was still alive. The social services visited him four times a day, so the odds were in his favor, but you could never be sure.

"Yes, yes, come in," came a groan from the bedroom. Julia let out her breath. Another shameful truth: She was less worried about him than about all the tedious practicalities she'd face if he died. His dementia was slowly getting worse, another reason she no longer took pleasure in her contact with him. He still recognized Julia, but other things were fading.

She crossed the kitchen, aware the cork matting under her shoes was sticky, and went into the bedroom that once had been hers. Her parents had slept in the living room. As usual, Papa sat propped up against a couple of large pillows. The TV at the foot of the bed showed a man in a vest and top hat preparing for his next shot on the snooker table. The sound was off.

Julia bent over and kissed her father on the cheek, then pulled up a wooden chair to seat herself at his bedside. The table on the opposite side was heaped with medicines, tubes and jars of creams, newspapers, and scraps of paper. Her father was perpetually scribbling on those scraps, noting in his illegible handwriting everything he was supposed to remember but immediately forgot.

"How are you doing?" asked Julia. "Should I turn off the TV?"

"Don't bother," Papa said, not watching the screen. As far as Julia was aware, he didn't even know the rules of snooker, but maybe the balls rolling across the table in their simple, predictable trajectories had a lulling effect. Without mentioning any specific annoyance, her father said, "Getting old is a hell of a thing."

It wasn't entirely clear just what her father's illness was. He consumed pills to counteract low blood pressure, nausea, dizziness, and more, but no specific affliction kept him bedridden. Maybe it was a combination, an accumulation of maladies. Or maybe he was just tired of life.

"Enough of that," her father said. "How are things with Jonny these days?"

Julia had stopped correcting him years before when his memory failed, because that merely upset him and made him anxious. Still, today she did know how things were with Jonny. "He's alive and healthy," she replied in an expressionless voice.

Her father shook his head and lowered his voice as if about to tell her a secret. "You could have done without that one, if you ask me."

"I'll think about it, Papa."

"Do that. And your job? Working on anything interesting?"

"No, not since that Millennium project was turned down."

He raised his bushy eyebrows. "Mill . . . what are you talking about? I meant your *job*. With the police."

Julia took a moment, then decided to play along. "I don't know if you remember Olof Helander?"

"Of course I do! Ran all about the neighborhood here."

"Right. He's just been murdered, and I'm trying—"

"Murdered?" Those bushy eyebrows went up again. "But he's just a little boy!" Julia sighed. This wasn't one of her father's better days, which was further confirmed when he leaned forward and confided in a conspiratorial tone, "You know I was a policeman too, right?"

"Yep, Papa. I know."

Her father put his thumb and index finger together. "I *pinched* 'em, I want you to know!"

Julia cut the visit short because an aching feeling of loss had begun to spread through her. It became more intense as she tramped heavily down the stairs from his apartment. She missed the father she'd known, she missed her mother, who'd died of cancer ten years earlier, she missed Kim Ribbing, who might never return, and . . . yes, she even missed Mikael Blomkvist and Lisbeth Salander, who were no longer hers to play with.

The staircase smelled the same as ever, but the Julia Malmros traversing it was different, a woman defined by everything she no longer had. Soon enough, she'd be the one sitting in bed and watching snooker.

10

The summer morning was clear and pure when Kim Ribbing parked his Honda in the uncovered lot closest to Arlanda's Terminal 2. He hefted his compact backpack to his shoulder and walked toward the terminal building. The air had that crisp but warm quality that maybe only Swedish summer mornings have. It was just past six. His flight with Norwegian Air was scheduled for 7:15.

He had that liberated feeling you get when you're carrying minimal baggage leaving one place on the way to somewhere else. That in-between status. The sun warmed his face, and the air he inhaled had a lovely blend of the smells of summer greenery and jet fuel. He was on his way.

VI

S

1

Christof Adler was already in the conference room when Carmen Sánchez got there. He sat hunched over the table, intently watching a small screen. His thumbs twiddled two little levers and pushed buttons to the reedy sound of electronic music.

Carmen stood behind him and watched. A little figure climbed obstacles, bounced over cars, and hopped from one roof to another with a cheery "*Yahoo!*"

"What on earth is that?" asked Carmen.

"Super Mario," Christof told her as the little man leaped through a row of golden coins, each one jingling. As if this required further explanation, Christof added, "Odyssey."

"Matilda loaned it to you, did she?"

Christof shook his head. "Mine. Mine alone."

Christof had been living for the past couple of years with Cecilia, six years older than he was, who had a seven-year-old daughter, Matilda. Christof stayed with them but hadn't given up his lease on an efficiency apartment because he wasn't ready to "commit fully," as he'd once explained to Carmen when she'd asked.

Carmen liked working with Christof, but sometimes she had the impression she was like a big sister to him or even a mama. The little man on the screen grabbed a blue moon, shouted gleefully, and swung around. Merry music played. Christof gave a fist pump and cried, "Yessss!"

"You're pretty childish. You know that, right?" said Carmen.

"So what? There's lots of grown-ups that play this, and besides . . ." Christof shrugged. "Might be good to retain a little childhood innocence." He nodded toward the whiteboard they knew was crowded with photos and notes. "Especially when you work on stuff like that."

Mario kept shouting as Carmen went to the board and removed the covering. The first thing she saw was the collection of photos of the aftermath of the Midsummer Eve slaughter. She rolled up the cloth and tilted her head.

The brutality of it.

The thought of having to fire her official weapon at another human being had always repulsed Carmen Sánchez. She couldn't stand the idea that her own hand would send a devastating little lead slug to rip through another person's flesh and maybe smash a bone. But here two individuals had stood and in cold blood fired two hundred rounds straight into a group of defenseless human beings, including a fourteen-year-old girl. What had been going on in those men's heads? Could one imagine even the slightest trace of empathy in their minds?

The photos had been enlarged and examined closely in the effort to identify some sort of intentionality of the victims, some foreknowledge or unusual behavior. Nothing had surfaced, other than Chen Bao's irrational attempt to protect his porcelain-cat-loving wife. They were completely, undeniably victims taken by surprise at the table and mercilessly mowed down. That was all.

Carmen remembered the dark beckoning force that had emanated from that dock, the mesmerizing whisper *Come and look, come see.* The photos had some of that same allure. She stood there with her mouth open, staring at the sprawled, stretched-out bodies, the broken porcelain, and the blood-soaked tablecloth, the blue sky and glittering sea in the background. She flinched when the door opened and Jonny Munther came in.

"Don't you ever get enough of that?" he asked.

"I got enough a long time ago," said Carmen. She sat down. "That's why I'm looking. To remind myself."

Jonny caught sight of Christof sitting with his tongue at one corner of his mouth. Christof must have realized he was being watched, because without looking up from the screen, he said, "I know, I know. I just want to . . ."

Christof smiled broadly as a descending melody came from the device. He turned the game off and stuffed it into his satchel. Jonny was tempted to lecture the lad about toys during work hours and how inappropriate it was to sit in this room playing games, but at that moment the door opened and William King entered. Jonny didn't want King to hear him scolding Christof, so he let it drop.

William King had dark circles under his eyes and an aura—or rather, an odor—of having guzzled too much booze the night before. "Aha," he said. "What are all of you sitting here buzzing about, huh?"

"The difference between right and left," Carmen said.

William King shook his head and plopped down in a chair with a groan. Ulrika Boberg came in next, and Jonny invited her to close the door behind her. He rose. "We might as well review anything new since last time. Carmen?"

"Right. The conversation with Astrid Helander turned up the fact that her papa had an iPad he tried to keep hidden. I was up at the Greenbase offices yesterday and talked with the employees, but they claimed not to know about any iPad. I searched his office but found nothing. I don't know if that makes him more suspect or less, but—"

"The little girl *may* be making it up," said William King. "Spinning a tale, just to offer us something. That's not a rare phenomenon."

"That wasn't my impression," said Carmen.

"Mine either," said Jonny Munther. "Carmen, you and Christof should go out to Knektholmen and see if you can locate it. Then we'll check the apartment in Stockholm. This is top priority. Ulrika?"

As ever, Ulrika carefully aligned the already perfectly ordered pages in front of her, as if symmetry were a prerequisite for speaking. "Yes, I was assigned the job of taking a closer look at that Frode Moe fellow . . ."

"I probably wouldn't put it that way," said Jonny.

"Oh?" said Ulrika. "How would you put it, then? I prefer to have perfectly clear instructions for my assignments."

"Forget it," said Jonny. "Continue."

For a moment it looked as if Ulrika Boberg had no intention of continuing, not out of childish pique but because she'd done a job imprecisely defined and therefore irrelevant. Then her face went through a sequence of impressive contortions, and she said, "There's lots that is not clear. Futurig, the parent company, is transparent, but beyond that . . . I doubt you can even imagine how complicated the concern's structure is. He must have battalions of accountants and lawyers. Futurig has a huge presence in the North Sea. I won't go into all the details about shell companies, subsidiaries, depreciation funds, and loss amortizations, but what jumps out is that there's an impressive amount of revenue that seems to come out of thin air. That does not conform with standard accounting practices."

"Excuse me," said Jonny Munther, "but what do you mean when you say 'out of thin air'?"

"The money just appears. I haven't been able to trace the transactions, so they *might* be legitimate, but I smell a rat."

"And we're talking about large amounts?" asked Jonny Munther.

"Many hundreds of millions. And in some cases they're used to cover losses they might have run up but hid by recycling them through several subsidiaries' depreciation accounts. It looks like this money arriving for no reason is sustaining the whole structure."

"This is all very interesting," said Jonny Munther, "but does it have any direct bearing on our case?"

Ulrika pouted. "You asked me to look at Frode Moe, I looked at Frode Moe. So now what do I do? Stuff the Norwegian in the closet?"

"No, no, not at all," said Jonny. "I also found something out, so that . . . you go on."

"What did you find out?" asked Carmen Sánchez.

"Give me just a moment."

All this gabbing so early in the morning about complicated financial transactions gave Jonny Munther a headache. He went to the coffee table and pumped a paper cup full of the stuff, poured in enough milk to bring it down to a drinkable temperature, and sloshed half of it down his throat. His mind cleared. He knew it was merely a placebo effect, because caffeine took several minutes to act, but a placebo effect was at least an effect.

He turned and saw Carmen Sánchez looking annoyed.

"Just needed a little coffee."

"Uh-huh. So, let's hear it."

"It's no big thing. I asked vice to lend us Geoffrey Chang twenty-five percent of his time, so he could spend a couple of hours a day checking Chinese media outlets, in case they mention something we don't know."

"And?"

"Maybe not directly related to our case, but there was one interesting detail about Chen Bao. In an interview he gave to the *China Daily* a few years ago, he said he had taken an interest in Chinese-made oil rigs and their effects on the climate, and he was on his way to becoming something of an authority. That was all, but if we think about it in connection with Frode Moe, then . . . after all, Moe gets his rigs built in China. So, well, that was all. Let's get back to work."

"And me?" asked William King. "What should I do?"

"What did you do yesterday?"

"You know perfectly well. I had my hands full dealing with the media after that stuff about Chinese soldiers came out. Had to twist and turn like a snake to keep bad from getting worse."

And then you drank yourself senseless, thought Jonny Munther, but all he said was, "Find the leak."

"Don't you think I'm a little overqualified for that?"

"Oh, I don't know. You might as well keep twisting and turning."

2

Julia felt a sharp sting of worry when she locked the door to her Tärnö summer cabin, as if she were shutting up something she'd lost. She didn't know what to think of her relationship with Kim. Nothing had become any clearer in the days they'd spent together.

She didn't know why Kim had come, and she didn't know why he'd left. And meanwhile, she didn't understand her own behavior. Her nighttime attack had been completely out of character, a desperate, violent attempt to break through the invisible barrier between them, symbolized by a sheet through which contact could be forced.

Julia's unhappy dilemma kept intruding and tormenting her as she made her way down the steep path to the ferry landing. She'd planned to stay longer on Tärnö, but after a solitary evening on the terrace, the cabin and its surroundings felt like the scene of a disaster. In her loneliness, the proximity of Knektholmen evoked horrible visions of those murder victims still lying out there, rotting on the dock. Of course they weren't, not anymore, but that's how it *felt* when she looked over the bay, thinking she could smell decay on the evening breeze.

Some of the people at the landing sneaked glances at her. Nothing unusual. No one said anything about Malou or Millennium or anything else, for that matter. She was left in peace with her bleak thoughts about Kim Ribbing, whom she might never see again.

There was one point of light in all this obscurity. That morning she'd gotten an email from someone called Moebius. It had a link to a program called Tracksuit and an explanation of how it was set up. Kim had assigned Julia to watch over him. That was a bit of consolation, at least. And he'd said "little by little." That gave her a straw to cling to.

Shanghai. Why did I let him go?

As if she could have stopped him. There was plenty Julia didn't know about Kim Ribbing, but she had grasped that he was a person who craved *movement* of one sort or other. When he sat still, his demons emerged and crowded around.

The ferry came gliding up to the landing. It was slightly absurd that Kim, of all people, had taken himself off to the other side of the world to locate the vanished Danny, but at least that was part of the private investigation. On her own side of the globe, Julia kept brooding on what she might be able to do. Correction: It was *their* investigation. If nothing else, at least they had that much in common.

3

Carmen Sánchez had just rung to report that she and Christof Adler were on site on Knektholmen, but the doors were locked. They had no keys. Who'd been the last to leave the island? Jonny Munther guessed it was the technicians or maybe the divers. Most folks had an extra key to their summerhouse hidden somewhere. He suggested they try to find one.

"Don't you think I'm a little overqualified for that?" Carmen said, echoing the reply from that morning's meeting. Jonny Munther rarely appreciated jokes made by his colleagues, but this one made him chuckle. Presumably that was because the jab was directed at William King.

"Otherwise, just call in a locksmith," said Jonny. "If the keys aren't with the rest of the confiscated stuff, it could take all day."

"Aye, aye, captain!"

Jonny Munther finished the call and heard a cautious knock at his door. Lennart Browall stuck his head in and asked if he was disturbing. The police chief's leadership style wasn't what you'd call authoritarian. Jonny invited him to come in and have a seat.

"Oh, no, just stopping by for a moment," Lennart said. "I was talking with Liselott, and it seems you've directed a team member to take a look at Frode Moe."

Despite Jonny Munther's initial misgivings about Liselott Ahrnander, he had to praise the fact that she didn't interfere any more than necessary. Jonny generally gave her a short briefing just before lunch, and so far she hadn't offered any objections to the way he was managing *her* investigation. But Jonny didn't miss that quizzical eyebrow when Lennart mentioned King Frode.

"It's a good idea to check," said Jonny Munther. "He has turned up, that's true."

"And I assume you understand that's sensitive?"

"What *isn't* sensitive in this matter?"

"Well . . . thousands of Swedish citizens depend on him for employment, both on the rigs and in his businesses in Sweden. The interior minister called me to express his concern."

Jonny Munther couldn't believe his ears. "Are you telling me to *ignore* him, just because—"

Lennart Browall looked shocked. He waved his hand. "No, no! For God's sake, no. What impression would that give? But I just wanted to make sure that there's not . . . another China situation."

"That it gets out, you mean? I'm relatively sure the leak didn't come from here."

"The minister more or less guaranteed it didn't come from anywhere in the government."

"What does that leave?" asked Jonny Munther. "The Chinese embassy?"

Despite his earlier remark that he was stopping by just for a moment, Lennart Browall now carefully lowered his lanky body onto a chair. He was always notably cautious in his movements, as if his mere presence could break things. It was hard to understand how such an unaggressive man had managed to get as far as he had. Well, appearances can be deceiving.

"That's unfortunate," said Lennart Browall, dolefully shaking his head. "That business with the Chinese. Extremely unfortunate."

"I agree entirely. But in what sense do you mean 'unfortunate'?"

"If it turns out they were the ones. Sweden's international reputation . . . we can certainly not give the impression that we would accept the Chinese government sending soldiers here to liquidate Swedish citizens on Swedish territory. We would have to make that absolutely clear."

"By declaring war, then."

Lennart Browall gave him a strained smile, but his eyes flashed dangerously. So, the man did have some gumption. "Maybe not *quite* as drastic as that," he said. "But it's unfortunate, in terms of diplomacy and business. Very unfortunate."

Jonny Munther sat his rump on the desk so he could look the police chief in the eye. "Just to make things *entirely* clear here. If you're implying I should forget about both Moe and the Chinese because they're 'bad for business,' I can't do that."

"Of course not. What would that look like?"

Jonny Munther thought that phrase probably summarized Lennart Browall's philosophy of life: *What would that look like?* Maybe that's how he got this far in his career. Jonny Munther made a noncommittal reply. "I'll keep that in mind." They shook hands, and the chief left his office.

What was all that about really?

Lennart Browall was probably covering his ass in case everything went to shit. If, for example, they were to detain Moe but couldn't prove their charges, the police chief could throw up his snow-white hands and cry, "I warned Munther! I told him exactly that!"

Carmen Sánchez phoned to report that Christof had found the key in a tin attached by a magnet to one of the gutters. "Congratulate him on his fine police work," Jonny Munther said dryly and ended the call.

4

After the refreshing sea air blowing through the house on Tärnö, her apartment in Stockholm Old Town felt airless and stifling. Dust particles danced in sunbeams, and her plants drooped pitifully. Julia sat in her armchair with her hands in her lap and looked around.

It was like the times she'd come home after a long trip. All her possessions looked unfamiliar; she needed to use them to get used to them again. There was the television she could watch, a sofa to sit on, a rug she could walk on. The last few days *had* been like a long trip, and she was suffering from something that really resembled jet lag.

Julia Malmros turned to her usual method of getting back in tune: making coffee. Simply fiddling with the espresso maker in the kitchen granted her a little feeling of returning home. Her restlessness subsided as she poured tap water, coffee beans, and milk, then ground, twisted, pressed, and skimmed. She took a few sips of her perfect coffee, put the cup down, and rubbed her hands. All right. Now what?

Julia's current project was to try to map out her childhood friend's life in as much detail as possible, financially speaking. She was almost sure Olof Helander's murder was related to his business activities. His and those of Chen Bao. There might be a third man as well; Montaigne could have been involved.

Julia's first thought was to investigate Olle's drone project. It seemed entirely reasonable that the boy who made paper airplanes had gone on to more advanced types of aircraft. It was doubtful the solution lay there, but it was something no one had considered. Julia took her coffee to her desk and had just turned on the computer when the phone rang. She glanced at the screen and was surprised. Jonny had been curt and contrary when she'd spoken to him at McDonald's. What had changed?

"Hello, Detective Superintendent. How are things?"

"Yeah, that video. The one that Ribbling guy sent. It was edited, probably he did it, and I'd like to see the original."

"I see."

Jonny said irritably, "Yeah, well, he's not exactly in the phone book . . ."

"They *still* publish the phone book?"

"You know what I mean. Can you fix up a meeting with him for me?"

"No."

"Why not?"

"He's not here."

"Where is he?"

Julia carefully weighed the pros and cons. She knew that if the Tracksuit alarm went off while Kim was in China, only international police cooperation could help him, so she said, "On his way to Shanghai."

A long silence on the other end of the line. Julia studied an African violet on the windowsill. It looked unexpectedly fresh and lush. After several seconds, Jonny Munther said, "No. No, Julia. The investigation needs to make progress."

"Seems to me that its progress for the moment is rather limited. You and your team have no way to do anything in China, but Kim does. I'm not terribly happy he chose to go, but that's just how it is."

"What is it between you two, really?"

"How is that relevant?"

Jonny muttered something under his breath, and the silence returned. Julia couldn't have answered his question even if she'd wanted to. What was it between her and Kim? Maybe nothing other than a little private detective work. Once Jonny had finished chewing and swallowing his gall, he asked, "What's he going to do there? Ribbling, that is. In Shanghai."

"Meet Chen Bao's son. If possible."

"I hope he knows that's not without danger."

"Yes, and speaking of that . . ."

Julia told him about the Tracksuit app. Jonny Munther said he couldn't guarantee anything since his current relations with China weren't the best, but if an emergency occurred, he'd see what he could do—provided Kim made absolutely no pretense of working for the Swedish government or police. Julia said Kim was aware of that.

"I hope you'll keep me informed," said Jonny Munther.

"That's my intention."

His long sigh made the phone rattle. Jonny Munther said, "I already told you out on the island, Julia, it's—"

"A mess. We're certainly aware of that."

"No, not a mess. A *goddamn* mess."

5

Astrid Helander opened the fridge and took out the open-faced sandwich with vegan cheese and pickles her uncle had made for her that morning before leaving for work. She seated herself at the table. Above her on the wall, the kitchen clock's plastic second hand jolted its way around the dial. Astrid took a bite. When she swallowed, the dry bread seemed to swell up inside her, making it hard to breathe.

She dropped the sandwich, got to her feet, and pressed her hands against her ribs, gasping for breath. Her legs started to buckle, and she had to hold on to the counter to keep from collapsing. A black spiral whirled inside her bowed head.

Panic, Astrid thought. *A touch of panic, that's all.*

It didn't matter how many times she'd experienced it. Each was like the first, stretching out before her like an endless night. The difference now was that she could recognize it. Naming the symptoms didn't make them go away. Walter had offered to prescribe Atarax or some other fast-acting drug, but Astrid had declined. She wanted to keep from turning into a pill junkie as long as she could.

Astrid forced herself erect. She went to her room. When she reached the doorway, she was reminded it *wasn't* her room at all; nothing of hers was there. Her throat closed, and for a moment she thought she was going to suffocate. She squeezed her eyes shut and staggered toward the living room. The cramping let up enough to allow her to breathe again.

Panic. Panic is my lot, grabbing me by the throat, my heart screaming into the world.

She wished she had her book with Pär Lagerkvist's poems, but it was still in the Strandvägen apartment. Even more than that she wished she had her Bippo, her plush toy hippo, but he was still in her real room. When a panic attack seized her, hugging Bippo tight helped her resist the worst of the gaping emptiness. Tomorrow. She'd go get Bippo tomorrow.

Her stomach heaved. It was crazy, with everything going on, but tears streamed down her cheeks at the thought of Bippo sitting all alone on her bed, not understanding why she'd abandoned him. She saw him weeping huge hippo tears.

But I'm the one who's crazy.

The first thing Astrid saw when she entered the living room was the print of the painting with the dead bird hanging from a hook in a noose. Her uncle had explained one time that a really famous artist painted it, but that meant nothing to Astrid. Someone had shot a bird, hung it up in a noose, and then painted a picture of it. *That* was sick.

Astrid sank to the floor and stretched out on her back. Her heart was pounding. She held her breath, kept holding it, and held it some more. The last thing she saw before passing out was Kim Ribbing's face.

Where are you now? What are you doing?

Then the darkness closed in.

6

Kim got his first glimpse of smog as the plane was on approach into Shanghai. The vast glittering city visible through the plane window was sunk in a foul haze that obscured the millions of lamps and streetlights and made them fade in and out. He'd read that on some days it could be dangerous to go outside, especially when the wind came from the ocean and brought with it pollution from the factories outside city limits.

He thought he could make out Shanghai's famous radio tower, looking like a round, deformed spider on three legs. He saw a skyscraper that resembled a bottle opener and must have been at least a hundred stories tall and another two skyscrapers close to it, equally tall and bizarrely shaped. He was intrigued and attracted by this beast, by the idea of taking its pulse close up.

"First time in Shanghai?"

The passenger across the first-class aisle, a well-dressed older Chinese lady, was leaning toward him.

"Yes," Kim answered in English. "First time. Anything I should know?"

She smiled. "Be careful crossing the street!"

"I will."

It was almost ten o'clock in the evening, but the air that struck Kim's face when he deplaned was a rough shock after long hours enclosed in an air-conditioned space. It was warm and humid and smelled faintly of exhaust. He carried the bag he'd bought at Schiphol down the stairs and boarded the bus for the terminal.

He took a seat all the way in the back corner, pulled his phone from his pack, and turned it on. He had a message from BL: Contact made. Instructions follow. Kim deleted the text. Julia had found it necessary to exert her charms, but Bruce Li had eventually agreed to help, commenting it was in his own interest to "make old Xi's life difficult," as he'd put it.

Since Kim had no checked baggage, he went directly to the taxi stand and asked to be driven to the Peninsula in the French quarter. He'd booked a suite on one of the top floors. Two thousand dollars a night.

When he got out of the taxi, he saw the woman on the plane hadn't been joking. Even at this time of night, the street in front of the hotel was jammed with cars, motorcycles, electric scooters, and lots and lots of electric mopeds. Crossing it looked impossible, even more so if a person had to *be careful.*

Kim declined an offer of help with his bag and went to the reception desk to check in. The courteous woman at the desk glanced at him just a *tiny* bit too long when her screen showed which room he'd booked. Kim's hair was black as ink again, and the T-shirt he'd found in Amsterdam was printed with a picture of a marijuana plant. But after Kim gave her his card for "eventual expenses," everything was fine.

"Beer," said Kim. "Send up a couple of beers to the room."

"What brand? We have Tsingtao, Singha . . ."

"Doesn't matter," said Kim. "Just make sure they're cold."

The first thing Kim saw when he entered the room was the reason he'd reserved that particular suite. One wall of the approximately five-hundred-square-foot living room bowed slightly outward and was made entirely of armored glass. He was on the fiftieth floor with the blinking, glowing city spread out at his feet.

He went to the bathroom, which was as large as the entire summerhouse on Tärnö and equipped with a Jacuzzi big enough to accommodate six persons comfortably. As Kim turned on the tap to fill it, he heard a discreet knock on the suite door. He crossed the big room and opened it. Outside stood a genuine bellboy in a red uniform and a pillbox cap held in place by an elastic band. Kim had thought such fantastical creatures no longer existed. The boy held out a tray with three Singha beers in an ice bucket. "At your service, sir."

Kim accepted the ice bucket and gave the boy a ten-dollar tip, which earned him a slight bow. He carried the bucket to the bathroom and shed his clothes after flinging a handful of bath salts into the water.

Ah, yes!

He sighed with pleasure as he slipped into the warm bubbling water. He took a gulp of beer. It tasted heavenly after all those hours he'd been obliged to breathe, first aircraft air and then Shanghai air. He stretched himself out full length and knitted his hands behind his head.

Now, this is the life. It should always be like this.

He reminded himself that he in fact *was* able to have it like this. He was an accomplished master at focusing himself but not so good when it came to mindfulness. He took another gulp of beer and envisioned Martin Rudbeck's living room. He'd inserted a bug into the television's system that uploaded the camera images to Kim's cloud account whenever it detected motion.

The thought of Martin Rudbeck left a sour taste in his mouth. With difficulty, he pushed it out of his mind. He'd examine the images in good time, but until then, *Begone, Dr. Shock.*

When the beer was finished and Kim's fingers and toes were wrinkled, he got out and wrapped himself in a thick white terry-cloth robe of a quality far surpassing Julia Malmros's simple wrap. He padded across the living room's wall-to-wall carpet to the panoramic window. Except for another skyscraper here and there, he was above *everything.*

He let the bathrobe fall and leaned against the glass wall. Its touch was cool against his Jacuzzi-warmed skin. He held his arms out to the side and placed his palms against the glass, then relaxed so his entire body settled against it. A quivering arose in his gut as he leaned out over the glowing, pulsating city with only a couple of inches of glass between himself and the dizzying drop. Kim's breath misted the pane as he grinned and showed his teeth to the monster over which he was hovering.

Catch me if you can.

7

Julia Malmros closed her laptop and stretched her arms toward the ceiling. Her shoulder joints cracked. She was significantly more knowledgeable about drone technology and pollution monitoring than she'd been two hours earlier.

Olof Helander's Greenbase firm leased and sold a drone that monitored methane emissions with impressive precision. The firm could operate the drones remotely if the client desired. The instrument they'd engineered was accurate to within 0.5 ppm—parts per million—which was extraordinary. An elegant bonus was the same drone's ability to measure wind speed and direction in the air, providing those measurements with greater accuracy than surface-based instruments. In short, Olle's drone detected the truth and reported it in real time.

Julia had even found a couple of photos of the little bugger. It was black and circular and looked like a robo-vacuum with propellers. The wind monitor was installed at the end of a long stem that kept it away from the propellers, while the rest of the monitoring equipment was integrated in the hull. The thing weighed just over ten pounds.

She'd learned that the demand for more accurate measurements had grown sharply because of firms' increasing awareness of the environment and a general desire to do something about climate change. Drones were highly efficient, so the market had grown quickly, and Greenbase's technology was simply the best. Add to that the fact that the firm had been the first to enter the market. Olle's company was quite profitable, but there was no indication that management was offering its employees lavish bonuses or profit sharing. Most of its earnings were reinvested. So Olle's wealth couldn't be attributed to the company.

Nor did the drone business explain his murder. Julia had pummeled her brain in the effort to establish a link between his flying robo-vacuum and the Midsummer Eve massacre. Her initial hypothesis was that Olle could have discovered that some industry was emitting far more methane than it reported, thereby considerably reducing its purchases of emissions rights, which were expensive. That theory fell apart when Julia figured out how much money might be involved. Not much more than a major industrial concern probably spent on coffee supplies. A hundred thousand a year, presumably not enough of an incentive to murder six people. It seemed more likely that an explanation might be found in Chen Bao's undisclosed activities, so she hoped Kim would find out something in Shanghai.

Okay, her findings were probably irrelevant, but this was still part of their . . . well, you might as well call it their *investigation*. Julia put together a summary of her findings, attached images, and sent it all to Kim.

It was after six when Julia shut down her computer. That evening's unwritten pages silently accused her. She thought about going down to the Angel Pub on the corner for an update on the local gossip. Then she realized that *she* was probably the hottest topic. That discouraged her.

She opened the computer again and called up the text of her rejected Millennium novel. In a moment of weakness, she weighed whether she really should revise it "with a different plot," but that possibility had probably vanished forever with her screwup on Malou's program. She sat staring for a while at a scene between Mikael Blomkvist and Erika Berger. Then she did a find-and-replace and changed their names to Mökööl Blömkvöst and Örökö Börgör.

She burst out laughing and shook her head. If only it were that simple!

8

The hotel's whisky bar evoked for Kim the stereotypical image of an English gentleman's club. Heavy tables of dark wood, oak paneling, and thick wall-to-wall carpet that dampened noise. The low lighting was golden yellow and caused the long marble bar's brass fittings to gleam.

Kim had found himself a table far in the corner where he could sit with his back to the wall. He'd ordered a whisky sour and a pack of Camel Blues and taken out his laptop. Surprisingly, smoking was permitted, a luxury as impressive as his hotel suite. It was one thing to smoke in some Cuban café with plastic chairs and rickety tables, quite another to do so *in da club*.

Kim took a puff, tapped the cigarette in a heavy glass ashtray, and took a sip of his drink. His eyebrows rose. He studied the tumbler of golden liquid with crushed ice. He wasn't at all particular about what he drank, but this taste—he had to admit it was goddamn good. Perhaps the drink was made with a finer whisky than what he was used to. It had a trace of juniper smoke.

A message had pinged his phone half an hour earlier. An address, a time—2 p.m.—with the cryptic note Corridor with the moaning lady. What could that mean? Was the meeting in some bordello? Kim googled the address and found it was a place in the Jiading district called Hospital of Horror, a haunted house advertising live actors "who will scare the hell out of you." It looked as if the moaning lady was one of the attractions intended to do just that.

Kim understood the logic. The place was accessible to the public, and the online photos showed it was very dark inside. Perfect if you want to lurk in the shadows but still have safety in numbers. He didn't like the idea very much. Something about the place made his skin crawl. That was probably the intention. But it wasn't the horror show that was making him apprehensive.

He logged into HackPack via the Pac-Man front. That day's spot was five rows down and four in from the right. He put up a post asking if anybody knew of a place in Shanghai where a guy could buy a Taser. Sale to private individuals was strictly prohibited. Kim's view was that his own shocking past entitled him to protect himself with electricity.

He checked his email and saw a message from Julia Malmros titled "Drones." The phone rang before he could open it. The screen showed *Astrid Helander*. He hesitated a fraction of a second, then answered. "Yes? Hello?"

A long pause followed, then a tormented sigh came across the line. In a tiny little voice, Astrid said, "Kim, I'm not doing well."

"Physically or mentally?"

"Mentally."

"I'm really sorry to hear that."

"I held my breath until I passed out."

"Ouch. You can do that?"

"Yeah."

There was a time in Vamlinge that Kim had tried to do exactly that. He'd learned to vomit without sticking his fingers down his throat, but other than refusing to eat or remaining mute, that could have been a tactic to get out of yet another electroconvulsive treatment. He'd never managed. Just as the darkness was closing in and his brain was starting to shut down, his body shuddered and inhaled, a purely autonomous reflex.

"Kim?" said Astrid. "When you were feeling like shit, what would you do?"

All right, what *had* he done? His survival strategies were certainly too complicated to explain, so he told her the only thing he could. "I toughed it out. I refused to let anyone get at me, and I toughed it out."

"Nobody's after me."

"It's the illness," said Kim. Then he corrected himself. "That is, if it really is an illness. It *might* be a demon."

Astrid gasped. "A demon? For real?"

"Whatever you want to call it. Picture it. And resist it."

"I don't know if I can."

"Astrid," said Kim. "You're strong. If you can hold your breath until you pass out, you can do more than you imagine."

"You believe that?"

"No, I don't believe it. I *know* it."

Another couple of seconds of silence. Kim waved to a waiter and made a circling gesture over his glass: *One more of the same.* The waiter gave him that little bow and went to the bar.

Astrid said, "That Martin Rudbeck guy. Who is he?"

"I'll tell you about it sometime. But not right now."

"Okay. I don't know if what you say about me is true. But it helps that . . ."

"What helps?"

"That you survived," said Astrid. "That you exist. So long, Kim."

"So long, Astrid."

Kim put down the phone. He couldn't remember anyone ever *praising* him for surviving his youth despite the crappy odds against him. Kim generally had no need of praise, but even so, it gave him a bit of a lift to hear that the hell he'd lived through could be an inspiration to someone.

The girl can hold her breath till she passes out. Kim felt nothing but deep admiration for an accomplishment he himself had never managed, despite all his efforts. Even if Astrid was feeling fucking awful, there was more to her than had met Kim's eyes under the dock that Midsummer

Eve afternoon. Kim knew Astrid was a survivor, no matter what the girl thought of herself.

Kim's drink was delivered, along with another bow. He lit another cigarette and went into HackPack. His question had been answered. Someone called MekaGodzilla gave the address to an electronics shop and commented that of course Tasers weren't something they advertised, but if he said Jimmy Bang sent him, they'd probably have what he wanted.

Seriously? Kim wrote back. *I want to buy a stun gun and I'm just supposed to say this Bang guy sent me? What if I want a grenade? Should I mention Benny Boom?*

The answer popped up a couple of minutes later. *Give them whatever name you want, Skalman, but if you want to buy what you're looking for, I recommend Jimmy Bang.*

Kim assumed that the guy—after all, who but a guy would call himself MekaGodzilla—was Chinese. He was beginning to suspect Chinese humor wasn't particularly convincing. He sent back a short *Thanks* and exited the chat room.

9

Julia Malmros sat for an hour poking and prodding at her *Sandstorm* manuscript without coming up with anything. There was a good story in it, but it lost most of its élan when it wasn't about Salander and Blomkvist. She hadn't yet figured out a way to ditch them. The story had come to her so vividly that she'd written it out as if reading it in her mind. It had an energy and freshness that should survive even without the dynamic duo of Micke and Lisbeth. She just didn't know how to alter it.

When it got to eight o'clock, she gave up and phoned Irma Ryding. Irma was pleasantly surprised to hear Julia was back in town, and they agreed to get together in fifteen minutes at the usual. Julia pulled up Google Maps, typed *Shanghai* in the search field and clicked Street View. She spent five minutes wandering through the streets where Kim now was, trying to imagine his long black hair among all those people with blurred faces. Then she shut down the computer and left her flat.

Stockholm Old Town was full of tourists. Crowds strolled past the brightly lit shop windows that summer evening, people took pictures of one another with their mobile phones, and a large group had gathered around a female juggler dressed as Pippi Longstocking. Julia pushed her way past the clustered group and heard someone say "Moomin!" Maybe that person thought the juggler was impersonating Little My.

Irma stood leaning on a crutch outside the Gråmunken. She saw Julia and nodded toward the locale. "Feels a bit stuffy in there. Want to find terrace service somewhere else?"

"Oh, my dear friend," said Julia. "What happened to you?"

Irma shrugged. "Fell down. Broke a hip."

"But why didn't you tell me?"

Irma fixed her watery blue eyes on Julia's. "Old ladies who talk about their aches and pains are the most boring beings on planet Earth. Except for engineers, maybe. Shall we go?"

They slowly made their way along Västerlång Street and turned toward Kåkbrinkenen to go toward Stortorget. Irma griped about the tourists who got in her way as she hobbled along. "Should get myself a motorized wheelchair," she grumped. "Run over the whole lot of 'em."

They found a free table at a terrace right across from the exchange building where the Swedish Academy had its offices. Irma sank into a chair with a groan and nodded toward the building that dominated the entire side of the plaza. "What do you think they're up to in there? Think they're back up to speed?"

Julia had much earlier stopped caring about the changes in the academy in the wake of the #MeToo movement. Irma had continued monitoring them almost as a hobby; she talked of setting her next detective novel in that milieu, a tale about a serial killer eventually revealed to be a member. Her working title was *The Swedish Academy Death List*. Julia assumed Irma was joking.

Each ordered a glass of white wine, and Irma added a double vodka. She patted her midriff. "Vodka for the hip, wine for the company. And what have you been up to lately?"

"Short version or long one?"

"Long, if you please. I'm right tired of the sound of my own voice."

It took Julia quite a while to recount everything that had happened since Midsummer Eve, and in the process they finished their drinks and ordered another round. Irma had sat uncomfortably erect, but when those arrived and the vodka had done its magic, she relaxed in her chair. "Alcohol solves all problems."

"Except for those it creates."

"Ah, no! You just drink more, and those go away too. Well, well, so you're conducting your own investigation? I thought you'd given up police work."

Julia smiled. "When I was a kid, I never dreamed of becoming a police officer, even though Papa was one. I wanted to be a private detective."

"And now here you are. How'd that happen?"

Julia had asked herself the same question and hadn't come up with a simple explanation. "Many reasons, but I believe . . . Olof Helander, that little boy I used to know. He got mixed up with powers too strong for him, and somebody had him killed. Olof was with me for part of my childhood, and now he's gone. Something of me disappeared with him, and I want to . . . oh, it's too hard to put into words."

Irma sipped her wine, and her eyes glinted. "So this has nothing to do with the breathtaking adventure with a certain mysterious young man?"

"Please, Irma. I mostly sit and fiddle with my computer, and Kim . . . I'm not feeling any thrills here. Mostly I'm worried about what might happen to him."

"Hmm," Irma responded. "I believe what I believe. And it seems you've gotten yourself involved in an honest-to-God installment of the Millennium story."

"That's not what it feels like."

"No. It never does as it's happening. Here's to Kim, then. And in hopes he'll come back."

10

Kim Ribbing's phone alarm went off. He found himself in a bed as vast as the sea, surrounded by soft pillows and embraced by a duvet. It was nine o'clock, but time no longer had any meaning for him except as a concept for scheduling.

He'd slept well, surprisingly enough. He'd had five whisky sours all told, and when he'd crawled into bed, he'd gone to sleep immediately. He hadn't awakened during the night. He felt rested and clearheaded.

He took a quick shower and went down into the breakfast room where a buffet table was loaded with enough to feed a small Cuban town. Kim made do with scrambled eggs, bacon, and a gigantic mug of coffee. Then he went out for a look at Shanghai.

He was astonished by all the trees as he walked along the main avenue through the French quarter. He'd expected Shanghai to be a traffic-choked metropolis with pestilential air. Both expectations were confirmed, but in fact the wide streets densely lined with trees alleviated the overall impression of steel and concrete. Kim found a crossing and walked across the avenue to explore the heart of the French quarter.

The streets teemed with people. Odors of noodle broth and meat grease hung in the air. A rotisserie was cooking spitted chicken in a shop window, and elderly men in hole-in-the-wall restaurants were busily preparing food in enormous woks. Signs in Chinese and English announced menus, and people hunkered in street-corner seating, slurping noodles, their chins almost inside the bowls. Kim stopped before a sign with a picture of an electric scooter announcing "300 CNY/day."

Fifteen minutes later he was ready to start his rented scooter. He put on the helmet he'd rented for another thirty yuan and familiarized himself with the controls. He put the address of the electronics shop into his phone's GPS. Result: twenty minutes to get there by car. Probably a bit more by scooter.

Kim turned it on, hit the accelerator, and swooshed silently out into the traffic. He quickly realized a Shanghai electric scooter was more powerful than the Swedish version. When he accelerated to the max on a straight stretch with less traffic, the speedometer hit 85 km/hr—better than 50 miles an hour.

There was something satisfying about a sturdy vehicle that was entirely silent. Kim swerved among the cars and pedestrians without the slightest stutter or shake. It was like hovering in the air. He felt exuberant. *Catch me if you can!*

The electronics shop was in a rough neighborhood. Broken signs, trash in the street, people peeking down from apartments with rickety balconies. The shop window was papered over with announcements in Chinese characters Kim couldn't decipher. He parked next to a fire hydrant and secured the moped with a chain. Another thirty yuan for that; if they'd thought of charging him for putting more air in the tires, they probably would have. He put the helmet under his arm and went inside.

11

If an absolute opposite to an Apple store existed anywhere in the world, this was it. Old and new electronics, computers, TVs, amplifiers, and Blu-ray players were piled hither and thither in closed or open cartons, all of it lit with randomly placed lamps. There was a smoky smell to the air, probably intended to mask something worse.

Kim made his way along a makeshift corridor between cartons to a counter where an old man sat smoking a pipe. He wore a simple black skullcap. He peered at Kim from behind the rectangular frames of his glasses.

"Good morning," Kim said in English. "I'd like to buy a Taser."

The man gave him a dismayed grimace and twirled a finger around an ear to signal that he didn't understand.

"I'm supposed to say Jimmy Bang sent me."

The man's face lit up, and he replied in excellent English. "Aha! That casts an entirely new light on the present situation. How is Jimmy doing?"

"Couldn't be better," Kim said.

"Come, come this way." The man beckoned. "Be so good as to accompany me to the nether regions." He lifted a partition in the counter.

Kim followed him to an interior space he assumed was a storeroom, even though the whole shop looked like a warehouse. There was certainly very little difference between the rear of the shop and the front, except perhaps that the rear was more poorly lit. Cartons everywhere. Kim wondered how the man knew which ones should go where.

In a space among the cartons stood a table with a lamp suspended over it. The old man switched on the light, which cast a brilliant white glare. "If you will be so kind as to wait a moment, I will bring the requested merchandise without delay."

Kim sat on a stool and placed his elbow on the table. A figure in the corner of his eye made him turn and look. A human-size mannequin stood in a corner across the room. Cable leads ran from its fingers to some sort of meter. Did they sell torture devices here too? The creepy figure reminded Kim of Vamlinge. He shivered.

The proprietor returned with three cartons and placed them on the table. Each was printed with a sketch of the contents. Kim asked, "Which one's the best?"

"Ah! That depends entirely upon the goal, or perhaps I should say upon your intended area of operations." The man tapped a yellow nail on the model that most resembled a pistol. "This one is the most powerful, if that's a concern, while this one"—his finger moved—"fires the darts, or shall I say, the electrical contacts, more quickly, and has the strongest battery by far. Then there's this beauty." The man tapped the smallest carton. "A somewhat more elegant model. Discreet, let's say."

"I like discreet," Kim said. "But it packs a punch?"

"Oh, certainly," the man said, opening his eyes wide. "A proper kiss, one might say."

He opened the carton and took out a small black box with a button on each side and two holes in the front. He gestured elegantly toward the mannequin. "If you will be so kind as to follow me over to Mr. Ling."

When Kim neared Mr. Ling, he saw that the mannequin's silicone skin was perforated with hundreds of tiny holes. The mere fact that Mr. Ling had a name suggested that he was frequently used. The man put the little box in Kim's hand and clicked a switch in Mr. Ling's metering instrument; its screen lit up. He pointed to the box. "Fire with the button on the left; the right button, shock."

Kim lifted the box, which had a reassuring heft. It was compact enough for him to put his thumb on the right button and his index on the left. He aimed at Mr. Ling's chest and pressed the left button. The box recoiled slightly; darts flew out and embedded themselves just beneath where Mr. Ling's heart would have been, if he'd had one. Copper filaments hung loose between the box and the darts.

Kim was about to press the button on the right, but the man threw out his hand and directed Kim's attention to the meter. "Watch!" Kim fixed his eyes on the meter and pressed the shock button. The needle jolted up about halfway. The proprietor tapped his yellowed nail on the glass. "Two thousand volts!"

"Now that's a real kiss," said Kim.

"I could not have expressed it more eloquently."

The man extracted the darts, then showed how to pop out a reel on the rear of the box to retract the electrical leads.

"The electrical charge?" asked Kim. "How long is the battery good for?"

The man gestured in front of him. "If I may use the gentleman's remarkable simile, one might estimate it would do for two passionate kisses, and a little more . . . how shall I express it . . . conjugal contact." He pointed to the table. "The largest model there delivers such a quantity of kisses that the character of the activity necessarily would change, if I may be so bold as to express it so."

"I have no need of that kind of activity at the moment," Kim said. "I'll take this one. How much does it cost?"

"Three thousand yuan. If you're interested in bargaining, perhaps, with grief in my heart, I might let it go for two thousand five hundred."

"Let's say three thousand. Will you take a card?"

"Regrettably, no. Transactions of this character should not leave tracks in the sand. If the gentleman can appreciate the figure of speech?"

"I can. Is there an ATM nearby?"

The man told him how to find the nearest one. Kim said he'd be back in two hours. He put the Taser to charge and asked if it was all right to charge the scooter as well. The man bowed and provided an extension cord long enough to reach the street. Kim asked for the price; the man told him it was on the house. It appeared that covert commerce was conducted on more generous terms than its overt equivalent.

Kim got his cash and spent two hours in a teahouse where a waiter provided more hot water for his tea leaves as soon as the cup was empty. He read through Julia Malmros's drone briefing and checked to see if Martin Rudbeck was up to anything in his living room. Unfortunately not, as the man in the electronics shop might have said.

The GPS indicated it would take about forty minutes to get to the place where he was supposed to meet Danny, so Kim returned to the shop just before one o'clock. He paid for the Taser and managed to stuff it into the waistband at his back, though it wasn't easy. The proprietor's vanishingly thin eyebrows rose. "Aha, the gentleman expects soon to come in contact with a clientele where kissing may become necessary, if I may be so bold as to express it so?"

"You might put it that way," Kim said. "But I hope it will be more . . . platonic."

"Naturally," the man said and bowed deeply. "I wish the gentleman all happiness and good health."

Kim unplugged the scooter from the extension cord exactly at one o'clock. He unlocked the chain, stowed it, and got onto the saddle. He knotted his hair behind him, waved goodbye to the proprietor, and silently swooped away toward the Hospital of Horror.

12

Julia Malmros awoke exactly at seven o'clock, the hour that Kim, seven time zones away, was scheduled to meet Danny Chen. She'd gotten Kim's message—Meeting X 14h tomorrow—the previous evening. Julia found his cryptic references to name and place worrisome, and perhaps that was what woke her. She picked up her phone, adjusted the ring volume to max and set the vibration to the highest possible level so she wouldn't miss a Tracksuit alarm. If there was one.

She brewed and drank her coffee, then wandered around her apartment, biting her nails. She assumed Kim could take care of himself, but he was alone in a foreign country where he probably didn't understand the rules of the game.

It got to be nine o'clock. Kim hadn't rung and the alarm hadn't gone off. Julia began to relax. Apparently things had gone well, and after all, why shouldn't they have? Her worry was giving way to curiosity.

Wandering around her flat wouldn't get her the answers any sooner. She had a little project to carry out that day, and she might as well get on with it. She called up the Greenbase website and found that its offices were in Sundbyberg.

She'd had quite a few glasses of wine with Irma the evening before, and she didn't feel up to driving. The Swedish Railways site showed she could get to Greenbase with only one change of underground trains. Before leaving, she checked and double-checked to make sure she had her phone in her breast pocket.

While waiting on the train platform, she thought of Irma as an example of how aging might affect her personally. She found it troubling that Irma had fallen and injured herself so badly but then didn't want to talk about it lest she be seen as a boring old lady. A lonely old lady.

Would Julia be that stoic when she got to that age? Or would she continue complaining about trivialities, as she was doing now? Probably the latter. Nor did it look too likely anyone would be at her side then. Kim least of all. He seized every opportunity to make himself scarce as soon as things got complicated. It'd probably be best for Julia to pull back a little and give in to the inevitable. She had repeatedly come to that conclusion, but never when she was actually in his presence.

The rails clattered as the train neared the station. Julia was so startled by a sudden savage vibration in her pocket that she thought she was having a heart attack.

13

Jonny Munther convened the first meeting of the day at nine o'clock by rapping on the table and saying, "Good morning. I hope that you all had a good night's sleep and are in fine health."

"You've been talking to the Chinese ambassador too much," said Carmen Sánchez.

"Could be. When I phoned him half an hour ago, he said we'd probably hurt the feelings of the Chinese people by spreading an unfounded rumor that their soldiers might be involved. He was considering taking the matter to a higher diplomatic level."

"You think they really are?" said Ulrika Boberg.

"Who are what?" asked Jonny Munther.

"The Chinese people. Their feelings. Hurt."

"Oh," said William King. "That's just diplomatic talk meaning nobody should say anything bad about the Chinese government. And, besides, do Chinese have any feelings?" Before anyone could respond, William King raised his hands in an *I give up!* gesture. "Since I have noticed it's necessary to explain, I wish to emphasize I was merely joking."

"An entirely inappropriate joke in the present circumstances," said Jonny Munther, but he let it drop and turned to Carmen Sánchez. "Didn't come up with anything on Knektholmen?"

"Correct. And we were very thorough. For example, behind a baseboard we found an emerald ring that must have belonged to

Gabriella Helander. Planning to take it to Strandvägen when we go there to look for the iPad today. It's Astrid's now."

"Good. Ulrika?"

Ulrika had no papers today, but she had carefully aligned her laptop with the table edge. She looked at the screen. "I asked my colleagues at the financial crimes unit to go into the underground maze of Moe's financial dealings. I took a closer look at Chen Bao and came up with some things that may be relevant. Futurig's oil rigs are constructed in China by a firm calling itself ChengBa, located in Chengdu. It's a huge concern that builds rigs for many countries. It has a turnover of tens of billions of dollars."

"I wondered about that," Christof Adler said. "How much does an oil rig cost, anyway?"

"Depends on the size and how deep it can bore," said Ulrika. "But somewhere between one and two billion. Dollars, that is."

Christof Adler whistled. "Now we're talking about sums people would murder for."

"Yes," Ulrika said. "And it so happens that in his research on oil rig construction, Chen Bao concentrated exclusively on ChengBa. There we have a horse worth looking at. There might have been payoffs when they landed their contracts, including with Futurig."

"They paid a little bonus to get the contract," said Jonny Munther. "Not so unusual. Illegal, of course, but common practice, if I understand correctly."

Ulrika was plainly aggrieved that the DS had tramped into her specialization with his banal remarks. "Sure," she said. "Correct. But think how much oil rigs cost, as was just mentioned. Let us say that's about fifteen billion Swedish kronor. Say that someone gets himself a little payoff of . . . for example, half a percent of the value of the contract. That's seventy-five million kronor, or about $7.5 million. There's a lot of wool on that there piggy."

"And those bribes supposedly went to Frode Moe?" asked Jonny Munther.

"Nothing suggests that. As far as I can see, it's an internal Chinese affair. More likely some minister or official."

William King made a pistol gesture with his index finger. "Summary execution for the rascal if it comes out. Winnie the Pooh himself will pull the trigger."

"Yeah," said Ulrika Boberg. "You might say that the incentives for avoiding detection in China are significant."

"Significant enough to mow down six people to escape detection?" asked Jonny Munther.

"I'd tend to agree. A person's got only one life to live."

"Okay," said Jonny. "So what have we got, then?" His phone rang. He checked the screen, excused himself, and stepped out into the hall.

"Julia," Jonny Munther said. "I'm in the middle of—"

"Something's happened," interrupted Julia Malmros. Her voice was frantic. "Are you sitting down?"

14

Judging from the outside, the Hospital of Horror didn't look likely to scare anyone out of their wits. A featureless industrial installation with a wide staircase of steel grating that led up to two glass doors. The sign over them was somewhat grimmer. White letters in a bold font against a black background: "Hospital of Horror." If the font had featured twisting, green, bloodstained letters, you'd have expected something spooky, but it seemed this hospital was taking a considerably more *clinical* approach to the art of scaring people.

Kim parked where several mopeds, motorcycles, and cars stood on the gravel lot. He walked around the building to look for rear entrances but saw none. When he came back to the entry, a group of five youngsters were ahead of him. The boys pretended to be monsters, and the girls giggled. Kim gave them a head start before he opened the doors.

He found the dim reception area barren of any cheap horror-house props. Kim paid the hundred-yuan entrance fee and was shown to a waiting room where about ten persons sat. A sign announced that no more than thirty persons at a time would be allowed inside "for sake of the experience."

Fortunately, Kim wasn't looking to have a horror experience. If he had been, the five tittering teenagers probably would have spoiled it for him. The others in the group were two pale tourists (a man and woman of his own age already looking scared to death), an older gentleman who seemed bored, and two young men with delicately feminine features sitting very close to one another. The whole group was watching a large television screen flashing reaction shots from inside the "hospital." People screaming in fright, their faces twisting with horror.

Five minutes later, a man wearing a doctor's coat beckoned Kim inside. The others had already been called, and new clients crowded the waiting room. Kim adjusted the Taser; it had begun to chafe his lower back. He walked through the door, and the man shut it behind them.

"Please. Welcome. Walk," said the man and pointed to a hallway dimly lit by red bulbs. A bier with a draped shape was visible. Kim walked. He heard shrieks and youthful laughter from farther inside. Kim disliked sudden movements and surprise sounds, so he tensed as he approached the covered figure. He expected it to sit up suddenly. The sheet over it was stained red and covered with bloody handprints. Kim kept his eyes fixed on it, but nothing happened.

He caught movement in his peripheral vision and realized he'd been tricked. The body was intended to divert his attention to intensify the scare when the real effect revealed itself. Kim flinched as a woman in a doctor's coat with long black hair hanging over her face came lurching toward him making a guttural hissing sound. Wide-open eyes and a bloody face were visible through the curtain of hair. The woman shuddered her way past Kim and disappeared into an alcove.

It occurred to Kim that a job as a professional ghost must be dangerous work. He'd instinctively grabbed for the Taser when he saw her, but he'd restrained himself. Some other client might have had less control. He continued around a corner into a new corridor. Surgical saws hung from the ceiling. Kim entered a room where a physician seemed to be rooting around in a patient's intestines. The patient was a very convincing mannequin, and the slurping intestines the doctor pulled out to inspect were just as realistic. The doctor lifted his head with a jerk and glowered at Kim as he passed.

The next room was a spacious, high-ceilinged hall where an ambulance was parked. A stretcher lay overturned, and a hand stuck out from beneath it. As Kim approached, a man and woman with stark white faces leaped out of the ambulance, sprang past him, and disappeared through an opening in the wall covered by a sheet. Kim assumed there was a system of corridors behind the public spaces so the ghosts could race about unseen.

The next passage led to a stairway where a person with a crushed head lay, presumably a mannequin. To the right of the stairs was an opening from which a woman's moaning came. Kim went there and peered into the dark. The woman groaned and moaned in proper phantom style, but she didn't reveal herself. Kim looked around to make sure he was alone, then turned on his phone's flashlight.

Before him a narrow hallway extended about thirty feet to a door. A loudspeaker was mounted above the door, and the moaning sounds came from there. A faint red lamp provided minimal illumination. Kim turned off his phone light and went in, since apparently this was the place.

He went to the door and squatted, leaning against the wall. Kim was so close to the speakers that the woman's noisy plaints drowned out any other sounds. He checked the time on his phone. Five minutes to two. He hoped Danny would be punctual, because sitting any considerable length of time deafened by this lamentation and distress would probably drive him crazy.

The door opened exactly at two o'clock. A faint light spilled into the hallway, and he saw a somewhat overweight Chinese man, probably in his thirties, cast nervous glances from behind rimless eyeglasses before closing the door behind him and sinking to squat across from Kim. Their knees almost touched.

"Danny?" asked Kim. The man nodded, so sharply that the flap of flesh under his chin quivered. Small talk was useless, so Kim went straight into the matter, raising his voice to be heard above the moaning racket. "Your father found something, didn't he?"

"Yeah," said Danny. "There's this businessman in Norway."

"Frode Moe?"

"That's him. He gets oil rigs built in Chengdu, and my papa found out that those rigs are manipulated somehow. He—" The man broke off and wrung his hands. "Long story, but Papa said it all started in Havana, at the Hotel Habana Libre in the nineties when that Moe and another man met some official from the Cuban government . . ."

"Is that written down somewhere? Do you have documents?"

"Yeah, sure, of course," said Danny and put his hand into the inner pocket of his jacket. "I have a memorandum."

A green dot appeared on Danny's temple. Kim knew instantly what it was and assumed that a similar one was on his own head. He lunged toward Danny just as two quiet pops were heard. Danny's head jerked to the side and slammed against Kim's shoulder.

Blood, black in the darkness, splattered on the door. Danny fell over, his glasses clattering against the cement floor. Kim glanced to the side and saw two slim silhouettes outlined by the stronger light beyond the hallway entrance, probably the two young men he'd taken for homosexuals. The laser beams from their silenced pistols shot through the dark.

For one mad moment Kim thought of checking Danny's pocket, but there was literally not a split second to lose. He cast himself against the door as two more pops sounded. One slug hit the cement wall and ricocheted with a zinging sound, and the other struck Danny, who didn't react, for he was dead.

Kim opened the door, hunched over, and rushed down a narrower hall that branched in several directions. He made it around the corner to the right just before the men fired again. The bullets flew past behind him.

Taser. Behind!

Right, but there were two of them. He could shock one, but the other one would calmly blow him away. *Two passionate kisses.* Okay, if he could separate them, but how? He took a left and came into a room where a hanged man swayed at the end of his rope. He took a new side corridor. Racing steps echoed behind him.

Kim grabbed a doctor's smock from a hook and clutched his upper arm. He'd been shot sometime in the fracas, perhaps struck by the ricochet. It was only a flesh wound, but he was bleeding profusely. He kept running, rubbed his fingers in his own blood and smeared it on his face. He took another side hallway and went through a cramped space where a man lay writhing on a stretcher. A hysterically laughing doctor administered repeated electroshocks as the bunch of kids stood giggling as they watched. If they only knew!

Kim scowled to see that his personal hell had been turned into entertainment. He pulled on the physician's smock and raced down another corridor, loosening the knot in his hair, veered to the left, and raced down a corridor that ended in a blank wall.

He stood there petrified. Then he pushed his long hair forward over his face and turned around.

The two men—no doubt about it, they were the two young men who'd huddled together—came racing down the hall and looked around.

Last chance.

Kim shuffled toward them, moving in abrupt jerks with his eyes open wide, gasping as if he were dying. The men gave him terrified glances and backed out of the corridor. They stumbled, then raced away. Kim retraced his steps, still jerking and swaying like a Japanese ghost. As he lumbered along, the implications of the encounter became clear.

They shot him right in front of me.

The image of the green dot on Danny's temple that morphed into a bullet entry wound haunted Kim as he jerked spastically through the room with the ongoing fake surgical operation. The surgeon glanced up from his handful of intestines, looked surprised, and said something in Chinese. Kim just groaned in reply.

Frode Moe. Habana Libre.

The fucking worst of it was that he had no hard evidence. Kim thought about going back to the moaning woman's hallway to recover the memo, but that was far too dangerous. By now the shooters had probably recovered from their fright and realized they needed a closer look at that zombie. He had to escape. They'd probably already grabbed the memo anyway.

Blood had soaked the shoulder of the smock. He had no trouble moving his right hand or arm, so he knew he wasn't seriously injured, but his shoulder burned as if someone was holding a lit Zippo to it.

How did they find me?

He'd been very careful, but the most likely explanation was that he'd been followed. He was almost certain that he wasn't carrying any tracker on him except the ruby pendant, and he hadn't activated it, but on the other hand . . .

The scooter.

He'd rented it at a random shop, and he instinctively trusted the man running the electronics shop. *Takes one to know one.* On the other hand, it had sat outside charging for two hours. Someone could have bugged it there.

But—they were here ahead of me!

True, but Kim had circled the building, inspecting it, before he entered. That had created a gap; his shadows could have slipped in ahead of him. *Fuck!* You could never be careful enough.

In the last corridor Kim came face to face with the woman for whom he was now an exact double. He stopped. She opened her eyes even wider and served him an indignant stream of Chinese, probably thinking Kim was auditioning for her job. Kim growled and moved toward the exit.

Only once he got to the waiting room and saw the two men weren't there did he gather his hair and twist it into a bun behind him. A couple of teenage girls sat with open mouths, staring at his bloody face.

Kim wrestled off the bloody smock and dropped it on the floor. "I . . . *escaped*!" He rushed to the exit.

15

Kim jammed on the helmet and started the scooter. He pulled off his belt and tightened it around his upper arm as a makeshift tourniquet. He twisted the accelerator and had just cleared the parking lot when the hospital door flew open and the two men came racing out.

Double fuck!

Kim hunched over and made himself as small a target as possible as he twisted the accelerator as far as it would go. The back wheel kicked up gravel, and Kim had to lean far over the handlebars to keep the thing from doing a wheelie. Kim swished by the men before they could pull out their pistols. He sped down a broad tree-lined avenue.

He looked back and saw them climb together aboard their own moped, which looked bigger and far more badass than Kim's scooter. There was plenty of traffic, and Kim was forced to slow down to keep from colliding with cars, mopeds, and pedestrians. He missed a man in a crosswalk by a hair's breadth. The man was okay, but his attaché case took a whack that tore it from his hand.

Kim looked back. The briefcase had broken open and sent papers flying. The killers drove straight through the whirl of documents. A paper plastered itself momentarily over the driver's face. They were getting closer.

Would they shoot him down amid all these people? If they were the Midsummer Eve killers—and they certainly resembled them—they wouldn't be particularly concerned about the sanctity of human life.

And if they'd attached a tracker to Kim's moped, it wouldn't matter what kind of daredevil driving he performed or whether he tried to elude them by whizzing through a labyrinth of back streets. They had him on a satellite-guided hook. He was done for.

I'm leaving the table. I'm out of the game.

Kim remembered those words from Julia on Kungsträdgården, and for a moment he wanted simply to give up. Release the accelerator, stop fleeing, just let it happen, get it over with. Fortunately, the adrenaline coursing through him urged otherwise.

A green signal invited pedestrians to use the crosswalk, and people surged into the street. Kim sighted a narrow gap between two of them, thought *Please keep walking at that pace,* and cut through the crowd at maximum speed. The shouts that rang out in his wake certainly weren't wishing him good health.

He glanced back and saw the men's presumptive attitude toward human life confirmed. They ran into an old woman, flinging her to the ground and leaving her arms twisted in positions that were painful to see. They were only a few yards behind Kim. He made a sudden right turn into a smaller street lined with food stands.

Maybe not such a good idea.

Food splashed in Kim's face. People holding plates and bowls leaped aside and flung their chopsticks after him. The scooter's front wheel sent low plastic pallets flying. Kim dug out the Taser from his waistband when the men appeared on his left. Twenty yards ahead of them, a man was crossing the narrow street, pulling a large cart piled high with chicken cages.

The man riding passenger on their electric moped stuck his hand inside his jacket. It was only seconds before a deadly green dot would mark Kim. He weighed his options, aimed at the driver's jeans-clad thigh, and fired. The passenger now had his pistol in hand but couldn't aim because the driver had twisted to look at the dart in his leg. Kim blew him a kiss.

In different circumstances it would have been comic. Correction: Even under *these* circumstances it was comic. The driver's arms and legs flung out and his face screwed up in the sort of agonized grimace you see in a Pilates studio. The handlebars went left, the moped turned around twice, the Taser lead went taut and pulled out the darts.

Kim succeeded in avoiding the cart with the cages, but the two men didn't. They ran into it at about forty miles an hour, and both flew over the handlebars and into the captive feathery mass. Kim heard wild cackling behind him as he swung into a side street and headed for his hotel with bright gold Taser filaments dancing behind him like long, thin Chinese dragons.

16

After confirming that her ex-husband was sitting down, Julia recounted her telephone conversation, what had happened in Shanghai and what Kim had learned about Frode Moe and the Hotel Habana Libre. She left out the juicier details about the moped chase and Kim's flesh wound because Jonny might conclude she was making it all up. She could hardly believe it herself.

Another underground train arrived at the platform, and Julia had to cover one ear to hear Jonny's question. "And where is that Ribbing guy now?"

Julia's face twitched with a little smile. It seemed that Kim's collection of new facts had made Jonny drop his infantile mispronunciation of the name. Though apparently he couldn't stop referring to Kim as "that guy."

"He didn't want to say. He thinks information about his whereabouts tends to leak."

"He suspects you?"

"No, but you've got to admit it's strange they were able to locate him and Danny both."

"Right. Yeah." Jonny released a sound halfway between a sigh and a sniff. "Frode Moe, then. And don't you say—"

"I told you so," Julia anticipated. "You think you might get serious about the Norwegian connection now?"

"Our sights are already trained westward, I can tell you that much. But we have nothing concrete to go on. It's a real shame Ribbing didn't manage to get hold of that memorandum."

How about that! Julia thought. *Before too long, Jonny will start calling him "Kim."*

"I personally prefer for him to get out alive," Julia said.

"Yeah, sure, naturally," said Jonny, not sounding terribly convinced. He changed the subject. "How did you two meet, actually?"

"Can't see how that's relevant to the investigation. On the other hand, there's some kind of monkey business going on with the oil rigs . . ."

Julia heard Jonny move to a place with less background noise and fewer listening ears. He lowered his voice. "Before you come up with quid pro quo or something equally stupid, I can let you know that we have strong indications that bribes occurred in connection with that contract. Payoffs that maybe Chen Bao found out about."

"A lot of money?"

"More than enough."

"Any government official involved?" asked Julia. "I've learned that the Chinese government is a major shareholder in all such enterprises." She heard a click on the other end of the line. "What was that noise?"

"The sound of my jaw dropping," said Jonny Munther.

They ended the call promising to keep each other updated, since Jonny noted that in contrast to Julia, he was not *obliged* to share essential information with her. Julia said she was aware of that and would be as transparent as a jellyfish, a remark that provoked a groan.

The next train arrived. Julia stuffed her phone in her pocket and settled on a single fold-down seat. For once, she didn't care if people looked at her or not, since she was absorbed in processing the new information from Kim and trying to fit it together with what they'd known before.

During her police career, her superpower had been seeing which bits of an investigation were relevant and which belonged together.

Jonny knew that, and it was probably why he was keeping her informed, although within what he considered to be reasonable limits.

So. Frode Moe and another man had had some sort of contact in Cuba. A Chinese firm was paying bribes to get contracts for the rigs that Moe was buying. In turn, those rigs were somehow—manipulated? Chen Bao had been unraveling that tangle.

That was one aspect. Another was International Credentials and Holdings, the partnership of Olof Helander and Chen Bao into which money came streaming from another firm that just happened to be owned by Frode Moe. What kind of money? Had the Norwegian been paying them to keep something secret?

And how did Olof Helander fit in the picture? The business in Cuba sounded unrelated, but why had Danny thought it so important that it was one of the few things he said before he was murdered? *Cuba. China. Norway. Sweden.* What linked those countries? The links had probably been sitting around that table on Midsummer Eve. Far-fetched possibilities stuck out their noses and ducked back into the darkness. Julia's head spun. She pushed away those thoughts and concentrated on Kim.

He'd delivered his report quickly in clipped sentences against a background of traffic noise, so in two minutes Julia had gotten only the barest outline of the developments. The Hospital of Horror, the shooting, the moped chase, the Taser. Kim mentioned something about chicken cages that Julia didn't understand and asked him to explain. He'd simply hung up. *Chicken cages?* Julia hoped that wasn't yet another missing puzzle piece she'd have to fit into the overall picture.

17

Kim Ribbing clicked off the call to Julia Malmros, checked his phone's GPS, and saw he was a mile or so from his hotel. He slowed the moped and turned into a street lined with stands offering clothes for sale. He snatched a huge silk scarf with a dragon motif from a hanger. Angry shouts came from behind him as he wrapped the scarf around his head and gunned the electric motor.

He dumped the moped in an alley half a mile from the hotel and went the rest of the way on foot. He'd wrapped the Taser leads around the box, and while walking, he let them out so he could rewind them properly, in case additional kissing should prove necessary. He doubted he'd get the chance now that he no longer possessed the element of surprise. When the guys located him, they'd gun him down immediately, if for no other reason than that they were probably a bit pissed at him.

Kim removed the scarf from around his neck and draped it around his shoulders as he approached the hotel entrance. His shirt arm was bloody from the shoulder to elbow and would not pass unnoticed in the lobby of a five-star hotel. Or any hotel, for that matter. Kim scanned his surroundings as he walked, seeking any anomalies. The task was more difficult in a foreign environment; one didn't know *what*, exactly, might be an anomaly.

In the suite he threw his things together and took the time to go into the bathroom and pull off his shirt to wash and inspect it. The bullet had barely touched him and hadn't injured any muscles, but his skin was laid open with a two-inch gash that wouldn't stop bleeding. Kim wrapped several thicknesses of toilet paper around his upper arm and found a paper clip to hold the temporary bandage together.

He tossed the bloody shirt into the trash can, pulled on a fresh one, stuffed a change of clothes in his pack, and abandoned the bag he'd bought at Schiphol. He left his hotel room with his pack on one shoulder and the Taser in his hand.

A *ding!* announced the arrival of an elevator. Kim held the Taser ready at his hip as the doors opened. It was empty. He stepped in and pressed the button for the ground floor. As the doors slid shut, he heard a *ding!* as the second elevator reached his floor.

He hurried across the enormous lobby and didn't bother to check out. Maybe his pursuers weren't getting into his room and finding his bloody shirt, but they *might* be doing just that. He was greatly disturbed that he couldn't figure out how they located him. He had no intention of letting them find him again.

He joined the stream of humanity in the street and saw no sign he was being followed. He stuffed the Taser in his waistband and walked swiftly to the area of the French quarter he'd visited that morning. He'd noticed a sign.

"Rooms hour or day" proclaimed the simple plastic plaque at the bottom of a narrow, steep staircase inside a hole-in-the-wall shop selling used phones. Clearly a fuckpad for adulterous adventures or for young couples with nowhere else to go. The exact opposite of the place Kim had just left but presumably an establishment where no one was inclined to ask questions.

Kim's shoulder pained him as he hauled his backpack up a narrow stairwell so steep the pack rubbed against the walls. He'd bled through the toilet paper by the time he got to the second landing. An elderly woman sat at a rickety wooden table, slurping noodles from a cracked bowl. She looked up when Kim stomped onto the landing, and her eyes took in Kim's face and the bloody shirt without a change of expression. In this hotel nothing surprised them.

"Good day," Kim said in English. "I would like to have a room."

"Day or hour?" the woman asked in heavily accented English without putting down her bowl.

"Day."

"Two hundred," the woman said, poking her chopsticks around in the soup for the last noodle strands.

"Two hundred for the room," said Kim. "Two hundred more not to check in."

"Not check in?"

"No. Just go to room."

"Ah. Yes." The woman nodded and lifted the bowl to her mouth to drink the broth. Kim put a five-hundred-yuan note on the table and showed her a couple of hundreds. Nodding at his shoulder, he said, "And I need a doctor."

"Hospital?"

"No. Doctor."

"Ah. Hard, hard."

Kim placed some more hundreds on the table. "Doctor. Now. Fast." He made a gesture as if sewing on his shoulder and then the international sign for money, rubbing his thumb and index finger together. "Doctor. Sew. Good pay."

The woman nodded, put down the bowl, and swept up the bills. She put them into the front pocket of a kind of apron knotted around her plump body. She groaned as she got up, holding the table edge, and waddled toward another flight of stairs.

"Key?" asked Kim.

The woman waved him toward a short hallway beyond the table where she'd been seated. "In door. Number four." She went slowly up the stairs, setting both feet on each step as she puffed and panted. Kim guessed that his payment was compensation for this monumental project of climbing the stairs.

Kim found a warped wooden door with the number four marked on it in ink. He turned the loose doorknob, and the door opened with a squeak. The room was about eight by ten and contained only a bed, a little writing table with an electric fan, and a stool. It stank of decades of sweat and other body fluids stewing in the warm, stifling air. A filthy window looked out onto a wall where someone had spray painted *No worry be hapy.*

Kim tried to open the window but found it jammed, so he turned on the fan instead, which produced an irritating rattle. He aimed it toward the bed and lay on his back with his right arm over his eyes. After he'd set the Taser on the writing table.

No worry be hapy.

Kim had been in a constant adrenaline rush since the green dot lit up Danny Chen's temple only an hour earlier. One of his strengths was that he seldom panicked in tight situations, but the events at the Hospital of Horror and in the streets of Shanghai afterward had just about *overstressed* him as his brain worked at lightning speed seeking possibilities and escape routes. Now he was allowing himself to come back to earth.

He lay unmoving with his arm across his eyes and allowed the fan's breeze to cool his burning face. The new shirt was sopping with sweat. Kim took deep breaths and imagined himself sinking into a black pool in the forest under a sky sparkling with stars. Down, ever deeper down in the blackness with his arms stretched out Christlike from his body.

18

Kim jerked when someone knocked at the door. He assumed he'd been asleep. He found himself lying in a hollow in the middle of the bed, the result of decades of humping and bumping. He rolled out of bed and was on his way to the Taser, but it occurred to him that no one hunting him would have *knocked*. He slipped the black box under the mattress, then opened the door.

The little man standing outside looked two hundred years old. A wasted face, frowsy white hair on his head, chubby, circular-framed eyeglasses, and a skimpy goatee. Behind him stood the woman Kim had spoken with. She pointed at the old man and said, "Doctor," and for some reason added, "Specialist."

The man nodded to confirm that he was indeed a specialist without revealing what he specialized in. Survival, maybe. The woman wobbled her way down the hall, and Kim let in the man, who bowed and introduced himself as Mr. Che. Kim sat on the bed. His visitor moved with surprising agility to seat himself beside him. From a leather medical bag shiny with age he took a glass bottle and a square of cloth. Fortunately, it looked clean.

"Show, show," he said. Kim rolled up his shirt. The man made a few tsk-tsk noises at Kim's improvised bandage and commented, "Bad. Very bad." With tentative fingers he carefully pulled at the blood-soaked toilet paper until Kim lost patience and simply tore the thing off. The man was shocked. He pointed disapprovingly at dark shreds of red, crusted paper stuck in the wound. Kim relented and let him pick them out with tweezers. He cleaned the injury with alcohol.

"How?" he asked.

"How what?"

"How hurt?"

"Bad luck."

"Bad luck?"

"Yes. Know who Che Guevara was?" Kim asked.

"Yes. Cuba. Castro. Friend. Bang, bang. Why?"

"Your name. Che."

The man's expression was completely uncomprehending. He said, "Not Che. *Che.*"

Kim couldn't hear the difference, so he dropped the subject. Comparing this man's conversational ability with that of the electronics store proprietor was like describing the difference between night and day.

The man fished from his bag a spool of what looked like ordinary heavy-duty sewing thread and an unnecessarily thick hooked needle. He held the object up before Kim's eyes like a torturer beginning his session by frightening the victim with his instruments. "Numbing?"

"Yes, please. Have something?"

The man nodded and handed Kim a glass vial with the same liquid he'd used to clean the wound. Confused, Kim shook his head. The man mimed to indicate he should drink it. *First-rate medical technology.* Kim shrugged and chugged some.

It was as if someone had stuck a flamethrower down his throat. The doctor's alcohol burned his gums and made his tongue curl, it even made his *teeth* ache before the liquid took its course and flowed like a stream of lava down his throat and left his chest a Pompeii in ruins before hitting his stomach and curdling the remains of his scrambled eggs.

"Good?" the man asked.

"Sure," Kim coughed. "Great. Start now."

The man reached with trembling fingers toward Kim's shoulder, while Kim stared through the window. *No worry be hapy.* The sharp stabs in his shoulder were like wasp stings, but the fire in his chest and stomach really did make it easier to ignore the pain. Kim sat quite motionless with his hands on his knees as Mr. Che hummed while sewing him up.

After about the third sharp sting, Kim began to consider his life. Here he sat in a sperm-crusted fuck room in Shanghai being patched up by a man with tremors who must have memories of the First World War. Was that good? Had he lived a righteous life, considering it had brought him to this?

Apparently not. But then the eternal question posed itself: *What is the alternative?* He was convinced he would never be able to achieve one of the "normal" lives he'd seen people living. Why? Because those lives came with obligations he wasn't willing to accept. It boiled down to a question of freedom, including and especially the freedom to destroy himself and end up in just such a room as this and in this situation. *No worry be hapy.*

Kim was sunk so deep in thought that he hadn't felt the next two stings. It was only when Mr. Che brushed his hands together to indicate the procedure was finished that Kim turned from the window and examined his shoulder. It was swollen and bruised, but the five black stitches holding together the edges of the wound were surprisingly precise and wouldn't make him look like Frankenstein's monster when they healed.

Kim thanked him and held out two hundred-yuan notes. Mr. Che shook his head, plucked up only one, and said, "Greed. Not good."

"Sure?"

"Very sure!" With a bow and a toothless smile, the man left the room. Kim remained sitting on the bed and let the fan cool his belly, since he'd started sweating again while being patched up. He looked out the window and thought about life. With conscious effort, he was able to view life as he'd conceived of it before, in terms of freedom versus obligation. But as soon as he let his thoughts wander, he saw only a wide, empty space covered with trails of footprints going nowhere for no reason. He thought about that picture for a while.

One of Thomas Aquinas's evident truths that he'd never bothered to prove was that existence per se was a good thing. From that it followed that since God is the highest good, then he must necessarily exist. That's where Kim took exception with Thomas. Existing wasn't a good thing; perhaps in fact it was better to cease existing or never to have existed at all. But existing just *was*. An empty surface marked with footprints, and then came darkness. That was all. Maybe there was a pattern to it, but that was hard to discern.

Kim got up, took his laptop from his backpack, and set it on the writing table. He moved the little fan to the windowsill and adjusted it so it blew on him as he sat on the stool. His right shoulder throbbed slightly. He opened the laptop and began to create a program he was designing specially for the Cuban market. Kim Ribbing had decided to infiltrate El Paquete.

19

Astrid Helander slowly climbed the stairs to the apartment on Strandvägen. They'd lived there for only three years, but she knew every worn surface and discoloration of the marble stairs, and that made her feel she'd lived there forever. Perhaps it was because of her age. After all, three years was more than 20 percent of her life.

She hadn't forgotten the old three-room flat on Birge Jarlsgatan, not at all, but those were abstract memories, like scenes from a film. That apartment couldn't have been worth more than a quarter of the value of the place she was about to visit. There'd been a kind of sea change several years earlier. First the new place on Knektholmen and then the new apartment. The money had come rolling in. From where? She didn't know.

She was doing better today. The brief conversation with Kim Ribbing had made a lot of the darkness go away, and then she'd done what Kim suggested. She'd imagined her anxiety as a leering demon with the face of a butcher, and she'd wrestled hard with it. That had helped some. Maybe not for the long term, but, like, whatever.

With every step she took up the stairwell she felt the dark load settling farther into her body. She was apprehensive about what the sight of the flat would do to her. She'd never live here again. Where *would* she live, actually? She was already feeling like an intruder at her uncle's place and was sure that sensation would only increase over time.

When would she be able to leave? At fourteen years of age, could she manage living on her own? Would she be allowed to?

She reached the door, put the key into the lock, took a deep breath, and turned it. Nothing happened. It wasn't locked. She couldn't remember Mama or Papa ever forgetting to lock it when they left. Astrid put her ear to the door and listened; there were people inside. She thought about calling the police, but then it came to her: They probably *were* the police. Astrid opened the door just a little and called, "Hello? Anyone here?"

Carmen Sánchez's face appeared at the door to the living room, and Astrid opened the front door all the way. Carmen smiled. "Sorry we're here rummaging around, but—"

"The iPad," said Astrid. "I understand. I just wanted to collect a few things. If that's okay?"

"Sure. And we already checked your room." Carmen Sánchez made an apologetic gesture. "Sorry! Hardly likely it would be there, but—"

Astrid again finished her sentence. "You had to be methodical."

"Right, exactly." Carmen snapped her fingers. "Oh, another thing: When we searched the place on Knektholmen, we found a ring. Don't know if you want it, but I left it on the kitchen table."

"Okay. Thanks."

"How are things going for you?"

Astrid shrugged. "I know I have what I need . . ." Carmen Sánchez frowned as if searching her memory, and Astrid helped her out. "That sounds like Olle Adolphson."

"Aha!" Carmen said. "Thought that was familiar. You listen to him?"

"Sometimes."

"I won't bother you anymore," said Carmen. "If there's anything you want to know, just give me a shout."

"How's it going?" asked Astrid. "With the—how do you put it—the investigation?"

"We're making progress," said Carmen.

"You know who did it?"

"Not yet."

"Not *that* much progress, then."

Carmen smiled. "If we could put our hands on that iPad, it'd probably give us a lot of useful information."

Astrid went to the kitchen where the ring lay glistening on the wide, squeaky-clean wooden table. The entire apartment was in apple-pie order, so Ivana had probably been in sometime between their departure for Knektholmen and Midsummer Eve. She'd certainly not come *after* Midsummer Eve, because she was terribly superstitious and believed in ghosts, portents, and—yes—demons.

Astrid picked up the ring and inspected it. She was pretty sure it belonged to her mother, but not entirely certain; she hadn't seen it for a long time. She held it up to the sunlight and watched the emerald glitter. Then she placed it on her right ring finger and flexed her hand. It felt just right.

Astrid went to her room. She'd gotten a little worried when Carmen Sánchez said they'd already *rummaged* around in there, making her think of a scene in some detective novel where thieves, including policemen, ransacked a place and left everything helter-skelter. She needn't have worried. The room was tidier than she'd left it, and that probably wasn't only because of Ivana.

Bippo lay in his place by her pillow. She picked him up and pressed him to her, looked around to make sure no one was watching, and gave him a little kiss on his broad nose. "Hey there, you," she whispered. "Want to come with me?"

Her room was large with high stucco ceilings. Everyone in her class at school came from more-or-less affluent families, but none of them had a room this size. There was even a piano in the corner *just in case* she ever felt like learning to play. That hadn't happened. Not yet.

She had a queen-size bed by Hästens. She had an armchair in floral chintz fabric and a designer floor lamp next to her bookcase. An antique wardrobe from Bukowski, a desk from Svenskt Tenn. There'd been talk of getting an antique desk chair, but Astrid had dug in her heels and demanded something comfortable and ergonomic, since she knew she'd be spending lots of time with her homework and other stuff. She had prevailed, and they'd come up with a high-backed variant from Kinnarps that her mama called "that whatchamacallit." And the TV, of course, a forty-two-inch Samsung Frame with a PlayStation 4 and, sitting before it, the Fatboy beanbag chair Astrid had chosen.

Yeah, I'm privileged, thought Astrid as she looked around. *Or, rather, I* was *privileged.*

But all of this and everything in the flat was *hers* now, wasn't it? Could she live here? Astrid visualized herself wandering like a phantom through the previously populated room and decided not to think about it just then.

She went to her bookcase and took out a couple of books by John Green. She took her diary and some pens from the desk. She thought about carrying off her Game Boy but left it for another day. More than anything, she'd have preferred to cart off her whole room and carry it on her back like a snail, but since that wasn't possible, she made do with a few small things.

She went to the towering bookcase in the living room in search of something to read. Most of the books on her own shelves were young adult fiction. They corresponded to her chronological age, but she'd outgrown them.

Carmen Sánchez and Christof Adler were in her parents' room, talking in low voices, perhaps out of respect for Astrid. She liked Carmen. Carmen was considerate and didn't treat her like a child. And she seemed smart.

Astrid ran her eyes along the book titles and stopped at Fyodor Dostoevsky's *Crime and Punishment*. Hugo, that kid in ninth grade who was a little stuck up, had mentioned it one time. She pulled out the book and held it with the little collection in her arms.

She was about to leave when she caught sight of a title that brought a smile to her face: *101 Paper Airplanes*. That had been a thing Papa and Astrid shared when she was little, folding paper airplanes. Astrid still remembered a couple of models, including the Phoenix. That one was Papa's favorite. It looked like a bird with a long tail.

Maybe she should take it and relearn a couple of the twenty or so models she could make when she was only nine. Astrid put down the other books and had to go up on tiptoes to reach the tall, wide book. She grasped it and found it bulged strangely. She pulled it out of the bookcase. An iPad slipped out of the book. She managed to catch it just before it hit the floor.

20

Jonny had just gotten back to his office after his daily brief for Liselott Ahrnander when his phone buzzed. He didn't recognize the number blinking on the screen. "Hello, this is Munther."

A slow voice with a dismal, falling tone came through the line. "Is that Detective Superintendent Jonny Munther?"

"It is, yes."

"Hello. My name is Bruce Li. I work at the Foreign Ministry, and I obtained your number from Julia Malmros."

"What did you say your name was?"

"Exactly what the detective superintendent heard, and it's of no particular importance. I'm phoning because I have information that may be of interest to you."

"You do? Tell me."

"It's not something I wish to say on the telephone. Can we meet somewhere?"

Fifteen minutes later Jonny Munther was waiting down at the reception desk. A stooped figure came through the doors. The voice on the phone had hinted at the dismal aura that hovered about Bruce Li. The man gave Jonny the impression he'd lost everything. Jonny Munther came forward, extending his hand. "Bruce Li?"

"Yes," said Bruce Li with a limp handshake. "Unfortunately."

They took the elevator to Jonny Munther's office. A faint shimmer of interest appeared in Bruce Li's expression when he looked at the picture of the two men in the boat Jonny had left on his wall. Li collapsed into the visitor's chair and fanned himself with the latest edition of the Stockholm police's in-house newspaper that had been lying on Jonny's desk.

"So, then," said Jonny Munther. "What's this information you have?"

Bruce Li wasn't one for small talk. "I have the names."

"Of the leaker?"

"Leaker? What leak?"

"Sorry. Continue."

"The names of the killers. From Knektholmen."

Jonny Munther's jaw dropped, but then he closed his mouth. Certainly, sometimes essential information for an investigation came down like manna from heaven, wrapped up nice and tidy, but this sounded too good to be true.

"And how did you get this information?"

"I have extensive contacts, and I understand the Chinese police have been sitting on this information for a couple of days."

"A couple of *days*?"

"Yes. And that's deplorable. I assume that the detective superintendent has been in contact with the Chinese ambassador?"

"Yes. And it wasn't all that fruitful."

"Then perhaps it is encouraging news," said Bruce Li with an expression more appropriate for delivering news of a death, "that the men in question were in no way related to the Red Army. They are killers for hire connected with the Mafia."

"The ambassador insisted that there is no Mafia in China."

"Naturally he did. And no political prisoners. And only a minimal number of executions. Deplorable."

"And the names?"

"Would mean nothing to you." Bruce Li dug in the inside pocket of his jacket and came up with folded sheets of paper stained with perspiration. "But here are photocopies of their passports."

Jonny Munther shook his head as he unfolded the pages. This was more than a package that tumbled down from heaven. If the information was accurate, it was birthday cake and party hats and the whole shebang.

As Bruce Li had predicted, the men's names meant nothing to him. Xi Li-Jiang and Bao Tsiang. According to the birth dates, one was twenty-seven, the other twenty-eight. They had delicate features that certainly might match those of the slim men in the boat. They looked impassively into the camera. Was Jonny Munther really sitting here with the murderers in hand, so to speak?

Bruce Li pointed to the photocopies. "I believe one can assume the passports are false. What is it they say? No reason to yell '*yahoo*'?"

Jonny Munther doubted that Bruce Li was in the habit of yelling "*yahoo*." "Excuse me, but if these men are, as you say, hired killers connected with the Mafia, aren't you putting yourself in danger by finding this information and sharing it?"

"The detective superintendent is not aware of my background, so we can content ourselves with the observation that my relationship with China is . . . difficult. We still have a bone to pick with one another . . ." Bruce Li shook his head. "That is a very, very strange expression. Why do you Swedes say that? An unpicked bone?"

"No idea," replied Jonny Munther. "But a difficult relationship with your homeland, then?"

"Yes. And the fact that the killers who murdered in Sweden are from China is most painful for the Chinese government, and I would prefer you keep that information strictly confidential. If I may say so, I would personally be more pleased if they'd been soldiers."

"Meaning you'd have really yelled '*yahoo*'?"

Bruce Li raised his eyebrows and regarded Jonny Munther with such a melancholy expression that the detective superintendent regretted his attempt at humor.

"There is a time consideration here," said Bruce Li. "I assume you understand that."

"A time consideration?"

"I do not know how . . . how shall I put it, how *intent* you are at putting these men under lock and key. But it was truly most ill-advised of the Chinese police not to have shared information about their identities. That is an indication that one would, so to speak, wish to resolve the situation discreetly and . . . what is the expression? *Expeditiously?*"

"Put them out of the way to avoid scandal, to put it bluntly?"

"One might put it that way. I speculate that may already have happened."

"It doesn't look like it."

"No?"

"I can't go into the details, but certain events indicate that they're still out there and active."

"That is most surprising," Bruce Li commented without the least sign of surprise, and Jonny Munther recalled William King's inappropriate question whether Chinese people even had feelings. Bruce Li, at least, appeared to have none, assuming pessimism didn't count as a feeling.

"Well, then," concluded Bruce Li, getting to his feet. "It won't take too long. I don't know what experience you may have had with the Chinese police; they are extremely effective and have . . . extreme means at their disposal." Bruce Li wrapped things up as if stating what he was planning to have for lunch. "And these men will be executed, no matter what happens. Now I must return to my duties."

"Then let me thank you for your help," said Jonny Munther. "If this is accurate, it will certainly be extremely valuable."

"It is accurate," Bruce Li said on his way to the door.

"And it's certain the gentleman himself isn't in danger now?"

Bruce Li paused before opening Jonny's office door and said something that was probably the guiding principle of his philosophy. "My life has no meaning."

Jonny Munther followed him to the elevator, since outsiders had to be escorted within the building. They'd just stepped into the elevator when Jonny's phone buzzed in his pocket. He saw the call was from Carmen Sánchez and apologized. "Have to take this."

"Of course," said Bruce Li, studying his own face in the elevator's mirror and slowly shaking his head.

"Yeah?" said Jonny Munther.

"We have the iPad."

"Olof Helander's iPad?"

"Right. Astrid found it."

"What's in it, then?"

"Not a clue. It's locked up tight, but we'll bring it in and give the techies something to chew on."

"Great. See you later." Jonny Munther stuffed his phone in his pocket.

With a voice suggesting he thought Jonny must have received catastrophic news, Bruce Li said, "Good news?"

"You could say that."

The elevator doors slid open, and Bruce Li left Jonny with a simple "Bye!" that confused the detective superintendent. Was that just a farewell salutation, or had the man in fact *mocked* him with the equivalent of shouting '*yahoo*'? Jonny tended to believe the first possibility.

21

Lady Luck kept smiling at Jonny Munther that day. When he got back to his office, Ulrika Boberg came in with a folder. "We got the passenger lists from the Norwegian police. I've found all the Chinese citizens who flew out of Norway on Midsummer Eve and the three following days and sorted them by the airports of departure and by chronological age, from youngest to oldest."

"Excellent, excellent," said Jonny Munther and gestured toward the photocopies Bruce Li had given him. "Looks like our search might just have been narrowed down considerably."

Ulrika Boberg studied the photos of the two young men. "Those are the guys?"

"Might be, as I said. We'll have to see if they're on your list."

"Ribbing can probably identify them."

"Right, I thought of that. But the less I have to involve that Ribbing guy in the investigation, the happier I'll be."

Ulrika nodded and left. She had done a thorough, flawless job arranging her data. More than five hundred pages of passport copies were perfectly aligned on top of one another, classified with tabs on which Ulrika had neatly printed *Oslo*, *Narvik*, *Trondheim* and so on. The neighboring country had nineteen public airports in all.

Jonny Munther placed Bruce Li's photocopies before him on the desk, assuming the information was accurate. He started by taking out the first third of the pages from each airport, where men less than thirty years of age were bound to appear.

It took only ten minutes to find them. Xi Li-Jiang and Bao Tsiang had flown out of the Stavanger airport on Norwegian flight NW163 at 7:45 p.m. on Midsummer Eve to Beijing where they'd connected to a flight to Shanghai. Jonny Munther nodded to himself. Nice and tidy.

But . . .

Jonny Munther stared at the tilted venetian blinds and saw slices of the sunlit greenery of Kronoberg Park, where summer continued its triumphant advance.

But . . .

He'd gotten excited at the possibility of finally identifying the two masked men who'd made a mockery of him for days. The *perpetrators*. Of course that was important, but what was he dealing with here? In all likelihood the two names were no more important than the brand of their automatic weapons; in fact, that's what the men were. Weapons. *Guns for hire.* Even if they were the ones who'd pulled the triggers, they were merely someone's tools. They might well have perpetrated the massacre, but they weren't the guilty parties. The chase had only just begun.

After hesitating for a long time, Jonny Munther picked up his phone, photographed the two passport copies, and sent them to Julia Malmros for forwarding to Kim Ribbing to see if he could confirm these were the men who'd attacked him in Shanghai.

Jonny Munther had just tapped send when his door opened. Startled, he straightened up as if he'd been caught doing something dodgy, which he probably had, and stuffed his phone in a pocket. Carmen Sánchez marched into the office holding an iPad over her head like a winner's trophy. "This is going to the techies, who can tell us what the Easter bunny left us!" She tilted her head. "What's that weird expression on your face?"

22

Julia used her phone to read up on Frode Moe as she rode the train toward Sundbyberg. She'd already researched the man's business activity, and now she was studying his biography.

Born in 1963 in Oslo to a middle-class family. Excellent school results. By the time he graduated from high school he already knew he wanted to work in Norway's rapidly developing oil industry. He took direct aim at it by studying geochemistry at the University of Stavanger, a course tailor-made for a job on North Sea oil rigs or in the laboratories in Stavanger. Frode got a job with government-owned Statoil, and for several years he was mostly out on the rigs and boats doing sediment analysis and prospecting for oil.

Then came the interesting part. In 1992 and 1993 Frode Moe had been hired as a consultant to an unspecified country in Latin America. That was exactly the period when Cuba was scouring its territory for oil after the collapse of the Soviet Union and the end of oil shipments from the USSR. The country was poleaxed by that development, and there were widespread shortages during the time Fidel Castro referred to as "the special period." If food were to be found, there was no fuel to distribute it, and the population was starving. Finding oil would solve certain problems. Some was discovered, but not enough.

Danny's last words to Kim Ribbing seemed to suggest the solution to the massacre was related to the fact that Frode Moe and another man had met a Cuban government official in Havana in 1993. That must have resulted in some agreement or pact that led, decades later, to the brutal murder of six persons.

In the winter of 1993, Frode Moe returned to Oslo. In 1995 he married Freja Lodalen, whom he'd met at university when she was studying geophysics. They had two daughters who now were frequently seen in Oslo's higher-class nightclubs. The beautiful people.

Around the turn of the century, Frode Moe had left Statoil and established his own firm specializing in oil rig repair and furnishing spare parts and replacement equipment procured from China. He was so successful that ten years later his company began financing construction in China of rigs leased to oil-producing countries, particularly Norway. In addition, he had investments large and small in Norwegian and Swedish industries and elsewhere in the world. For example, the paper mill in Skutskär on Sweden's east coast would find itself in trouble if Moe were ever to pull out.

Julia got out at Sundbyberg's central station and took a bus toward the Ulvsunda industrial zone. After settling into a window seat, she took her phone out again, typed *Frode Moe* into Google's search field, and tapped Images.

The photos that filled the screen in tiled display showed that the Norwegian wore traditional sweaters most of the time. That was his trademark. His patterned sweaters weren't surprising in pictures of him on tour, but he showed off his collection of many versions of Norwegian national garb even in boardrooms and annual general meetings. He appeared wearing a suit or formal evening attire principally for theater premieres, dedications, and other red-carpet affairs. You could imagine him hurrying home afterward to get back into one of his comfy sweaters.

Julia zoomed in on a picture of Frode and Freja taken at the National Theatre premiere of a Jon Fosse piece several years earlier. They beamed with that almost offensive *healthiness* that may be unique to Norway. Mountains and fjords imbibed by the skin made it shine. Broad smiles, brilliant white teeth. Okay, little crow's feet at the corners of the eyes and a few extra lines along their mouths, but the overall impression was that the two were at least ten years younger than their real ages.

Julia zoomed closer, so that King Frode's face filled the screen. He had sharply chiseled features, closely trimmed silver-gray hair, and the hooked nose of an eagle. If he'd been wearing a uniform instead of a tuxedo, he could easily have been mistaken for a senior military officer. His smile didn't quite reach his eyes, but that was more the rule than the exception among successful CEOs. A ruthlessness that shaded the pleasure of the moment. Or perhaps he'd never experienced real enjoyment and hadn't needed it to succeed.

What were you up to in Havana, Frode?

Even though Julia had trouble with the Norwegian's appallingly healthy appearance, it was still difficult to imagine him ordering the murder of six human beings. On the other hand, maybe she was looking at it from a typically Scandinavian point of view. Nobody had imagined that the grown Norwegian man who stayed home with his mama in what he called his "fart room" and played *World of Warcraft* for days and nights on end would, some years later, take himself to an island a few miles from Oslo and murder sixty-nine young persons. Things like that don't happen *here*.

And then it did happen.

The bus was approaching the outskirts of Sundbyberg. Julia shut off her phone, pressed Stop Requested, and got off at the Ulvsunda industrial zone. The scene that stretched out before her was a 1960s industrial landscape, the architectural equivalent of a clinical depression. Tall, boring buildings with roofs of corrugated metal and sheet metal walls in shades of gray. *Abandon all hope, ye who enter here.* Julia checked her phone and found that Greenbase should be somewhere in a radius of about a hundred and fifty feet. It was; it stood out as the only green-painted structure.

Greenbase probably managed its contacts with clientele by phone and internet, since they obviously hadn't made the slightest effort to provide a welcoming front, unless you counted the green paint. The only indication that Olof Helander's firm was headquartered here was a small sign next to a pair of coldly institutional glass doors.

Julia opened a door and stepped directly into an open-plan office where perhaps ten persons sat before their computer screens, mostly men in their late twenties and thirties. Julia went to one of two men working in the foreground. He was closer to her age. Skinny, wearing glasses, with the air of somebody who'd been around when the Commodore 64 came out.

"Hi," said Julia. The man looked up, and something in his expression said that he recognized her. She introduced herself anyway. "My name is Julia Malmros, and I was childhood friends with Olle."

He got up and shook her hand. "Thomas Wahlqvist. Yes, sure, he mentioned you sometimes."

"Really? What did he say?"

"Gosh, about your books and all that. He was pretty proud of it all. You two threw lots of paper airplanes from Traneberg Bridge, didn't you?"

"Yes, that's right." Julia felt a warmth around her heart when she heard that Olle's memory of that day was so special he'd described it to others. That meant it hadn't disappeared entirely.

"Sorry for your grief," Thomas said.

"Same to you," said Julia. "Have you worked here for a long time?"

"Since the beginning. It was me, Olle, and"—Thomas pointed toward the other middle-aged man, who confirmed his existence by waving—"Staffan, over there, who got together for the startup fifteen years ago. But not here, of course."

"What's going to happen with the firm now?"

Thomas's shoulders sagged as he took off his glasses and polished them on his shirttail. "Looks like there'll be a restructuring over time. For the moment we're filling existing orders but not accepting new ones." Thomas pointed toward an area with empty desks. "We're usually twice as many employees, but . . . well. Coffee?"

They went through the work area to a kitchenette at the far end. They passed a structure that Julia assumed had been Olle's office, the only space separated by glass walls. The blinds were down. "Is that where Olle sat?"

"Yes. The police were here a few days ago and took his computer. We haven't heard anything since."

The kitchenette consisted of a counter, a coffee machine, and a microwave. There was a table big enough for six people. Julia dropped into one of the chairs. Thomas asked if a cappuccino would do, and Julia told him that would do just fine.

"What did they ask about? The police, I mean."

Thomas set a paper cup in the holder, pushed a button, and the machine began humming and shaking, proclaiming *Look how hard I'm working!* Thomas had to raise his voice to answer. "Everything imaginable, but mostly if Olle could have been mixed up in some . . . well, something that led to things winding up the way they did. We understood they meant something illegal."

"Any idea what?" asked Julia. She took a sip of coffee. It had a watery machine-made taste. Half as much water would have been the correct proportion.

"He certainly seemed to have *plenty* of money," said Thomas. "On the other hand, I haven't a clue how he managed his private finances. He could have made good investments a long time ago."

"Did he ever mention Frode Moe?"

"The businessman? From Norway? No. Why?"

"Nothing. Just a thought I had."

Thomas sipped his coffee. His expression showed he had the same opinion about it as Julia did. "And what brings you here?"

"Wanted to see where Olle worked, and . . .well, to be completely honest, I'm actually working on my own little investigation on the side."

"You were with the police before, weren't you?"

"Yes, exactly. Old habits die hard, I guess. Could I look at his office?"

"Please go ahead."

23

Olle's own office was better equipped for representing the firm, so perhaps he might have held client meetings there. A couple of framed posters with the Greenbase logo and the slogan "For a better tomorrow" hung on the wall alongside diplomas and awards. Two leather visitor chairs sat in front of a large desk.

Julia looked at the swivel chair behind the desk and felt a phantom touch at the nape of her neck, as if something of her childhood friend lingered in the air, the lightest possible wisp, as if from a passing paper airplane.

The office door was closed, so no one outside could see Julia. She approached the desk with hesitant steps and sank into Olle's chair. This was where he'd sat. A wireless keyboard sat before her on the desktop alongside a mouse and before a large monitor. Its cable hung loose because the police had taken the computer.

Was it here you sat when you did what got you killed, whatever it was?

Julia ran her finger across the desktop, leaving a track in the thin layer of dust. No one except the police had been in his office for days, so maybe Julia wasn't the only one to feel spooked in here. She pulled out desk drawers and found office supplies, brochures about Greenbase activities, and an almost full package of blank printer paper. Nothing personal. Had the police taken personal items as well? Julia checked the trash can. Empty. She drummed her fingers on the desktop.

Nowadays people use computers to manage that part of their lives dealing with numbers and letters, so that's probably where the evidence would be found, assuming there was any. *Even so.*

Of course it was pure superstition, but there was that feeling; the fine hairs on Julia's neck had risen at the sight of the desk. Nonsense. Nothing to act on. *Even so.*

She didn't know what prompted her to lift the ream of blank pages and turn it over. She gasped. The bottom sheet was completely crammed with numbers and letters.

0327HI1RV324AV365110
HI2RV275AV30196
HI3RV221AV24273
0328HI1RV332AV367111
HI2RV282AV30397
HI3RV230AV24474

And on and on. Julia sat for a while, staring at what for her were odd meaningless scribblings. The only thing she could guess was that 0327 and 0328 were probably dates: March 27 and March 28. The series continued: 0329, 0330, and 0331, but none after that. Julia went through the rest of the ream but found no other notations. She had before her an accounting of *something* for the end of March of some unspecified year.

She took a photo of the page, then went out to Thomas's desk and showed him the paper. "Do you have any idea what this might be?"

Thomas pushed down his eyeglasses and peered at the page full of notations. His lips twitched as he scanned up and down until at last he said, "No idea. Where's it from?"

"Olle's desk. And it looked as if he'd hidden it there."

"Hmm. Say, Staffan? Can you come here for a moment?"

Nothing about Thomas's reaction made Julia think he was acting or lying. He seemed as genuinely confounded by the paper as Julia was.

Staffan was so short and pudgy he looked as if he'd stopped growing sometime around sixth grade. He shook his head after studying the page. "Let's see. You might suppose they're some sort of measurements," Staffan said. "But it's impossible to say, since there are no units. Could be in bars for atmospheric pressure, in pascals for other pressures, or anything at all."

Julia nodded. Without asking for permission, she folded the page and stuffed it into her trouser pocket. The two men made no objection, another indication that Olle hadn't sworn them to secrecy. And what said the page had any bearing at all upon the investigation? Just that spooky feeling in the office.

"Thank you for your help," said Julia. "And for the coffee."

"There's literally nothing to thank us for," said Thomas. "Good luck with . . . whatever you're doing."

Julia left the building and walked back to the bus stop, staring into the distance and feeling the mysterious sheet burning in her pocket.

HI1, HI2, HI3? What were you up to, Olle?

24

It was nearing five in the morning. Kim had almost finished programming when the room next to his was rented. A door slammed loudly and in just a couple of minutes the rusty bedsprings began creaking and squeaking.

Not much foreplay in there, thought Kim. He clenched his jaw when a woman started making a rhythmic peeping. Kim concentrated on assigning values to variables the program would use to search, while the woman kept peeping. Good God, what kind of a sound was that to be making? It sounded like a dog chewing a rubber duckie.

Kim popped in his noise-canceling earbuds without putting on any music. He wrote *Moe*, he wrote *Futurig*, but then realized the earbuds couldn't cancel the peeping sound. Probably no design engineer had imagined a sound like that was possible. He'd just started to think about banging on the wall when the peeping rose in intensity. A groan was heard, the bed gave a tremendous squeak, and the woman exclaimed suddenly, probably when the man collapsed on top of her. Kim wrote *Greenbase* and *Klintec*. He added *Frode*, just to make certain.

He'd designed the spy program to search for those five words. He'd send it to Fly, who'd take care of inserting it into as early a version of El Paquete as she could. Preferably the daily first edition, since that would mean maximum dissemination.

As soon as someone in Cuba decided to download something from El Paquete, Cuba's "hands-on" version of the internet, they'd get Kim's program as a bonus. It was designed to search computers, including their back files, for those five words. When it found any of them, as soon as the computer user connected to the net it would send up a search balloon in the form of a message to Kim. This business probably involved a very senior person, so that individual would also have access to the internet.

But would such an individual use El Paquete? Would he have his own Wi-Fi router? Probably not. And here came the clever bit: Once a computer was infected by Kim's program via contact with El Paquete, it would infect every other computer with which it came in contact. Whenever an infected computer transmitted an email or photo to another device, like magic, Kim was there as well, and that computer would in turn infect others.

In purely technical terms, it would also have sufficed to infect a single computer, provided it belonged to a person who was in contact with lots of others, but infecting El Paquete gave a kick start to exponential growth and would make the whole process go faster.

Kim closed his laptop and took the passport of his alter ego Sven-Erik Magnusson from his suitcase. He'd asked Moebius to fix it up several years earlier just for fun, but he hadn't found an opportunity to use it until now. Kim had entered China with that passport and used it at the hotel. He had no idea who had set the killers on his tail; the trail might lead back even to the airport staff. He didn't intend to take any risks. He sent a message to Julia Malmros before leaving the room.

25

It was just after 1 p.m. Julia was sitting on the bus from Sundbyberg when her phone gave a *ding!* She checked it and saw she'd received an SMS from Kim Cracker.

Perhaps Kim suspected someone had tapped his phone. The short message was expressed so enigmatically that Julia had trouble interpreting it. Kim had told her of his diving companions. The message was short and sweet: Skalman flying to Fly.

Kim was on his way to Cuba.

VII

Guanabo

Five months earlier

1

It was purely by chance that Kim Ribbing found himself in the tiny town of Guanabo along Playas del Este in Cuba. He'd taken a taxi from the airport and made the choice for better or worse to head east. He'd bounced around in the enormous back seat of a Plymouth from the 1950s for about half an hour when a collection of houses along the beach appeared on the left side of the vehicle.

"What's that place?" he asked the driver.

"Over there?" the driver answered. "Guanabo. It's nowhere. Nothing."

"Sounds good. Take me there."

The taxi driver dropped him off on a street that ran along the beach, then vanished in a cloud of dust with a pealing *da-dada-da*—the opening notes of "La Cucaracha" for the Cuban's automobile horn. Kim looked around and found a house with a sign identifying it as a *casa particular* available to rent.

Most often an owner would have only a single room to offer, but here the entire house could be rented. It was situated at some distance from the village of Guanabo. For thirty-five CUC (convertible Cuban pesos) per day he got himself a little wooden house with a terrace twenty yards off the beach. Not big, about twenty by fifteen feet, but complete with bedroom, kitchen, and bathroom. He rented the place.

No Wi-Fi, and that was a problem. Using Google Translate as his intermediary, Kim learned from the landlady that there was a hot spot in the village. He tried it out that evening and found it so slow it took almost a full minute to download an image. He gave up and decided simply to take it easy and enjoy the place.

He went shopping in the afternoon. Beer was in plentiful supply but not much else was available for the moment. He bought a carton of Cerveza Cristal, produced in Cuba, and started to carry it back under the blazing sun. He was soaked in sweat in less than a minute. He accepted the offer of a man on a horse-drawn cart to transport him and the beer the half mile to his new home in exchange for two CUC.

Kim worked a can loose and stowed the rest from the carton in the otherwise empty fridge. He popped open the can and sat himself in one of the two wrought-iron rockers on the terrace. He took a big gulp of the tepid liquid and looked out over the Cuban sea. It was covered with whitecaps, even though he didn't feel the slightest breeze. He rocked a little, took another gulp, and rocked some more. Here he was, king of his own domain.

His parents and grandfather were dead, and he had no living relatives. He had no friends, other than a few online acquaintances. He had enough money for whatever he wanted for the rest of his life. He was completely free, all possibilities were open to him, and nothing appealed to him. There was a single, solitary loose end in his life. Namely, Shock Doctor Martin Rudbeck, torturer of children.

Someday, Kim vowed to himself as he had so many times before. *Someday you'll pay.*

When had he ever really felt good in recent years? When hadn't he felt a darkness perpetually lurking behind him, ready to devour him? Kim went to the fridge for another beer and took out his Spanish phrase and grammar book.

He switched on the outside lights and scanned the pages. His memory was excellent, so he retained things easily, but he needed to concentrate a bit more to understand the grammar. He reckoned he could still absorb some basic Spanish in a week and could become comfortable in two if he put his mind to it.

2

Kim worked hard on his Spanish for several full days to get to a level where people could understand him. He didn't need to stock the fridge with anything but beer and rum, for he found a restaurant with four tables only fifty yards from his house. That's where he had his morning coffee with a bit of bread and his dinner. Chicken or fish with rice or beans, depending on what the owner had scrounged up that day. He didn't mind the monotonous diet. For him, food was merely fuel.

On the seventh day after his arrival in Guanabo, Kim went looking for a dive center. He asked several people, who waved him along to a shack on the beach. Kim went there and knocked. An elderly man came out from a nearby house. Kim asked if the shack was a dive center, and the man broke out in cheery toothless laughter. No, it wasn't a *center*, but it was the place where he, Ernesto, stored his ancient diving gear that people sometimes came and rented. Kim could rent it too.

The state of the gear wasn't terribly reassuring. The hoses were mended with vulcanized rubber patches, the mask was scratched, and the BCD was antiquated. The tanks couldn't have been originally intended for diving, since the meter showing remaining air was fixed to the top.

Kim pointed to a tank, then to his own eyes. "How do I see if there's . . . time?" He didn't know the word for air. Ernesto opened a drawer and took out a small hand mirror. He held it up and gestured behind him. *"Aire, sí?"* Cuba was the land of improvised solutions; when you couldn't purchase something, you came up with a workaround. And "air" was just *aire*.

Kim screwed the gear together, and Ernesto brought out a wetsuit with tattered cuffs. The torn zipper had been repaired with sailing thread. Kim tested the regulator and was surprised to find it fit his mouth well and worked perfectly. The air flow was strong and cooled his mouth. So how did Ernesto fill his tanks?

"Umm . . . *aire*?" Kim asked. "Where do you get air? For tank?"

Ernest slapped a large tank behind the shack. His wedding ring made it clang. "Big truck comes," he said and unexpectedly yelled, "*Bam!*"

Kim felt Ernesto's gaze on his back as he changed into swim trunks and pulled on the wetsuit. The old guy had the discretion not to ask or comment. He helped Kim carry the gear out of the hut to the beach, where it was easier to heft. Kim had just clipped the weight belt around his waist when he heard a woman's voice. "Hey, Ernesto! Are you out there killing tourists again?"

Ernesto shook his head. "Don't listen. She's crazy. *Loca.*"

An odd pair came walking along the beach. A skinny woman who probably didn't weigh more than ninety pounds and was less than five feet tall. Almost invisible hips and breasts, and a tiny little face except for the eyes, which were enormous. Or at least looked enormous in that setting. Long black hair not unlike Kim's own, but probably natural in color.

Alongside her lumbered a giant of a man. At least six and a half feet tall with a chest as big as an oil drum. Huge arms thick as pier bollards that swayed as he walked. His face was the opposite of the woman's, with small eyes in deep sockets but thick lips and a big nose. A mop of unruly dark-brown hair on his head.

While the woman looked thin and sharp, the man seemed like a friendly bear with a constant little smile on his lips. He was lugging a complete set of worn diving gear without the least trouble. The woman had only fins, a mask, and a speargun. She walked up to Kim and looked him over.

"Um-hum. You some kind of hard rocker or something?" She used the English words, "hard rocker." Kim knew it would be absurd to declare his preference for Swedish top-forty hits, so he just held out his hand and said, "Kim. *Me llamo* Kim."

The woman's hand was small, but her grip was powerful, like a skeleton hand endowed with muscles. "I'm called Fly," she said. "*La Mosca.* And this is Fedo."

Kim almost panicked when his hand disappeared into Fedo's mitt, but fortunately this colossus seemed to be aware of his potential for harm. He held Kim's hand lightly and pumped it up and down. "I'm Fedo," he said and nodded to himself. "Fe-do!"

"Kim."

There was a childlike simplicity in Fedo's gaze and a marveling incomprehension in his voice. Kim would later learn that Fedo's brain hadn't developed beyond that of an eight-year-old, because he'd nearly drowned at that age when his family tried to flee Cuba aboard a raft. His mother and father had died, which was probably part of the reason Fedo never escaped his childhood.

His real name was Gerardo García, but everyone called him Ferdinando, subsequently shortened to Fedo. Nobody remembered whether that was a comparison to the good-natured bear or to the popular Czech clown *el payaso Ferdinando*. Probably both.

Fedo released Kim's hand and pointed to Kim's wetsuit. "Awful," he said. "Awful things."

Fly agreed. "Really crummy. You gonna drown. Guaranteed."

Ernesto snorted. "Like yours is any better?" He followed up with what sounded like it was probably an insult involving Fly's mother's sexual parts. She came right back at him. Fedo just stood beaming at Kim with irresistible friendliness.

When Fly and Ernesto had finished insulting each other's families, Fly turned to Kim. "Where you from, Kim?"

"From Sweden."

Fedo clapped his hands, eyes gleaming. His smile went up a notch. He shouted, "Ibrahimović!"

Kim was impressed to hear the name of the former Swedish soccer champ.

"Eh, Ernesto," said Fly. "Give Zlatan here your speargun so he can hang out with us."

Kim was taken aback. Why would he need a gun? Ernesto went muttering back into the dive shack. Fly stuck her face into Kim's and delivered a harangue from which Kim gathered that he should stay close to her so she could pull him out when he sank. Kim hoped she was joking.

"He showed you the mirror?" she asked.

"Yeah."

"Okay, so you understand."

Ernesto came out of the shack holding a harpoon gun that probably had seen its best days back in the 1980s. Fly took it and wrinkled up her face when she tested the tension of its rubber band. "Shit, Ernesto, this thing's looser than the sack you keep your cojones in."

Fly showed Kim how to pull back the band, set it, and make a test shot. The arrow flew seven or eight yards before burying itself in the sand. Fly sighed. "With that kind of *puta madre* gun, you got to get close. Twelve or, better, ten feet. Ever use one of these?"

"Never."

"Just do what we do."

Kim went into the shed and brought out the mirror, but when he was about to put it into his vest pocket, Fly discouraged him with a wave. "No danger. I'll watch."

They went out into the water and put on fins and masks. Kim didn't know how it had happened that now he was supposed to go out spearfishing with two Cubans; Fly and Fedo acted as if it were the most natural thing in the world. For example, they'd never asked if he *wanted* to come along. Though he certainly did. He was just so unaccustomed to having people accept him.

They paddled out to the reef and submerged. Kim felt clumsy alongside Fedo. Despite his massive body, the man slipped through the water like a sea lion. Not to mention Fly, who sped forward like an arrow, ducked under the surface, bobbed up to breathe, then plunged again. She speared her first fish within five minutes. Meanwhile, Kim hadn't even gotten within range of anything.

He heard a clanking sound and looked all around, because it was impossible to tell where it was coming from. Sound traveled too fast underwater. He caught sight of Fly tapping his tank with a knife and pointing to one side of him. He looked in that direction and saw an almost perfectly round fish swimming lazily along the reef.

The fish's coloration made it a living target. Add its rotundity, and it was as if nature itself had set up a practice shot for him. Kim raised the harpoon gun, aimed, and released. The gun recoiled as the harpoon shot forth and passed a couple of inches above the fish, which immediately fled.

Kim saw Fly jam one thumb down into her other fist, a gesture Kim hadn't seen before. It had to be a swear word in Cuban sign language, presumably with a distinctly sexual connotation.

Ten minutes later, Fly swam up to Kim to check his air. She gave him a thumbs-up sign, not to approve of his skills but to indicate it was time to ascend. Kim inflated his BCD and rose to the surface.

Fedo looked delighted when he came up. He pointed to Kim and shouted, "Zlatan missed!" He held his hands up to indicate a rectangle and explained. "Here's target. Here comes Zlatan. Pum! Sky high! Awful, awful."

Kim wanted to make some jolly reply, but he didn't have the vocabulary, so he just shook his head woefully. "First time. Awful Swede."

That alarmed Fedo. "No, no, not awful Swede. Good Swede. But awful shooting!"

Fedo had scored two fish, and Fly had three. On their swim back to shore, Kim asked what they did with their catches.

"Eat 'em," answered Fly. "Sell to restaurants sometimes."

Fish with rice at Kim's nearby restaurant cost seven convertible pesos, so he assumed they didn't get very much for the basic ingredients. "You can live on that?"

Fly blew a raspberry at the thought. "No. No way."

An argument broke out between Fly and Fedo on their way back to the beach. Kim didn't understand all of it, but he thought he heard Fedo say he was tired of eating fish, so couldn't they just sell them? Fly resisted at first but finally gave in. Their relationship resembled that of a mother and son in many ways, but it turned out that they were the same age, just a couple of years younger than Kim. It was simply inconceivable that Fly could have produced a giant like Fedo.

Kim later learned that they'd grown up in the same barrio, and Fedo the kindly giant had acted as Fly's guardian angel since they were toddlers. That relationship was inverted by the accident that killed Fedo's parents. Fedo was taken in by a maternal uncle but in effect became part of Fly's extended family of many brothers and sisters. He went "home" only to sleep.

When they came ashore, Kim took off the diving gear and paid Ernesto the ten convertible pesos they'd agreed upon. Kim wanted to delay pulling off the wetsuit to avoid the predictable reactions, but Fly and Fedo stayed, chatting with Ernesto. Nothing in the tone of their conversation indicated that they'd just been casting the crudest possible insults at one another and maligning their respective families. All was peace and concord.

It was starting to get hot inside the wetsuit, and Kim's face was awash with perspiration. There was no avoiding it. He started pulling off the thin, nubbly rubber fabric. He'd shed the top when Fedo noticed.

It wasn't uncommon for people to pretend to be unimpressed by the sight of Kim's scarred hide, but indifference was certainly not Fedo's thing. His little eyes flew open as wide as they could, and he made the sign of the cross. When Kim's legs came free, Fly asked, "What happened to you? Fall into the *cosechedora*?" (Kim later looked up the word and discovered that it meant "harvester.")

Standing there on the beach, he assumed it was some sort of machine designed to inflict injuries, so he affirmed it. "Exactly."

"Bad hurts?"

"No."

Fedo's gaping mouth swung shut. "Somebody try to kill you? Lots of times?"

"Right."

Fedo was about to ask more, but Fly saw the matter should be closed. She signaled Fedo to hush. Fedo looked disappointed but shut his mouth. Kim thanked them for the guiding and managed a joke: The real Zlatan wouldn't miss a fish.

As Kim got ready to leave, Fly said, "Same time tomorrow?"

3

Kim's subsequent weeks were devoted to strolls along the beach, studying, and fishing expeditions with Fly and Fedo. His Spanish language ability improved, as did his spearfishing skills. He managed to spear his first fish on their third outing and presented it to Fly and Fedo.

"Don't you want us to pay?" asked Fly.

"No need."

"Why?"

"My way of saying thanks for letting me come."

To his surprise, Fly accepted that without further comment, and after that day it became the practice for them to accept Kim's fish, even though Fedo kept calling him "total crazy" for giving them away. Perhaps it was a dismal thought, but it occurred to him after a couple of weeks that Fly and Fedo were the best friends he'd ever had.

Afternoons, he went to his usual restaurant, then sat on his terrace drinking Cristal and smoking cigarettes as the sun sank and set. When he finished the carton of Camel Blues he'd bought at the airport, he switched to Popular, the local brand with tobacco so dark it made him cough.

One evening out on the terrace he made a serious effort to decide what he was going to do with his life. He had no interest in getting back into computer work again. Should he choose something to study, get himself a place to live? One question prompted another, eventually swamping him with doubt and tormenting him with anxiety. His chest tightened so intensely that he could hardly breathe. He thumped his fist over his heart and got up but had to grab the veranda railing to keep from falling over. He felt a strong urge to plunge into the sea and drown, fulfilling the wish that had failed him when he was seven.

Kim stumbled out on the beach. It was lit by a crescent moon. His breathing eased somewhat when he approached the water. Sounds of surf filled his ears. He hugged himself and felt unbearably alone.

Halfway to Ernesto's shack he sank to the sand. The worst of his panic had subsided, leaving emptiness vaster than his torso could accommodate. He pulled out his pack of Popular, lit one, and immediately began coughing. The coughing fit was unusually violent. He stretched out on his back on the beach. An upside-down face appeared above him.

"That can't go on," said Fly. She reached down to help him into a sitting position.

Kim stubbed out the cigarette in the sand. "It's this stuff. Popular."

Fly sat down beside him. "Nobody but Cubans can smoke those. Ever try this?"

She held out a black metal tube with a mouthpiece. Kim took it, then held it up in a questioning gesture. Fly nodded. Kim found a button and pressed it. A filament glowed; he took a puff. Cool smoke filled his mouth and created a pleasant tickling in his throat. When he exhaled, a dense cloud surged across his lips. He handed the vape pen back. "Didn't know that you . . . smoked. Or whatever it's called."

"Fedo doesn't want me to. He's scared I'll die."

"Where is he?"

"Home. Sleeping. Likes to sleep after the last children's program. Gives me a little time for myself."

"You're always together except then?"

"Always."

"But are you . . . *together* together too?"

Fly pulled back, a shocked expression on her face. "Of course not. I'm not a pedophile!"

"Sorry."

"It's okay," Fly said. "You have a girlfriend?"

"No."

"Boyfriend?"

Kim gave her a look. In Cuba, same-sex relationships were kept deeply concealed. Fly's direct question implied she had unusually broad-minded views on the subject.

"No," Kim answered. "Not that either."

"Okay. Wanna fuck?"

Kim looked into Fly's enormous eyes. They reflected the stars as she looked up at him. He remembered how her body slid through the water. His mouth went dry.

"Is that a good idea?" he asked.

"I think so. Not wanting to be your girlfriend or anything, but I wanna do it with you. Right now."

Kim had been feeling totally isolated in the universe. Now here was another human being next to him, offering the warmth of her skin. The strange thing was that it didn't make him feel less alone; the opposite, in fact. He was incapable of extending himself beyond the limits of his own body to take in another person. The momentary spark of attraction he'd felt was purely theoretical. A reaction he'd felt only because he was *supposed to.*

"I'm sorry," he said. "I don't think I can."

"Can't or don't want to?"

"Mostly can't, I think."

"Okay."

Fly took a couple of vapes and sat with her arms wrapped around her knees, looking out over the sea. There was an offended look on her face Kim was sorry to have caused. He said, "Can I ask you something?"

"Go ahead. Ask."

"What's your real name?"

Fly looked at him, and a challenge glinted in her eyes. "Will you go to bed with me if I tell you?"

"No."

"Then I won't."

Kim laughed out loud. He was feeling a lot better than he had ten minutes earlier. Maybe he thought himself so banal he was reassured when someone wanted to have him, even if he couldn't give himself.

Fly got up and pushed the vape pen into a pocket. "Gotta go home to Fedo. He gets worried if he wakes up and I'm not there."

"You're a wonderful person, Fly."

"Absolutely. Totally fantastic. You have no idea what you're missing."

"I do. I'll walk with you a bit."

For some reason Fly seemed reluctant to be accompanied. She sighed before replying. "Yeah, yeah. Come on, then."

They chatted idly as they walked along the beach. When they reached the house that marked the outskirts of Guanabo, Fly said, "Thanks for the company. I'll manage alone the rest of the way."

"You sure?"

"Hundred percent. Come here." Fly put a hand on Kim's shoulder and pulled his face down to hers. She kissed him lightly on the cheek and whispered "My favorite Swede" before she continued toward the town. Kim waited until she'd gone about a hundred yards, then trailed after her. He wanted to make sure she got home safe.

Fly turned inland. The houses there were ramshackle, worsening as she went up the street. She turned into a cross street you couldn't really call a street; it was a dirt path off an unpaved road. Kim trailed her another couple hundred yards. She walked out into a field where a lonely shack stood. It wasn't much better than Ernesto's.

Fly pulled open a squeaky door of random hammered-together planks. A faint flickering light came on inside, filtering through gaps in the wooden walls. Kim stood there for a while looking at the shack, trying to imagine what might be inside. Then he turned and walked back to his place.

Kim got himself a beer. He took it out to the terrace and sipped it slowly as he assessed himself. His anxiety was gone. He thought about

Fly. Maybe he should have gone to bed with her, but that would have been a mistake. It would have affected their friendship. Yet . . .

Was he sitting here feeling relieved that he'd been faithful to Julia Malmros? There was no pact between them, no expression of mutual responsibilities, and he hadn't seen her for several weeks. Oh well . . . being faithful to a memory was also a kind of faithfulness. *Whatever gets you through the night.*

Kim went to bed. Fly's proposal must have had some trace of an impact, for the last thing in his mind before he fell asleep was the vision of her supple body gliding like a dolphin above the shimmering reef. *Disappearing . . . oh, yes, if only . . .*

4

Fly was sitting on the terrace when Kim came out the following evening. He went back into the house without a word, fetched two beers, and handed her one. She pressed the chilled can against her cheek for a moment before opening it.

"Should we make this a habit?" asked Kim.

"Maybe. Would that bother you?"

"On the contrary."

Over the following evenings Kim learned more about Fly's upbringing in dire poverty. One evening he asked what jobs her mother and father had had. Fly stared at him for a long time.

Then she nodded, as if deciding something. "Got any rum?"

"Sure. Want to mix it with something?"

"Nothing else. Just rum."

Kim went in and came back with a water glass full of Havana Club. A quarter of a glass was enough for him, mixed with tuKola. Fly whistled, impressed, when he gave her the glass. She took a big swallow, cleared her throat, and said, "I was born during the special period. You know what that was?"

He did. Kim had heard the term and read about it. The special period had lasted several years after the 1989 collapse of the Soviet Union. Cuba's economy had depended upon the sale of Cuban sugar to the USSR at inflated prices and the purchase of subsidized oil. The Russians wanted to maintain their Caribbean outpost as a threat perilously close to the

USA. The Soviet Union collapsed, and the trade essentially vanished; the Cuban economy went into a tailspin, and within months there was famine in the land. Human beings shambled around like living skeletons. Many died of related illnesses. People feared US President Ronald Reagan would grab the opportunity to invade the weakened country.

Shelves in state-run stores were practically bare except for rationed rice and beans. Black market prices soared, and many women were forced to turn to prostitution just to stay alive.

"My mother was a *jinetera*," said Fly. "She had no choice. She waited in the Habana Libre lobby. She told me"—Fly's smile was grim—"that she used to paint her lips with red chalk, the kind that kids write with, because there was no lipstick. She got pregnant with me right away, and afterward . . . she had to keep doing it so I wouldn't starve. Then my siblings were born. All from different fathers, I think."

"So your father's a foreigner?"

"Yeah. My mama is a lot darker than me." *Mucho más negra.*

"Is she living?"

"Yeah, but now she's selling other things to tourists. Not her body." Fly took a big swallow that almost emptied the glass. "Don't tell Fedo. He thinks she sold baskets in Havana. He'd be really upset." She straightened up. "What were your parents like?"

Kim had mentioned his parents were dead but said nothing more. "They sold *me*. To my grandfather." When Fly leaned forward, he held up a hand. "It's a long story that I don't want to tell."

"Okay. But if you ever do, I'll listen." Fly drank the last of her rum and rolled the glass between her palms. "We all have our crosses to bear."

"Yes. I like you a lot, Fly. I'm sorry we can't . . ."

"Marislady. My name's Marislady. You laugh, I kill you."

Kim didn't laugh. They met as usual the next day to go fishing. It turned out that Fedo had followed Fly the previous evening and now was convinced she and Kim were a couple. He made childish hints and kissing sounds till Fly shouted that yes, she offered her body to the Swede, but he'd turned her down like she was an old dishrag.

Fedo looked deeply shocked. "But *why*, Zlatan?"

Kim tried to find an explanation Fedo could understand. At last he said, "I don't know how to do it."

Fedo peered all around, then leaned down to Kim and whispered, "I can tell you."

Kim saw Fedo was about to provide a pedagogic illustration with his fingers. He carefully pushed aside Fedo's hands and said, "Some other time, Fedo. Not now."

"Okay. But if you want to know, come to me. I saw on TV."

Fly had told him Fedo watched children's programs, nothing else, so either Cuban children's programs were really special or Fedo had misunderstood something.

Kim's visa was about to expire, and when Fly came over that evening, he told her he'd be going home in two days. Fly took it with equanimity but said Fedo would probably be very unhappy. He'd been including Zlatan in his evening prayers. Fly had pointed out that the Swede wasn't really named Zlatan. Fedo said God was sure to know who he meant.

"Do you believe in God?" asked Kim. He took a puff on the vape pen Fly had handed him.

"Sure. You don't?"

"No."

"Why not?"

"He or she isn't needed, that's all. God is an empty concept. You might as well believe in space aliens."

Fly twisted her neck to unkink it. "I believe in space aliens. You think we're *alone*? And we can get along without God? That's just bigheaded madness."

"I don't know, Marislady."

"You really need to think about your attitude toward life, Kim Ribbing. And don't use that name with me."

"I'll do the one, and I won't use the other. But one thing I *will* do is invite you two to a farewell dinner."

5

The following evening he took Fedo and Fly to Pizzeria Piccolo, which Tripadvisor said was the town's best restaurant. Fedo and Fly looked worried as they studied the menu. They were used to getting pizza slices from stands and hole-in-the-wall eateries, paying between five and ten Cuban pesos. Piccolo charged about the same amount but in convertible pesos. In other words, twenty-five times as much.

"Hello?" said Kim. "*Oye.* Order whatever you want. It's on me."

"I can't—" began Fly.

Kim interrupted her. "*Cállate.* Not another word. I'm leaving for Sweden tomorrow. This is my last evening. I'm in charge. And I'm telling you to choose exactly what you want, and I'm inviting. *Basta ya.*"

Hunger lit up Fedo's eyes as he studied the menu, moving his lips. He looked up at Kim. "Can I have two?"

"Fedo, you can have *five* if you want."

Fedo rubbed his belly, pondering, and said unhappily, "Can't eat that many."

"Start with two, then."

Each of them ordered a Diablo, the most expensive pizza on the menu, which Tripadvisor had highly recommended. Fedo added the Quattro Stagioni. Then they ordered drinks. Kim had assumed Fedo liked only soft drinks, but the big man surprised him by ordering not one beer but three, causing Fly to glare threateningly at him and give a wordless growl.

"What?" said Fedo. "Didn't Zlatan say—"

"Never mind little Fly's buzzing," said Kim. "Would you like to have a mojito?"

Fedo wrinkled his nose. "Naw. Don't like booze."

"I'll have one," said Fly.

"Now we're talking," said Kim. "Me too!"

The pizzas arrived, and Tripadvisor hadn't lied. Even though Kim wasn't interested in food, he could confirm that the Diablo with its slices of fiery chorizo bits was the best meal he'd eaten in Cuba and maybe the best pizza he'd ever had, period. Fly consumed her slices with elegantly spread fingers, while Fedo so gobbled his that you'd think he was grazing. His mouth was constantly moving. Before Kim and Fly finished, Fedo had devoured both of his and ordered another Diablo. Fly just sighed.

They ordered several more beers after the meal and talked about their times together, fishes they'd speared, and fish that got away. After a few beers, Fly started going on and on about the fact that she knew Elio Sánchez, the designer of El Paquete, Cuba's alternative internet provider, and she was a bit miffed Kim wasn't sufficiently impressed by that glorious fact.

"You understand?" she said. "The whole goddam Package, *el Paquete de puta madre*!"

For many years the only access to the internet for Cubans was the Package, a hard disk with more than a terabyte of memory that was loaded weekly with content from the leading US television channels—series, sports, and films that then were sent out and distributed by thousands of retailers. People would put a flash drive in a computer holding that week's Package, pay one convertible peso, and download whatever they wanted. Since internet connections were so slow, the Package was the first choice of many.

"I understand," said Kim. "I do understand, Fly."

"I helped him with the programming," Fly said, with a nostalgic glimmer in her eye. "Programming the damn Package!"

"The damn Package," mumbled Fedo and gazed listlessly at the collection of cans in front of him. He'd refused to let the waitress take away the empties because he regarded his fifteen empty Cristal beers as a performance worthy to be shown to the whole world. When he asked for another, the waitress said that there was no more beer and they'd be closing soon.

Fly put her vape pen and little plastic vial with liquid tobacco essence on the table and said it was a farewell present. Whenever Kim sat and vaped, he'd think of her and their evenings on the terrace.

"When's he gonna think of me, then?" asked Fedo.

"All the time," Kim said as he fished out his own present from his shoulder bag. It was a plastic container tightly wound in duct tape and wrapped in newspaper. "This is for you two, but on one condition. You don't open it until after I'm gone. Pinky promises?"

In turn and with proper ceremony, Fly and Fedo each wrapped a little finger around Kim's little finger. The plastic container held five thousand convertible pesos, which was the maximum amount Kim had been permitted to take out from the bank. He assumed Fly would refuse to accept the present if she knew, even despite the conditions in which she and Fedo lived. The cash should be useful.

As they stood on the road under a streetlamp, both Fedo and Fly were a bit unsteady on their feet. Fly gave Kim a long, warm kiss on the cheek, after which Fedo wrapped his arms around Kim and covered his head with so many kisses that Kim's hair felt drenched. When Kim managed to free himself, he saw the wetness was from Fedo's tears. Kim felt an unfamiliar squeeze in his heart.

"Don't be sad," said Kim. "Maybe I'll come back."

"Yeah, do that," Fedo said, wiping his eyes. He winked. "And I'll tell you how to *do it*."

"Do what?" asked Fly.

Fedo winked again. "That's between me and Zlatan."

VIII

Havana

1

Olof Helander's iPad had been hooked up to a Graybox server that ground away for twelve hours and succeeded in extracting its six-digit passcode in the middle of the night. They found that except for the operating system, the iPad was almost empty. The only item that might be of interest, in fact extremely high interest, was a single document titled *Moe*. They opened it, and the monitor display filled from side to side and top to bottom with letters and digits that looked completely meaningless. It was encrypted.

IT expert Linus Tingwall, adept at recovering deleted and encrypted data from phones and computers, attended the morning group meeting. He'd come in early to start tussling with the iPad before the gathering. Linus was twenty-five years old. He had long red hair and a heavy beard that made him look more like a character from *Game of Thrones* than a data geek.

But that's how data geeks look these days, thought Jonny Munther. He addressed Linus. "So, where do we stand?"

Linus leaned back in his chair. "In a pile of shit."

"Can you be more specific?"

"Just as I thought, it's standard operating procedure when someone wants to protect something: symmetrical encryption with an asymmetric key that's also encrypted."

"Which means?"

"That we're in a pile of shit. Of course, there's a possibility it's using a simple patterned encryption, but I doubt it. I certainly can't find any pattern at all."

Carmen Sánchez leaned forward. "But isn't there some kind of, what do you call it, some logarithm, one you can use to . . ." Her voice faded away.

Linus gave her a pitying look and finished her question. "Decrypt it? 'Algorithm' is the word you mean. Decryption without a key is theoretically possible, but it's impossible in practical terms."

"What makes it impossible?" asked Jonny Munther.

"Our limited time on earth," Linus said, a cryptic enough remark. "Without getting too technical, encryption is based on two extremely large prime numbers. If we suppose that a key a hundred and twenty-eight bits long is the product of those two—"

"Now we're getting into the weeds," said Jonny Munther. "You mentioned our time on earth. That's more my speed."

"Okay. It's like this. Say we've got a box that can try a hundred billion keys a second . . ."

"What kind of box?" asked William King.

"A computer, obviously," said Linus irritably, pulling on his beard. "With a hell of a fast processor. It sits there hammering away, and suppose it comes up with the key halfway through the process. It wouldn't get there before the earth as we know it falls into the sun. We're talking about billions and billions of years."

"But that Graybox server that pulled out the passcode, it took only—"

Linus Tingwall just shook his head. "That's completely different. A six-digit code generates nine-to-the-sixth-power combinations, only about half a million. But now we're talking about astronomical numbers. Like the number of atoms on earth. Those dimensions. Lots and lots of zeros. Practically impossible without the key. Provided it's not a patterned encryption."

"What does that kind of key look like? Where's it found?"

"It's a file, that's all. Could be in a computer or a hard disk, in a flash drive or in the cloud."

Jonny Munther turned to Ulrika Boberg. "Do we have Olof Helander's log-in information?"

She shook her head. "From his computer, it looks like he *has* an account in the cloud, but we don't have a password. I rummaged around in both computers looking for one, but I didn't find anything."

"That maybe I can help you with," said Linus. "If you'll loan me the computers, maybe I can break into the password list. Maybe."

"You have time for that?" asked Jonny Munther.

"I don't really, but . . ." Linus shrugged. "I have to admit this is a bit more interesting than credit card fraud."

"We'd appreciate it. We'll have them delivered as soon as we've finished here."

Linus Tingwall didn't budge and looked at Jonny Munther expectantly. The detective superintendent's experience dealing with staff from the IT branch was that a greater number of them than average in the general population lacked social awareness and the ability to read subtle signals. He saw he'd have to be blunt. "So, thanks, that's all for now."

2

Linus Tingwall slouched his way out, and Jonny Munther again turned to Ulrika Boberg. He saw Christof Adler bouncing a little in his seat, obviously with something to say, but this seemed an appropriate moment for a probationary officer to learn the importance of patience.

"Ulrika? What do you have?"

"I'm still bothered by this Futurig firm's unexplained revenue, and I think I may have found something, but I want to be sure before sharing. Is it okay if I keep working on it?"

"If you think something might come of it. Take today and see if you can dig something up, but then we'll need to redirect your resources. Christof?"

Christof Adler almost bounded to his feet, but William King noisily cleared his throat and rose majestically. "It's time now for me to raise another matter."

Christof looked up at Jonny Munther with a look of childish disappointment. *But it's my turn!* Jonny thought about giving Babyface Billy a reprimand but remembered Carmen Sánchez's words about using kid gloves. He let the King take the floor. The man swayed back and forth, shifting from toes to heels. "Have the killers definitely been identified?"

"Yes," said Jonny Munther. "We're almost a hundred percent sure."

"And how, may I ask?"

The previous evening Jonny had reached out to Julia, who was in contact with Kim Ribbing. Kim had told her the passport photos were of the men who'd tried to shoot him. Jonny Munther saw no reason to weasel out of answering. "Kim Ribbing was able to confirm they were the men who tried to kill him in Shanghai."

"Aha!" exclaimed William King. He sneered. "That raises a question: Why don't we quite simply turn over the whole investigation to Julia Malmros and Kim Ribbing?"

"Unless you have something else to discuss—"

"Yes, in fact I do. This is a hunt for murderers, right?" William King pointed at the whiteboard where the photocopies of the men's passports were taped up. "And there they are, the killers. Shouldn't we make sure they're arrested? That's the whole point, isn't it?"

"No," said Jonny Munther. "Those two are hired killers operating on someone's instructions. I consider them criminals but not the party or parties responsible for the murders."

William King threw out his arms, feigning dramatic desperation. "And what do you think I'm going to tell the media? *Yes, we know exactly who they are, but we're not planning to arrest them because after serious philosophical reflection, we realize they're not guilty.* Really? You think I can get away with that?"

Jonny Munther silently counted to ten before answering. "It's of no interest to me what you can get away with. This is a *real* ongoing investigation, and that means we don't consider what some random outsider might criticize. In other words, we don't take the attitude you've manifested for years now. That's like an outsider looking at a war and saying, *But why don't they just stop fighting? My God, they're stupid!*"

Carmen Sánchez gave Jonny a warning glance. He took it down a notch. "This has become a diplomatic problem in Sweden's relationship with China, and I'm more than pleased to turn over to you the job of contacting the Chinese ambassador to work out a solution. You might well get better results than I have. The ambassador seems to be getting tired of me."

King nodded and sat down, pleased to have received an important assignment. Jonny Munther didn't believe for a second that William King would do any better, since the man was an oaf. There was nothing the ambassador disliked more than impolite behavior.

"Christof?" said Jonny Munther. "I see you're on the edge of your seat. Go ahead."

"Finally!" said Christof Adler, giving the side-eye to William King, who merely waved his fingers in a la-di-da gesture. "Right. I went through the call list from the telephone company, and it turns out Chen Bao called Olof Helander two days before Midsummer Eve."

"Not too surprising," said Carmen Sánchez. "Must have been getting ready to travel."

Christof smiled patronizingly. "What's interesting isn't the calls, it's where Chen Bao called from. A four-minute call from Stavanger."

The room fell quiet as they tried to see how this new information fit with what they knew.

William King drummed on the tabletop. "Has anyone checked Chen Bao's itinerary?"

It hadn't occurred to Jonny Munther that Chen Bao's route to Sweden might be of interest. Had they gotten to the moment when William King would bolt and take his waiting taxi to a television studio? Jonny saw no signs of that. Maybe William King was looking forward to his chat with the Chinese ambassador; or maybe he just found it too difficult to get out of his seat.

"Hold on," Carmen Sánchez said. "If we assume Chen Bao traveled to Sweden from Stavanger, that means he used the same airport the murderers left from three days later. Do we know how they got to Sweden?"

"That's in process," said Ulrika Boberg. "We've got lots of airline companies and airports, but for now I limited the inquiry to Arlanda and Bromma. We should have the results this afternoon."

Carmen Sánchez looked at Christof Adler. "Is it possible to trace that call? I mean, to see exactly where he was calling from?"

"I think so. When we're finished here, I was planning to contact Telenor, which handles digital traffic in Norway."

"Let Carmen do that," said Jonny Munther. He did feel a moment of sympathy when he saw Christof's disappointed expression. Just as the boy was about to protest, *But I was the one who . . .* Jonny Munther steeled himself and said, "Christof, I want you to search Olof Helander's office and residences. And this time you're looking for a storage device of some kind or maybe a password written down somewhere."

Christof clutched his temples. "That's so *boring*!"

"As time goes on, I think you'll find that a lot of fundamental police work is boring. And with that, let's—"

"One thing more," said William King. "Kim Ribbing. Where is he now?"

"On his way to Cuba, the last I heard," said Jonny Munther and forestalled William King from asking follow-up questions to which Jonny had no answers. "And that's all for the moment."

3

Fly and Fedo were waiting outside Hotel Habana Libre when Kim got out of the taxi from the airport. Fly had been watching the street, while Fedo sat on a wall, dangling his feet. He was concentrating on licking an ice cream held in his big hand. Kim felt a little surge of warmth around his heart.

Fly saw him as soon as he got out, but she made no move to approach. Only when Kim walked up and gave her the obligatory kiss on the cheek did her attitude soften. Fedo lumbered forward and gave Kim a bear hug and then exclaimed, "Thanks for the money, Zlatan!"

Fly nodded with a bitter expression. "It's bad manners to give a present without giving a person the chance to say 'No, thanks.'"

"It's not," said Kim. "That's exactly why I did it that way."

"It was great!" said Fedo. "We started fixing the house, and Fly bought a new computer, and lookee!" Fedo held up his half-eaten cone. "I got ice cream! And a new bed, and—"

"I want to pay you back," Fly said. "It'll take time, but—"

Kim waved toward the hotel. "You'll repay me by helping me out with this. If you give me even a single peso, convertible or not, I'll toss it in the sea."

"Good!" said Fedo. "Then we can dive for it!"

"You don't understand," Fly said to Fedo. "This is a matter of—"

Kim put a hand on Fly's shoulder. "Marislady, it doesn't matter; I'm rich. Helping you two out means much more to me than money. I'll be really, really upset if you try to give it back."

"Don't upset Zlatan," Fedo whispered. He turned to Kim. "You know her *real name*?"

Fly kept protesting for a while, sounding less and less convinced. Fedo intervened with happy comments that made it clear the cash had really been of use, which pleased Kim no end. Fly shrugged at last. "Yeah, yeah. So, thanks. There. But if you give me even one more centavo, it goes right into the sea."

Fedo winked at Kim and mimicked putting on a dive mask.

Kim smiled. "Shall we go in?"

The doorman seemed reluctant to open for them, but the sight of Fedo's looming bulk made him change his mind. They came into a vast lobby lit by a chandelier twenty feet overhead. When Kim caught the eye of a woman standing by the reception desk, she slipped away into a back room. Kim assumed that his long black hair provoked certain assumptions about raving debaucheries and *la vida cabrón*.

"What are we doing?" asked Fly.

"Checking in," Kim said. He addressed the man standing stoically at his terminal with a stiff smile on his lips. Kim put his Sven-Erik Magnusson passport on the counter. "I have a reservation."

The man opened the passport and took a while to examine it before he turned on the computer. His eyebrows shot up at the search result. He repeated the search, obviously with the same result. In a congested voice, he said, "Two rooms. *Premium* rooms?"

"Yes," said Kim. "Already paid for, right?"

"Yes, certainly . . ." the man replied, scratching the back of his head as he looked from Kim to Fly and Fedo. They looked like ordinary Cubans, clean and properly dressed no matter how poor, but even so, their appearance didn't correspond with a premium room in what had once been Havana's most luxurious hotel.

The man appeared to weigh his alternatives, maybe thinking he could say that all those rooms had been destroyed after Fidel Castro confiscated the hotel during the revolution. At last he heaved a sigh, put his hand down, and handed over two key cards. He pointed to the elevators. "Twenty-fourth floor." He made a real effort and said, "Welcome."

Fly looked around the exclusive surroundings with a mocking little smile. Fedo was wringing his hands and seemed ready to take to his heels. Fly took his hand and drew him toward the elevators. On the way up, Fedo's eyes flickered all around, and Fly said, "*Cálmate,* relax. Everything's okay. We're having an adventure, like when we were little kids. Okay?"

Fedo nodded and seemed a bit reassured. His gaze got less jumpy, and when he stepped out of the elevator he looked around, marveling and interested. The wide hallway had wall-to-wall carpet. Doors were set at lengthy intervals because each room measured well over six hundred square feet.

"We need to talk," said Kim. "We'll go to my room."

"I wanna see *my* room first," said Fedo.

"I guess Fedo and I are sharing," said Fly. "Or, Kim, maybe you . . . changed your mind about some things?"

Fedo must have caught Fly's meaning from the tone of her voice. "Remember? Zlatan doesn't know how to *do it.*"

"Right," said Kim. "So, you two will be roommates."

The rooms were adjacent. Fedo hopped in expectation as Fly put the key card into the slot. It clicked, she opened the door. Fedo cried, "Wow!"

"Come over when you're ready," Kim said and went to his room. Behind him he heard shouts. *"Cojones!"* and *"No me jodas!"* He opened his door and entered a room humble in comparison to the suite in Shanghai but probably unimaginably luxurious for the two young Cubans. Blond parquet floor, white walls, two huge double beds, pastel-upholstered armchairs, and sliding glass doors to the balcony.

Kim took a quick shower, then tossed his backpack onto the bed and took out a Santa Muerte T-shirt he'd found at Heathrow. The "Death Saint" was a female skeleton in a billowing blouse wearing a crown of roses. Kim put it on and went out on the balcony.

It had been hot as hell down there in the street, but up on the twenty-fourth floor a cool breeze was blowing from Havana Bay. Fly came out on the adjoining balcony, grabbed the railing, took in the view, and muttered, "*Que comemierda . . .*" That expression, literally as "what a shit eater," was usually a negative comment, but Kim suspected that wasn't Fly's intention. He asked if they were ready. She said Fedo didn't seem to want to leave the room. Unless he had to.

"Okay, then I'll come over there."

In the other room Kim found Fedo lying in bed, arms and legs flung out, wearing a white robe that reached only to his elbows. He rolled onto his side when Kim came in, smiled brilliantly, and exclaimed, "Look! We got bathrobes!"

Fly sat cross-legged on her own bed, her back against the headboard and a nearly new laptop in her lap. "Really good connection here," she said. "Anyway, better than all the *puta madre* hot spots."

"Find him?"

"Sure did. I have a number here."

Kim had been able to read his email during the flight despite the plane's spotty Wi-Fi connection. Three hours before landing, a message had popped up from the spy program Fly had planted in El Paquete. Someone had received an email reading Due to recent events in Shanghai, there is concern that Futurig might be implicated. We strongly urge you to do away with any documentation regarding past affairs.

Someone was worried that Kim might have come up with information in Shanghai related to some dirty business of Futurig. He wanted all documentation to be shredded. The message had been sent by gtrJL7532, presumably a randomly generated username for someone no longer on the system. But they knew who'd received it: Ramón Socarrás, an official in the Cuban Ministry of Energy. Fly had just come up with his phone number.

"Wow, lookee here!" Fedo had found a minibar stocked with soft drinks, beer, liquor, nuts, and chips. "Is that for free?"

"Sure," Kim lied. "Take whatever you like."

"It's not—" Fly started to say but broke off when she saw Kim's stern expression.

Satisfied, he said, "You want to call, or should I?"

"Guess it's better if I do," said Fly. "Your Spanish is . . . not perfect. But go over all this again for me."

Kim had phoned from the airport, waking Fly. He'd given her a quick summary of what had happened and what he was planning. She'd been groggy at first, and he'd had to repeat himself a couple of times because she thought he was pulling her leg. Since they'd last seen each other, there'd been a massacre in Sweden and a murder attempt in Shanghai? *Que comemierda.*

Fedo munched peanuts and drank a Cristal while Kim went through the whole story again as best he could in his *not perfect* Spanish. Fedo stopped chewing when Kim described the scooter chase and the kisses that made his pursuers crash. "*Coño,* Zlatan," he said. "You're, like, James Bond."

"I don't know. But that's what happened."

"Really?" asked Fly. *"En serio?"*

"Yes. Everything I told you is real and serious, and that's why I want you to think about it before you phone the man or help me out. I have no idea how far up this goes, but there are huge sums of money involved, and that means it's going to be dangerous. No kidding."

"Why are *you* doing all this?" asked Fly.

"Honestly, I don't know. I got dragged into it, and . . . maybe I've got this sick tendency to finish up whatever I start. Plus, I want to catch those ugly fish. Is that the way you say it? Ugly fish? *Peces feos?*"

Fedo burst out laughing, slapped his thigh, and repeated *peces feos,* so that probably wasn't the correct idiom. Fly confirmed it. "No, but I understand. And I'll tell you I'm pretty tired of all the *peces feos* who do their shit protected by the system and get away with it." Fly picked up her phone from the bedside table. "What am I supposed to say?"

"Are you sure about this?"

"Yes. What should I say?"

"Say we know about his business with Frode Moe and will expose him if he doesn't meet us. Tell him to come to the bar here in the hotel. *Where it all began*—stress that. Say he must come alone." Kim patted the front of his T-shirt. "And tell him to watch out for *la Santa Muerte.*"

4

Half an hour later, Kim Ribbing sat in the bar in an armchair upholstered in gray imitation leather. The bar was just as vast as every other space in the hotel, but its furnishings were noticeably spare. It had seating for thirty in a space that could easily have accommodated two hundred. There was a raised stage in one corner. Along an inner wall was a series of murals depicting human figures in naive style. A bartender stood looking bored at the circular bar in the middle of the space. The only other clients were a couple of Asian tourists concentrating on their phones.

Natural lighting came through a lengthy floor-to-ceiling glass wall that looked out over the pool area, where a few people lay stretched out in lounge chairs placed around the irregularly shaped swimming pool.

Kim studied his phone, which displayed a photo of Ramón Socarrás he'd found online. Most Cubans, young or old, had something *sharp* about them, as if they'd been blasted by the sun and chiseled by the scarcities, but Ramón Socarrás seemed bloated, maybe even pudgy. In contrast to most Cubans, he seemed not to have the slightest drop of African blood in him. He could probably trace his family tree directly back to a bunch of Spanish ancestors.

His round face beamed contentment and his little mustache was carefully trimmed. His mouth was small and tight, what you might call *miserly*, but there was no sign of ill will in his dark-brown eyes. Quite the contrary, he looked like someone's kindly uncle who'd served himself a little too much at a Christmas buffet. The only feature that might possibly hint at a nefarious nature was the presence of some hard lines around the eyes.

Kim clicked away the photo and leaned back in the armchair. In his experience, every human who looked like a crook really was a crook, but most crooks had perfectly ordinary faces. Like this Ramón guy.

Kim swiped the screen and found Julia Malmros's photo of the sheet of enigmatic letters and numbers from Olof Helander's office.

0327HI1RV324AV365110
HI2RV275AV30196
HI3RV221AV24273
0328HI1RV332AV367111
HI2RV282AV30397
HI3RV230AV24474

According to the usual way of arranging things, the digits to the right would be some form of result, the consequence of the digits and letters that preceded them. But if, for example, you took the last row and imagined it was indicating the difference between 230 and 244, which would be 14, there would still be no way of guessing what that had to do with the terminal figure of 74, which would be the outcome of some calculation.

The only pattern Kim could perceive was that the larger the difference between the AV figures and the RV figures, the larger the number at the end of the line. But he couldn't discover a veiled constant. And he had no idea what HI stood for.

His phone vibrated in his palm, and Fly's sharp features appeared. "Coming in now. And I don't see anybody with him. He looks really . . . *indeciso*."

"Don't know that word."

"Yeah, well, like . . . doubting. Like he doesn't know what to do."

"He's nervous, then. Good."

"Hold on, I . . ."

The sounds in the background changed. Kim understood from the echoing footsteps that Fly was following Ramón into the lobby. "He's going up the stairs. Nobody with him."

"Great. We'll talk later."

The fact that the man had no security detail probably indicated that his activity, whatever it was, hadn't been approved by the leadership. That simplified things. If Ramón was on the stairs, he'd enter the bar in thirty seconds. Kim whistled to attract the bartender's attention. The man looked up. Kim nodded, and the bartender returned the nod. Kim had given him fifty convertible pesos to surprise hotel guests out at the pool with free drinks. That way the bartender wouldn't be there to intervene if things somehow got hairy.

The bartender set out toward the pool. The two Asians had left. Kim stretched out in his chair. He was feeling epic jet lag after days of crisscrossing the globe. His body was confused and couldn't tell if it was day or night. Kim felt detached from reality, and he kind of liked the feeling. He wasn't particularly worried about life and death. That gave him a strong negotiating position if push should come to shove.

The man who appeared at the entrance to the bar was a somewhat older version of the photo Kim had examined. He didn't look tough at all; the accumulating years had given him an even softer face and a potbelly. Ramón stepped into the bar, and Kim stood up. Ramón's eyes fixed on the skeleton woman on Kim's chest, then lifted to his face. Ramón's eyes opened wide. He turned on his heel and left.

Just outside the bar Fedo stepped in front of him. Ramón's face slammed into Fedo's massive torso. He staggered back, tried to grab an armchair but missed and sprawled onto the floor.

"Uy," commented Fedo.

As Kim had suspected, things had gotten hairy.

5

William King was the first one in the conference room, and Jonny Munther noticed just too late to turn around. He sauntered across the room and busied himself at the coffee counter.

"They're dead," William King said behind him.

"Who's that?" asked Jonny Munther, putting a splash of milk into his coffee.

"The killers." Jonny Munther turned to look at William King, who gave him a nasty little smile and added, "If one is to believe the ambassador."

"They've been found, then?"

"Yep. Garbage dump outside Shanghai. Shot in the back of the head. Executed, obviously."

"Have the Chinese police confirmed this?"

"Nope. As you're aware, it's not at all easy to get hold of someone over there . . . looks like we have to involve the embassy. There's a press meeting in an hour. Think I can make this public?"

"No, hold on to it for now. I'll talk to Liselott Ahrnander to see what diplomatic channels we can use. When you say 'executed,' you mean after a judicial process? They were sentenced to death?"

"I very much doubt it," said William King. "That would have been lightning fast in any case, even for the Chinese. And they've given up on shooting people; now they have panel trucks where they administer fatal injections. What a horrible way to die."

"Hmm," responded Jonny Munther, lost in thought. He took his seat at the end of the table. *The killers were killed.* Was that punishment for letting Kim Ribbing get away, or had it been the plan from the beginning? To get rid of the weapons, so to speak?

When Carmen Sánchez and Christof Adler came in, it turned out that William King had already informed them there was no need to keep trying to locate the murderers, assuming what the Chinese ambassador had said was true. It was entirely possible that the Chinese government simply wanted to sweep the problem under the rug.

"Okay," said Jonny Munther. "We'll leave that till later. Christof, want to begin?"

Christof Adler sat with his chin propped up by one fist. His eyes were tired. He didn't bother to lift his head. "Yeah, what should I say? I know that apartment like the back of my hand by now. I'm going to be dreaming about it at night, but I didn't find anything. Please, please, *please* don't send me out to go through the house on Knektholmen again."

"Pleasing people isn't something we do in police investigations," said Jonny Munther. "You must do your pleasing on your own free time. You're going back out there tomorrow, unless something new turns up."

Christof moaned, lowered his head to the table, and carefully knocked his forehead on it a couple of times. "I didn't join the police to—"

Jonny Munther sharply cleared his throat, interrupting Christof. "How about you, Carmen?"

Carmen opened her laptop. "Something, but probably trivial. I went through Chen Min's Instagram account and found this. Taken six months ago." She turned the computer so the others could see Chen Min proudly holding a porcelain cat.

"Shit!" said William King. "A porcelain cat! There's the smoking gun!"

"Look at the background," Carmen Sánchez said. She touched the screen to enlarge the image. Behind Chen Min was an open door through which a desk was visible. An architectural diagram of an oil rig was on the wall of the office. Carmen zoomed until the image pixelated. She put the cursor on some wiggly shapes. "This looks like text. Sent it to the techies to see if they could clean it up enough to read, but no luck."

"And what does this tell us?" asked Jonny Munther.

"Nothing more than we already knew, unfortunately," said Carmen Sánchez. "Chen Bao's business had to do with oil rigs. The only possibly relevant thing is that this image helps date that activity. It was taken this year on January 14."

"Not a terribly tasty bit of news," said Jonny Munther.

"Sorry, boss," said Carmen. "You can send me with Christof to Knektholmen, punishment island."

"Hmm. And you, Ulrika?"

"Ah, I indeed have something a bit better to chew on," said Ulrika Boberg, her face lighting up as she straightened her blouse's collar points and checked to make sure the stack of pages before her was perfectly aligned. "I've been in contact with the Norske Bank, and they were much more willing to help than the Chinese chamber of commerce. About a thousand times more willing. They sent me everything they were able to release concerning Frode Moe's personal finances."

Ulrika gently stroked the stack of pages, which caused the top sheet to slide just a bit to the side. She realigned it. "With these printouts of account movements as a basis, I was able to . . . let's just say I probed a bit in the gray zones yesterday afternoon." Ulrika moved her hands as if feeling her way through a thick fog.

"I hope you're not saying you broke the law," said Jonny Munther. "If this eventually goes to court . . ."

Ulrika shook her head. "Didn't *break* it. Just bent it a little and strength tested it to see if I could track the cash flows. It's a consummately constructed merry-go-round. In some cases, money was washed through as many as seven banks before getting to Moe. In all modesty, I can declare that there aren't many who could have managed to hang on tight long enough to track it."

"Okay," said Jonny Munther. "But what conclusion did you come to?"

"Ah—in light of certain activities of persons associated with the investigation, it may be interesting to know that the money comes from Cuba."

William King laughed at that. "Ribbing, you mean? Fascinating, the way he keeps turning up! When we come up with a place, he's already on the scene."

Jonny Munther ignored William King and asked Ulrika, "But what are the Cubans paying for?"

"The money comes from CUPET, the government petroleum company. Among other activities, it extracts oil, so one shouldn't discard the thought the payments might have to do with that. The strange thing is that the money goes into Frode Moe's personal account."

"You mean they're employing him as a private consultant or something like that?" asked Carmen Sánchez.

"If so, those would represent the highest consultancy fees ever charged," said Ulrika.

A knock on the door. Walter Berzelius poked his head in. "Sorry, just wanted to let you know we're here now."

"Thanks," said Jonny Munther. "We're just about finished. You can use my office in the meantime."

Jonny Munther had asked Astrid Helander to come by, hoping she might know something that could help them with the encrypted text. He knew it was a long shot, but sometimes that was all you could do.

"What were you saying, Ulrika?"

"In fact, this is a matter of more than a hundred million kronor a year. Of course, there's never that much in the account at once, it's sent out in every direction and all over the place, but all told, it's a real birthday goose."

Jonny Munther assumed that Ulrika was referring to the goose that laid golden eggs, but she tended to mix up a thing or two in her metaphors.

"What does all that mean?" asked Jonny Munther. "Isn't it illegal to do business with Cuba because of sanctions, or what?"

"Nope," said Ulrika. "It's more a matter of whether you want to take a chance of offending the US and getting your own firm sanctioned, but it's not illegal."

"Ah, I see," said Jonny Munther. "So how do we use this information?"

"Don't know," said Ulrika. "If nothing else, it might be good to know that King Frode has his own secret treasure room."

"Granted," said Jonny Munther. "But there's nothing to indicate that all this has anything to do with our case."

Ulrika's mouth twisted into a pout. "'Research without foregone conclusions,' I seem to recall hearing."

"I didn't mean to criticize, I . . . good job, anyhow. Let's end with that."

6

Jonny Munther grumbled to himself as he went down the hall toward his office. It was astonishing that people needed so much praise to motivate them to do their jobs. There was no one praising him, was there? Nobody at all! *Face it—that's what happens when you're the boss.*

He found Walter Berzelius sitting in a visitor's chair while Astrid Helander stood staring at the wall. Her makeup was less garish than the last time he'd seen her. He followed her gaze and saw it fixed on the printout of the stew of numbers and letters he'd pinned to his bulletin board.

"Well now, that's fine," said Jonny Munther. "That's funny. Those are exactly what I was wondering if you could—"

"Look here," said Astrid Helander, stepping forward and tracing a long diagonal line of numbers with her index finger, then a shorter diagonal of capital letters, and then additional vectors running across the page in different directions.

"I don't understand," said Jonny Munther. "You know what that represents?"

"No," said Astrid Helander. "But I know what it is. That's Phoenix."

"Phoenix? The bird?"

"No, the paper airplane. These are instructions on how to fold Phoenix."

7

Julia had gone back to her real profession, writing, for the first time since the publishing firm's crushing refusal. It was going slowly and maybe it was only a way to fill in time while waiting for Kim to call. But she *was* writing again.

Julia was finding Åsa Fors terribly tedious after the intense months of living in Salander and Blomkvist's world. She pondered whether to let Åsa take up *krav maga* defense training or contract some thrilling illness, but it finally occurred to her that Åsa's monotonous existence was probably the selling point. That's what her readers wanted. Unlike many other heroes and heroines in contemporary detective fiction, Åsa had no flashes of inspiration. She just slogged on and did her duty.

Julia provided graphic descriptions of crimes and violence, of course, but when it came to the actual investigations, she described the many dismal meetings, pointless interrogations, and the exhausting job of following paper trails. Just like in real life.

Julia always began with an opening scene. She described in great detail the man staggering across the Rinkeby marketplace. He was clutching a paper bag creased and worn from use, its handle mended with tape. Those were the sorts of details that attracted the reader and made him—or her—really *see* the scene.

She described the man's collapse down to his slightest shudder and twitch and the way a single orange went rolling across the pavement as the light in his eye went out. For about ten minutes she succeeded in entering a writer's trance, smelling scents from vegetable stands in the market and hearing cries of horror in several languages.

The work got harder when she'd finished that two-page opening. Now the reader gets to meet old Åsa Fors again and discover how her life is going. Julia leaned back and closed her eyes. She found it difficult to recall where she'd left Åsa at the end of the most recent novel. Wasn't there something about a cat?

She pulled the book down from the shelf where she displayed her many editions and skimmed through the last thirty pages. Yep, there was indeed a cat that belonged to the senior physician at the Karolinska Hospital who'd turned out to be the murderer. A cat named Truls. Åsa Fors had adopted Truls.

A cat. How thrilling.

Julia soldiered on and produced a page about Åsa Fors's life with Truls. She knew that many of her readers, especially the older women, adored scenes like that. She'd often heard comments like "All that violence was horrid," but Julia described ordinary life so well that they toughed it out and kept on reading. People asked if she'd ever thought about writing something "without all that nastiness?"

No, she had not. Julia didn't know how to keep a plot moving unless horrible sudden death figured into the equation. The simplest approach was the popular formula replicated in *The Little Engine That Could.* Someone engaged in an insignificant activity or business found it threatened but managed to save it by the end of the story. Maybe Julia might write something like that if someone was threatening to cut her throat, but no one was brandishing a knife. So she forgot about it for the time being.

Julia had written five acceptable pages by the time she shut down her computer just before 4 p.m. Stiff after sitting and leaning over the screen, she massaged her neck. Later, when she was about to print out the text for easier editing and had to reload the printer's paper tray, she remembered.

Olle's notes.

She'd intended to go to police headquarters with the puzzling sheet of paper from Olof Helander's office as soon as she finished her morning coffee. She thought that contribution might be repaid with a hint of how the investigation was going. But she'd forgotten. Before leaving her flat, she checked and rechecked her phone to see if Kim had called or sent a message. Nothing. She walked to the underground station.

8

The officer at the front desk called upstairs, and Carmen Sánchez came down to meet her. Julia shook her outstretched hand. "Carmen, right? How are things?"

"That's right," said Carmen and returned to the elevator with Julia following her. "I spent half the day looking at porcelain cats."

"Do tell. Things are that slow?"

They got in, and Carmen Sánchez pressed the button for the fourth floor. "Chen Min's Instagram. The woman was obsessed."

"Uh-huh. Anything come of it?"

"A little something, but it's probably trivial. And how are you?"

"Doing okay. I'm back to writing. But I found this thing I probably should have handed over right away, but I forgot. Probably means nothing at all, but you never know, do you?"

"What kind of thing?"

"A sheet of paper from Olof Helander's office."

"We searched it."

"Then somebody was a bit sloppy."

"Hmm."

The elevator door opened, and they found themselves face to face with Jonny Munther. The detective superintendent looked pleased with himself. Julia extended her hand, a tactic to ward off any kissing of cheeks. Jonny pressed it briefly, then stepped into the elevator Julia and Carmen had just exited.

"I just wanted to—" Julia began, but Jonny waved her away.

"Got to swing by the IT unit. Wait in my office." He was about to say more, but the closing doors cut him off.

Julia turned to Carmen. "Has there been a breakthrough?"

"Not as far as I know. But he sure seemed in fine spirits."

Julia pulled the sheet of paper from her trouser pocket and unfolded it. Carmen Sánchez squinted as she studied the tidy columns of letters and numbers. "What's this thing?"

"I have no idea, but I found it beneath a stack of printer paper, so it's probably something Olle wanted to hide. Or maybe it's just trash. What do I know? But I thought that if the investigation comes across numbers that match these . . ."

"Right, thanks. I understand," said Carmen and handed it back. "Might be better if you give it to Jonny yourself."

"Why?"

Carmen gave Julia a slightly mocking look. "Don't you want to shine and be seen as competent? Maybe get something in return?"

"You know me that well?"

"By reputation. I've got some things to take care of, so . . ."

"I'll wait in his office."

9

Julia found Astrid Helander in Jonny's office with a much older man. Julia tried to recall what Olle's older brother Lasse had looked like but couldn't remember. That became irrelevant when the man introduced himself as Walter Berzelius, psychologist.

Julia held out a hand to Astrid, who was leaning with her back against the wall. "Hi, Astrid. Julia Malmros. Don't know if you remember me."

Astrid's hand was small and fragile in Julia's grasp, so Julia pressed it carefully. "Sure," said Astrid. "You gave me a puzzle on Knektholmen when I was ten. A thousand pieces. Took me a month to finish it."

"Oh, right. Probably a few too many. Sorry."

"And you were there when . . . with Kim. How is he?"

"Fine, as far as I know."

"Are you and Kim, like . . . together?"

Julia rubbed her neck, which was feeling unusually warm. "That's a question that doesn't have a simple answer."

"Okay." Astrid dropped the subject, much to Julia's relief, and turned her attention to a tacked-up sheet of paper completely filled with incomprehensible typing. She turned to Walter. "You can leave if you like. I can manage."

Walter checked his wristwatch. "Are you sure?"

"Yes. You have a patient at five thirty, don't you?"

"I do, but I can cancel and stay here if you want."

"Not necessary. See you the day after tomorrow. Hop to it, go cure."

Walter's mouth turned down at her expression. He got up from the visitor's chair, said a few words of farewell, and left Julia and Astrid together. Julia sneaked a peek at Astrid, who wore jeans torn at the knees. Her thin jacket might have come from some uniform. Under it she wore a T-shirt with the slogan "I think, therefore I'm vegan." Her eyes were heavily lined with kohl, so it was hard to make out her expression.

"How are things with you?" Julia asked.

Astrid shrugged. "Lots of folks want to know. Usually tell 'em 'I know I have what I need.'"

"Olle Adolphson."

"She hit the target! Two more and the little lady gets the cigar."

Julia remembered ten-year-old Astrid as a clever little thing, small for her age and looking much younger, but smart and verbally precocious. Looking like an eight-year-old and talking like a thirty-year-old. And she'd been sufficiently self-disciplined to complete a thousand-piece jigsaw puzzle.

"Are you okay staying with Lasse?"

Julia was impressed at how collected and easygoing Astrid seemed, considering what she'd gone through, but now the girl's expression darkened. A more resentful personality emerged. "It's all right. Don't want to discuss it."

"But he's nice to you?"

"Yeah. Nice. It's not that. Don't want to talk."

Astrid turned away and studied the enigmatic sheet on the announcement board. Julia looked at the Marc Chagall print showing the embraced couple flying high above the roofs of the town. Nothing more was said until Jonny Munther came in a few minutes later. He ignored Julia and went to Astrid. "Sorry you had to wait. I think that your . . ." Jonny sneaked a look at Julia before continuing. "Your insight is likely to be very useful. Thanks for taking the time. Carmen Sánchez will take you downstairs, if that's okay."

"It's okay," said Astrid. She adjusted her jacket, gave Julia a look, and said, "Say hi to Kim."

10

"What was her insight?" asked Julia after Astrid left.

"Nothing I can discuss, unfortunately," said Jonny Munther. "But I can go so far as to say that the net is closing around our beloved Norwegian."

"Frode Moe?"

"Did you mention any other Norwegian?"

"Do you have enough on him to—"

"Like I said, the investigation is moving along. What was it you wanted?"

The detective superintendent was curt and appeared impatient, so Julia took out the sheet of paper, put it on his desk, and repeated what she'd already told Carmen Sánchez. Jonny looked at the sheet. "Couldn't you just have sent us a scan of it?"

"I don't know. I thought that—"

"That you'd take the opportunity to snoop around a bit."

"Now you're being downright rude, Jonny. I'm really trying to help."

Jonny Munther sighed and rubbed his eyes. "Yeah, yeah. Sorry about that. But sometimes, Julia, you seem to forget that now you're a private individual who really shouldn't have anything at all to do with a police investigation. How's it going with that Ribbing guy?"

"Another private individual," Julia said bitterly. "Who's also made some contributions."

"And?"

"And—nothing. I don't know. Hasn't been heard from since Shanghai."

Her mention of Shanghai made Jonny Munther shake his head unhappily. "Yeah, that was a hell of a thing. You fished up a real pearl of a boyfriend for yourself."

"He's not—"

"Not? Really? What is he, then?"

Julia scowled. "A separate investigation would be needed to determine that."

11

Ramón Socarrás was sweating like a pig by the time Kim Ribbing got him into an armchair with Fedo's help. Large dark stains were obvious in the armpits of his white guayabera when he struggled out of his jacket and said, "I don't understand what you want with me."

In the last thirty minutes, Fly had looked up Ramón Socarrás's house in Miramar and discovered that its dimensions and gated community were far beyond what should be possible for his level in the hierarchy. Google Maps showed a guard tower at the entrance to the extensive grounds, a courtesy typical of ministerial residences.

"We know about your business with Futurig and Frode Moe," Fly said. "And that it's likely some of your superiors must also know. It wouldn't work, otherwise. But I don't think they're aware"—here they were staking everything on a win-or-lose bet—"that you're skimming off money and putting it in your own pocket."

Ramón's expression was the giveaway. They'd won. He cast all around to see if anyone could hear. What Fly had carefully neglected to mention was that yes, they knew there was dirty business going on but no idea what it might be.

"Let's take it from the beginning," said Kim. "You and Frode Moe met right here in 1993."

"How did you find that out?"

Kim leaned into Ramón Socarrás's face, opened his blue eyes wide, and snarled, "I ask the questions; you answer! You have just *one* chance to save your skin. *One* chance, that's if you tell me what I want to know. Otherwise, you're *fried.* Understand, buddy?"

Ramón nodded, gulped, and asked in a quivering voice, "Can I have something to drink?"

"No bartender here right now, unfortunately. Talk!"

Ramón Socarrás fumbled with a jacket pocket, pulled out a red handkerchief, and used it to wipe his face. Perspiration soaked the handkerchief with dark stains that Ramón inspected, shaking his head. "I really don't want to be part of it anymore. Wanted to get out for a long time. I want out of the whole business."

"That's fine," said Kim. "So you can regard this as an opportunity instead of a problem."

"Who are you guys?"

"I'm losing patience, Ramón," said Kim. He held out his phone to display a message in Spanish he'd drafted with Fly's help. It was addressed to Ramón Socarrás, Frode Moe, and Futurig. Attached were a couple of empty files to which he'd given ominous titles. Kim's thumb hovered over the send button. "Should we just get done with all this?"

Ramón Socarrás held up his hands as if the phone were a pistol aimed at his head. "No, no! Don't send it! I'll tell you everything!" Ramón's face was bright red, his lips were trembling, and he was fumbling so desperately at his shirt that Kim was afraid the man was going to have a heart attack right there in the bar.

"It was 1993," Fly said. "During the special period."

"Yes," said Ramón. "Hard times. We needed petroleum, and consultants and experts came from all over the world to help us prospect for oil. Frode Moe was one."

"We already know that," said Kim. "Continue."

"Yes, and Frode and I drew up a kind of special contract, and one evening he invited me here for a couple of drinks." Ramón nodded toward a spot in the room closer to the pool, presumably the place where the tête-à-tête with Frode Moe had taken place. "We talked about all sorts of things, but mostly we decided to stay in contact about how things were going and developing, to see if there might be possibilities of doing business in the future."

"And when did those possibilities materialize?"

Ramón tightened his lips. Kim sighed and held up his telephone again, his thumb hovering over the send button. "You're half an inch from blowing yourself away."

Ramón waved to forestall him. "*Cálmate.* Relax. It was in 2014 that . . . we'd had good relations with Venezuela and bought oil at good discounts. In return, we sent doctors and medical personnel, but after Hugo Chávez died, it all went to hell and we couldn't get fuel. Couldn't transport goods, couldn't—"

"I know the story," said Kim. "Keep going."

"Right, and by that time Frode Moe had gotten to a position where he could . . . make it available. *Proporcionar.*"

"I don't know that word."

"It just means 'sell oil,' that's all. But surely you know that."

"Naturally, *por supuesto*," Kim deadpanned. "What we're missing are the volumes."

Ramón shrugged. "Trivial in the overall situation but important at the margins. Maybe two hundred thousand barrels a month, about the same amount Venezuela had been delivering every two days at the best of times. But it was something."

"How many people know about this?" asked Kim.

"Just enough for it to work. The higher-ups don't ask questions provided we get our hands on the oil. So, now I've told you what you want to know." He got up, breathing hard. "I hope that you also . . ."

Kim flicked a finger at Fedo, who pushed Ramón back into his seat.

"We're not finished until I tell you we're finished," said Kim. The bartender, back from the pool, frowned uneasily at the little group. Kim signaled OK with his thumb and index finger and called, "A glass of mineral water, thank you." He didn't want Ramón Socarrás to die of heatstroke.

"Okay," said Kim. "So, you're handling the contacts with Frode to buy the oil from . . . who? Statoil?"

"No, no. This is a strictly private arrangement. We buy oil directly from him. Statoil doesn't sell oil to Cuba, because they don't want to have trouble with the United States."

"But where does Frode Moe get this oil?"

"That's up to him. He offers to sell; we need to buy. I don't know any more than that, and I don't need to know."

"Okay, I'll accept that," said Kim.

The bartender came over with a tray holding a glass of bubbly water. "Everything all right here?"

"Wonderful," responded Kim, giving him a banknote worth five convertible pesos. Ramón Socarrás seemed about to protest that there was nothing wonderful about the situation, but he shut his mouth when he saw Fedo stand up. Ramón gulped the water so greedily that liquid spurted from one side of his mouth and wet his collar.

"Just one more thing," said Kim. "You say you met Frode Moe . . . over there. But I happen to know that another person was present. Who was it?"

Ramón Socarrás put down the glass so suddenly that it slammed against the table and water sloshed out. He frantically shook his head. "You can threaten me however you want, evil man, but *that* I won't tell you."

"Because?"

"Because if you . . ." Ramón Socarrás pointed at Kim's phone. "If you send that to the wrong people, I'll go to prison for years and lose everything I own. But if I answer what you're asking now, I'm *dead*. Nothing you can say or do—"

"So you say, and you're quite convincing. But I'm extremely curious about this mystery man."

"Believe me, Santa Muerte. You don't want to know. Can you let me leave now?"

"Go," said Kim. "And can we agree that it's best for everyone that this conversation never occurred?"

When Ramón Socarrás got to his feet, his guayabera wasn't just blotched; it was so soaked with sweat that all the fabric had darkened. He wiped his face with his handkerchief again and glanced anxiously at Kim's phone. "Are you planning . . . to send that?"

"That depends," said Kim. "*Depende.* If you keep quiet, tell nobody about this conversation, and keep doing your job as usual, then you can get out of this with your sweaty hide intact."

Kim remained seated, pondering, after Ramón Socarrás had staggered out of the bar on rubbery legs. Frode Moe was selling two hundred thousand barrels of oil a month outside official channels. Kim checked oil prices and found that a barrel of crude was worth about fifty dollars. A million dollars a month, maybe more if Cuba had to pay a higher price because of the embargo.

"What was all that about a third person?" asked Fly.

"Something I learned in Shanghai," said Kim. "From a very reliable source."

"Can't you contact that source, then?"

"Not possible, unfortunately. That's the guy I mentioned. He was shot. But I need to locate that third man before he finds me."

"How will we do that?" asked Fly.

"I have an idea, or at least a possibility. Are you still in contact with your mama?"

12

Jonny Munther sat at his desk, examining the sheet of paper Julia had left. Maybe he'd been unnecessarily hard, but the detective superintendent generally disliked private detectives with their imaginings, and when the private detective in question also happened to be his ex-wife . . . still, Jonny Munther couldn't deny he'd given Julia a peek into the investigation. It was hardly surprising she was now assuming she'd be welcomed in.

The text that filled the page meant absolutely nothing to the detective superintendent. It wasn't encrypted, that was obvious, but the patterns indicated that it had been copied from something, but who knew what? HI? RV? AV? Why couldn't they come up with at least *one* thing in this case written out in plain text?

The phone rang and Jonny Munther answered. An excited Linus Tingwall exclaimed on the other end, "I've got it! I got it!"

"And that means?"

"I can read the text! There's a file called *Phoenix* in the office computer, just like that girl said, and when I uploaded that file to the iPad—"

"Better come up and show me," said Jonny Munther. "I'll tell the others."

Five minutes later they were all in the conference room except for William King, who was at his press briefing. Linus Tingwall was proud as punch when he plugged Olof Helander's iPad into the big screen so everyone could see.

The iPad display appeared. Linus Tingwall brought up the encrypted text. "This is what we had, right? Complete gibberish." He closed the file and opened a file titled *Phoenix* instead. A complicated set of instructions for folding a paper airplane came into view.

"I thought this was just what it seems to be," said Linus, pointing to the pattern of lines, "but I never checked the source code."

"And what's that, then?" asked Jonny Munther.

"The Rosetta Stone, animation and all."

"Rosetta Stone?" asked Christof Adler.

"The one they used to figure out Egyptian hieroglyphics," Linus Tingwall said. "It had a text written in three languages."

"Maybe the history lesson can wait," said Jonny Munther. "You mentioned animation?"

"Yeah, it's a pattern encryption, exactly what we'd given up hope for, and so all you need to do is upload the paper airplane's key pattern to the encrypted text, and *zap!* it's decrypted. Olof Helander even took the trouble to create an animated representation of the process. Watch this."

Linus Tingwall grabbed the *Phoenix* file and dropped it onto the encrypted document. The chaotic text appeared on the screen but then began moving. It folded progressively as if it were a sheet of paper someone was using to make a paper airplane. New combinations of letters and numbers formed and then folded again across one another into new combinations. Linus Tingwall chuckled. "Completely unnecessary. But cool!"

When the process had produced the image of a paper airplane, the page flattened and the fold lines stood out in bold, then aligned themselves in tidy rows.

"Ta-da!" said Linus Tingwall.

Ulrika went right up to the screen to examine the numbers and letters. The document's entries were listed chronologically, and on the fifteenth of each month a lengthy list of unidentified account numbers had transferred funds to a bank account Ulrika recognized. "The receiving account, that one," she said, "is the IBAN code for International Credentials and Holdings. Jointly owned by Olof Helander and Chen Bao."

"You got it, sister!" said Linus Tingwall and ran the mouse pointer down the list of other numbers. "And it won't be hard to track these, since we've got the numbers. Anybody want to take a guess? Who is making these cash payments?"

"Frode Moe?" said Carmen Sánchez.

"King Frode *in person*," said Linus Tingwall. "Every single one of these accounts belongs to him."

Ulrika's eyes moved down the long rows of numbers. She commented, "Not particularly large transfers, but taken together, they amount to more than a million kronor a month."

"Hold on," said Carmen Sánchez as Linus scrolled up through the document. "Let's see the end again." Linus went there, and Carmen pointed. "The last transfers are from April of this year. Nothing in May, none in June."

"Static on the line?" suggested Christof Adler.

"Oh, my God," said Jonny Munther. "Is that what your grandfather used to say?"

"I mean maybe something went wrong with the arrangement," Christof explained. "Maybe that's why Chen Bao flew to Stavanger."

"Maybe they got greedy," said Carmen Sánchez. "Wanted more."

"Could be," said Jonny Munther. "But we still haven't resolved the crucial point: What was Frode Moe *paying* for? And the first of you who says 'consulting services' gets busted to probationary status."

The room fell silent as they all sat staring at the screen as if another combined mental effort could get the numbers to reveal their secrets. Finally, Ulrika Boberg said, "My experience in the financial crimes unit was that it's typical to use complicated transfers like these for bribes."

"Okay," said Jonny Munther. "Suppose we test that hypothesis. Frode Moe was bribing Olof Helander and Chen Bao. To get them to do what?"

"Nothing at all," suggested Carmen Sánchez. "To keep their mouths shut."

"Possible. But in that case . . ."

"Wait, wait," said Ulrika Boberg, pointing at the screen. "Give me just a couple of minutes." She hurried to her computer, opened it, and started entering something, occasionally stopping to look up at the big screen, then tapping away again.

"Do we know by now how the killers arrived *in* Sweden?" asked Jonny Munther.

"Yes," Carmen Sánchez said. "No surprises there. They flew from Stavanger to Bromma the day before the massacre."

"Meaning the day *after* Chen Bao was in Stavanger?"

"Correct."

"Again, just hypothetically," said Jonny Munther, "we could imagine a meeting between Chen Bao and Frode Moe that didn't turn out well. Let's say, for example, that Chen Bao was insisting on more money for something involving the business with the oil rigs. The Norwegian guy refuses, the Chinese fellow flies to Sweden after threatening to expose some big dirty business if Moe doesn't reconsider. And then things happened the way they did on Midsummer Eve."

Carmen Sánchez shook her head. "That sounds plausible except for the idea of Moe calling in two professional killers from China. It's hard for me to see him picking up his phone and saying, *Hello, is this the Chinese Mafia? Could you murder a few people for me?* That's beyond me. And not practical at all."

"Do we have a printout of Frode Moe's phone calls?" asked Christof Adler.

"Hardly likely he'd be stupid enough to use his own phone for something like this," said Carmen Sánchez, "if he's as slippery as we think he is. But sure, I'll check with Telenor if Liselott approves it."

"Somebody should check the Bromma Airport security cameras too," said Jonny Munther. "It's not impossible someone might have met them there to give them instructions about the job. Do they keep video recordings this long?"

"I think they do," said Carmen Sánchez. "Nowadays."

Ulrika Boberg snapped her fingers. "Aha, got it! You've got a woman here with a super memory! Holy smokes, am I good!"

Everyone around the table sat in silent astonishment at Ulrika's unexpected crowing. When she looked up and saw their expressions, she realized what she'd just said. She hunched over just a bit. "It's actually *okay* to give yourself a pat on the back from time to time."

"Absolutely," said Jonny Munther. "What is it you came up with?"

Ulrika pointed to the screen. "Okay, so if you add together all those smaller payments, the way I just did, you come up with a monthly sum. It varies by up to two hundred thousand, but the interesting thing is when you compare them with the money Frode Moe receives from Cuba every month." Ulrika gave Linus Tingwall a look. "As we say around here: Anybody want to take a guess?"

"It's a certain percentage," said Carmen Sánchez.

"Exactly!" cried Ulrika. "Cuba's CUPET pays Frode Moe monthly, and each following month he pays exactly ten percent of that amount to International Credentials and Holdings. They had him by the balls and were squeezing tight!"

Another lengthy silence around the table. Again Ulrika hunched over when she realized what she'd said.

13

The dark den of the Angel Pub seemed to reach out to Julia as she walked back from the underground station, but she resisted. She could have a glass or two of wine at her computer. She'd been intrigued by something Carmen Sánchez had said.

Once she'd settled at her computer with a wineglass within reach, she tapped *Chen Min* into Google Translate and copied the Chinese characters into Facebook's search field. A long list of users appeared, but she quickly located the woman she wanted because Chen Min's profile image showed her hugging a porcelain cat.

A few minutes of scrolling through Chen Min's photos left her feeling dizzy. It was incredible and grotesque to see how many different sorts of porcelain cats she had, and Julia didn't see how that menagerie of small beasts with frozen expressions could have any relevance at all for the investigation.

Chen Min looked fragile and nervous as she stood holding what Julia assumed was her latest acquisition. She seemed to plead *Now do you like me?* or *Do you at least like my cat, please, do you?* If there'd ever been the slightest suspicion that Chen Min was the target of the Midsummer Eve attack, surely these images had blown it away. This woman probably wasn't capable of slapping a mosquito, even if it was biting her.

A new cat every single day. Julia studied the images intently, which meant it took quite a while for her to get to the one she assumed Carmen Sánchez had referred to when she said she'd found "a little something."

That was probably the open door that revealed an office. A diagram showing the cross section of an oil platform. Julia clicked on the photo, took a screenshot, and zoomed in on that part. The image melted into colorful dots and the text was illegible, but there was something familiar about the rig's *shape*. Julia stared at the thin lines, trying to extract a pure form. For some reason, the name of a Norwegian author popped into her mind.

Of course! I'm a moron!

When they'd investigated the disappearance of Edward Dahlberg, they'd learned that the rigs Frode Moe leased were named after Norwegian writers, Bjørnstjerne Bjørnson and Sigrid Undset, but there were three named after the author who was probably the greatest of them all: Henrik Ibsen. Those were Henrik Ibsen One, Two, and Three—HI1, HI2, HI3—and those must be the references on the page she'd found in Olof Helander's office.

Julia picked up her phone to call Jonny Munther. This was the sort of tip from a "private individual" that her ex-husband might be able to use.

14

Fly flagged down a Lada with a hand-painted taxi sign on the roof. She crammed herself into the back seat with Fedo. Kim sat up front and said, "Plaza Vieja." The taxi rumbled off and squealed like a dying dog as it turned the corner and went down toward the Malecón.

They approached their destination five minutes later. Since no vehicles were allowed onto the plaza, the driver let them off a couple of blocks away. It was a relief to get out of the taxi; the vehicle was hot as a pizza oven and the reek of gas fumes rose from a hole in the floor.

The houses around them looked about to collapse. Large chunks of stucco and mortar had fallen off the facades; a couple of balconies were propped up with wooden beams. Clothes were hung to dry on lines across the street that competed for space with tangles of electric cable swaying freely in the air. Birdsong reached them from small wooden cages on the balconies.

They walked only one block and found themselves in another world. The facades were undamaged and painted in warm pastels, window grilles were free of rust, and front doors were of polished wood with glittering brass handles. Even the birdsong sounded more cheerful.

"Tourist zone," Fly muttered. "Really *authentic*."

The street was crowded with shops selling cheap souvenirs of Cuba. License plates, T-shirts, caps, metal models of old American cars crafted from tin cans, and paintings of Ernest Hemingway. And Che

Guevara, Che Guevara—Che Guevara's image rendered on anything and everything imaginable.

Fedo started singing. With a surprisingly light, clear tenor, he sang a lovely melody about *la clara* and *Commandante Che Guevara.* They reached the Plaza Vieja and walked up to a statue of a naked woman astride a rooster with a pitchfork over her shoulder.

"Your mama works *here*?" exclaimed Kim.

Fly's expression was sullen. "Wait and see!"

Fly brought them into a street crammed with tourists. Kim saw the street sign: "Mercaderes." They had to step aside to get by a big group of Chinese tourists wearing visors. The group followed a guide holding up a banner at the end of a long pole. Kim realized he'd automatically begun scanning their faces to detect anyone looking hostile.

Buskers and choir groups stood playing here and there along the street. Kim heard the notes of the unofficial national anthem "Chan Chan," which he'd never been able to decipher. Stands offered garments and paintings for sale, and before they'd gone less than a hundred yards, Kim had to say "*No, gracias*" to five persons who offered either nightclub tickets or taxi services.

They reached a street corner where a couple of tourists were snapping photos of a rotund older Cuban woman in "traditional" dress, a cloth bound on her head, a cigar in her mouth, and a little parrot on her shoulder. The sign next to her made it clear that the charge for each pose was one convertible peso. Tourists clustered around to have their portraits taken with this *unique* personage they'd found on the street. They posed holding their thumbs up.

"My mama," Fly said.

The woman sitting on a little stool was darker skinned than her daughter, and the black hair shot with gray that stuck out from her headcloth had a slight curl. Though she was overweight, tending to fat, her movements were graceful, and she had remarkably small hands with small fingers. Responding to tourists' encouragement, she used them to take the cigar out of her mouth before firing off a bright, practiced smile.

When the session was finished, Fly went to the woman and said something about "the Swede." The woman looked up, and this time her smile was genuine. Her parrot flapped its wings as she got to her feet, embraced Kim Ribbing, and pressed him into her bounteous bosom.

"Gracias, mi amor," the woman whispered into Kim's ear. "My girl bought herself a proper front door, and now she's talking about going back to her studies."

"That makes me happy," said Kim once the woman had released him. She kept hold of Kim's shoulder so she could inspect him. She gazed at his long black hair and then down at Santa Muerte on his chest. Even the parrot cocked its head as if it found Kim extremely interesting.

"Mother of God, my boy," the woman said. "You surely do look like a ghost."

"Thanks," said Kim. "That's my, how to say it, my intention. *Mi objectivo.*"

"A ghost sent from heaven, then," the woman said. "My name is Celia."

"Kim."

The woman repeated his name and let him go so she could pat Fedo's cheek. "And you there, my favorite big bear. How are you?"

"Good," said Fedo. "I got ice cream. But Zlatan asked about something."

"Zlatan?"

"The Swedish guy."

"Aha," Celia said. "Let's get into the shade. Marislady, you take Hector."

Fly rolled her eyes and placed her index finger on her mama's shoulder. This seemed to be routine, for the parrot quickly stepped onto it and allowed her to lift it. Fly squatted and held Hector out to the open door of a little wooden cage next to the platform. Hector said "Auck!" and went inside.

Celia jerked a thumb at two other women in traditional garb stationed a little farther down the street. "Twice as many people want to take my photo," she whispered, "and that's thanks to Hector." She picked up the cage, Fly collected the stool and the sign, and the group moved into a side street shaded from the sun.

Celia dropped onto her stool, and the others sat around her on the sidewalk. Kim said, "It's about something that happened during the special period."

Celia made the sign of the cross. "Mother of God, may such days never visit us again!"

"No," agreed Kim. "Fl—Marislady told me you used to . . . work at the Habana Libre."

Celia gave Fly a reproachful glance; Fly shrugged. Kim took out his phone, where he'd pre-loaded an image of Frode Moe from the end of the 1990s. He held it out to show Celia. "Did you ever meet this man? He's from Norway and his name is Frode Moe."

Celia leaned forward for a closer look. She probably needed glasses but didn't want them to interfere with her look of "authenticity." Kim put the phone closer to her eyes. Celia nodded slowly. "*Sí.* I recognize him. Never had him as a client."

"Know if he used to be seen with another man?"

Celia shook her head. "Sorry, son, I don't remember anyone else. But there were so many of 'em who came and went, if you know what I mean."

Kim nodded, feeling his heart sink. He'd known this was a shot in the dark but had hoped for the best. With Celia's negative report he'd probably reached the end of the road as far as information about the third man was concerned.

Then Celia's face lit up. She tapped her temple. "Ah!" she said. "Now I remember. Lizaveta used to go off with that Norway man. Maybe she'll remember something."

"Lizaveta?"

"Right," said Celia and pointed down the street. "She lives a couple of blocks that way. She . . . doesn't get out too often, but we can make a little house call." Celia turned to Fedo. "Can you stay here to watch Hector?"

"Naw," said Fedo. "I wanna come too. But I can carry him." Fedo picked up the cage with exaggerated ease and added, "I'm really strong."

"Does he talk at all?" asked Kim, pointing at Hector as they made their way down the street.

"Only two words," answered Celia. "That's why I'd prefer not to have him with us." She looked at the cage swinging in Fedo's hand. "Talk!"

"Puta madre!" said Hector.

15

An example of Cubans' usual optimistic calculations of distance, the "couple" of blocks turned out to be seven. To get there, they'd left the tourist zone behind and gone deep into a rougher Old Havana neighborhood where another maze of clotheslines and electric cables stood out against the sky.

They went to a doorway where a warped wooden door hung partly off its hinges and went up a dark stair so narrow that it accommodated only one person at a time. Celia's broad haunches brushed against the walls and the rickety handrail as she moaned her way upward, the others following after. Her wide buttocks shook and quivered in Kim's face like an undulating beanbag.

Celia had to stop on the landing two floors up, leaning over to clutch her thighs and catch her breath before she could press the buzzer by a door painted blue. There was no response. She knocked instead. "Veta? Are you in there?" She turned to reassure Kim. "Don't worry. She's *always* at home."

Silence for a moment, then there was a squeaking and a sigh from within. The squeaking came closer. A key turned in the lock, and the door opened. You might call the woman sitting in a wheelchair just across the threshold Celia's exact opposite. Celia was hugely round and healthy, while this woman was skeletal and seemed afflicted by some grave disease. The skin of her legs was wrinkled as gray silk, and her skull was clearly visible behind her face. She peered out into the dark stairwell. "Celia? Is that you?"

"It's me, my love." Celia leaned over to kiss the woman's sunken cheek. It wasn't unusual for Cubans to call anyone, even foreigners, "my love," and between friends it was almost obligatory. Fly did the same. Lizaveta pointed a trembling finger through the doorway toward the unlighted landing and asked, "What kind of people did you bring up here?"

"Friends," Celia said. "They wanted to ask you something."

"*Sí, sí,* come on in." They did. "Ah, it's you, Fedo. You can push my chair for me."

Fedo handed the parrot cage to Fly, took the wheelchair handles, and turned it to face inward.

"The kitchen," said Lizaveta. "Push me into the kitchen. And who's that one, looking like a demon out of hell?"

"His name is Kim," said Fedo. "But we call him Zlatan, 'cause he's from Sweden. Zlatan comes from there too."

As the squeaky wheelchair rolled toward the kitchen, Celia whispered into Kim's ear. "They used to call her the Skinny Girl, *La Flaca,* even back then. Then she fell down the stairs, and . . . Mother of God, that's just how things can happen."

The apartment was as shabby and dilapidated as the rest of the building. The wooden floors had settled and were buckled and warped, the wallpaper was peeling, fissures and cracks were visible in the ceiling. In contrast, the rooms were sparsely furnished but well kept, so Lizaveta must have had some sort of housekeeping help.

The kitchen looked out over the street and was far better lit than the interior hall. Maybe the power was out, as often happened. Fedo pushed Lizaveta to a little table with three stools. Celia settled onto one with a groan as Kim and Fedo took the others. Fly sat on the counter with Hector's cage beside her.

"So, then?" said Lizaveta. "What was it you wanted to ask?"

Celia nodded toward Kim. He said, "Celia told us you worked at the Habana Libre during the special period, and also that"—Kim held out his phone with the photo of Frode Moe—"you used to . . . accompany this person."

Lizaveta's body was a ruin, but there obviously was nothing wrong with her vision. She glanced at the photo, nodded, and said, "That's right. Harald. Don't know if that was his name, but that's what he said."

Not surprising. Already back in the 1990s King Frode had taken as his alias the name of the Norwegian head of state for his amusements.

"His name's Frode," said Kim. "Frode Moe. But what interests me more is that he used to go around with another person. Right?"

"Hmm," said Lizaveta. She looked from the photo to Fedo. "Hmm, hmm."

"What's the matter?" asked Kim.

"If I'm going to discuss it . . ."

"Puta madre!" exclaimed Hector, which made Lizaveta raise her thin eyebrows. "Couldn't have said it better myself. What I'm going to say isn't fit for your ears, Fedo. Go wait in the living room."

Fedo felt wronged. "Sure it fits them! And I don't wanna be all alone in the living room. It's dark and creepy in there!"

"I'll go with you," said Fly. She tugged his arm and got him up. When Fedo got to the kitchen door, he changed his mind and came back to pick up the cage so Hector wouldn't stick his beak into the conversation again. After they'd closed the kitchen door behind them, Lizaveta said, "This here's not appropriate for children's ears, and Fedo . . . well, you know how it is with him?"

"Sure," said Kim. "I know."

Lizaveta nodded, and shifted her weight in the wheelchair, making it creak, before she said, "Sometimes men came along with . . . special requests. Harald there did that one time."

Kim didn't bother to correct Lizaveta about Frode Moe's name. The elderly woman threaded her fingers together and pressed them to her chest, sighed, and said, "A person had to take whatever was on offer, if you know what I mean. Those were hard times and . . . anyway, one day Harald came and asked if I would agree to a *triangulo*. Understand?"

"An extra man."

"Yes. He and this other man had some important agreement and wanted to celebrate it by getting . . . so to speak . . . together."

"I understand. People have astonishing ways of celebrating."

Lizaveta tilted her head, and her eyes got hard when she looked at Kim. "I'm not at all comfortable telling this to a man, but you don't seem to be one of *those* men. You look more like a woman, in fact."

"Thanks. Guess it's better than a demon from hell."

"Sorry about that. Where was I?" Lizaveta grimaced in annoyance and looked at the wall. "Yes. Harald was in front, and the other man was behind . . . *sí*, the other one wanted to get in by the back door, you understand . . . that wasn't part of the deal, and when I tried to stop him, he got violent, really violent, and took what he wanted."

Lizaveta rubbed her paper-thin eyelids and loosed a deep sigh. "Those were hard times. Horrible ones, sometimes."

"Horrible times," Celia echoed her.

"I'm sorry," said Kim. "But can you describe that other man?"

"Asian," Lizaveta said. "As for his face . . ."

"This him?" said Kim and held out the phone to show Chen Bao.

Lizaveta shook her head so hard that the skin beneath her sharp chin shook. She put her index fingers to the corners of her eyes, squinted, and turned down the corners of her mouth as far as possible. Since the chase in Shanghai, Kim had been bothered by a nagging suspicion, and now he pulled up a photo of Bruce Li from around the time he'd started to work for the Foreign Ministry. He showed Lizaveta. "This one?"

Something grim came into Lizaveta's expression. "Yes. He was the one. You don't forget a face like that in a hurry."

16

Julia Malmros's doorbell rang, so she went and opened the door. Bruce Li was standing on the landing, his hands in the pockets of a thin summer jacket. He gave Julia a look that seemed to say that all his worries and sorrows stemmed from the woman in the door before him.

"Hi, Bruce. Come in."

Bruce Li nodded and stepped into her hall. He continued directly into the living room without removing his shoes or taking his hands out of his pockets. Julia followed and asked, "What was so important that you couldn't discuss it on the phone?"

Bruce Li sank into an armchair and nodded to indicate Julia should take the sofa. His behavior was unheard of for a visitor in Sweden, but there was lots about Bruce Li that was unheard of. Julia sat on the very edge of the sofa and rested her elbows on her knees as she looked inquisitively toward Bruce Li. He said, "I really despise sounding melodramatic, but in the current situation . . ."

From his pocket Bruce Li pulled a Glock with a silencer and aimed it squarely at Julia's chest. "I need to know how much you know. And how much the police know."

Julia sat up in surprise. Her jaw fell and trembled. Eventually she managed to say, "Good God, Bruce, what are you doing?"

"What I must, in the current situation."

"But why . . . how?"

Bruce Li rolled his eyes. "Can you try to focus? *I'm* the one asking the questions."

Julia gulped and tried to keep her voice steady. "Why do you think I know anything at all?"

Bruce Li grimaced. "If you please, can we skip this step? I don't want to kneecap you and blow off your elbows to make you talk. I don't know if I mentioned that I like you and would gladly have . . . but, whatever."

Julia's voice fell apart. "But how . . . do you . . . know I . . . know anything?"

"Ribbing. My contacts in Shanghai and Havana have explained to me he has dug up a great deal more information than is appropriate. And I presume he has shared his information with you."

"But you—why? Who . . . are you? Are you . . . China?"

One side of Bruce Li's mouth twitched. "You're asking if I'm China?"

"No, I mean . . ." Julia put her hands to her face and took several deep breaths. She lowered her hands and her voice was steadier. "Working . . . are you working for China?"

"Of course," said Bruce Li. "But pay attention now: I have the weapon, and that gives me the right to ask the questions."

"This explains a lot," commented Julia.

"So glad to hear it," said Bruce Li without changing expression. "What did Ribbing find out in Shanghai?"

"Are you planning . . . to *kill* me?"

"I'm planning to shoot you right here and now if you don't get yourself together and start talking," said Bruce Li, aiming directly at Julia's forehead.

Julia held up her hands. "Give me just a moment, please." She grabbed her thighs tight, straightened up, and inhaled deeply. Finally, she let out the air in a long, noisy exhalation and said, "Kim found out that everything started at the Hotel Habana Libre early in the 1990s. Frode Moe and another man met a Cuban official. The second man, was that you?"

"Yes. Those were happy times." It always seemed absurd when Bruce Li mentioned happiness or good fortune, because his expression never showed any hint that he'd ever experienced those emotions. He waved the pistol at Julia. "And how did he find Ramón Socarrás?"

"He hacked El Paquete."

"What package?"

"It's Cuba's version of . . ." Julia let it go, made a fist of one hand, and thumped herself on the chest a couple of times before continuing. "Kim monitored internet traffic for certain keywords. That's what led him to someone named Ramón Socarrás."

"From whom Ribbing learned that . . . ?"

"That Frode was selling oil to Cuba illegally." Julia shook her head and almost sniffled. "That was so *simple*."

Bruce Li had seemed determined to ignore any comments from Julia, but now he shrugged and asked, "What was simple?"

"Your agreement with Moe about the future. How everything fell into place when you rose in the ministry and he started buying oil rigs. You could manipulate ChengBa into paying bribes to get contracts with Frode Moe, contracts that were already set up." Julia appeared momentarily to forget the gun as she giggled nervously. "So simple. A senior government employee in one country and a big businessman in another have a secret agreement. That opens up so many enormous opportunities."

"That's true," said Bruce Li, nodding thoughtfully, as if he'd never considered it quite that way. "That is true. And may I ask how much you've documented of what you learned?"

"All of it."

"Excellent. If you'd answered differently, I'd have assumed you were lying." Bruce Li gestured with the pistol toward Julia's computer. "May I ask you to be so kind as to delete that documentation?"

Bruce Li stood at her back as Julia moved all the documents about Futurig, Frode Moe, and other subjects associated with the investigation into the wastebasket and deleted them permanently.

"I assumed you used the cloud as well," said Bruce Li and pressed the gun's muzzle to her neck. "And no lies, please."

It took several tries for Julia to log into her cloud service because her hands were trembling and her fingers were sweaty. Bruce Li watched closely as she permanently deleted all relevant files before returning to the sofa. Bruce Li picked up the half-filled glass of red wine she'd left by the laptop and poured it over the keyboard. Crackling sounds came from inside the laptop, the screen flared several times, and then it went dead.

"Of course, I will take this with me. Afterward," said Bruce Li once he'd returned to the armchair. "A person can never be too careful."

"After what?" asked Julia in a whisper.

"You know," said Bruce Li. "*Those who see the face of the Phantom* and so on."

"May I ask one question?" asked Julia.

Bruce Li glanced at his wristwatch as if he had some important appointment to attend after shooting Julia. He waved, giving her permission.

"Those tampered rigs," said Julia. "I assume you arranged that by coordinating with ChengBa."

"Oh dear," said Bruce Li. "You knew about *that*, also? That's bad, very bad. It was truly lucky for us that I made this little visit."

Julia couldn't really agree, but she took the opportunity to ask, "The tampering was with measurement of volumes, wasn't it? Something in the metering equipment was altered so the rig extracted more oil than was recorded. And the extra was sold on to Cuba."

"What more can I add?" asked Bruce Li.

"What I don't understand is how Olof Helander and Chen Bao—"

"*One* question, we said," said Bruce Li. "I think you'll agree with me that it's best if we handle this business *simply*, as you said, and as effectively as possible." Bruce Li tapped the pistol barrel on the floor. "So, will you be so kind as to kneel and turn your back to me?

I assure you that this is the most . . . merciful way to proceed in these circumstances."

"Please, Bruce, I don't want to die."

"No, and I must admit that it's unfortunate that you must, but that's how it is. Drawing it out is meaningless. Onto your knees, Julia."

Julia slowly knelt. She asked, "It was you who hired the killers, wasn't it?"

"Of course. Frode Moe isn't particularly squeamish about such things, but he lacks the right contacts."

Julia slowly began to shift to turn her back to Bruce Li. She signaled.

"Don't move!" shouted Jonny Munther as he stepped out of Julia's bedroom holding his Sig Sauer. Carmen Sánchez came behind him, scowling and holding out her service arm. "We have two weapons aimed at you," said Jonny Munther to Bruce Li's back. "Put yours down!"

Bruce Li nodded heavily as if he'd been expecting exactly this. He leaned over Julia's coffee table and deposited his pistol. Then he sagged back into the armchair and emptied his lungs in a sigh so deep that it should have covered him in a black cloud.

Jonny Munther picked up the Glock, took out the magazine, and set the safety before stuffing it into his pocket. "Good Lord, Julia. How much ice are you carrying in your guts? I wouldn't have waited another second, even if you hadn't signaled."

"No ice," said Julia. She held up her violently shaking hands. "Paralysis. If I'd had ice, it would have melted by now." Julia's body seemed to have turned to jelly. She remained on her knees because she knew her legs wouldn't hold her up. During her police career she'd been threatened at gunpoint a couple of times, but she'd never faced *execution.*

Carmen Sánchez lowered her weapon and holstered it with a relieved expression. She got down next to Julia, put a hand on her shoulder, and asked, "How are you? Can I help you up?"

Julia shook her head. "I . . . I'll be okay. Got to just . . . take a moment."

Before Carmen got up, she gently punched Julia's shoulder. "Well done. I don't think I could have managed that."

From the depths of the armchair, Bruce Li said, "May one be allowed to ask a question?"

"We'll have plenty of questions to ask *you*," said Jonny Munther. "But sure. Go ahead."

"All of this," said Bruce Li with a gesture taking in the living room and the last few minutes, "was obviously a lie. Theater from you, Julia. Quite convincing, let me congratulate you. But—"

"Not much acting required," said Julia, hugging herself to stop her shaking.

"No," said Bruce Li. "But even so. How was it that you *knew*? About me?"

"Kim telephoned from Havana. He told me," said Julia, pushing up onto the sofa without using her hands. Even *sitting* straight was difficult in her present condition. She swallowed a couple of times. "And just after we finished our conversation, you called to say you wanted to see me. I phoned Jonny and Carmen."

"Aha," said Bruce Li. "That's why you didn't agree to meet immediately. So you would have time to prepare everyone's little . . . surprise. I understand and thank you for the explanation."

"That time you came to the station," said Jonny Munther, "and gave us the killers' identities. You knew that we'd find them sometime, and you wanted to appear helpful so no one would suspect you after the incident in Shanghai."

"Certainly. Ribbing had seen them, after all, and I presumed you weren't so dumb as to forget to go through the passenger lists."

"It's touching to hear that you have such confidence in our police work," said Jonny Munther, unclipping a pair of handcuffs from his belt. "Can you stand up and put your hands behind your back?"

Bruce Li clambered out of the armchair and did so. Jonny Munther cuffed him and prodded him toward the front door. Carmen Sánchez gave Julia a full salute. Julia nodded stiffly and tried to smile.

17

Kim Ribbing, Fly, Fedo, and Celia sat around a table in the Habana Libre lobby, with farewell mojitos. Fedo had a Cristal. Before leaving Lizaveta's flat, Kim had tucked a little money in her breadbox. A *lot* of money, calculated in local currency.

"You really have to go already?" asked Fly, sucking the last of her drink through a straw so that it made slurping noises in the bottom of the glass.

"Don't *have* to," said Kim. "I choose to. There's still things to take care of, and I think they're best handled in Sweden. Besides, I'm starting to feel a little homesick. Or maybe it's triple jet lag, I don't know."

"What was all that about, really?" asked Celia.

"My taxi's waiting. It would take me too long. Fly can tell you."

"I can tell you too!" exclaimed Fedo, sounding slighted.

"Okay," Kim said and finished his drink. "Got to go. I told Ramón Socarrás I'd keep his name out of this as long as he keeps quiet, but I don't know what the Swedish police will turn up. Let me know if there's a problem."

Fly flung her hands up toward the chandelier as if putting her fate into God's hands. "What could you do?"

"I can do a lot," said Kim. "Didn't you notice?"

Kim didn't much care for formal farewells. All too often they involved a lot of unnecessary body contact. When he saw both Fly and

Fedo were getting up from their chairs, he backed away a step and said, "That's good, let's leave it at that. *Hasta luego,* we'll meet again."

Fly lifted her empty glass as a toast. "A pleasure! Just to get to live for a time in this place. It's a shame we never got to try out the pool."

"Oh," said Kim. "Speaking of that. I paid for your rooms for a week. Breakfast and minibar included. Enjoy yourselves."

Kim turned and left, but he did see Fedo raise both arms high in victorious celebration.

IX

Stavanger

1

The book *101 Paper Airplanes* lay open on the kitchen table before Astrid Helander. She was sitting with a stack of blank pages, trying to relearn patterns that had once been familiar. For the moment she was concentrating on folding a Phoenix, and the precise motions, remembered from childhood, brought tears to her eyes. The tears overflowed, dropped, and spotted the paper.

Grief had gradually taken a serious hold on her. Her angry conflicts with her parents had given way in her memories to scenes and images from when she was younger. Now there was no one else who remembered them. She alone would remember her childhood.

Astrid sniffled, wiped the tears from her eyes, and kept folding. It didn't help that she'd gradually begun to dislike living with her uncle. He never said he considered Astrid a burden or an intrusion, but she was reading subtle signs. He'd made it clear she wouldn't be allowed to leave "home" before turning sixteen, and she needed to learn basic skills before that. She was going to have to endure two years of living in this unpleasant alienation.

Astrid fidgeted with the emerald ring and then pulled it off her finger. She wouldn't be allowed to access any other assets until her eighteenth birthday. But she had her ways. As a twelve-year-old, she'd begun conning people to augment her allowance. Astrid contemplated the glittering jewel. A genuine emerald ring could be useful for a scammer like herself.

She slipped the ring back on, did the last fold, picked up scissors, clipped out tail feathers, and held up the paper airplane. The shape wasn't quite right and it was tearstained, but it looked flightworthy.

She went to the living room and opened the window that looked over the Karlberg Canal. A mild summer wind caressed her face and dried her cheeks. She took a deep breath and felt the lump in her throat start to loosen. She held the airplane over her shoulder, moved her arm in a gentle arc, and let it go.

Farewell to my tears.

Phoenix's wings caught the breeze, it rose, dipped, and rose again on its way toward the canal. As it went gliding over the water and the Kungsholm shore, an invisible jolt sent it diving. It struck the sidewalk right in front of a girl the same age as Astrid.

The girl squatted, picked Phoenix up, and looked around. She saw Astrid in the open window and waved in greeting. Astrid smiled and waved back. The world was out there after all. Someday she would fly free as well.

2

Liselott Ahrnander had requested an arrest warrant for Bruce Li the previous evening, and in the morning the judge immediately approved it. Bruce Li was now officially in custody, and they'd confiscated his computers and phones. Those were expected to provide irrefutable evidence of his criminal activities.

Jonny Munther doubted that the man was so careless as to hire the killers in a manner that could be traced, but even if nothing else turned up, they had his admissions to Julia Malmros in her apartment. The conversation had been recorded via a telephone hidden in Julia's bookcase, and two police officers had heard every word.

Jonny Munther was now seated in Liselott Ahrnander's room in the public prosecutor's offices. It was airy and full of light, but Jonny Munther preferred his own with its view over Kronoberg Park. Liselott's view was limited to the Östra Real high school gym.

Liselott put down Jonny Munther's preliminary report, which she'd just read. "This idea of using a private individual as bait isn't something I'd have approved."

"We were forced to move fast," said Jonny Munther. "Wasn't possible to run it up the flagpole. And Julia knew exactly what she was getting into."

"And what if it had gone wrong? Let's suppose that this Bruce Li individual *hadn't* behaved like a film gangster but just stepped in and gunned Malmros down?"

"I would have taken full responsibility. But we had our sights on him the whole time. Literally. Our pistol sights."

"Hmm. Hmm. Did the detainee say anything when interrogated?"

"Silent as the Great Wall of China. I talked to people at the Foreign Ministry who mentioned suspicions someone was leaking; the Chinese often seemed to be informed in advance of Swedish diplomatic initiatives. They, at least, are pleased as punch. The ministry guys, that is. And of course the Chinese deny the existence of any informer."

"Naturally. Can that be established as evidence?"

"Depends on what we can shake out of Bruce Li's electronics, but it's likely a whole lot will come loose if we shake hard enough."

"Let's cross our fingers," said Liselott Ahrnander. "And the Norwegian? Frode Moe?"

"We've got enough to draw up charges for major financial crimes but probably can't tie him to the murders. He's gone underground, but we're looking for him and so are the Norwegian police."

"Should I report him to Europol? Interpol?"

"No hurry. His bank accounts are frozen. He'll have to stick his nose out from somewhere eventually."

"All right, that'll do," said Liselott Ahrnander. She got up, went to the window, and looked out. When she turned back to Jonny Munther, a little smile was playing around her lips. "And William King? How did that go?"

"Oh, him," said Jonny Munther. "He's bounding around happy as a spawning salmon, since this afternoon he gets to tell the press we detained someone and have strong evidence. The King will probably spin the story to imply he himself carried out the arrest."

"But you know what you did."

"Sure," said Jonny Munther. "My bit. I did my bit. Like I always do."

3

Julia Malmros held her phone as she wandered around in her flat. Kim Ribbing's connecting flight from Paris was due just after two o'clock. By a quarter past two Julia was getting worried and regretted she hadn't taken a taxi to meet him. She knew that would have made Kim feel uncomfortable. He wanted to come and go without ceremony.

The problem was that Bruce Li had destroyed Julia's laptop, and if an alarm message came from Kim, she wouldn't get it. He'd phoned right after boarding and was going to call when he arrived. Nothing bad was likely to happen, but Julia had been glad to have that emergency signal as a contingency. Just in case. She'd never had such a device before, but the signal's inaccessibility now worried her. Probably for nothing.

After Carmen Sánchez and Jonny Munther had taken Bruce Li away, Julia had drunk a couple of glasses of wine, taken a sleeping pill, and—to her own surprise—slept through the night, serenely unaffected by disturbing memories.

In the morning she'd taken out her old tower computer to work on the new Åsa Fors story but had managed only a few edits of the text pulled down from the cloud. She'd made a stab at writing a new beginning to *Sandstorm* introducing the characters who'd replace Blomkvist and Salander, but it felt flat and bloodless. Throughout this, her thoughts kept wandering back to Kim.

Julia had given up her writing exercise by about half past two and concentrated instead on monitoring her phone. From time to time she called up the photo of the page of notations she'd found in Olof Helander's office. Jonny Munther had commented the night before that Ulrika Boberg believed the letters RV stood for "reported value" and AV meant "actual value," but they'd made no further progress. Julia had sent Kim that information. She didn't know what it meant, but she was relaying everything that came up.

Julia's heart skipped a beat when her phone rang just before two thirty. She grabbed it up. "Yes? Hello?"

"I'm here," said Kim. "Arlanda Airport. On my way to the bike."

"And it's . . . everything's calm?"

"Yeah."

"I've—" began Julia but put an imaginary pistol to her temple. "I thought about you. A lot."

"Uh-huh, sure. Gotta go now."

Julia pulled the imaginary trigger, *bam!* but asked anyway. "Coming here?"

"We'll see. Got some stuff to deal with. Maybe later. We'll phone."

Kim ended the call before she could say anything more. It was so easy to imagine things about their relationship when she fantasized alone but a lot harder when Kim himself was involved. Julia remained seated on the sofa for a long time, feeling baffled.

Then she quickly got up. Kim was back, and all was well. She could stop circling round the phone and relax a bit. Julia set her phone on the desk and left the apartment for an undisturbed afternoon of enjoying the summer.

I'm leaving the table . . .

4

"Maybe later. We'll phone."

Kim ended the call and dropped the phone into his backpack. *I thought about you. A lot.* Sounded like reaching out to encourage a closer relationship, didn't it? Kim didn't know what attitude he should take to that.

Kim set his backpack over one shoulder, passed the parking garage, and walked toward the open lot where he'd left his Honda. From the taxi on the way to Havana's airport he'd called Jenny Martling and learned that the former Haitian embassy was now his property and had been furnished by two different firms. He planned to go there and see. Maybe settle in. The keys were at the office of one of the interior design firms.

His motorcycle was where he'd left it. A man was struggling with some suitcases in the trunk of the car in the next parking slot. Kim opened the Honda's top case and stuffed his pack inside. He didn't hear the man working with the suitcases until the guy was directly behind him. He felt a sharp sting in his neck.

He turned to see an athletic-looking man of his own age holding a syringe. The man grinned, exposing bright-white teeth in a face that glowed with that unmistakable vigor of mountains and fjords. Not Frode Moe, but probably a younger countryman. Kim's head spun, and he grabbed the Honda's top case. His vision narrowed. Darkness spiraled around him the way a camera aperture closes. Kim's hand slid across the plastic lid of the top case, and he slumped forward into the man's arms.

The last thing he heard was a car door opening. The last thing he thought was that it had probably been a mistake to fly Norwegian Air.

5

Kim Ribbing didn't know how much time had passed when the darkness began to dissolve. The world offered itself to him one pixel at a time. He heard a thwack-thwack-thwack over his head and the sound of running liquid behind his back. He forced his eyes open a crack and found himself belted fast in the rearmost seat of a helicopter. His hands and feet were bound with half-inch plastic cable ties.

He pushed and pulled, but the leather straps holding him in the seat didn't budge. The pilot in the front seat turned to look at Kim. He was wearing mirrored sunglasses, headphones, and a Circle-K baseball cap. He gave a thumbs-up and called, "Everything okay?"

"Jus' grea'," Kim mumbled and closed his eyes. The gushing sound behind him stopped. The helicopter stood in an open field, probably for a refueling that was now complete. Where had the killers' helicopter landed? Karlstad? Were they in Karlstad? Was this the pilot who'd flown those guys?

The man who'd used the syringe on Kim climbed into the helicopter, took the seat next to him, pulled the door shut, and gave the pilot that thumbs-up sign. Why were Norwegians always sticking their thumbs into the air? The rotor blades accelerated, and they took off a moment later. Kim's neck muscles felt loose, and his head bobbled.

"Whe . . . where are . . . we going?" he asked his assailant.

"Bet you can guess," the man said. "There's somebody who'd like to meet you."

"Frode? Moe?"

"Mm-hmm. What's that funny word you Swedes use? 'Peeved.' He's a little peeved at you. That's putting it mildly. Looks like this day's not going to end well for you. Sorry about that."

Kim nodded and faked even greater sluggishness, letting his head fall limply forward. His chin searched until he found the little ruby charm. He pressed the tip of his chin against the pendant, pushing it against his rib cage. He sensed the gem sliding into its recess.

He'd set off the alarm. All he could hope was that someone would receive it.

6

Moebius was idly reading through a HackPack chat about the Linux operating system when the alarm went off. He sat up in his chair before double clicking the Tracksuit icon. His phone also started bleating.

A blue box with a white field full of digits appeared on the screen. Moebius frowned. The first coordinates shown were 59.136650, 11.414687, but they changed quickly. The first coordinate, latitude, was almost constant, but the digits for longitude were diminishing rapidly. Moebius wasn't familiar enough with the system to translate the latitudinal changes into an equivalent speed of movement, but one thing was sure: Kim Ribbing was rapidly on his way westward.

He highlighted and copied the coordinates, put them into Google Maps, and saw Kim's position had just been somewhere near Halden in southeast Norway. Moebius bit his ragged fingernails. Why hadn't Julia Malmros called? They'd agreed to contact one another if the alarm went off so they could double-check before Julia initiated anything.

Moebius fumbled at his phone and managed to mute it to stop the bleating. He couldn't just hit Received on Tracksuit because the coordinates kept changing. He tapped in Julia Malmros's number. Five rings; no one answered. He started sweating. He tapped a quick message about the westward movement and added the current coordinates, then wiped his face with the tail of the short-sleeved Hawaiian shirt he'd worn for the last three days.

Moebius waited several minutes more, chewing nails so short that his thumbnail started bleeding. What should he do? Ring that Jonny Munther guy? Some folks called his absolute aversion to the police nothing but paranoia, but he considered it entirely reasonable and merely precautionary. He didn't want to have anything to do with those guys.

He phoned Kim Ribbing's number, but as he expected, no one answered. If Kim had access to a phone, he'd have used it instead of setting off the alarm.

Moebius looked at the filthy window with its lowered venetian blinds and broke out into a serious sweat when he realized the inevitable: He had to go outside. Out among the *population*, to try to get hold of Julia Malmros. He had her address in Stockholm's Old Town. Moebius hyperventilated for a long time before managing to work his shapeless bulk up out of the captain's chair. He tottered out to the kitchen and splashed his face with tap water to keep from passing out.

Moebius wiped his face with a kitchen towel. He grasped the counter with both hands, put his head down, and closed his eyes to focus on breathing. When he was a teenager, he'd had therapy for social awkwardness so extreme that it bordered on agoraphobia, but nothing had helped. Only when he found he had something in common with faceless internet acquaintances had he gained a semblance of social interaction. *You can do it, man. You can do it!* Kim Ribbing was one of the few people he'd encountered IRL, and now Kim was in danger. Moebius had to act *now*, or it would be too late.

He pushed off the counter and went into the hall. He sat on a stool. He picked up his sneakers and found spiderwebs in them. When had he last put them on? Two months ago? Three? He'd been forced to go to a dentist for a terrible toothache, and that had been one of the most horrific experiences of his life.

His stomach was heaving. Moebius huffed and puffed but succeeded in getting his shoes on and knotting the laces with his clumsy fingers. The sour stink of sweat both old and new rose from his shirt. He got up, stood swaying for a couple of seconds, stared at the knob of the front door. Then he threw open the bolt and turned the knob.

The short walk through the center of Sundbyberg was a real trial. People stared at him as he inched along the walls, dazzled by the brilliant sunshine. He needed sunglasses, but he didn't have any. He moved forward step by step, keeping his eyes on the ground as much as possible. Moebius got to the Sundbyberg underground station, where he found himself obliged to download the Stockholm Transport app and figure out how to buy a ticket. He had considerable difficulty getting to the platforms.

The train arrived. Moebius went to the section at the end of the car reserved for the disabled. No other passengers there. He gazed rigidly out the window, glancing down from time to time at his phone. The longitudinal coordinates kept falling. Kim was still in motion; surely that was a good sign? Unless that flight was transporting a dead body. Moebius shivered.

The train pulled into Central Station, Stockholm. Moebius watched via the reflection in the window as a woman coming to sit in his section wrinkled her nose and chose somewhere else. Moebius was little aware of his body odor, but it clearly affected other people. *Okay, good!* On the net he was a respected data expert, an authority, but in this so-called reality he was an outcast. It wouldn't matter if only people would stop *staring* at him.

Several people got out at the Old Town station. He did too but hung back to let them climb the stairs before he followed. Moebius shivered; it was chilly below ground. He was really feeling lousy. He had to hold tight to the handrail on the way up to keep from collapsing.

He emerged onto the street, and the heat struck him in the face. Crowds were passing in all directions, people of many nationalities. He took a few awkward steps. He looked toward Old Town and broke into a sweat again. The sun's burning rays spotlighted hundreds of people moving about in all sorts of unpredictable ways.

Moebius choked up and put his back to a wall. For a moment he thought he was dying. Walking through those narrow streets would finish him off. He squeezed his eyes tight and huddled over. He couldn't do this. He just couldn't.

Steadying himself against the wall with one hand, he pulled out his phone. Tracksuit showed that the longitudinal movement had stopped. Kim had gotten to his destination, wherever it was. Moebius's fingers left moist prints on the screen as he copied the coordinates and sent them to Julia Malmros. Then he hugged his big gut and staggered back down the stairs to the underground station.

7

Kim Ribbing's mind had cleared during the flight. The open spaces, fields, and buildings that sped past far below said nothing to him, but he assumed they were over Norway. His guess was confirmed after a while when they left the coast and flew out over the open sea. So that city down there must have been Stavanger.

The helicopter descended so suddenly half an hour later that Kim's gut lurched. Through the window he saw a structure in the sea that looked like something a kid might put together from a Meccano set. A platform littered with a chaotic disorder of pipes, towers, and cranes was supported by four thick gleaming legs. An oil rig. A large sign on its side read "Henrik Ibsen Three." The helicopter approached a landing pad.

Kim's hands, bound behind him, were stiff and numb. He tried to rub his wrists together, but they hardly moved. He clenched and unclenched his fists to improve blood circulation before trying to press his hands together. The cable ties allowed less than a half inch of movement. He was hog-tied.

The helicopter jolted down onto the platform with a whoosh, and the beat of the rotors changed. Kim's assailant leaned over and peered out the window. Quite a few men in red coveralls and bright-yellow hard hats were moving purposefully about the platform. Kim's captor said something to the pilot, who nodded and got out. A few moments later Kim saw the pilot shouting, gesturing, and waving away a crane, attracting attention and drawing a crowd.

Kim's assailant released the straps around Kim's torso and waist, opened the door, and grabbed his right arm. He dragged Kim out of the helicopter, checking to be sure no one was looking in their direction. The strong wind would have drowned out Kim's voice if he'd tried to shout. The pilot's distraction of the workers suggested they weren't aware of what was going on. Kim was clad only in his jeans and Santa Muerte T-shirt. The icy blast of the howling wind made his arms cramp.

Kim looked around in search of anything he could use, but his assailant instantly grabbed him up and physically carried him off to what looked like a toolshed. Kim considered twisting upward to try to set his teeth into the man's jugular, but the steely grip on his shoulder granted him no possibility of movement. He looked around, taking in everything he could see.

The man kicked the door open and carried Kim into what indeed turned out to be a toolshed. Aviation coveralls and high-visibility vests hung on the wall with helmets and fire extinguishers. The tools lying on a table included a pair of pliers.

The man carefully deposited Kim on the floor and brushed his hands. "Can't offer you a chair. Sorry about that."

"That's okay," said Kim. "I've been through worse."

"I believe it. You've really been *opptatt*."

"Which means?"

"Travel. How do you say it in Swedish? Busy? Diligent, maybe. If you wait here, Frode will see you soon."

"I'm not going anywhere."

The man nodded and glanced around. He noticed the pliers, which he stuffed into his back pocket. "Just to make sure you don't go anywhere, *nei*?" He found a screwdriver, held it up, and pocketed that too. He did a last sweep and appeared to find nothing else Kim might use to remove the cable ties. He left and locked the door behind him.

8

A couple of minutes later, Kim heard the vibration of steps approaching across the deck grating, and the door was pulled open with a screech. The figure dressed in jeans and his traditional Norwegian sweater carried a plastic folding chair. Kim's assailant accompanied him.

Frode Moe unfolded the chair, settled in it, and studied Kim. Kim studied him back. Frode Moe's pale blue eyes, sculpted features, and well-trimmed gray hair gave him the aura of an actor or that film star usually cast as the father of the romantic lead. The sweater of the day was black and white with a red collar and geometric patterns across the chest. Frode leaned forward, clasped his hands, and said, *"Men gutten min, hva du ser forferdelig ut!"*

"If you want me to take you seriously, you'll have to speak Swedish," said Kim.

Frode Moe's mouth turned down. "Want to get yourself whacked?" Still in Norwegian.

"Listen to yourself," Kim said. "Even when you guys *threaten* someone it sounds like you're talking to a puppy. And I'm not asking for a whack, thank you."

Frode Moe made a sign to the man who'd kidnapped Kim. Without changing expression, the man took a couple of steps forward and gave Kim a tremendous kick in the belly. Kim's lungs emptied, he coughed and gasped, a ball of fire burst in his gut, and his mouth filled with blood. He'd bitten his own tongue. He spat out a bubble of red slime that landed inches from Frode Moe's brilliantly polished shoes.

Moe ignored Kim's request concerning Swedish. Continuing in Norwegian, he said, "As far as I'm concerned, Swedish sounds like a language for morons, so I stick to Norwegian."

"Okay," Kim wheezed and replied in English, "it's your funeral."

"Yours, more likely, I'd say. You'll be buried at sea, sailor fashion." Frode Moe sat up straight and shook his head. "I'm almost impressed by your ability to collect information."

"It won't disappear if you kill me. I already passed it on."

"Yes, I thought so."

"So what's this all about?"

Frode Moe looked surprised. He glanced at the other man as if Kim's question were incomprehensible, then turned back to his prisoner. "Revenge, of course. Useless, meaningless revenge for destroying my businesses. Destroying my life, I might even say. You think I can just let you get away with that?"

"That would probably tarnish your reputation."

Frode Moe slapped his knee. "Nope. I just wanted to see you before you disappear."

"And here I am. Now what?"

"With you? I already told you that—"

"With yourself! You say your life is destroyed. What are you planning to do about that?"

"Don't worry about me. I have resources stashed everywhere and all kinds of transport at my disposal. I'll pick some place where your so-called justice can't reach me."

"And your wife? Your daughters?"

Frode Moe clenched his jaw. His expression darkened. He got up from his chair. "Maybe now you understand why I want to see you dead." He folded the chair and handed it to the other man, nodded at Kim, and said, "Wait until the crew goes down for dinner."

9

Kim didn't know what time it was or how long it would be before *the crew goes down for dinner.* That could mean hours; it could mean minutes. So, he'd found out the hard way what had happened to marine biologist Edward Dahlberg, whose fate he shortly would share unless he found a way out.

Kim had once seen a video of a woman who'd moved her handcuffed hands from her back to her front in four seconds by revolving her arms over her head. Intrigued, Kim had bound his own wrists with duct tape, tried the maneuver, and found it impossible. Her trick required the ability to rotate her shoulders so her arms momentarily popped out of joint. Kim didn't have that ability. Or perhaps that peculiar deformity.

Continuing the experiment, he'd cut off the duct tape, laced his fingers together behind his back, and tried to shift them to his front by sitting and pulling joined hands under his rear and feet. Not too difficult. He'd taped his wrists together and tried this approach but failed. The few inches of difference between joined wrists and intertwined fingers rendered that move impossible.

The plastic ties binding him were narrower than duct tape, so that gained him a little maneuvering room. He kicked off his shoes to get maybe an inch more leeway. It still didn't work. By compressing his body to the utmost and stretching his arms out as far as possible, he managed to get the ties past his heels, but then they stopped under the arches of his feet and could go no farther.

Fuck, fuck, fuck . . .

Kim lay balled up on the floor and banged his forehead against his updrawn knees. He had no intention of letting that Norwegian sweater conquer him, so *think!* Kim shut his eyes and pulled from memory an exact image of everything in the room around him. Then he pushed himself to his feet and hopped to the tool table. A plastic bottle of engine oil stood there.

He seized it with his teeth, sat down again, and clamped it between his knees. He used his teeth to unscrew the cap. He tipped sideways and let the contents run out across the floor.

Kim rubbed the bottoms of his feet in the sluggishly flowing liquid and went back to work. This time when the cable tie slipped past his heels, the slippery oil helped them slide farther. Kim grunted "Ha!" in triumph when the ties slurped past his big toes and his hands were in front of him.

At home he'd had a knife nearby when he'd tried the maneuver, in case the experiment didn't succeed. No knife now, but that wasn't a major problem. Kim fumbled in his jeans cuff, pulled out the vape pen, and unscrewed it to expose the glow tip.

If he'd been locked in handcuffs, the vape wouldn't have helped, but now he was dealing with plastic. Plastic and a glow tip were a fine combination in these circumstances. It took him only about a minute to burn through the binding on his wrists. The room stank of plastic fumes as he liberated his ankles as well. He was free.

Kim studied the lock on the door. It was far too sturdy a contraption to yield to any tool he had at hand. Kim looked around and once again assessed the objects in the room. He thought for a moment, weighing various possibilities. Then he put on his shoes and began preparing.

10

After leaving her apartment, Julia Malmros wandered through the Old Town streets. As so often happened, she eventually found herself in the main market square. She perched on a bench and watched the passing population—or, to be precise, the strolling tourists. Chinese visitors were taking photos of one another with the Grand Church in the background, and an obviously bored man used a selfie stick to preserve forever an image of himself before the stock exchange building.

Julia peered covertly at the Chinese, who seemed to have an unquenchable thirst for pictures of themselves posing in front of Old Town's best-known buildings. She didn't feel the least bit tense, which pleased her. She'd heard that some people suffer from the syndrome labeled Sinophobia, fear of the Chinese, but despite recent events, it wasn't affecting her.

She had that soft but empty feeling in her heart that something had come to an end. The confrontation with Bruce Li the previous evening had been terrifying and disruptive, but it also served as a sort of finale to the events that began on Midsummer Eve. Maybe that was why she'd finally gotten a good night's sleep. Despite everything.

Thoughts of sleep glided into thoughts of bed and from there slipped inevitably onward to Kim Ribbing. Julia focused on her emotions. A flame still burned somewhere inside, but Julia didn't know if Kim would see it as warmth or threat. Or just something that needed to be extinguished. Julia recalled that rough act of proxy intercourse on Tärnö and sighed morosely. Had that changed things forever?

Julia got up from the bench and took a turn around the square. The soft spot in her heart began to harden. No, she wasn't suffering from Sinophobia but from a different and thoroughly contemporary fear: nomophobia, the fear of having no mobile phone, of losing coverage. She'd thought it'd be liberating to leave her phone at home, but now her restlessness was rapidly becoming a bad case of nerves. She walked toward Svartman Street and accelerated her steps as she passed St. Gertrude's Church.

She was feeling the same eerie malaise she'd experienced in Olof Helander's office. It was nonsensical, of course. People called it intuition, but it was really the unconscious assimilation and interpreting of known variables that roused an uneasy feeling, a warning. Because this was happening in her unconscious mind, Julia had no idea why she broke into a gentle jog to get home as soon as possible.

When Julia got there and picked up her cell, she saw her intuition had been anything but nonsensical. She'd gotten a text from Moebius: KIM'S ALARM! 59.136650, 11.4525687 FAST WEST. Several more texts followed urging Julia to call NOW, each with a new set of coordinates.

Julia rushed to the stairs, clutching her phone. Plunging downward, she took the steps two at a time, already calling Jonny Munther.

11

A couple of hours had passed since they locked him in, so Kim Ribbing had had plenty of time to get ready by the time the steel grating vibrated with approaching steps. Kim wiped his hands on the flight coverall he'd pulled on and held the fire extinguisher nozzle tight.

Kim's kidnapper pulled the door open, and the pilot was close behind him. The sunlight was dazzling. Kim aimed the nozzle at his face. The man managed to exclaim "*Hva faen!*" before Kim pressed the release.

The extinguisher hissed like an enormous snake and pushed the man backward. He lost his footing as the stream of foam blasted his face and turned him into half a snowman, a thick layer of white goop covering his shoulders. He bent over, pressed his hands to his face, and screamed something about his eyes.

Kim stepped past him onto the grating. The pilot had his hands up to shield his face, which was okay with Kim. He dropped the nozzle, grabbed the extinguisher's neck with both hands, and slammed the heavy steel tank into the man's crotch. A high, broken squeal burst from him, and he put his hands between his knees before falling forward and joining his colleague on the grating.

The wind blew Kim's hair wildly as he tossed the fire extinguisher aside and ran across the helicopter pad. The oversized flight suit hindered his movement. The area where the rig workers had milled about was empty. Kim looked around and caught sight of Frode Moe staring through the glass window of the observation tower from which he'd obviously expected to enjoy Kim's burial at sea. Moe's mouth was a big *O* as he put his mobile phone to his ear.

It seemed unlikely the two he'd put down on the deck were the only ones involved in Frode Moe's darker doings. You'd need plenty of help to fill an oil tanker destined for Cuba. Those who'd come to kill him would soon be discovered, and Kim didn't know if others would be armed. He had to get away. Now.

His plan was ready. Looking around the work area upon arrival a couple of hours earlier, he'd spotted a small rubber dinghy fastened to the platform railing. Kim ran toward it now, the coverall flapping at his ankles and the wind roaring in his ears. He unlashed the dinghy and looked back toward the shed they'd put him in.

Both men were on their feet. The kidnapper was wiping foam from his eyes with one hand but fumbling behind him with the other. His vision probably wasn't the best at the moment, but Kim was an easy target on the open deck. Kim lifted the dinghy and looked down over the rail. The sea at least sixty feet below was breaking furiously against the rig's massive supports. The entire structure was swaying.

Fuck.

Kim heard a shot and a loud *zing!* as the bullet struck the railing beside him and ricocheted out over the sea.

Fuck.

Kim took a deep breath and lifted the dinghy over his head. His arms quivered with the effort. He climbed onto the rail, thought *Fuck* one last time, and threw himself over. As he'd hoped, the strong updraft caught the rubber boat and slowed his fall a little as he dropped toward the surging whitecaps below.

This was probably the craziest thing he'd ever done. Kim Ribbing felt time cease as he rocked through the air between two of the rig's enormous legs.

He felt the wind in his face and the elasticity of the rubber oarlocks his fingers clutched as he tried to keep the dinghy positioned directly overhead to slow his fall. He saw the sun standing high in the heavens, casting a heaving, flashing layer of light over the churning water.

Time resumed flowing with oily viscosity as he neared the surface. He saw swirling rainbow-colored oil stains moving and changing shape in slow motion. For a split second he saw the *pattern*. His eyes widened, and suddenly everything became obvious.

There was the rectangle of the oil rig and the distorted rhomboid shape of the drilling mechanism. There was the rectangle of an oil tanker waiting for oil and there was a circle. The circle was one of Olof Helander's drones. That's what he hadn't understood.

A difference between reported value and actual value occurred when they extracted more oil than they logged. Those values weren't in ppm, particle concentration in the air, and none of this had anything to do with climate compensation payments. The numbers had to be quantities of unreported oil. Maybe the number in the right-hand column indicated the number of barrels of corresponding difference. Olof Helander must have discovered the scam and blackmailed Frode Moe. Mr. Film Star in the Norwegian Sweater told his Chinese partner to solve the problem.

No rational, carefully deduced chain of insights had enlightened Kim Ribbing in midair, no, sir; it had come to him in the flash created by the *pattern*. Then the pattern dissolved, and Kim saw the sea surface approaching at great speed. He clenched his teeth and got ready for impact.

At the last instant he succeeded in swinging the dinghy beneath him. That was probably a tactical mistake. It hit the water, and he slammed against the rubber flooring. That knocked the wind out of him.

Fu . . .

His eyes dimmed as he rebounded and was flung overboard. Kim's numbed body splashed into the icy water, his head went under, he gasped involuntarily and inhaled sea water. His arms and legs were virtually paralyzed by the impact, but fortunately the flight suit buoyed him up. An insistent throbbing was like a church clock in his head. He felt his consciousness slipping away. The rubber boat bobbed in the waves, moving away from him.

No! Not possible!

Kim shook his head, retched, and coughed up salt water. He gathered his strength to send energy from his impaired torso into his arms and legs. He swam one stroke toward the dinghy. And another. He couldn't feel his arms, but he could still move them. Another stroke brought him to the boat. He put an arm over the edge and dragged himself out of the water.

The waves rocked him so violently that his stomach rebelled. He vomited over the gunwale into the sea and then collapsed onto the bottom of the dinghy. He lay inert for several seconds. When he looked up, he saw a large inflatable boat being lowered from the platform toward the water.

Double fuck.

He was probably lost, but it wasn't in his nature to give up before all possibilities were exhausted. Kim looked at the tiny outboard motor set in the dinghy's stern and couldn't see where the fuel came from. No hose, no tank. Then he saw a cap on the rear side of the motor and realized the fuel tank was integrated into the housing.

He set the choke on full and yanked the cord. The motor started immediately. He reduced the choke and turned the dinghy toward the mainland, guessing the direction from the angle of the sun.

Despite his desperate situation, he couldn't keep from grinning at himself. There wasn't a chance in the universe of reaching land. That helicopter had flown over the sea for maybe half an hour, and a copter was capable of speeds of more than two hundred miles per hour. He could be a hundred miles or more from the coast. He'd be lucky if the fuel in the little motor was enough for a tenth of that distance. Add to it the fact that the larger boat with its stronger engine was halfway down to the water surging around the rig. Not much to hope for.

Sweater Guy wins. Goddamn it!

The rubber boat heaved in the waves, rose up and slammed down, drenching Kim's face with salty seawater. He wiped his eyes and saw bright spots that seemed to dance up and down in the distance. He rubbed his eyes and peered at them. The dinghy's movement was making the brilliant white dots of light dance. They were getting larger and larger.

Kim steered into a wave so tall that for a moment it blocked the gleaming dots. The wave surged, propelling the dinghy to the crest and throwing Kim upward. Only his death grip on the starter cord kept him from being cast overboard again. The dinghy's propeller snarled when it was lifted clear of the water, then caught the sea again and sent the boat hurtling down into the hollow between waves. It slammed into the next wave with a bone-shaking impact.

The dots became as intense as searchlights. There were three in all, and after a few seconds, despite the roaring of the waves, Kim heard the regular beating of approaching helicopters. Kim looked over his shoulder and saw the larger rubber boat had stopped and hung suspended about six feet above the sea.

The thump of the rotors was directly over Kim now. He looked up and saw two Norwegian police helicopters head toward the oil rig as a copter with Swedish markings descended toward him. The side door slid open, and a very familiar face appeared. Julia's gray hair swirled as she leaned out as far as she could. Kim laughed out loud and shook his head.

Julia Malmros, back in the game.

12

After informing Jonny Munther, Julia grabbed a taxi to the police helicopter base at Arlanda Airport. The detective superintendent had arrived a couple of minutes earlier in a squad car.

Jonny Munther strongly objected to having Julia aboard the helicopter. What use was that? And the participation of his ex-wife in an official mission hadn't been approved! Julia argued that she was the one with the phone, she was getting the location updates from Moebius, and this was no time to quibble about authorizations. Nor was it the first time Julia had been aboard a police helicopter. The detective superintendent gave in. They took off minutes later.

Jonny sternly warned Julia that she was there only as a consultant and not allowed to intervene in any way. He sat staring grimly out the window before contacting the Norwegian police. The helicopter had been in flight for half an hour when Moebius sent Julia the text with the coordinates pinpointing Kim's location. Julia googled them. She understood when she saw they were far out in the North Sea.

"Kim's on an oil rig," Julia said and kept googling. "Henrik Ibsen Three, if this information is correct."

Julia put down her phone and did something she should have done long before. Since receiving Moebius's first message, she'd been obsessively watching the coordinates as he updated them, seeing them as a *function*, an ongoing process she was afraid of disturbing. Now she messaged Moebius. Good job. We're on the way. Thanks. Fingers crossed.

Julia pressed a hand to her chest where her heart had been hammering ever since she rushed back to her flat. More than an hour had passed since Kim activated the signal, and they were still at least two hours away from the rig. Anything at all could happen in that time.

Three hours. Julia put both hands over her heart trying to reassure and calm herself. She was finding it difficult to breathe. Jonny Munther had told the pilot to fly as fast as possible, but Julia had the sensation the landscape beneath them was *crawling* past. Much of the time Jonny was talking to Norwegian law enforcement, trying to convince them the situation was dire. It was no easy job persuading them to mount a coordinated intervention against King Frode.

The pilot pushed his bird to the max, and by the time they stopped for refueling at the Norwegian police base in Stavanger, several warning lights were flashing. Jonny Munther briefed the Norwegian colleagues while the tank was refilled. Five minutes later, three helicopters lifted and set off in formation toward the North Sea destination.

The stress and the view over the open sea almost gave Julia a heart attack. Kim was alone, isolated somewhere out in this nowhere, in the hands of a man without the least respect for human life.

When at last they were on approach to Henrik Ibsen Three, Julia pressed her face to the window and peered toward the graceless steel structure protruding from the sea like a curse cast down from heaven. She scanned the rig and the sea. She gasped when she spotted an orange shape tossing in the waves. "There!" she screamed into her headset so loud that the pilot grabbed his ears. "There, I think . . . over there!"

The pilot brought the helicopter down toward sea level while the Norwegian helicopters continued toward the rig. When their altitude was no more than sixty feet, Julia saw the figure in the little rubber boat really was Kim. The pilot brought the copter down even closer. Julia made sure her flight harness was extended but securely attached and pulled back the door.

"Julia, for God's sake!" said Jonny Munther. "You can't . . ."

Julia looked Kim straight in the eye. He was mouthing some words. Incredibly enough, considering the situation, there was an ironic twinkle in his eye.

"We have to pick him up!" Julia told the pilot.

"We don't have the equipment for air-sea rescue," he replied.

"Get down as far as you can," said Julia. "I'll grab him."

A strong yank at her harness dragged Julia backward. Holding it, Jonny Munther shouted, "Calm down, Julia!" He grabbed his phone. "I'll call Norway Sea Rescue, and they can get here with the right gear if . . ."

Unless the sea rescue team was nearby, which was unlikely, it would take hours for them to arrive. Kim's little dinghy tossing about in the powerful waves would probably have capsized by then. Julia resorted to her personal defense maneuver, jabbing her stiff fingers up beneath Jonny's ribs. A sound somewhere between a gasp and a giggle erupted from him, and he lost his grip on her.

Julia pushed him away and stretched down as far as she could. She got her right leg out onto the landing skid. The downdraft from the rotors and the wind over the sea sent her hair blowing wildly, half blinding her as she reached toward Kim, who'd gotten to his feet, balancing with difficulty against the pitching of the dinghy.

"Jesus, Jesus, Jesus . . ." Julia heard the pilot groaning in her headset as he brought his craft down another three feet, countering the howling wind and adjusting position precisely. He brought her right down to Kim's outstretched hand.

"Damn it, Julia," shouted Jonny Munther. "Is he so goddamn important that you've got to . . ."

His tug on her harness wasn't convincing. She thought, *Yes, he is that important.*

A strong gust made the helicopter lurch. Julia's hand dipped a couple of feet, and her fingers brushed Kim's. She stretched out as far as possible, Kim went up on tiptoe, and they grasped each other's wrists.

Julia's jaw clenched and her teeth ground against one another; the sharp taste of amalgam filled her mouth. She pulled as hard as she could. Kim's flight coverall made him heavy, but with the help of a swell that lifted him, riding the impetus of its thrusting energy, he leaped from the dinghy and got one knee up on the landing skid. Julia stretched out her other hand, Kim grabbed it, and with a tremendous jerk she got Kim through the door and onto the copter's deck.

"Jesus, Mary, and Joseph!" the pilot said and lifted the craft to a less perilous altitude as Julia dragged the door shut.

Julia put her hands on Kim's back. "How are you? Are you okay?"

"Apparently," Kim answered and clambered up into the seat. He gave a nod of recognition to Jonny Munther, who grunted and shook his head.

Adrenaline kept surging in Julia's bloodstream, and when Kim turned to look at her, she put her hands on his cheeks and pulled him to her. She put her lips to his. For a moment his lips were chilly and reluctant. Then his mouth softened and he returned her kiss. Julia pressed him closer and nibbled at his lips. Their tongues played with one another, and Julia's body filled with a cloud of red warmth as Kim breathed into her mouth.

"For Christ's sake," muttered Jonny Munther. "Get a room somewhere."

Kim carefully disengaged his lips from Julia's and replied, "No problem. I have a whole house."

X

Stockholm

1

It was well past ten o'clock in the morning when Julia Malmros awoke in Kim Ribbing's huge, comfortable, top-of-the-line Hästens bed. Kim was already up, and the tempting aroma of coffee came from the kitchen. They'd sat up late the previous night talking, drinking wine, and then making love. There'd still been an initial reluctance in Kim's body, but it went away as desire took hold.

Julia looked around, amused by his place's schizophrenic style. The two interior decorating firms had gotten into a serious disagreement and refused to coordinate their concepts, each of them taking liberties. For example, in the bedroom an antique seafarer's trunk from Bukowski was set by a round, seventies-style plastic armchair, and next to them stood a floor lamp that could have been swiped from a spaceship.

When Julia had delicately remarked to Kim that his residence looked as if it had been decorated by a five-year-old with a few million kronor in the bank, he'd shrugged. "So? It's just furniture." Julia had spent a lot of time in the place since their return from Norway and was starting to get used to it. The place was just as multifaceted and contradictory as its owner, so maybe there was a certain logic after all.

The Norwegian police had detained Frode Moe just as he was boarding his helicopter. Kim's statement was more than enough for an arrest warrant for Moe and both his buddies. They were at Oslo's central prison for the time being. Frode was scheduled for trial in Norway for major financial fraud and later in Stockholm for hiring killers for the Knektholmen massacre. Certain telephone records showing conversations with Bruce Li were likely to create difficulties for the Norwegian.

Julia put her legs over the edge of the bed, then put on the morning robe that was one of the few things Kim had allowed to "move in," as he'd expressed it. They'd never sat down for a serious talk about their relationship or where it was headed. They might never discuss that. It was a thing, it was ongoing, and that was all.

Julia looked out the window and saw the Kaknäs communications tower sticking up above the treetops a couple of miles away. Kim's villa was on Lido Street in Gärdet. Amusingly enough the Chinese embassy was a stone's throw away, and the Djurgården zoo and museum district was just around the corner.

When Haiti's embassy had been active, the country hadn't had the resources to purchase a separate residence. They'd set up an apartment on the upper floor of the embassy, and that was the living space Kim had allowed the firms to decorate "in a blend of old and modern," to use an appropriate euphemism.

The areas on the ground floor that had contained embassy offices sat empty, and Julia couldn't understand why Kim had purchased a place with so much unused space. His only comment was that he "liked the joint." Maybe that had to do with the tall iron fencing surrounding the grounds and the surveillance cameras that were still functional. Or maybe it was something else.

Julia crossed the parquet floor where Persian carpets competed for space with the homey geometrical patterns of traditional Swedish Röllakan rugs. She found Kim at the kitchen table with a cup of coffee, intently focused on his laptop.

"Good morning," said Julia.

"Mm-hmm," answered Kim. "There's coffee."

Julia poured herself a cup. "Did you give up that sum thing?"

"What sum?"

"The theological one."

"*Summa Theologica*? Five hundred pages was enough. Boring. And there's no God. I'm more interested in that Ces person. Seems they have been messing with the Swedish Royal Bank. Pretty impressive, really."

After finishing her coffee, Julia went back to the bedroom and dressed in dark blue. The funeral service for Olof and Gabriella Helander was scheduled for eleven thirty at Skogs church. Whether God existed or not, Julia was going to be there to honor her deceased childhood friend.

When she was ready, she followed Kim down the stairs to the ground floor. Their steps echoed as they walked through the empty space.

"I wouldn't mind living here," said Julia.

"Ha!" said Kim. "That's a good one."

Julia's suggestion hadn't been serious, but she took a childish pleasure in testing Kim's boundaries. He disliked any reference to formalizing their relationship and bristled whenever Julia hinted at that.

High summer weather seemed it would never end. It was yet another day with cloudless blue skies, but there was no sign of drought. An overnight shower had blessed the city's greenery. The fresh scent of grass rose from lawns, and more intense, luxuriant odors came from the woods behind the residence.

Kim trailed after Julia down the gravel path to the tall gate crowned with spikes. He unlocked it with a heavy key; the gate slowly creaked open. They exchanged a quick kiss before Julia walked toward the bus stop and Kim returned to the house.

He started to go to the basement door with the heavy padlock but decided *that* project would take a few hours. He went upstairs to the kitchen and assembled an open-faced sandwich instead. He returned to his task of hacking into the records system of Danderyd Hospital.

2

About a hundred people had gathered in Hope Chapel, and Julia Malmros was one of the last to arrive. Several looked around at her when the doors closed behind her, including Astrid Helander, who was sitting in the front row. Julia didn't detect anything special in the girl's gaze. Julia lifted a hand in implied greeting, and Astrid returned the gesture.

She slipped into one of the rear pews, a bit relieved. Over the previous week the newspapers had served up some of William King's information along with additional details they'd dug up on their own. Olof Helander's role was known. He'd blackmailed Frode Moe with information from drones Olof had piloted from his office. Julia's role in the exposure of Astrid's father wasn't minor, and she'd feared the girl might be furious at her. Perhaps she was; but at least she'd responded with a greeting.

Two coffins in light-colored wood stood side by side before the altar. Julia wondered how Astrid was feeling at that moment, sitting and gazing at two boxes containing the bodies of persons she'd grown up with. The priest spoke, the music was played, and a couple of Olof and Gabriella's relatives gave little talks about what fine persons the deceased had been and described the consternation caused by their deaths. Nothing about the circumstances surrounding the deaths, of course.

When those in attendance were allowed to approach the coffins, Astrid was the first. The sniffling and sobbing in the chapel space rose in volume when Astrid placed a rose on each coffin. *Orphaned.* Julia felt a lump in her throat, but she still couldn't read anything from Astrid's expression. The girl looked resolute, more than anything else. Lips tight. In control.

As everyone filed past the coffins, Astrid remained seated in the front row, accepting the many condolences. Julia hesitated but then advanced and joined the queue. When she reached Astrid ten minutes later, she found the girl pale and exhausted. Astrid seemed indifferent when she saw Julia.

"Are you willing to talk with me?" asked Julia.

Astrid shrugged. "Only if you don't cry and talk about how sorry you are for me."

"No. I mostly wanted to express my dismay that . . . it came out the way it did. About Olof. In the newspapers and all that."

"I was part of it too," said Astrid. "With the iPad. Anyway, it was mostly Kim, wasn't it?"

"Yes, maybe. Are you angry at him?"

"No. I'm going to go visit him. After all this."

"Just like that?"

"He phoned. Said I should come."

"Oh, are you two . . . uh-huh."

Astrid leaned forward and sighed when she saw the long queue behind Julia. "I have to accept some more sympathy now, if you don't mind."

"Of course. Naturally. And . . . I'm sorry for your loss."

Astrid nodded and straightened up in her pew. Julia made way for the kind remarks of the next relative or friend of the family. She perceived a latent strength in Astrid, who sat firmly upright in her black tulle dress. Julia expected things would fall into place for Astrid. If they didn't, then Astrid would put them into the order she wanted. She was somewhat like Kim.

3

Kim left his residence just before one o'clock and walked up Lido Street, which ran toward the Gärdet bus stop. The narrow street was lined with trees, and it was the closest you could get to living in a forest in central Stockholm. Scarcely a house was in sight, except for the Academic Rowing Association down by the shore a hundred yards away. That suited Kim. Neighborliness had never been his thing.

Astrid arrived on the number 69 bus at 1:05 p.m. Her hair wasn't much different from Kim's own, and the black tulle dress was a garment Kim could have worn during his youth before he gave up dressing in female clothing.

"How was the funeral?" asked Kim.

"It happened."

"Great. Want to walk?"

Kim had asked Jonny Munther to keep his involvement in solving the Knektholmen murders out of the media, but it had leaked somehow. Kim suspected that the leaker was named William King. Kim had been mentioned in a few articles, and it turned out Astrid had read them all. She bombarded him with questions throughout the walk to his place. He provided short but polite answers. When Kim unlocked the gate, Astrid just stood there and stared. Then she said, "Shit, seriously? This is *yours*?"

"Yeah."

"But what, are you rolling in dough?"

"Yeah. But so are you."

"Not like *this* and, anyway, not till I turn eighteen. Where did you get all that money?"

"Like you. Inherited."

"Your family . . ."

"Dead. They're all dead."

4

By the summer Kim turned fourteen, his grandfather's abuse had become both less barbaric and less frequent. Not for any lack of desire, but because the old man was less able. Age had begun to catch up with the count after his long life of debauchery, and Kim's increasing strength and agility allowed him to escape by leaping, ducking, feinting, or simply running away.

In recent years Kim had spent most of his free time on gymnastics. He'd come in fourth in his age group in the Stockholm Marathon and had been chosen as an alternate for the national junior gymnastics team. It was only when he pushed his body to its limit, when a leap or a landing depended upon absolute precision and demanded total concentration, that his inner chaos subsided briefly.

No, that's not entirely correct. Another activity could provide him occasional relief, and that's what he spent the rest of his free time on. Computers. Kim had gone beyond online gaming and started searching the internet with an extremely well-defined goal. In the summer of 2004 he achieved it. He knew he could accomplish what he'd set himself to accomplish.

The summer weeks at Roshult had been devoted to playing a horrible variation of hide-and-seek with the count. His grandfather would stand in wait and suddenly jump him or try to hit him with some weapon. Kim was constantly on high alert and practically always escaped. He'd received a few blows and gotten a few bruises, but he'd never been overcome. Kim suspected that his grandfather really wasn't so interested anymore but was harassing him out of habit.

His parents came to visit in early August. Kim kept his distance, but from the tone of the talk over the luncheon table audible all the way out in the garden, he gathered that his parents' privileges were at risk now that the count wasn't enjoying Kim's summer stay as much as before. Kim sat in a garden chair and smiled a smile that was no more than a twitch of his lips. His parents' privileges were the least of their worries, but they weren't aware of that yet.

After lunch it was time for the hallowed custom of a boat tour in Grandfather's immaculately preserved wooden cabin cruiser. Kim didn't join them. During such expeditions his grandfather was generally tender, loving, and affectionate, pretending he had a fine, normal relationship with his grandson, while Kim's parents accepted that charade. That was the most disgusting part of all.

Kim stood hidden by the lilac bushes and watched the little group make its way across the lawn, Grandfather leading and all of them wearing old-fashioned orange life vests. He watched them go out on the dock and get into the boat, heard the noise when the spark plugs fired and started the motor that puttered loudly while propelling the boat out into the still waters of Horn Lake.

Kim returned to the residence and its former ballroom and stood there for a moment staring at the hated horse the count hadn't had the opportunity to uncover that summer. Kim's jaws tightened as he remembered the hours he'd endured on its sharp edge while Grandfather stood chuckling and calling, "Giddyup! Giddyup!" and Kim was gradually cloven in two by indescribable pain.

Kim turned his back to the horse, took the tamer's coat down from its hook in the wall, and put it on. Grandfather's torture costume fell as far as his ankles, and its weight on his shoulders pressed his feet into the ground, providing him stability and solidity.

Kim returned to the garden, the coat swinging around him as he walked. He stood in the center of the lawn, straight and tall like a shadowy statue looking over the lake. He rubbed the sweat from his hands onto the coat's fleece lapels and took out his mobile phone, a simple Nokia 1100.

It had taken him two years of searching through the pages of the dark web to learn how to put together a small explosive device and another year to get hold of the components and assemble a functional bomb. By then he'd made so many helpful contacts that remote control turned out to be no problem at all. The components for a detonator controlled by a mobile phone came from someone using Moebius as a pseudonym. Bought and paid for, of course.

That strategic bomblet now sat fastened with industrial adhesive beneath the cabin cruiser's gas tank. The boat approached the center, where the lake was deepest. Kim whispered, "Giddyup. Giddyup," then tapped the code into his phone. The heat from the explosion and raging fire swept across the bay where he'd tried to drown himself all those years ago, reached the shore, and warmed Kim's face. Something shattered in his soul.

5

When Kim and Astrid walked through the ground floor's empty office locale, she commented that not many people had their own roller-skating rink. They went upstairs and Astrid dropped a few comments about the interior decoration. She considered it *a little bit much*.

"There's, like, a . . . I don't know," said Astrid. "There's a kind of *war* going on between the pieces of furniture. Like, they're standing there, just glaring at each other. *You lookin' at me?* the sofa says to the table. I like that."

"Great," said Kim. He went to a door next to the kitchen and opened it. Astrid peered into a room furnished spartan style with only a bed, a desk and chair, and an armchair with a floor lamp. A wide window looked out into the forest.

"Is this your office?" Astrid asked.

"Nope," said Kim. "It's yours."

"My . . . office?"

"Nope. Your room. If you want."

Astrid's hands dropped to her sides. She gaped. "What do you mean . . . Should I . . . ?"

"You have to live with your uncle, but you can spend as much time here as you want. If you want more furniture, I'll pay for it."

"But . . . why?"

"You already said you didn't like it there. Maybe you'll like this better. But I'm not your daddy, and I'm not expecting to—"

Kim couldn't complete that thought because Astrid burst into tears and threw her arms around him. Kim awkwardly patted her back. "It's okay. Everything's fine."

Through her sniffles, Astrid said, "This is the nicest thing anyone's ever done for me."

"I'm not being nice, I'm just . . . uh, can you let go now?"

Astrid's lips pressed against his cheek and moved toward his mouth. Kim carefully pushed her away. "No, Astrid, no. Not that."

"But I thought . . ."

"Stop thinking like that. You're still a child. I don't know, maybe I feel some kind of kinship with you, but that's all and that's all it'll ever be."

Astrid hiccupped. "But, like, I've got a kind of crush on you."

"I'm sure you'll get over it."

Astrid looked like she wanted to say more, but Kim gave her a stern look. She nodded and wiped her eyes, smearing her mascara, and heaved a long sigh. At last she said in a choked voice, "Thank you, then. Thanks ever so much. You have no idea what a relief it is . . . to have somewhere to go."

"I do understand," said Kim. "Starting the day after tomorrow you can be here as much as you want. I'll order a key for you. But first I have some things to do."

Astrid made a quick inspection of her room. Kim saw she was visualizing her existence there. She stood looking out the window for a moment before turning to Kim. "Now it'll be fine. It'll be great. I thought this would never happen."

6

After Astrid left, Kim went through the empty downstairs to a smaller door in what once had been the pantry. It was secured with a heavy padlock. Kim took the key hanging from a hook and undid the lock.

One of the details of the residence that had attracted Kim was that it had a vast basement with several rooms. Kim switched on the light and descended a narrow stair that ended at a humid concrete floor. The basement smelled of mold. It would eventually need to be renovated.

Kim turned to the left and went to what had appeared at the last click of his mouse after he'd found the place on the internet. A heavy metal sliding door framed in steel was very much like the one that Leatherface in *The Texas Chain Saw Massacre* closes behind him after carrying out his first murder. God only knows what the Haitian embassy staff had been up to in the room with bare cement walls behind that door.

Kim unlocked yet another padlock and had to use all his strength to move the door. It rumbled ominously as the heavy metal scraped along a rusty floor track. Kim flipped breakers on the electric panel just inside the door. A fluorescent tube hanging from the ceiling blinked into life.

The room didn't hold much more than a cot with leather straps. On that cot Dr. Martin Rudbeck lay belted, clad only in a T-shirt and boxer shorts. The room stank of urine. That was another detail that would need to be attended to. The Shock Doctor blinked at Kim, and his lips twisted into a grimace. "What are you planning, you pitiful person?"

Kim's voice was neutral. "We're going to have a conversation now, you and me. A proper conversation. After my grandfather, you are the evilest human being I've ever met. He's not alive anymore, but now I have you." Kim pulled the heavy sliding door, and it slammed shut with a satisfying crash. He walked up to Martin Rudbeck, leaned over the man, and said, "I want to *understand*."

About the Author

Photo © 2022 Thron Ullberg

John Ajvide Lindqvist—dubbed Sweden's answer to Stephen King by the *Daily Mirror*—is a Nordic horror master who leaves readers terrified yet craving more. With limitless imagination and a keen sense of language, he creates new worlds, tempting you to laugh in the middle of darkness even as he leads you into the unknown.

Born in 1968, John grew up in Blackeberg, a suburb of Stockholm. A fan of magic, he started out as a conjurer, then did stand-up comedy for twelve years before finding his true calling: writing. In 2004, he debuted his now internationally acclaimed novel *Let the Right One In*.

Since then, John has written more novels, as well as works for stage and screen. Published in thirty-one countries, his writing has earned awards like the Selma Lagerlöf Prize and Best Novel in Translation (Norway). His work has also been short-listed for the August Prize, Book of the Year, and Swedish Radio Literature Prize.

To learn more, visit www.johnajvidelindqvist.com/english.php.

About the Translator

Photo © 2017 Steve Rogers

After a thirty-year career as a US diplomat, which included lengthy assignments in Europe, Africa, and Latin America, Michael Meigs settled in Austin, Texas. His literary translations have been awarded the American-Scandinavian Foundation's annual translation prize and the American Translators Association's Lewis Galantière Award. His translation of Dolores Redondo's *The North Face of the Heart* was short-listed for the Queen Sofía Spanish Institute Translation Prize. He has reviewed live narrative theater in Austin and elsewhere in Central Texas since 2008, when he established his website www.CTXLiveTheatre.com. Michael is a production coordinator for an Austin opera company, a finance director for the Austin Area Interpreters and Translators Association, and a member of the Austin Theatre Critics Table.

Julia Malmros and Kim Ribbing return in *The Room in the Ground*, book 2 of the Bloodstorm series.